Epic Adventures
Of A CableGuy

Epic Adventures Of A Cable Guy

Seasons of the Witches

Book 1

Angel Mikey Michael Ruiz

Mill City Press

Mill City Press, Inc.
2301 Lucien Way #415
Maitland, FL 32751
407.339.4217
www.millcitypress.net

Library of Congress Control Number: 2021908671

ISBN-13: 978-1-6628-1545-4
Ebook ISBN-13: 978-1-6628-1546-1

Acknowledgments

It is the glory of God to conceal a matter, but the glory of kings is to search out a matter.
Proverbs 25:2

Dedicate this book and give special thanks to the big guy upstairs.
Envy was just an objection
It was
Kindness that was the true reflection

Table of Contents

1

Keep Austin Weird

Psalm 91:11
Once there was a young man who didn't think he could come to terms into adulthood

NOW I KNOW WHAT YOUR thinking Epics adventures but mostly about a cable guy, but trust me I know I know… but trust me it gets better, and I promise it gets weirder.

What if I told you everyone has a purpose and somewhere there's a place with secrets and magic, a place where the world revolves around its diversities, where all the weird and the unknown come together and meet in one exact time and place?

A place in Texas that is, Austin Texas, to be exact. Where do you think Austin got its reputation "keep Austin Weird," in the middle of the mighty Lone Star State, but to understand the whole concept we'll have to start from the beginning…

RADIO*–"Who is God? What is good? Why do we fear the unseen and the flickers in the shadows? For what matters, what do we really know? Matthew 7:7-8 my brother and sisters…

It felt like it was déjà vu just yesterday Stevie thought, changing it to the same radio podcast that was broadcasting the same rerun topic over and over when it's been a year, radio podcast announcer, "What's next after the severe global pandemic of 2020 that laid an after effect catastrophic across the world revealing the great awakening following into the next year to the sick sad world disclosing the corruption of today's world leaders as

1

the parties have been exposed to be high end criminal mafias with their occult agendas and global domination control called the great reset towards humanity a demise to their great deception of the draconian NWO that has come to past to an end some time ago, with the planets shifting its paradigm everyone is asking WHAT'S NEXT TO BE REVEALED, aliens, waking gods, how about dinosaur people?"

Stevie would hear over again the same re-run topic news at the same hour yesterday asking himself humorously as he tuned out the radio to the next station click on his seat belt before he drove off the parking lot like any ordinary maniac tragically escaping the nine to five matrix of orderliness society enslavement to labor, "I guess I'll take that as a sign?"

Stevie felt over-exaggerated about his lifestyle he was known to be the precocious one around his family having older siblings he always felt he wasn't understood.

Coming home from his daily boring routine from his work, a fifteen-minute drive was the only thing Stevie always look forward to the end of his tiring shift, he always turned to music rising his vibration frequency jamming up the volume to a few of his favorites on his smartphone auxiliary connected to his stereo in his truck with windows down blazing through the summer sunset as west Texas's wind hitting his face wearing his favorite shades.

It's the little moments like these Stevie would cherish after a long exhausting day of pushing carts at his local grocery store where originally he was supposed to be a cashier but he always got the short end of the stick maybe because he was one of the youngest at his job. Mostly every day coming home from work Stevie would take solitary moments to himself being raised as a Christian with Hispanic values and tradition he always turned to melodies introspectively music has always been part of his life connecting his mind and heart to the beat of the rhythm usually ending his thoughts from a prayer.

From being in a small town he felt stuck in a hole feeling doubtful for his future the thought of getting nowhere in life with no reason or meaning. He always felt like an adventurous guy stuck in a box, fear of being claustrophobic and being a bit tad dramatic in a small town with no directions or goals feeling desperate as if he wasn't going anywhere with his life.

Being only twenty years old with his birthday being near diagnosed with Hyperthymesia, it's a superior autobiographical memory at an early age. There have been a few to have accused Stevie of residing an old soul as he always claims he felt wiser than he should be, always feeling like the oddball out of the bunch of his family that can manage to crack a few jokes.

In a blink of an eye, it all of a sudden happen when his prayers were answered.

Turning onto Montague St. coming up towards north a block away from his home jamming in his pickup a street where he grew up with his elementary school being up the street that he use to attend living up northwest of San Angelo just inside of the out-skirt city limits, pulling into his block being about hundred yards from his parent's front driveway as their house faced the south.

Stevie contemplating addressing himself enjoying the loud music slowly strolling by he then bowed his head closing his moment with an "Amen."

Then within seconds looking up from retrieving control of the wheel swerving to an immediate left almost plowing down his parent's mailbox from running over the across street neighbor's spontaneous white cat, as a random song plays on the radio "anything can happen." (SC Music/1)

The whole neighborhood block knew the owner of the white cat was an old widow that had recently passed away knowing they had a special bond, so the neighborhood took upon the responsibility of leaving cat food for the cute little puffy fella with irresistible adorable blue eyes that uniquely crossed its eyes sometimes almost became pancake roadkill.

Fluffy was the name of the mysterious white cat that then runs onto his parent's pavement drive through under a vehicle he did not recognize as he pulls into the driveway parking his truck taking a couple of groceries into the house.

Stevie knew it was the cable company car, a black Hummer EV with a logo on the side of the Hummer that read, "Infinity Cable," which was a unique choice of a vehicle for a cable guy he thought. "Looks like dad's finally upgrading his cable services."

"Hey mom, is dad still at the farm? I got the groceries you wanted."

Stevie's mother always had a heart of an angel known for her hospitality always helping strangers in need. "Thank you mijo, put the eggs in the fridge please." Passing by the kitchen as he kissed his mom hello on the cheek who was stirring up a storm in the kitchen for dinner.

Stevie gave out a sigh, "Oh my gosh mom I almost ran over Fluffy just now pulling up to the driveway." Stevie's mother stops her dinner chores and turns to Stevie with her hands on her hips wearing an apron while holding a spatula in one hand like any other concern mom would with their motherly stern look. "I hope you weren't on your phone Steven, Lord heavens anything could be right in front of you!"

She smiled shook her head and gave a sigh. "And yes your father is at the family farm checking the water for the cows." Stevie pouring himself a glass of orange juice, "What's wrong with the cable, mom?" She then said turning back to her cooking on the stove in her green pink polka-dot kitchen apron, "A nice cable guy is outside at the back of the house by the outside basement cellar next to the windmill, I really don't know, he said he had to do some cable repair behind the house but I didn't see anything wrong with the cable on the television?"

Stevie then said and looked confused, "there's cable behind the house?"

Twenty-six years ago his family moved from his parent's first house that was located in the middle metropolitan area of the town moving into the outskirts of a Victorian farmhouse with antique huge old fashion high tall windows with high walls, and a wooden porch with white columns surrounding the porch from the front to the left side of the house.

Stevie's house face the south sitting next to the street

He always figured his parents thought it would be a good investment to move into a three acres lot size with an antique home built in 1896 by a well-suited family farm the Holliman's, which there is a school down the street was named after. Before the town grew around the farm it was the two-story house that was once the headquarters to a three thousands-acre ranch that use to have their own water system having an old rundown windmill standing beside a ruin old water tower pump house made out of bricks with a old septic tank place on top located behind the house being a couple of yards from a underground tornado cellar.

They say the house is haunted the only one on the block with pastures and trees between their neighbor's homes, not too long ago the house property used to be just outside city limits but now San Angelo has grown over time with new homes being built overtime on what used to be fields of pastures around the community and neighborhood. Down the block across the street from the school is a playground park located behind his folk's property.

"I didn't know there was cable at the back of the house, mom? Stevie's mom washing up plates replied, " I don't know… He seems nice." She continued, "Stevie can you run out and get the mail" Stevie then rushes gulping down his juice, and sighs "ok, mom."

Now, this is where it all started, and where it all got weird.

Coming back from the mailbox walking towards the front door of the front lawn glancing through the mail was the cable guy at his front porch.

As they walk past each other Stevie stepping onto the brick stairway he glances from the wooden porch and couldn't resist commenting randomly rolling off his tongue, "cable guy huh?"

The cable guy just nods his head and smiled to reply, "yes sir."

The odd thing about the cable guy and what shock Stevie was finding Fluffy the white cat all stirred up comfy occupied in the cable guy's arms purring as being scratching behind its ears knowing the cat was afraid of everyone and everything.

Stevie began to massage his left freezing hand, Stevie has always found it to be a comforting habit to warn his left hand when he tends to get nervous or suspicious, not only was Stevie amused by the stranger who was able to pick up Fluffy he just knew something was off about him.

Charlie was his name, label on his dark blue company polo shirt with the logo of infinity symbol representing Cable Company.

Stevie could see why his mom said he was nice cause he resembled features of an angel to a hero with a strong chin that belongs in one of those GQ magazines with all the American looks going for him. Wearing light brown sole high boots with blue jeans that looks like it was out of Levi's ad. He's one of those guys who's got a killer smile and could pull off a great Captain America costume for Halloween.

He wore a black arm sleeve spandex on his left arm assuming to cover up his tattoos.

This is where it got so weird where Charlie the cable guy lifted fluffy above his head while reaching for a blue shiny orb, an aura that was floating above them.

The white cat started pawing at the glistening blue orb shining above and seconds after fluffy snatch the blue orbit burst and evaporated into blue shiny sparkles glistening into the clear blue sky.

Ever since Stevie was little he had always had a gift he kept to himself able to see these so-called orbs in many places some in different colors like red, green, and even purple. Just like your flash photography with your camera catching those unexpected light orbs you sometimes see in your photos. Stevie never knew why he could see them but he has brought up the attention to his family a couple of times back when he was around six and eight years old. Like any other family "kids with their imaginations," his parents would say.

Even his sister nicknamed him a weirdo. A couple of times he would bring it up and would get shot back down with the same remarks since then he's never brought the strange subject up or hasn't spoken one word to anyone about it.

Now, this was different, Stevie knew he just bare witness proof of years of self-therapy that he wasn't going crazy. Stevie looks away immediately hoping the cable guy Charlie didn't recognize what he just witnesses. Stevie took a double look at Charlie who gently puts down fluffy "special cat you got there," he said as the cat runs off.

Flabbergasted as Stevie was caught off guard Charlie then says, "well good day sir" he nodded again and smiled and even his teeth had a sparkle to them.

As watching him walk away back into his black Hummer Stevie then abruptly asked, "Hey, are you guys hiring?" Charlie turns opening his car door before getting into his vehicle smiles and says, "We're always hiring."

As the black Hummer drives off Stevie then notices a bumper sticker on the back of his window, "Keep Austin Weird" and that ever since has always stuck with him.

Ever since then it was history from there, after that it was an epiphany, Stevie was too eager that he applied immediately online and that forever changed his life. Stevie took the chance with the cable company and made the big change that surprised his family and friends. Hired as cable tech support in a call center over the phones in Austin, the state capital of Texas, the Lone Star State.

Prior two months after applying and that weird incident he'll never forget, Stevie pack all his belongings feeling nervous and excited about the big change that he was finally making even though it's a four-hour drive away from home this was his first life-changing adventure but he had no clue… it was going to be epic.

Everything fell into place like it was meant to be, Stevie ended up moving in with a family friend Shay, who was his sister's best friend who moved to Austin a year ago. Shay has a degree in Associates of Applied Science in Nursing, but rather and loves to be behind the bar bartending. She had a vacant two-bedroom apartment after she had split with her boyfriend and was gracious to add Stevie to her lease splitting up the rent.

Six weeks passed, living in Austin was already a great start for Stevie. He enjoys the thriving urban city known to be "The Live Music Capital of the World," a reference to the many musicians and live music venues within the area.

Austin is one of the fastest-growing cities in the nation with distinctive flourishing cultures, along with many historical sites and a thriving growing economy for business and technology.

Austin is a diverse mix of Austenites, government employees, foreign and domestic college students, and high tech workers, with law enforcement, business folks like blue-collar workers, and most are artist and musicians.

At work Stevie was already taking cable calls after training four weeks into the job, it's a good job with just mandatory customer service request of simple tasks for billing issues and TV tech repair. Never did Stevie get a chance to see Charlie again after that weird encounter back in his hometown, "if it weren't for him I wouldn't be here," Stevie thought.

Stevie's abilities with encountering spheres and orb auras were remarkably too many in Austin, especially old sites and historical places. Stevie couldn't figure it out if it was due to the population with many old histories throughout Austin mostly seen in cemeteries or old sentimental monument sites. One thing Stevie learned throughout the years was able to adapt his gift to summon or abscond the orbs at his will, which he's gotten pretty good at shielding away these spiritual orbs from home. He always kept his secret to himself learning to accept it and keep quiet knowing he didn't want to sound like a nut-head keeping his insanity to himself.

Stevie could tell when an aura is near that's when his left-hand tingles it then turns icy cold very quickly. He could always feel a force or an invisible bubble that he can conjure suppressing the orb auras to vanish.

Never did again Stevie seen Charlie or anybody else to have the ability to see auras or better yet evaporate them with a cat!

The Infinity's cable tech support call center is located up north right off of Mopac and Duval road uptown city of Austin.

The call center looks like a shopping mall from the outside with a couple of trees surrounding the parking lot occupied with company vans and vehicles with other major shopping areas and markets across the interstate and surrounding areas.

The call center has a vast main lobby and two floors with a secret elevator that seems to have never work or to be used but there is a silly rumor among the employees that it leads to a secretive underground society or cult.

Even from the inside, the lobby looks huge walking in the entrance seeing high ceilings all-white tile floors with marble bland walls echoing every footstep throughout the lobby that can be heard.

When you first walk in the lobby looks like a shopping mall to the left is another small lobby with a line of customers either for exchange or pickup/drop off cable equipment and services.

To the right of the entrance, the lobby is a high rise security front desk, sitting behind it in a high desk chair was a short odd little fella who looks rough in his old ages maybe in his late eighties with a white beard and a leathery eye patch on his left eye. Stevie didn't bother to stare but his right eye had a unique bright blue twinkle. The little old man never did once look up always stuck his nose in a Sudoku puzzle book. It read "Janitor" as well as "security" along with the company's Infinity logo with no name badge to be seen on his blue janitor overalls where his uniform was over his Hawaiian aloha shirt underneath with a janitor push broom beside him on his high chair.

The janitor wasn't always there at times but when Stevie would pass by him his senses oddly would leave his left-hand freezing having to place them in his pockets, it was perfect fit in the category "Keep Austin Weird."

His aloha shirts were the opposite of what you would think it was covered with snowflakes or winter tributes.

Towards the back lobby white wall is a huge blue and white round time clock raised above the steel secretive elevator doors, which no one ever paid attention to or seen anyone used by an employee.

On the first floor to the left of the hall next to the steel elevator door is a red bench next to a stairway leading up to the conference room that was on the second floor. The rest of the hallway leads to the call center floor where Stevie's desk and about a hundred of a handful of employees taking service calls.

To the right of the steel door elevator is a small yellow trashcan next to a tall green plant in a purple colored pot.

Stevie's job is fairly easy to help and resolved the issue for the customer with their cable services. Little did he knew his weird special ability would come into play while working in a cubical desk with a headset on in front of his computer all day. Not far from his cubical is a high wall window that he dazes outside from time to time where down his row of desk cubicles is Stevie's supervisor's cubical who seems to always be absent from her desk from time to time.

Sitting at his desk he was one of the lucky ones to have a low cubical wall facing the window. Stevie's left hand would go into a frenzy cold at times leaving it to be one of those weird senses that he learned to grow up with knowing something unusual is going on around him.

He then spotted a green aura orb floating just right outside the high wall windows into the view. Oddly him being used to be the only one that could see these orbs floating Ashley his supervisor so happens to be there while Stevie not knowing she was watching him sitting quietly through her desk window cubical studying Stevie.

Stevie calmly closed his eyes taking a deep breath inhaling clinching his left cold hand. Exhaling, opening his eyes slowly the green aura orb was gone but surprisingly replace in front of him was his supervisor Ashley.

"Were you praying?" My supervisor is a recent graduate from Lubbock Texas at Texas Tech. Everything about her is bubbly to her Texan charm with blonde hair natural perm curls to her shoulders that bounce when she moves. One thing that stands out about her is her unique single streak of platinum white hair curled up in the middle that parts her hairline at the center top of her head. A white single streak hair in front of her face dangling with the other blonde curls. Stevie replies "oh no I'm sorry." Her round cute bubble face with high red round cheeks matching her bubbly big blue eyes and a smile that goes with her bubbly attitude.

Being from Lubbock Texas a graduate in her mid-early twenties she mostly wears dress attire with boots that suites her personality style.

"Oh well I do love a prayer, anyhow Mr. Ruiz, just wanted to say you've been up on your numbers and your scorecard is exceeding results on your job performance."

Stevie wasn't paying any much attention quickly trying to look over his supervisor's shoulder checking for any signs of the orb. She then said "you're meeting your quotes and metrics," rumbling on how well Stevie performance on his work ethics while Stevie was still constraining multi-tasking desperately trying to focus looking over behind his supervisor probing the window concerned as his left hand was still cold.

"Stevie is everything ok, is your left hand ok?" Stevie looking down at his left hand realizes it's cupped to his left chest over his heart with his right hand covering his left hand. Stevie got focused "ah… yeah… I'm sorry yes, everything is ok."

Ashley turns to the window checking out what Stevie was desperately trying to see. "With that being said, I know we're way too early for your six-month review but I want to offer you a position on behalf of myself and the cable company would love to use your skills and abilities in which I know you would be a great asset for the company."

Stevie was surprised "I know this is too sudden but we would love to have an interview with you tomorrow if you're up for the opportunity?"

Stevie was speechless replaying the scenario in his head of what his supervisor just hit him with. Stevie adjusts his hands down to his lap after his left hand was warmed up, "you're talking about me."

"Yes silly," she giggled. "Meet me at the steel elevator tomorrow no later than 5:30 pm sharp. I'm going to be out all day tomorrow in a conference meeting upstairs" Stevie rushed to say, "Wait?" He looked confused and shocked. "We're meeting at the elevator?" Ashley turns back with a grin as walking away from his desk, "is there a problem?" Stevie then snaps out from being shocked thinking of all the rumors and myths stirred among the employees about the steel elevator.

Stevie replied late, "No, I mean I want to say thank you!" His supervisor then last said, "Great I'll see you tomorrow at the steel elevator, and remember don't be late!"

Later on, that evening being too anxious Stevie texted his roommate Shay who was the only friend he knew at the time.

They ended up meeting at Austin's latest nightlife downtown on West sixth street which is the west side of Congress Street an area called West 6th Street District not mistaken for the actual sixth street known as dirty six a party fame street of music and bars located on the east side of Congress Street.

The west side is more high-end bars and clubs where Shay bartends at one of Austin's downtown hot spots since it opened about a year ago.

Meeting around early evening they decided to stroll down Dirty Six before shay went back to work. Shay was the same age as Stevie's sister around twenty-three years old and is recently seeing a guy who also bartends.

Standing outside the club Rio off of 6th Street Shay came out to greet Stevie from her break, "hey Stevie congratulations!"

Stevie's roommate is ginger with freckles that most definitely fit in with the urban lifestyle that dresses between chic and punk rock that skateboards with a piercing noise and a few tattoos. Shay was a dashing firecracker in her own way also works part-time gigs in the modeling industry around the city, she has a talent for keeping her hair color different shades of red every couple of months matching the seasons.

She reached for a hug, "congrats on your upcoming promotion I know you'll do great in your interview tomorrow you deserve it." Stevie then replies, "Yeah I know… Thanks, I'm a bit nervous about this interview. Not sure what I'm applying for but my supervisor who is a bit young but defiantly older than me, did mention I would be a great aspect to the team." Shay then replied, "That's great!" Stevie interrupted, "but wait there's more, I did become friends with an odd colleague of mine whose name is Allen but people call him crazy Al who is fascinated about a conspiracy of a steel elevator at our work in the middle of our lobby."

After waiting in line grabbing a few slices of pizza from Sixth Street, they were heading back to shay's work. "So you don't know what to expect coming out of that elevator? Better yet, you don't know what you're applying for?" Stevie replies, "Crazy Al has been working there for a few years, weirdest thing he tells me is that he's seen strange things come and go out of that elevator but who's to say no one believes him. He then goes on believing there's another world out there a secretive society that's hidden from the human eye, an old race we don't know about who ascendancy the stories we hear about tall tales of myths and legends around the world. I just don't know... then he goes on rumbling how it's all under our noses and we're all too blind to see it all."

Shay was skateboarding alongside Stevie as they walk back to her work.

"Wow that's crazy, what do you think?" There was a pause of silence then they both look up at each other and started laughing.

Stevie asks, "How's working at one of the hottest bars in Austin?" Shay replies, "well... there's this new club at the Warehouse district that's raking up all our customers for the past few days but today was the first time that business was slow. Supposedly this new club is a new alternative dance club like a magic cabaret show of some sort, I hear it's something new never before seen in Austin drawing a lot of crowds with having professional exotic dancers from all around the world I hear, performing their stunts of magic wonders whatever that means? I just call it entertainers." Stevie asked, "Aren't they called go-go dancers?" Shay answered, "No this is different, I hear there more like professional performers that sync dance routines and entertain with magic tricks something right out of Hollywood I guess." Stevie was intrigued, "cabaret dancers with magic huh?" "That's not all..." Shay continued leaving Stevie to briefly interrupting asking, "Wait there's more?"

"The owner who runs the club is rumored to be a secret ancient high priestess so my boss told me or a princess maybe who supposedly is an international supermodel from across the world." Stevie laughs, "Is there such a thing wow this all sounds really big. I wonder who she is?" Shay answered, "well whoever she is she's doing it right, she's bringing something new to Austin that the world has never seen."

Ending the conversation he escorted Shay back from her lunch break, "I don't know what to expect, but all I know is I got to kill this interview tomorrow." Stevie started to walk towards his vehicle.

"Go home and get some rest, I get off around three in the morning. I'll try not to be loud coming in tonight and good luck tomorrow." Stevie answered "no worries and thanks."

Shay marched up the stair entrance to her club as Stevie turns away heading back to his truck. Stevie's truck pulling out of the parking lot with the radio music coming on playing "Anything can happen" by Ellie Goulding.

Stevie couldn't shake the feeling that deep inside, in his gut, there was a little part of him that knew Crazy Al could be right.

2

The Interview

5:14

WALKING INTO THE PLAIN MAIN front lobby after Stevie had a long day of a work shift taking calls troubleshooting cable over the phones and the very first thing he did was look up at the clock to see the time.

Stevie notices he was early for his interview meeting with his supervisor at the steel elevator after work being a nervous wreck with sweaty palms all day.

He then seated himself on the red bench next to the steel elevator surround by white plain walls nothing out of the ordinary that no one recalls it ever being operational or even seen it open thoughts of the elevator being broken mostly people just think to assume it's for display show.

The day went by so fast never did Stevie see Ashley at her desk today but he did hear she was held up in the conference room all day. Nor did it help that the word got around the call center floor congratulating Stevie on his upcoming interview promotion for which he was still unaware unable to answer what he was applying for.

No thanks to Al but Stevie calls him Crazy Al for keeping his nerves in check, an older guy that sits next to Stevie in a desk cubicle in his well late forties into conspiracy theories that acts like he's in his twenties holding conversations questioning Stevie throughout the day.

Crazy Al was a nice guy possibility just lonely who works next to Stevie taking trouble calls on the call center floor and desperately looking for a friend, but all day before Stevie's interview crazy Al kept nagging him repeatedly over and over till it started to be a bit of a nuisance. "You have to tell me what's down there, what are they like, and you got to tell me what they up to?" Crazy Al pointed at Stevie with a pause hysteria look on his face, "but why you? Your one of them aren't you, they must know something about you? What did you do? What and who do you know? You'll tell me what's down there. Right? You promise, right?"

Being overwhelmed and exhausted from today's commotion waiting patiently on the red bench next to the mysterious steel elevator with his hands over his lap feeling a little skittish with his thumbs circling each other.

Stevie would stare straight up above the elevator door was a big blue clock remembering the exact time he arrived. It was just past 5:16p and suddenly Stevie's left hand started to freeze up placing it in his pockets knowing personally something unnatural was around nearby.

As he sat on the red bench never did take notice but out of nowhere to his left in a high-security desk sitting in it was the scrawny old security janitor who looks like a pirate on vacation while working. His long white beard had two white braided locks link to his bottom bearded from his chin. Wearing a right eye patch and a Hawaiian aloha snow shirt was revealing underneath his janitor jumpsuit uniform.

Stevie swore he remembers seeing the eye patch on his left eye before then suddenly the old man janitor got out of his security seat and grabs his long push broom hunching forward on it almost relying on the broom to support his balance.

You can tell by the old man's stance that he uses the broom as a walking stick most often wary of his old age. He was a little man no taller than 5'ft standing up to Stevie, he gradually walks over to Stevie with a little limp as the old man looks down at Stevie as he sat on the red bench who then looks up at the old man in shock.

Being mesmerized staring straight at his right twinkling empty eye socket it was filled with tiny cosmos stars like looking into a ignite toy telescope.

Stevie being paralyzed unable to move was amazed and daunted by the old man's sparkling eye, silently with the push broom in the old man's right hand and a clipboard in the other hand as he handed Stevie the clipboard that woke him up after being bewilderment over janitor's sparkling eye.

The janitor started sweeping and whistling in a high melody that seemed to put Stevie in a relaxed trance. The old man kept sweeping towards down the left side of the hallway until he was out of Stevie's view with his magical trance whistling throughout the hallway until it faded away with him.

Stevie didn't think twice about the odd recent event where he was focusing on his interview glancing at the clipboard he notices it was a sign-up checklist.

The INTERVIEW was the heading and it read,

"Name: Date:"

On top the left corner and the top right corner was

"Time: and Rev:"

The checklist wasn't much of an application, in the middle were four checkboxes lettered A, B, C, and D, with a red line between B and C. Stevie filled out what's requested filling in his Name as it requested, Steven Ruiz, and then the Date, 2/22/20, and time Stevie wrote, 5:30p.

Stevie was clueless to what (Rev:) meant on the application, Stevie placed 17:14 in military time, which was the actual arrival time when Stevie first walk in taking notice of the blue clock time and was taught to never leave applications blank so he thought no harm done.

Only a couple of few minutes went by sitting on the red bench silently too eager and nervously thinking of the rumors flying around in his head about this so called special mysterious elevator.

Stevie started to giggle at his ludicrous ideas more never less thought the opportunities would open for him being just a coincidence out of the blue.

Could it be true that Special Forces like elites have access to this mysterious elevator that's quoting from Crazy Al? "I know they're all authoritarian who have secretive meetings and upholds the ordinance that affects the majority of our world's everyday lives!"

There was a sound of click… click… click… echoing from the stairs that lead up from the second-floor conference room just to the left behind the elevator.

Just right around the corner of the elevator coming down from the stair steps appeared his supervisor Ashley being from Lubbock Texas she was in her brown boots that always seems to collaborate with all the colorful outfits of dresses she wears.

Today's outfit was different she was wearing book glasses looking smart with her frames that settle her round face wearing a yellow daisy sports dress which matches her bubbly attitude and bouncy blond curls. "Steven, you're here early."

Stevie being a nervous wreck was speechless. "Oh sorry for the whole four eyes thing going on here on my face." She chuckled, "my contacts dried up, you know how that goes." Ashley was smiling ear-to-ear, "You do go by Stevie as your name, don't you?" Stevie then broke his silence "ah, yes please, my friends call me Stevie." Handing her the clipboard and with her other hand she pulled out a company badge swiping her card into the elevator magnetic lock with a sound "bing," and the steel elevator doors opened slowly.

Ashley step into the elevator began to speak as her naturally perm blonde hair bouncing to her shoulders side to side steadily with her stepping pace going along with her motions. "Oh, I didn't realize you have a clipboard ready for me look at you ready for your first interview."

Ashley was studying Stevie and then asked, "nervous?"

Stevie was numb staring at the opening entrance to the enigmatic steel elevator doors before stepping in. Losing his track of thought he was reminiscence all the stories at work that were told about this eerie elevator which looks quite normal from the inside that can hold eight, with its walls having steel sides with full glass mirrors having a faint distinctive clean smell to it.

Ashley was smiling holding the elevator's door open for Stevie to step in. Hesitating for the moment Stevie caught himself staring at his reflection from the elevator's back mirror-wall and could have sworn he saw his reflection wink at himself.

At that split second before Stevie stepped onto the elevator, thoughts stirred from the back of his mind feeling the sudden warmth of consciousness comforting him that feeling deep inside of his gut that was telling him to jump, leap, step forward.

"Psalm 121:8

The Lord will watch over your coming and going both now and forevermore." Ashley then excused herself for sharing hugging her clipboard as she watches Stevie hop into the elevator, "It's a quote that I love to remind myself now and then when I get anxious."

Stevie listening to his instinct stepping into the elevator he notices and was surprised at the magnitude of the elevator's buttons, that there were one hundred and one level floors to be exact.

"The elevator is quick and simplistic actually" Ashley saying as she sees Stevie's reaction to the elevator buttons. She then says, "Below underneath every floor, we pass is two seconds per floor that's how prominent this elevator is.

With Stevie then asking, "how deep does this go?" Ashley continued to say, "Believe it or not it's ocean deep approximately about thirty seven thousands feet below I presume." Stevie quick on his math replies, "That's seven miles deep!

Ashley then responds and chuckles as if she's used to seeing the participant shock after the effect coming to a realization, "looks like somebody knows their math."

Ashley then sounded precautious "These elevator doors are the only one of the few entrances to come in and out to the inside world from underground." Stevie wondered what she meant by the inside world but more closely what was inside the deep underground.

There are four rows of buttons vertically counting twenty-five buttons for each row with a special single star button located in the middle of the elevator's buttons diagram.

She then selected button number twenty-five that lightened up with a bell sound, "bing."

"The twentieth floor is our intern block testing it's for your first interview." Feeling unease Stevie was startled doubting the situation with the elevator lights flickering for a split second starting with a little bump start grabbing ahold of the side rail feeling the falling impact plummeting straight downward. There was a countdown with a small ring that sounded for every floor they passed. Stevie nervously stirs up the courage to ask, "Ashley, if I may ask what is it exactly am I applying for?"

"Bing," the elevator passing through the fifth floor.

Ashley fixing her curls off the reflection from the elevator mirrors and replies, "oh, I thought I told you." She quickly continues, "Were promoting you as an authoritarian mystic or just a specter, a Christian like myself, or wizards, and knights, maybe warrior, or just a security guard but our profession is called (Specialize Elusive Entity Rudimentary) better known as Seers."

A secret society of intelligent agency of protectors known to the government as the adjustment bureau aka Seers that can see things and do things no one can do for we are the custodians of this planet.

She then goes along and explains, "among other things Seers do but mostly manage Austin Texas, which is a refuge to such a magical creatures and places of some sort for a lot of people who are that we like to say a little different in their magic elements."

Those words hypnotically drew onto Stevie as Ashley went on excitedly furthermore to explain.

"Most Seers are selected from the tales you've heard from are either lineage of witches, vampires, werewolves, to nomad warriors, saints, and wizards. We are the front line forces when grace falls and protection requires against the supernatural that goes bumping in the night. Everyone here has something special in ways the outside world wouldn't understand." Ashley quoted again showing her strong attributes of being a Christian that she loved the habit to shine her bible quotes.

"1 Corinthians 2:5

That your faith should not stand in the wisdom of men, but in the power of God."

"You've been chosen to an audience of one of the world's oldest rarest organization that maintains order among the supernatural along the side of being innuendo from the world as undercover cable guys hidden from the mortal eye that you'll also be providing trouble calls for cable service," she chuckled and said proudly. "Isn't it the perfect cover? Oh, that part always gets me, it's cute!"

Stevie then asks being clueless, "you're kidding?" Ashley responded, "not kidding." Stevie then replied, "These Seers that you have me out to be for an interview seems too much of a big responsibility I don't even know if I'm too sure what you guys still do?"

"Why it is a big responsibility not everyone can do it," Ashley then said excitedly making it sound so easy! "It's a one of a lifetime experience hand on hand filled with engaging magic transactions with the unexpected world of the supernatural." Ending her last word rolling her L's in her slang country accent. "It's always those who find their gifts first are the few that are chosen on this planet living in a world of secrecy."

Ashley then said she had time to explain what a Seer is even though she told him you'll go through the explanatory once more again if you pass the interview. "Amending through the millennia we managed to keep humanity protected learning to adapt to our worlds to protect and augment our powers. We, Seers, uphold our sacred law called the Covenant Code 9:12-17 better known as the Arc law." Ashley then hinted and said "Genesis" with a wink at Stevie and continued with her sentence.

"It's a binding agreement fulfilled over almost four millennia years ago among all creation to bind all archons who are also called gods and spirits for that matter and every magical creature that was left to walk the earth are forced by the Aether binding them to its rules where the Arc law is unseen found in every element matter that dwells on this planet. On that high note we Seers, are the ones that stands in between the reality of this world and the supernatural of their worlds. Since the time of the great biblical flood we have always been the last resort for the protection of humankind restoring balance and peace to this world from those unbinding the Arc law who are of the unnatural." She had said making a sour face at the end of her sentence.

"Bing," passing the twentieth floor reminding them they were still plummeting downward.

Stevie just nodded thinking how crazy this all sounds to him with Ashley's expressing much passion for the cable company he wasn't sure if she was serious. Stevie then trying to backtrack, "I'm sorry did you say supernatural, as in Gods, magic creatures, and having powers?" Ashley smiling back and said, "more on that subject later if you pass your interview which I'm sure you'll do fine."

"Bing," the twenty-fifth floor. "Ah, we're here…"

Being distracted she would glance over at the clipboard reserved in her arms slowly reviewing the application sheet that she received from Stevie.

She had a sudden pause to herself eyeing the clipboard while gathering her thoughts Stevie notice her brief moment and asks, "Supernatural huh?"

Ashley didn't entirely focus on Stevie as she was still glued to the check sheet application on the clipboard, "it is beyond what is natural honey," with her eyes still fixed on the checklist even though there wasn't much to look at.

"Ah… Isn't that the same thing," Stevie asks?

She turns slowly at Stevie smiling, looks upon Stevie again this time to study him, then her eyes fix back to the clipboard once more. "You prayed for this didn't you," she said swiftly being a strong Christian that is she with such faith pulling a question out of the air?

Stevie looks back at her dumbfounded, "If you mind me asking darling, do you go to church?" Stevie replied nervously, "I'm Catholic, I try when I can." He wasn't sure where she was going with the questions but he did notice some interest in her face that showed grace.

"It doesn't matter you're here now." She smiled.

Stevie was clueless about where the awkward conversation was going leaving him spellbound, her left eyebrow gave off an admonitory gesture arching a high perceptive above her brow starring at the checklist fishing for an answer.

Ashley then asks, "5:14 military time huh?"

Stevie was puzzled and answered, "Sorry, wasn't sure on that part of the sheet. I just didn't want…" Ashley interrupted blinking her eyes smiling to finishing Stevie's sentence. "To leave an application blank…"

Letting out little laughs as Stevie then said, "That's right… that's the time I arrived here for the interview."

She pulls out a red pen with a click having Stevie ask, "I wasn't sure what "REV," meant."

Ashley again interrupted with a big smile on her face, "no worries, it's nothing to worry about." With that she took her red pen marks a check onto the application check sheet clip to the clipboard in her hand, "pass."

She then turns to Stevie smiling with her eyes reading his reaction studying him leaving Stevie to wonder if it's possible she could read minds as he quickly tries to change subjects.

"What's down there the very bottom?" Ashley "what floor 101 why It hasn't been used for some time, no one has managed to go to the pit, so I hear it was a cell block at the beginning of its time and then used as an intern block back in the day for interview testing's, oh wait…!" She then looks at Stevie with an epiphany look, "what a great idea lets test it out!"

Hitting the special star button that leads to the bottom pit as they drop again plummeting faster to the bottom this time passing floors by the second as the elevator lights flickered again for the second time having Ashley saying "we really got to get that fix."

"Bing," rings passing the 58th floor. "Listen to me carefully there are three interviews to initiate to become a Seer two you must pass. The first one will be a test in the intern block testing's and the second interview will be the congregation of the tri-paradox. Whatever happens, just know to keep your faith pious for we are all chosen for a purpose. As a Christian, we have to keep our heads up high when the proof comes to those who do not ask for it living in a world of secrecy."

Stevie was a little bit taken back "How and why me?" She then easies herself and calmly states, "because something greater than you sent you here, either it chose you for a reason or you ask for it but if you were to ask me quite frankly everybody has a gift you just need to find your destiny."

There was a pause silence. "Bing," they arrived again this time under the ground of the bottom pit of the one hundred and one floors.

Breaking the silence, "now…" she said being cheerful with her rosy cheeks blushing with her bouncy blond perm "we're here," as the elevator door opens slowly.

An astonishing cold breeze was in the air with earthy aroma filled Stevie's nostrils, much as he wanted to get out of that awkward setting in the elevator, the 101th-floor was pitch black in an eerie way. Stevie could only make out what looks like a dark hallway noticing Ashley was analyzing him waiting for his next move as if this were a test.

Feeling his left hand stirring up in coldness he places his cold numb hand in his pocket anxiously taking a step into the dark hallway as a long fluorescent light bulb above comes on following with his steps. There were three more fluorescent light bulbs lighting up the dark hallway that was about twenty yards long. Ashley then said, "let there be light," she giggled.

"We would call this place the reformatory, aka the black hole, some call it the pit or the cell." Ashley then fastens to mend her skirt dress standing behind while Stevie took a look around taking it all in at once.

"Sorry for the quick geographic lesson but we've reached the very last floor underneath these Texas hills if you want to know, are numerous wonders of caves founded on a Balcones fault under the Quachita Mountains that range as far out from here throughout central Texas that formed about 300 million years ago during the continental collision from what we know about."

It didn't look much just a creepy calm cold long white hallway and on the right side of the hallway are four big wall panel windows.

Stevie couldn't see on the other side of the dark windows, for all four of them were pitch black in a dark room. A red line is awkwardly painted in the middle center of the hallway, dividing the pair sets of dark windows. At the end of the hallway was the last fourth window boarded up painted caution in red collecting dust and cobwebs, it looks like something straight out of a twilight light zone.

It wasn't much of a room with the hallway being twenty yards long and seven feet wide with a dead-end white wall.

On the left side of the hallway is just a back white wall.

Each of the four wall windows has its panel box of buttons to the side, one red and the other green that was located upper left of each dark windows.

Ashley walks over to the first dark window to the panel box and opened up the clear panel lid. At this point, Stevie was confused and a bit terrified watching her reaching to push the red button and she said, "Once the light comes on, I want you to tell me what you see?"

Stevie watches in dismay as his adrenaline was racing. Reaching for the box she pressed the red button and the lights in the first window came on, lighting up a nine by nine feet squared empty white room fit for an interrogation room.

With the clipboard adjusted in her hand to her side, she then looks at Stevie with a steady stern face waiting for his answer.

Not once did she ever turn to look at what's on the other side of the window she asks again with her red pen ready to mark on her checklist she began testing Stevie through the interview asking again, "What do you see?"

This was a life-changing moment for Stevie, as he knew right there and then he had to make a choice.

Speechless and confused, he was reminiscing through his head thinking to himself this can't be surreal.

On the other side of the first window in the white interrogation room were two colored aura spheres, red and blue. Ashley then asks again, "One more time, but I'm going to make this simple. Do you see anything?"

Stevie looks to Ashley who never took her eyes off Stevie, and then he looked at the color sphere auras at the window.

Stevie always had a hard time with his secret, never had shared or revealed his personal secret with anyone except with one or two occasions with his close family but here at this moment, he was finally being exposed.

Momentarily whispers were filling up his head and his heart leap.

With his jaw open he nodded yes trying to get a word out flabbergasted about what he just shared revealing what he saw as the whispers that were calling him to answer in his head got louder till he shouted, "yes!"

Never in his life has he ever meet anyone else besides the one-time meeting, Charlie, the cable guy, or even relate to anyone else at what he could see.

Ashley giggled and clapping with excitement trying to keep her happy composure. "This is great!" shriek Ashley.

Stevie paused with his palm hands up in the air and began with a stutter, "wait, wait, wait? You can see that? Who are you? What are you?"

"See what?" Ashley asks.

Moment of silence was stirred, Stevie finally answered and said, "I see two colored sphere auras one blue the other red."

Ashley then turns to the window and asks, "Really, what else do you see?"

Stevie looks onto the color orbs once again and then Ashley said, "If you look harder what do you see?"

Stevie was concentrating starring harder into the color orbs and suddenly the orbs started to take shape of damned souls left on this plane dimension to drift alone forever. The red orb formed to be a ghost of a little paperboy that looks to be from the early 1920s, and the blue orb appeared into a gentle granny knitting in her rocking chair.

Stevie paused reopening his eyes from taking a deep breath before he answered, "A paperboy and a granny in a rocking chair." Realizing the ghosts can see Stevie both spirits recognize that Stevie could see them having his left hand unfamiliarly went very warm from cold as if he was wearing mutton.

Stevie then faced the huge panel window as he shut his eyes clenching his left fist taking another deep breath and the damned souls started to smile and were both glistering in a shiny aura as they turned to look up above them was a pure white light appearing upon the two aura souls and then they were gone.

Ashley again looked shocked as if she was amused at what she too just witnessed. Shaking her head snapping out of her deep thought and she continues, "you're not a witch or saint are you? Never mind," she said and went on with the next test.

"Now let's move on," Ashley checking off the interview checklist.

Smiling twitching her nose pushing her large glasses back to rearrange her bridge nose. "Those orbs we like to call them shades. In Latin, it's the word umbra, or ghost, energy, spirits, phantasm whatever you like to call it they are damned to roam the earth until the end of time. You were never alone and you're not going crazy, it's a gift, a specter that is blessed to see under the veil, most Seers are specters. "

A blessing Stevie thought, he always found it a nuisance but Stevie had a lot of questions that stirred up and decided to go along with the interview and to ask afterward.

Ashley looks at her watch and was wrapping up her sentence, "The whole veil thing with Seers we'll get to that here shortly but right now we're on a tight schedule."

Walking to the second dark window with its lights being off, Ashley then reaching with her hands opening the second window clear panel box lid, behind her was the middle centered red line to not cross dividing the other two windows with the fourth window border up.

The second dark window was a little off Stevie could hear vibrations from the other side of the glass window. A humming sound or more of a loud buzzing sound leaving Stevie a dreadful feeling that came over him wanting to get this interview over with. Stevie took a step back facing the second window as Ashley pressed the window's red button that illuminated the whole room. Immediately he backed up with his back press against the white wall, "Bees, honeybees!"

Filled with honeycombs of bees in the second room. Frozen in place above Stevie on the window he notices air vent holes were opening releasing the bees into the hallway.

Ashley hadn't moved from her spot being calm as ever her eyes were fixed on Stevie. Never had he had issues with bees nor was he ever afraid of them that never has he witnessed this massive of bees before.

Stevie had no clue what all this interview was about, still expecting to wake up from a dream any moment now and within seconds the whole hallway was filled with bees trying to fill up every space of the hallway.

Stevie stood there, calm, eyes fix onto Ashley copying cat her every move.

The whole hallway was laden massively covered with bees, but yet not one bee has touched Ashley or Stevie. They seemed to be protected in like a force field of a bubble shielding them from the bees. Stevie could barely see Ashley through the shades of bees with buzzing sounds barely seeing her smiling ear to ear.

Her clipboard was up to her hips, marking her second check on the interview checklist. "Check," she said.

Stevie started to shut his eyes clenching his left fist again. Ashley then went to say, "Honeybees are tiny trustworthy farmers of our planet, the bees are the ones that sort out the good and the bad just like honey, hmm… Well what you know we're sweet!" Suddenly Stevie was conjuring back the same warm feeling he encountered at the first window wishful thinking for all the bees to be back in their honeycomb feeling a warm tingle sensation in his left hand again. The progression of the bees seemed to be swarming back into the vent holes above the window.

Ashley was still rumbling on how the bees connect to the world, "Bee's are royal rumor has it that Bees were naturally earth's first living creatures and the acceptance of the bees can sense one with bravery and compassion for the world. They can sense earth… followers…" Ashley being distracted, less than a minute subduing all the bees, Stevie open his eyes and all the bees were back in their honeycomb room where Ashley presses the green button closing the window vents.

Stevie then blinks livelily amazed at what just happen, with Ashley standing there this time her jaw open like she just saw another ghost while Stevie still blinks livelily amazed again at what just happen.

Ashley abruptly passed Stevie heading straight to the elevator signaling the end of the interview.

Thankfully Stevie was hoping that was the ending of the interview, he followed after her then she paused feet away from the elevator door. Hoping to get back on the elevator, "was it something I did, what am… I " Stevie said interrupted by Ashley turning her head, looking over Stevie's shoulder facing at the third window.

She looks down across the hallway at the red-painted line like it's some barrier line for your protection. It's was centered in the middle of the hallway between the second bee window and the third darken window.

Wanting the interview session to end Stevie was hoping to get back on the elevator as Ashley looks at her watch and says "one more test."

Right before passing the third window, Stevie notices a red caution sign hang upright on the white wall that reads, "WARNING PLEASE DO NOT FEED IT FEAR." Stevie rolled his eyes thinking to himself, "it's so time to get back on the elevator hoping to snap out of this dream."

This time following Ashley walking over the red line to the third dark window Ashley did seem a little edgy, reaching the red panel button, Ashley mentions, "FEAR is False Evidence Appearing Real."

Stevie was double-checking reading the WARNING sign again as he read, "Please Do Not Feed it Fear."

"Hey, Ashley what does…"

Lights went out in the hallway, but a light in the third window was the only empty room that was illuminating an eerie dim light into the hallway from the window. Oddly Ashley was nowhere to be seen in the dark hallway as if she disappeared, "Ashley?" Stevie's left hand went icy cold and he could sense something wasn't right. Stevie could see from the corner of his eye and could hear a shuffle movement in the dark at the end of the hallway towards the elevator door.

Stevie thought he was going crazy and swore he saw a glimpse of a familiar redhead doll in small blue overalls from his childhood nightmares scamper into the dark corner shadows at the end of the hallway.

Then Stevie was startled taking his full attention after hearing what sounded like someone crying in another corner at the other end of the hallway from the exit of the elevator.

"Ashley," He said in an alarm tone walking slowly towards the whining cry trying to make out the figure coming to life within from the dark corner with the only dim lights illuminating to cast light from the third window.

Stevie reaching out his hands towards the crying mysterious shadow figure taking shape, then the crying stops, as his fingertips were about to tap its shoulders as Stevie froze petrified at what he witness from the dark corner that it felt like his heart was in his throat. Stevie was looking at something bad or someone bad, a very peculiar familiar at the backside of its dirty, torn, old stripe red and green sweater with brown khaki pants also barley can see through the dark making out to be wearing what looks like a dark brown fedora hat.

The dark shadows that came to life were the mysterious figure that let out a malevolent laugh as it spins around slashes at Stevie with its right-hand glove with claw dagger knives.

Before being slashed Stevie lunges back falling backward onto the ground barely missing Stevie leaving a little slash rip on his shirt. Being on his back terrified Stevie began crawling backwards looking back at his childhood nightmares raised as a kid watching summer movies from the eighties having older siblings the shadows were coming to life before him.

The highly well-known character of the American nightmare with the creepy fedora hat began laughing historically with its presence being alive while peering out of the dark second window was a second terrifying character in a white Halloween mask in blue overalls with a huge kitchen knife in its hand.

Stevie shuffled on the ground crawling backward quickly to get up staggering onto the first dark glass window where he made out to see the aura-colored shades at the beginning of his interview.

Stevie could make out another shadow nightmare taking place in the first dark window beneath the flickering lights, as it approaches the dark figure in the first window appeared to be wearing a white hockey mask with a chainsaw being crank up aiming at the first indestructible window igniting sparks to fly.

In a panic as Stevie was on the other side of the first window sheltering himself crouch with his hands over his head realizing there was no broken glass that broke through.

"What's going on?" Stevie realizes then that the windows could not be penetrated with the nightmare burnt face character patronizing and still laughing from at the other end of the hallway with Stevie notices his nightmares couldn't cross the painted red line barrier.

Panicking Stevie didn't know what to do and started to clap, "Ok guys the gigs up hahaha, you all got me, guys." Thinking to himself he thought for the fourth time he must be in a dream closing his eyes with his left hand going crazy with a feeling of an icy/hot chill throughout the inside of his bones clearing his thoughts taking a deep breath and counted to three. "One, two, three," he opened his eyes and to his surprise, no one and nothing was there just an empty dark hallway with an obscured light by the third-panel window.

Suddenly running at him from the dark corner coming from the end of the other side of the hallway hollering psychotically it was one of his worst nightmares the small peculiar red hair demon boy doll famously known from the movies was the killer possessed doll.

The nightmares he began to notice were all main antagonists from Stevie's childhood American horror movies. Shockingly the American demon doll nightmare from Child's Play ran screaming past the red line on the floor towards Stevie as he screamed in shock with his quick instinct kicking the light-weight cursed red head demon doll at the other side across the hallway disappearing into the darkness. Everything went silent again like a roller coaster waiting to be surprised with Stevie backing up to the elevator door pasting to catch his breath desperately to open the door feeling for any button in the dark.

Spontaneously pressing the elevator buttons there was a loud annoying flat high pitch crackle laughing that he remembers from his very young childhood years that it echoed with dark shadows that were appearing to be moving across the walls along the indestructible four large windows was darkness liquefying to form to take shape.

The heinous afloat shadow started changing making its way towards Stevie shifting over the walls gliding and soppy onto the floor like black tar melted dark boiling liquid bubbling barely lifting itself making into shape with a familiar sinister crackle it made again and suddenly the dark was gone with the hallway lights coming on.

Stevie shielding his eyes to adjust his sight to the light with his back to the elevator door dragging on the floor looking up at Ashley, "yep, we're not doing that" she quickly added to say. Again Ashley with her familiar astonished look on her face blushing red with her eyes wide open blinking in awe standing at the same spot where she first vanished just a while ago with the lights on reappearing with her clipboard in her hand.

"Check!" With her eyes filled with concerns and certainty, she began writing notes. Stevie abruptly had to ask and said, "WHAT THE HECK WAS THAT?"

Ashley was quick to answer," oh that, well that's some annoying residue stuck here in this underground cell the reformatory it's a black hole." She nodded drastically as her delightful curls bounced she continued. "That use to resides in and out from our dimension from time to time once part of an ancient deity that was destroyed and broken a very, very long time ago leaving its darkness to be consumed by all the shadows of human hearts. You did create those monsters by fear made up of shadows that lurk from every dark corner of this very every room, closets or even under your bed, you may have heard of its other well-known name also called the Boogieman."

Stevie asks, "you were there the whole time, wait, I did what?" Ashley was serious in tone manner with her Texan accent, "it was all you darlin', you're gifted, you have a gift. What you have is special, never seen anyone like you before who could order a nightmare."

"So it's true what they say," Stevie asks? "What you mention about Seers, you're not joking?"

Ashley replies with a nod and said, "the supernatural."

Stevie answered "the supernatural right… so all this was some kind of test? I almost died!" Ashley smiles at Stevie walking towards the elevator "but you didn't."

Stevie was taken back by her answer as she turns around giggling and signaling her hand at Stevie to step forward to the elevator with the other hand holding the clipboard to her hips. "No worries they're harmless…" she then spun around while Stevie examined down at his fresh tear in his shirt and she whispered to herself, "so I hope."

Glancing at her watch again, "All in time we'll talk later to fill you in but right now I got to get you back up to the main library the congregation final interview of the tri-Paradox the council chambers, its the MAIN EXAMINATION where all the first Seers gather."

She then presses the elevator button "Bing" the elevator door opens allowing Stevie to pass through. Ashley then asks, "Hey I do have to ask about your nightmare?" Stepping into the elevator Stevie then went to say, "wasn't it the American classic Boogieman." Ashley then asks, "Let me guess you have older siblings?"

As Stevie notice, she selected elevator floor buttons number fifty followed by the star button and Stevie shrugged his shoulders and nodded yes.

"Bing," the elevator response to alert it was ready to close.

Ashley was quick to say, "oh my gosh you're doing so great you pass all your intern block interview test, by the way, if you keep it up you might just get the job. All this examination was a test to move onward to be ready for your third final test following after your last interview with the congregation of the tri-paradox.

Stevie was thinking, "great another test."

Ashley continued, "you and a few select gifted others like yourself that pass the first test are up against each other for the position, now off you go to the library council chamber to the fiftieth level."

She winks at Stevie releasing her hand letting go of the elevator door leaving Stevie strained alone in the elevator to his last interview. "What is the third test," he asks?

Ashley rushed to say before the elevator closed, "you'll know if you pass the final interview, it will all make sense later I promise but right now you're late to your congregation of the tri-Paradox your final interview good luck!"

3

Final INTERVIEW

"Wow" was the first word that came out of Stevie's mouth when the elevator doors open.

Stevie was flabbergasted at the first view of this so-called majestic library that he realized he was standing in the middle of a vast huge million years old subterranean city that lays deep underground complex being on the fiftieth ground below floor.

The library is what they call this secretive underground ancient city, it being so magical in different ways it was viewed as a museum library cavern with its grand sepulcher foyer above a comprising vast network of giant tunnels that leads to chambers, mines, and huge halls to behold with mass division mansion spaces that ran under and ultimately through the Balcones fault under the Quachita Mountains across Texas.

The underground library hall chambers were exaggerated with tremendous pillars immeasurably high above up to the ceiling of the cavern following to make out to be an enormous cave with multiple numerous shiny gems trough out with crystals of all kind.

There been giant caverns seen around the world but never has Stevie seen anything like this before visiting a few caves in his past with family vacation trips but thinking how remarkable the view of the main library that looks to be a repository museum with multiple-story floors indescribable level parts on the outer side of the cavern having most of the floors shelved with cases of numerous books and secured glass boxes displaying unique collectible objects.

If Stevie had to describe his amazing discovery of the bewildered unearth underground city cavern it was a beautifully plan domain that belong to a mysterious lost civilization that is complete with temples, pastel painting dwellings, workshops, stables, and other buildings including a palace. Complete with hydraulic underground waterways it has a perfect water drainage system along without other modern maintenance.

Compared to the underground city humongous size of space were nestles with permanent lighting is provided by large crystalline balls by the thousands sparkling radiant with glowing rocks and scattered crystals set in the walls and ceilings among the cavern and floors with full luminosity lights shimmering lighting up every dark corner. Stevie found it oddly weird sticking his arms out he notice there were no shadows to cast anywhere with no indirect lighting fixtures none just perfectly illuminated by the fused crystals of the library cavern.

Strolling through the greatest library Stevie has ever seen there were a couple of hanger rooms with huge castle doors partially open among the great corridor hallways as he passed by some look like classrooms filled in their chambers with sets of tables and chairs. Another chamber looks like a computer lab occupied by several TV sets displayed with every coverage news channel and media with computers monitoring all social media networks around the world.

All awhile most of the computers were being used by Seer colleagues where one Seer was watching a YouTube video of a toddler who caught on video of an actual fairy that landed on a toddler's hand laughing together all caught on a videophone having the Seers commenting to cover its tracks, "It's Photoshop, this is fake," tracking down and commenting multiple related supernatural videos that were exposed.

To the other side of the great corridor halls, were other rooms with some occupied in session with an over-seer mentor demonstrating to a few Seer trainees how to use their ultimate weapon against the supernatural with using the cable-guy controller remotes, a well hidden device tool disguised as a simple remote that is issued to every Seer for help as well as to be used for cable service for televisions.

There is a lair in the center of everything were various stairs of different stages with different kinds of types of stairs leading to somewhere. Some stairs are stone and concrete, some made out of old wood and some were short, some stairs were long and some were spiral and even some were upside down. There were also a part section of some stairs with magic and some were steep with old ruins having aged stone rocks that were leading to other corridor halls and doors with other vast chambers resemblance of underground castle warehouses is best to be described as a funhouse maze within the world's biggest library museum located within over hundreds of feet underneath the ground known to be a secretive temple base that holds one of the hidden oldest libraries of the world.

Stevie came to a vast chamber hall with so many unique antiquity streamers were garnished with different colors upon banners strung up high across throughout the sanctum library.

So much folklore and history were also among the adroitness of the interior decor hung on huge canvas paintings some were above marble statutes telling a story with so many monuments that were also decorated throughout the halls.

High above the inner chamber halls, technology being used never before seen with vibrant electric torches adorn onto the massive pillars of stones making up the inner light sanctum of the library.

Scattered around among nearly every majestic natural stone pillar resides a mass of viewing screens which could only be described as an amalgam of medieval arcane technologies, and the sleek futuristic tech machinery of tomorrow.

Every screen insight is illuminated with various scenes each different viewing of the constant stream of all of the world's news simulcast in a steady cacophonous hum.

Throughout the hall, most of the Seers were disguise as cable guy employees in their uniform polo company shirts and some wearing t-shirts with a branded company infinite logo.

Some were buried in their work while others were in teams filing papers and documents doing researches with books and using the computers.

Passing along the way there was even a department quarter called Inquiries, Stevie swore he could have seen through the window oddly a team of three Seers in their three books killing time he thought as they were all watching a well-known children movie on their computers taking notes on the classic of Alice in Wonderland calling themselves as a team called the ace of spades.

Stevie was found to be impressed by the main long quarters a causeway arch of the library cavern that Stevie could see clear out of sight as far as the human eye could see so vastly long the hallway would stretch and it would curve with a curvature of the earth.

In another hanger chambers were more training rooms with a few offices assisting special clients at their desk. Awkwardly there were a few random citizens spotted that were not Seers, they too were a little bit odd and out of place.

A tiny plump grandmother in a Sunday's morning church outfit wearing all in pink with blue polka-dots matching head to toe including her purple hair wearing a rose blue diamond brooch pin with a blue flower rain bonnet over her purple head was pushing a baby pink piglet in a blue baby stroller coming out of the office.

The old grandmother seemed to be a little off guarded talking to her self-mumbling with a quick glance at Stevie with curiosity while passing by each other who then rushed off.

Then Stevie was crossed by an express mailman who had blonde curly locks wearing a brown uniform with a caduceus symbol and with shorts above his knees that look outdated as if he was a retro fifties telegram rushing in and out as if late to his next destination.

The most awkward thing Stevie notices about the mailman is that he glowed about him, a vivid light surrounding him like silver blazing metallic color lining outlining his whole body. The deliveryman quickly looks at Stevie while Stevie was lost in the stranger's misty eyes that would flash with a silver gleam. The mailman then winks with a smile at Stevie and vanishes with a gust of wind following him.

Stevie was easily dazed and confused after running into the eerie incident with the deliveryman keeping his pace continuing to follow a straight path leading towards the middle of the library hall.

Place in the middle of the library hall was displayed a huge sphere dome with octagon shapes among the walls displayed centered middle of the library was a huge stone carved table from the inside look to be an ancient altar, a round marble stone table covered in ancient scribe markings and symbols.

Stevie was breathless at the sight of the library stone table with an enormous blue crystal in middle spiked up high enough to reach about six feet coming straight out from the marble stone table.

Place around on the marble table were ten white candles among standing in front of the candles were nine people waiting with other Seers gathering around them.

Above them were floors surrounding the enchanted small dome where there were also a few more library shelves with a collaboration of books.

Other Seers were taking the approach from their busy daily tasks to be of an audience and some were up on high on the story floors above ground to view the new select participants standing around of the middle circle of the library stone table.

Then out of nowhere from the only corner that was dark by shadows coming from one of the entrances approaching Stevie was Charlie the cable guy.

Charlie then appears behind Stevie whispering to him, "This is the congregation final interview of the tri-Paradox, and here you and nine others will be tested to move on forward.

Breaking out of his professional character when Stevie looked back to see who had spoken, "Hey your Ashley's guy right? She recruited you?"

He slaps a nametag sticker to Stevie's chest that had his name on it giving him a good pat on the back.

"Made me forget what I was supposed to tell you but hey here you are and welcome." Charlie pointed the way, "they've been waiting on you, and good luck!" Charlie rushes Stevie escorting him to an open spot at the round stone table presented in front of him with a white unlit candle.

Stevie's heart was racing as he walked up towards the round stone table approaching his spot already feeling the pressure of being the late guy taking notice thinking he wasn't alone lost in this confusion as they called it the "second interview" clueless to their about's contemporary with the supernatural occupation.

When Stevie approach the large stone table looking down trying to avoid eye contact as he could feel all eyes piercing at him then for a moment looking up at the rest of the candidates who all had nametags.

He then notices all the participants had looks of confusion and eagerness on their faces as well.

After a few seconds, a guy who had beads of sweat building upon his forehead in a business suit with a tie standing across from Stevie from the other side of the stone table was getting agitated, Stevie wasn't certain if it was due to his tardiness but he could tell everyone was starting to get restless.

The gentleman in the tie suite yells in frustration exaggerating the tiredness of standing around at the stone table tries to finish his sentence. "WHAT THE HECK ARE WE DOING HERE…"

Interrupted by a loud "BANG!"

Bursting loudly open a set of huge heavy ancient hall doors abruptly forced open that echoed and winded throughout the cavern halls of the library having a few Seers chasing after their scattered client papers.

Standing under the huge ancient doorway studying the scenery afar stretch from on the other side of the library table was a frightening dark sophisticated character whose attire came right out of the Victorian era dress in a late black silhouette with a high neck tight blouse that can pull off the world's scariest nanny.

Wearing a black-netted shawl over her stern pointed padded broad shoulders, with long black sleeves vested up like an hourglass covering every inch of her white pale skin except her left hand and her face barely exposing the neck wearing a high black old fashion brooch.

What made her presence even creepier was she wore a black leather glove on her right hand only carrying a stern austere look of a scary strict Librarian that of her age was obscured with hidden wrinkles dissipated but everyone knew she must have aged gracefully.

She raised her left hand flaunting with a black pearl ring she brought her index finger to her lips in a form to signal quiet as she hushed, "shhhhh…"

She wore black square spectacles that fits her oval sharp face, with her dark gray hair blended with light shades of gray and a few white frost strips pulled back tight up in a high old fashion bun tied in with a black ribbon displayed on the back of her head.

She held up high firm manners walking with strict posture Stevie could tell with among the other Seers she was very condescending and coarse at least to know he knew who runs this place drawing his curiosity that stirring upon Stevie.

Within the Librarian's possession grasping a pretentious dark staff in her right gloved hand made out of Black walnut wood design with black wooden roots stretching around the black staff reaching to the tip at the top shape into a hallow pyramidal with black root arches.

The black staff was equivalent to its wielder left with a few battle scars and scorches resembling how ancient and grandiosity its power can behold, there was the silence that fell upon the room seizing everyone's full attention momentarily after she raised her black staff striking the ground with such a blow that it echoed throughout the library hall.

Striding in black leather high pointed boots with each step echoing among the halls her conservative long black dress would cast flaring shadows of herself growing rapidly spreading its darkness eating up all the flame lights upon the room one by one with each step she took closer to the library stone table soon all will be consumed in her complete darkness.

Shadows from beneath the Librarian were casting dark tentacles eliminating the rest of the few fire torches mounted on the pillars and walls.

After a few seconds, all in total darkness with magic fire torches on the pillars burst into blue flames revealing more seers were gathered around and attentive from up above the story floors preparing to watch some exposition.

The alarming librarian approached the steps of the enchanted stone library table and took turns to look at each participant with a façade smile. She then looks upon at Stevie with a cold stare for a few seconds longer than anyone else and he wasn't sure if it had to do with him being tardy but it sure was hard for Stevie to swallow with a dry mouth reading guilty all over his face.

Stevie could sense something was conjuring where his left hand went from nervously sweaty palms to ice-cold placing his freezing hand in his pocket to keep it warm.

The Librarian posed like a statue posture by raising her black staff about to speak but barging in interrupting the ceremony tripping over his untied shoelace catching his fall who was wearing a long white lab coat unexpectedly spilling his paperwork and pens with tools scattered onto the floor from dropping his brown tech bag that hung over his shoulder.

The clumsy fella was a bit of a clatter but also a little bit of fresh air for the participants, for being a nosey guy and very mettle he seems to be the only one that doesn't let the Librarian faze him, or maybe he just looks at magic differently. The scientist was is in his early twenties with ashy white gray short hair wearing underneath his white lab coat he wore rolled up ankle blue jeans with high converse snickers also wearing a white plain V-neck t-shirt with black suspenders wearing huge oval retro thick spectacles over his green eyes that fit a little too big for his face. "I've done it, I've done it! He then was waving a remote in his hand as he gathers his thing s quickly as he could, "I've managed to compute scientific molecules of the dominant eminence of the beholder reflecting it interfaces all into one format chip that includes…"

He was then interrupted by a shot hand gesture at the scientist by the Librarian signaled him to stop.

"The short version and quickly," she demanded as she shot a glare at the scientist. "Yes Madam," he replied then he chuckled at his dispense and said, "Basically manage to supply extent magic properties bestowed by its beholder into a single remote and this one I made just for whoa…!"

The nerd scientist was transfixed on the library table that began to glow with its blue hieroglyphics lighting up with having a look on his face that read he had a million questions.

"This is the tri-Paradox that holds the Tricongreation and its quality of power is ironically summoned of an evocation spell at an accelerated vibration, the ancient stones of this table possessing the ability hologram of the plain dimension!"

Pulling out his tools and magnifying gadgets from his man brown tech bag and began testing examining the glowing blue crystal coming out from the middle of the library stone table.

You couldn't tell if the scientist nerd was trying hard to please the Librarian or if it was just his interest that got the best of him but the Librarian wasn't having any of it rejecting the scientist looking at his remote tool that was given.

"I have no need for this," snapping her fingers demanding fast results rushing in Ashley suddenly appeared from the other side among the other Seers watching from the backside who followed the librarian's orders escorting the tech nerd scientist out of the ceremony as the librarian announces with sarcasm, "yay for the world of technology," as she rolled her eyes with her passing the remote to the closest innocent victim to a participant at the library table next to the librarian who then the stranger looks at remote tool clueless.

A grand introduction ruined by the clumsy tech scientist who probably wouldn't even know it if he walks into a wedding or a funeral too busy functioning his gadgets and tools recollection data from almost everything.

The librarian ushering an epoch event upon her audience waving her arm across the magical bluestone table that began to glow eerie with more lustrous symbols, writings, and hieroglyphics appearing with the radiant blue crystal embedded in the middle of the stone library table.

"The ten of you are chosen whether it was destined or just coincidence all favorable by the paradox so let it be the Tricongreation to sniff it out."

Stevie thought for a moment about the last remark that didn't sit well with the participants, "sniff what out" he thought?

Everyone then was received a quick glare from the Librarian giving off such a brusque manner, "a ceremony is held once every three years conducting recruitments staff hopefully this time we can have an addition to the library if necessary. Here you are to lite the candle at your own will the choice is yours to make, now let the Tricongreation decide."

Most of the participants were flustered looking at each other skittish while others were uptight uncertain of their task but all decided to go along with the ceremony. Stevie notices there were two who stood out very calm a girl wearing scrunchie with her hair tied back into a tight ponytail and a young lad wearing a black sweat top hood jacket with a rad look having a scar over his left eye that looks to be a year younger than Stevie.

They pass the matches around one by one taking turns lighting up each of their own candles places in front of them.

As they thought all the hocus pocus was finished the Librarian had one more trick up her sleeve waving her right arm over the library stone table with her black shawl and they all look at each other and magically appeared on the library table from her shawl was an old music phonograph.

It scratched and began to play a melody by itself instantly sounding the halls as if the amphitheater was instead with surround stereos that were in sync with the enchanting music from the phonograph.

A glowing mystical blue light appeared above the glowing blue crystal in the middle of the stone table taking shapes arising above them. It was so magical all they could do was stare in awe seeing many blue auras that look like snow flurries infusing with few light bright colors with different shapes, sizes, and some brighter than others coruscating above and around the library table.

The phonograph was playing a cue song of Scott Mescudi vs. The World.

(SC Music/2)

Ashley among other Seers watching from the side standing back in the dark she was thrilled and excited as she was resisting her excitement quietly clapping her hands silently tugging on Charlie, "this is my favorite part and I love this song!"

Suddenly surrounding the library stone table a blue glistering typhoon with striking sparkling colors circling those around the table for the final interview synchronizing with the music played aloud from the phonograph.

Stevie was fascinated in a surreal moment witnessing colors harmonic with the music lyrics that began telling a story showing visions overhead above the stone library table as they watch.

It was a remarkable sight to see like a third was open, he wasn't sure what he was looking at but he could sense a clouded truth of the knowledge from the world and his surroundings surging through him like a big curtain was lifted watching the magical display revealing the truths of the world's saga of myths, legends, and lore that cloaks over the world.

All the participant's eyes were cloudy with a bright blue radiant light as they stare above in wonder at the magical display.

One of the participant's flame lit candle sparkled into a blue silver flame that started to arise floating midair in front of the blonde girl with the tight scrunchie standing next to Stevie with a nametag that read Valarie.

The young girl Valarie did possess an athletic robust look about her with a feminine touch having her blonde hair pulled back into a ponytail with the black thin scrunchie showing a soft side of adroitness.

The library table's blue luminous lights were now circling around her with her arms being stretched out reaching for her magical blue flame zipping around her body appeared a strip piece of her pulled-back yellow blond hair began to frost into a streak color white as snow almost the same resemblance as Ashley's blond hair with her white curl frost streak.

One by one most of the participant's candle flames were burning back from the enchanted blue-silver flame to its original burning flame fire color, as well as their eyes changing back from radiant cloudy eyes to normal with only a few candles still left burning with its magical blue silver flames.

One guy couldn't even get his candle to lite as the Librarian began escorting those out one by one before they vanished captured into the dark shadows disappearing there be vibrant multicolor rainbows with fiery confetti colors showered over them.

The Librarian would appear behind out of the darkness consuming them one by one into the dark sinstering shadows as their candlewicks blew out.

Stevie wasn't sure if all the participants were able to witness the final supernatural interview the same way he did. Place in front of Stevie his candle was still lit burning with a blue flame on its wick leaving two more left with their blue flames floating eye level right before them.

The second participant who wore the black sweater hoody jacket looked a little emo being around Stevie's age with having fair pale color skin with his black hair styled to the side wearing black skinny jeans and a dark V-neck shirt. He wore his nametag that read Kris looking a bit dark and mysterious having a small thin scar that was noticeable that runs over his left eye through his black thick eyebrows shape like a crescent moon.

The other third participate was a short round Latina named Lisa who looks to be in her late twenties.

They too both were getting a white frost hairstreak makeover while their blue flames were also circling around them.

Lisa's white frost pigment was dyed over her right side bangs.

Unfortunately Kris's pigment white color was unpredictable but it suited him, the forces of the Paradox did not frost Kris's hair over his head but instead, it chose a frost white stripe down his left scared bushy eyebrow making his moon crest scar shape more vivid.

Off to the side, Ashley was standing there checking her clipboard analyzing the interview with the Librarian standing along with a few other Seers.

Stevie was the only one left at the library table motionless in deep thought staring into his blue flame that was flickering fighting to stay lit.

Ashley hugging her clipboard waiting in dismay she uttered softly, "he has to be the one."

After twenty seconds of silent pause, Ashley nod and look down signaling the Librarian that proceeded to go up behind Stevie ready to snatch him up into the darkness. Ashley immediately said, "wait!"

Stevie started to feel his left hand turning icy cold, clinching his cold fist taking a deep breath, and shortly his blue flame started to sparkle.

The blue flame finally left Stevie's wick and started to rise above the library table pullulating blue sparkles illuminated throughout the whole library hall with twinkles of mystical streaks shooting out from Stevie's afloat burning blue flame like a firework show making all other candles alit into blue flames floating off its wicks. Dread came over Stevie when he took notice at everyone's facial expression with most of the Seer audience's jaws dropping with all were looking up above Stevie cause everyone knew this was not normal.

Unable to move the remaining other blue flames started to dance around Stevie as the inside of his left hand was a burning but the outside of his hand was freezing. Looking up slowly to see what everyone was looking at in awe, above Stevie was a radiant constellation of stars displaying an enchanted map of the planetary system glistering with multiple stars and galaxy shimmering throughout above the whole library hall.

To everyone's astonishment at what was displayed above Stevie while the music was still playing the librarian who didn't look amused raised her right hand with her black wooden staff up in the air and poke at the constellation stars up above them.

Just then the music stops and somehow the Librarian paused the magical display of the solar system from rotating freezing shooting stars at its place, letting her staff drop-down slamming it onto the marble ground floor as it echoed causing the luminous twinkling lights of the constellation to vaporized into snowflakes.

There were all sorts of shapes and sizes of snow falling upon everyone with having some blue-white crystal flakes.

It was an odd scene to observe with the whole library hall looking like a white Holiday covered in snow with flakes falling upon everyone and everywhere, whereas the Librarian who too was getting snowed upon took steps backward backing down from steps of the library stone table with her eyes still fixed on Stevie.

The librarian squinted her eyes and muttered softly, "Impossible."

Among the crowd was Charlie with his familiar smile that no one could forget, Charlie, walking up to the library stone table steps towards the final four while clapping congratulating and everyone who attended the ceremony followed his lead and began clapping.

Charlie announced, "Ladies and gentlemen introducing our four newest members." Within seconds after the ceremony Ashley rushes out from the crowd of Seers that were scattered making their way back to their daily routines, she ran up to the library table to the remaining final group congratulating the four in amusement. Ashley being joyful and bubbly runs over with Charlie warning Stevie, "watch out she's a hugger." Hugging Stevie Ashley turns to her fellow Seers and towards their matriarch the Librarian raising four fingers counting. "He's the one, that's four, that makes four. Did you see that he must be the one?" She said calmly holding her excitement as best she can. Ashley couldn't hold her tongue and felt she had to share her truths, "you are God's great mystery of how he works!"

Clueless about what Ashley was talking about but Stevie was ready to wake up from this surreal dream experience thinking this all must be a dream but deep inside he knew he wasn't dreaming.

That's when Stevie just reconsidered and he knew he spoke too soon with Ashley holding and aiming a Seer remote straight at his face and he sees red shine after blacking out after she fires and said, "DELIRIUM!"

4

Genesis 19:12-17

IT WAS A QUICK COLOR red flash that came over Stevie finding he had the hiccups and was at his work on the first floor suddenly delirious after realizing he was sitting in his chair in the middle of broad daylight.

Did he just skip a whole day he wondered not remembering anything just after he blackout from his lucid dream?

Momentarily it was Ashley getting up from her desk coming out from her supervisor cubical and motion's Stevie to follow her and ironically to the steel elevator doors as she began to advise how to get rid of silly hiccups upon arriving to see Lisa, Kris, and Valerie were already occupied waiting inside the elevator from Stevie's dream.

"We were wondering when you would wake up, it's only been fifteen mintues, do you remember the last words I said to you?"

Ashley asks the group, as they were alone with Ashley in the elevator shortly after the steel doors closed.

Stevie was first to speak, " You said the word, DELIRIUM."

Ashley began to read out from the cable guy booklet as the others caught on to reach into their pockets to obtain each their own set copy of the cable guy booklet to read along until they reached their rational destination ground floor coming out from the elevator to the Seer's grand library.

They read a script straight out from the Seers booklet, (SEERS- has the power to hypnotize those who are normal human mortal seeing the supernatural to fog their mind enhancing the dopamine that creates a happy alternative reality that makes the real reality like it never happen sometimes causing them to sneeze or get the hiccups.)

Valerie blurted out the word, "Erasure," as she was reading ahead and was caught off-guard surprising her self she then stuck her nose into the booklet keeping quiet while following Ashley as she continued to read.

(The word **DELIRIUM** is characterized not as a spell but cast by Seers to chastise, its primary functions is to erase the memory of its target to forget its recent supernatural disturbance replace instead with cloak new memories concealing with common insipidities memories, this known memory tool attributes to make one forget.")

Ashley being politically polite about it almost sounds like sarcasm. "It's how a seer maintains hidden from the mortal world and even though it was a test it should never be used again against a Seer."

They followed Ashley through the great corridors of the Seer's library trying hard not to be distracted by their surrounding of supernatural events within the pre-historic labyrinth of the underground palace sanctum.

Lisa then blurted out, "eew is that what just happened to us?"

Valarie was quick to her senses, "wipes your memories away."

Lisa then gasps at Valerie's answer.

Ashley then reassured the answer, "yes, but not as horrible as it sounds, like you are here today went on with your normal lives till just now, except Seers don't forget, it replaces the victims memory with a happy ordinary thought of what they weren't supposed to see, and erasing the human's current disruption memories that were not to be. It's made of the very essences of the prism Arc law the Aether the sacred covenant light of this world."

Ashley taunted her group to keep as they continued to follow her throughout the mesmerizing underground temples with a majestic castle.

"This part is important guys so listen up, Seers are renowned in the world of the supernatural however given amnesty among the human race your willpower will be tested throughout your occupation as a Seer to uphold peace with the supernatural among humanity and to never reveal the hidden truth to humankind for breaking the pact will inclination the Seer's will to lose its potential of sight under the rainbow arc law which is the veil and by next sunrise, your memory will be erased to never remember the glorious gift of sight as a seer. Your memories will be replaced with Normies aka normal human thoughts as if it never happens before you become a Seer living your lives as if you were."

Lisa immediately asks, "wait… what, we can't tell anybody?"

"In doing so we would lose our power as Seers and become normal among the human world having to forget all its magical secrets of the hidden world going on with our little pathetic lives." Valarie shared to exaggerate and quoted with her hint of an eerie foreign accent.

Ashley answered with a nod and was signaling the four to follow her lead leading them around the underground cavern library touring upon stairways up on high cliffs mazes walking on a height-high arch pathway going above and under corridor bridges as she spoke. "I wouldn't call it little." Her words echoed as she replied to Valarie who was taking a peep down below the abyss to the unknown that no one knows standing from a steep arch moon bridge.

"Not pathetic just a simple life but yes you'll return right back to your desk job on the first floor as a Normie taking calls for cable tech support with not a thing to remember to identify you as a Seer."

Stevie who was never afraid of heights then too took his turn to peer down below from the steep moon bridge into the deep dark and was startled by the thought of poor Al a Normie who he works with before becoming a Seer at the call center on the first floor.

Lisa then asked an essential question for the moment that was on everyone's mind. "Exactly how many Seers are there?

"There are one hundred forty-four thousand and one lightworkers of Seers employed right now including you four," Ashley replies and she indicates to answer the question, "Seers are spread throughout the world and across America, we have five known high commands of base operations with Austin Texas is known to be the fifth."

Ashley continues to tour her group coming to a chamber of an airlift cliff hanger being off-topic about the Seer employees they witness and continued while she chauffeurs her group around the sanctum library as they watch a few Seers testing out flight control wearing special gadget gears that could make them float on air, which only lasted a few seconds.

"That needs a little more tinkering of fixing to last in the air a little longer one would think but let's move on and I must regulate that in the past we had a few Seers that have to renounce whether their will was tested or resign to never come back."

It made Stevie think who would ever want to let go of this magical lifetime experience of being a Seer?

Then out of nowhere appeared Charlie he claps Stevie on the back, "I like to start off by…" then he was interrupted by one of the newest members the short round Hispanic girl who was blushing all over Charlie. "Hi, my name is like Lisa" who was pink-red to the nose and started to portray like a little girl with a crush having a dramatic scene over Charlie keeping her eyes glued onto him. "I'm like so… honored to be chosen and to be here, I'm so glad to be part of you, I mean the team."

Ashley just nods and smiles cutting off Lisa rushing to get a few words into a sentence, "Ahmhm… first of all, congratulations, never before has the TRI-paradox congregation pick four participants to be chosen Seers. Traditionally the Paradox has always chosen three or less but here we are extremely excited to add four newcomers to the world's top minority eminences that are chosen for the oldest hardship job known to mankind."

Charlie shared his brief outline, "Austin Texas, has its perks how it's a little weird place for a community of supernatural to coexist among the humans without any remorse obeying the code a place where the gods can be who they are and creatures to roam in free areas. But there are limits and rules and we are the protectors front line if anything happens."

Lisa who wasn't shy then asks a question regarding Charlie's statement pretending to be bashful, "like a police force?

Ashley took the lead to answer for Charlie with her Texan accent and then replied and continued, "Sorta but sometimes when the supernatural steps out of line we're there to remind them of their place and we the Seers guards the realm of men from those that wish to harm our way of life. For that, I take as the highest honor of being a Seer. Just know you each were well selected and passed our interview requirements testing your knowledge and your special ability skills.

The new assemblies of chosen Seers were smiling among themselves with much gratitude as they felt they belonged.

"So no further a due this is Charlie… and I'm Ashley. We are known as the Beta overseers second command who oversees this establish institution known as T.E.C. support short for Tribulation Ensorcell Clairvoyance but we all prefer to call it the library."

"Isn't it obvious" Charlie shrugged suggesting the newcomers look around at the unique underground cavern-library welcoming them to the new base command center for Seers as the rest of the crowd employees audience of Seers began continuing their daily routine.

Then Stevie ask, "Does this mean we get unlimited cable?"

Charlie laughed and wasn't sure if Stevie was serious, "we are still a cable company assisting outstanding services to our normal human customers aka Normies is what we like to call average people of our society but our secretive department is also a secluded job for special protocol T.C. for exclusive occasions dealing with the supernatural."

Ashley butted in, "T.C. is a short name for Trouble Call."

Charlie finishing his sentence he then said, "I know it sounds ludicrous but hear us out on a short genealogy history by the power of the Seers. Since the time of the great flood, an amnesty pact with God and man was made to keep order on earth. As history passed, the pact was later followed by the legendary Knights of the Templars but then later was passed onto what is known now today as Seers."

Ashley continued to finish for Charlie as they explained, "Seers are to uphold the Arc law better known as the covenant law 19:12-17 patrolling the supernatural secret world disguise as the cable guy under the human eye."

Everyone then abruptly out loud after a few seconds of awkward silence from collecting their thoughts, "Why keep it a secret," Stevie ask?

Lisa was quick to asks, "Genesis?"

"What law?" Kris had to ask.

Ashley giggled with excitement signaling her new crowd to settle down while passing out small guide booklets. "There's always more questions after quoting that verse," Ashley said with a charming smile to Charlie. "You can cover the Arc law in the Seer's cable guy hand booklet, but imagine ninety-seven percent of the human population get hit with the supernatural and that would be chaos. Humanity would not be able to comprehend or fathom the truths behind the veil of the physical realm, with tare dimensions leaking celestials and deities under our noses as it happens throughout the history of our planet and guess who you think is there on the front lines to stop them?

"WE ARE!" Charlie said excitedly.

Ashley then replies as she leads the group to an underground waterfall chamber with other Seers experimenting with water nymphs having remote tools such as water learning to use spells and gadgets seeing one Seer that took after a water nymph with a portable remote that cast human-size bubbles that was resistant to fire. "What you saw at the tri-Paradox congregation is a brief of the supernatural world that isn't just your tall tales, of magic, monsters, fairies, and mythical gods. It would cause fear and utter chaos onto every corner of the earth disrupting the order of life unbalancing our everyday human lives."

Valarie with a stern gaze with her hair back in a ponytail ask, "but we also service cable television?"

Ashley answered Valerie's question, "So bringing about peace and order what better way to disguise ourselves as an innocent cable guy among the human eye contacting the world when encountering the supernatural, it's the greatest cover."

Stevie's interest caught the best of him and muttered out as they were reviewing their small Seer guide booklet better known as the cable guy booklet with an infinity logo on the cover, "Wow this is unbelievable so everything we were told about myths, tales and legends are."

"True! Well most of them." Ashley interrupted Stevie in her Texan accent whom then she pointed and touch Stevie's three-sided red emblem necklace he wore for his faith with a tiny symbol of a halo cross right above an open-winged dove.

"In fact did you know it was our Lord who places that taboo approximately twelve thousands years ago almost wiping out the entire human race after the great flood including all them sups and I mean supernatural folks, that's why most of the Supes aren't too fond with Christians?"

The new colleagues all had faces of disbelief except for Valarie who always kept a strong attribute with her face.

"The Seer's handbook is filled with an encyclopedia of all the magical creatures from beasts to monsters all the way to the GODS. The book is an anecdotal treatise with bed-time stories to your mythological history all categorized in bestiary to magical spells."

The word monster that came out of Ashley's lips left Stevie looking around for the superstitious dark Librarian who then vanishes among the crowd as they scattered.

"Charlie and I will be your guide mentors from this point on and with those given Seer guide hand booklets that cover all the fundamentals and instruction of being a Seer with its tools. All newcomers are recruited as Begin Seers, which means beginners, and there you will be trained involved with requirements with necessary tools until you achieve hierarchy rank to assist without an overseer. For if anyone other than a Seer was to ever get his or her hands on the Seer's guide key booklet it would then appeared to be just scanning through a regular Sudoku book hidden to the human eye."

Charlie chuckled a little and included, "like everyone in here we Seers are believers and most of us here have encountered or come across some abnormal phenomenon at one time of our lives before becoming a Seer like yourself. With each one of us Seers having our own special unique qualities were also chosen by the tri-Paradox and inter-viewed with passing two requirement test."

Ashley didn't hesitate quickly glanced over at Stevie as if she thought Stevie had picked up a clue.

Lisa then looked down with shame on her face, "my uncle Tio Rolando is a brujeria." Valarie then ask Lisa with concern, "what's is that?"

Kris answered for Lisa "it means witch, a demon witch."

Lisa then made an unpleasant sad face. "I've seen what my uncle is capable of, I first couldn't believe what I saw then"

Kris sounded skeptical, "you have a problem with that."

Lisa wasn't sure how to answer back, "He wasn't a good man but I did learn a few spells from him."

Charlie cutting in before the topic got deep, "The sight of a seer is a blessing but to some, they may see it as a curse. From within this sanctum library, this underground cavern is a sacred ground that holds a pristine force, which you already know as the Paradox, and within its power is the great phenomenon you just witness that has chosen you at the library stone table revealing your sight to have the ability to see the unveiled world. Detailed in your Seer guide booklet on page two under the Arc law, is made up of what we call the Aether. A powerful substance of the unique celestial matter in every element that flows throughout this world to protect and bind all human body and soul from contacting the supernatural world created from the very exact rainbow from the biblical times."

Ashley reminisces through her own pages of her Seer guide booklet, "Covered in your cable guy handbook in the Seers guide section," she then licks her finger through her pages. "On the first few pages are the history of Seers that came to be of how it all began." Ashley then quoted, "T.E.C. support follows up to its reputation in the supernatural world as SEERS that has been around ever since the great flood that was founded by Noah and his sons the patriarch of the ark himself. Centuries later it was modernized under Emperor Constantine in 330 AD and later colonize into the legendary Knights of Templars that came to be, centuries later it was divided better known today as Seers and here we are today carrying on the disguise as a cable guy." Ashley then rushing to read through the Seer guide hand booklet while catching her breath.

"For those that haven't notice Seers are imprinted with a frost streak of what we call ensorcell wisdom leaving white tips randomly choosing any part of your hair body as its mark. A contract emblematize by the Aether, it's who we are and what we represent."

Ashley then was revealing her blonde perm curls with one curl having a single white frost mark in her curly bang while Charlie was brushing his fingers through his right side of his head revealing his frosted pepper sideburns.

The newcomers took a moment to look at each other taking it all in.

Kris's crescent moon scar on his left eye shape above his brow curve to the bottom of his eye highlighted his scar leaving white frost on the scar eyebrow stripe to his eyelashes.

Lisa turning to Kris, "wow your left eye looks like a crescent moon, it fits you."

She frantic turn to herself grabbing her hair, "oh no what about me? What do I look like?" Ashley handing Lisa a mirror who was admiring her new independent frost bangs while Kris gave her a sarcastic look. "It looks good," said Ashley.

When the mirror was handed to Stevie looking at himself with curiosity but could not trace to recognize his Seer's mark with no white frost over his head nor his eyebrows but only wondered.

Ashley was quick to recap to say when the mirror was handed back. "This part is important guys so listen up, remember Seers are renowned among the world of the supernatural however given amnesty among the human race your will is going to be tested throughout your occupation to uphold peace among humanity and to never reveal the hidden truth for breaking the contract the willpower of being a Seer will lose its potential of sight under the rainbow law and your memory would be erased never to remember the glorious gifts as a seer replace with memories as Normies before becoming a Seer.

Lisa immediately ask, "wait what, we can't tell anybody?"

"In doing so we would lose our power as Seers and become normal among humanity and the supernatural world having to forget all its magical secrets of the hidden world going on with our little pathetic lives." Valarie quoted.

Ashley was signaling the four to follow her as she was leading them back to the beginning around the library cavern touring around the stone library table as she spoke. "I wouldn't call it little." She replied to Valarie. "Definitely not pathetic just a simple life but yes you'll return right back to your desk job on the first floor as a Normie taking calls for cable tech support with not a thing to remember to identify you as a Seer. I must regulate that in the past a few Seers has to renounce whether their will was tested or resign to never come back." It made Stevie think, who would in their right mind ever want to let go of this magical experience?

Passing many halls and chambers through the corridor hall were some Seers in training stuck in research with books and computers and others learning in a separate combat training room. "You'll go through basic training working your way up to become powerful potential seers among the few are wizards, specters and witches, and very few monsters, possibly one day you could become an over-seer in no time like Charlie and myself."

Stevie had the audacity question that was a concern stuck in his mind for a while and he had to ask, "Why have monsters and witches aren't they bad?"

Ashley then follows up with the question and states, "the first rule of the Seers Guild, unite against a common enemy, and not all monsters and witches are bad."

Charlie praised over where he stood proudly like a showman, "Here on these scared grounds, this underground temple library is almost like a castle cavern with a massive library that has chambers magically changing its course for trespassers leading to a huge maze and trap doors still yet unknown to many. There's a lot to discover and explore about this defensive magic of the underground temple that is called the Durga and that's why we like to stick to the main floors and being Seers you cant get lost unless you go exploring, so we encourage everyone to stick to the high grounds."

The library is so large, thirteen stories high built with ancient structures inside a majestic cave that was supported by magic with a good example of hundreds of moving arch bridges and trail staircases throughout it mazes with many chambers of the great hall of towers and turrets and very deep dungeons.

"Come along…" Ashley clapped signaling the group to keep moving as they explored the great Durga halls and she continued, "We Seers use every asset of each other's power for its resources so it may be preceded for peace that is potential and necessary in maintaining balance and order."

They passed a hall chamber full of historical artifacts and weapons with painted canvas walls of many Gods and attributes to myth and legends. Indeed this enchanted library was like no other and is magically full of knowledge with history and within just like every library it has it's Librarian.

Kris was the one that finally broke the silence and brought up the white elephant in the room, "excuse me but who's the scary Mary Poppins?"

It dawns on them that the dark Librarian was nowhere to be seen, she vanished after the congregation tri-paradox during the congratulation commotion.

"The ALPHA" Charlie said as Ashley nudges Charlie at his side ribcage with her elbow and said, "She goes by the name Madam for her real name has never been revealed. She is the matron of this library well known for her vast skills in the sorcery of witchcraft with her special ability of magic is bookbinding which is literary manipulation that's quite scary if you ask me, but for many may know her as the Librarian who is the head-mistress supreme Alpha of all Seers of this post." She then looks at Charlie finishing her sentence, "Of this sanctuary library overseeing us all." "Basically she's YO BOSS," Charlie exclaimed throwing in the sense of humor in their recent dark topic throwing duce's signs with his hands. "And trust me, be glad she's on our side."

They were all taken back not sure what Charlie meant coming a lot from a muscular tough guy covered with tattoos.

Valarie out of nowhere abruptly spoke out, "who's the Omega that subsists the Durga?"

Awkward scenes of looks were exchanged between Ashley and Charlie hiding their shock disclaimer as much as they can like the cat was out of the bag.

"I'm sorry who recruited you again?" Charlie quickly asks, with Ashley beside him quickly coughs and whispers to Charlie loud enough for everyone to hear, "it was Madam the Librarian." Ashley then rushed in to say halting her hands up studying Valarie, "We're rushing into things way too fast here guys, but I will tell you this. Since the time of the Great flood, there is ancient magic that the paradox binds the Omega for its source of power that creates the Durga of this temple for its defensive. Valarie then said under her breath, "the Sacrosanctity bind spell."

Charlie then too began to study Valarie squinting his eyes while Ashley continued. "No one actually knows or ever seen the Omega so we keep it collective and call it the gatekeeper."

Stevie pointing to the round stone table objectifying the topic, "Is that what that is?"

Ashley was tinkled pink with amused, "that is the Paradox Nexus, the beginning of the end," She chuckled. "Oh never mind and yes that's the Paradox magic it's a mirage of magical mysticism plasma that creates our defensives of the Durga, it's the very magic essences that protects this sanctuary temple."

"A temple underground? No one would of aspect it." Lisa said.

Ashley went on, "yes and no one actually knows how deep the underground tunnels are, it runs deep miles down below with numerous enchanted passage with mazes that could trap its enemies. Why it's important to stay within the perimeters that permits you. In your booklet, the last chapters cover all its secret corners and chambers that have already been discovered. This temple including the Durga and its labyrinth is one of the many first few to ever be built on earth it's one of the many wonderful secrets of this world."

"Wait there are other underground temples?" Kris was stirred into the curiosity of new news being asked.

Ashley- "well there are a few, no one knows when or how old the temples are, some say been here around before the great flood."

Stevie- "So you keep mentioning this great flood is it like the one in the Bible with Noah and the ark?"

Ashley then nodded to reply, "yep, that's the one, it's my favorite story by the way."

They were all taken back again in silence as the wheels were turning in their head every time being reminded of the biblical event.

"For generations, the Seer's has been the world's greatest archivist, and here you see many historical artifacts of the supernatural and resources of many diverse cultures of the world. The visions you saw from the paradox are real, those ghosts, witches, mystic creatures, fairies, elves, and monsters are real, and the gods and forces you saw are among us, and once again this is a recap we call them Supiens."

Charlie had to revise once more to share his views of truth, "We are what stand's between the Supiens and the human world. We are protectors, gateways to the other side. Remember our main job is to keep control and balance from what is reality."

Lisa points to the stone roundtable, "so what we felt earlier and saw are real?" Charlie was glad that they were getting to the point, "what you just saw is the great divine order, the paradox reveling sprites, monsters, and Archons."

Things were cooking up when Kris began to start asking the right questions, "Archons?"

Charlie and Ashley began to clap with excitement and synchronized to reply together with one word, "Gods."

Charlie began to share once more, "What you saw is the truth of those among us that the natural human eye can't see. It's forbidden for a Archon to reveal its natural self among the human eye and therefore it dings the divine order." That's when Ashley then said, "Angels."

Charlie was finishing his sentence getting to the main point "remember Angels are the divine to keep the order intact and if the divine order can not fulfill its protection that's where we come in."

Valarie then chimed in to break the ice and asks, "So were the backup?"

Ashley then explained, "We Seers have been around for millennia of years secretively keeping the order in balance. It's why some of you can see and do what you can do. Some are talented and gifted while others are bloodline descendant from their ancestors passed down from generations." She turns to take notice at Kris and Lisa, "some are in the arts of magic in wizardry and witchcraft."

She then turns to Valarie and points out, "some are skillful in combat."

She then looks at Stevie and smiled at him, "and some of those who are unique in their own special ways. Some of you are fully aware but all this may be a bit too much to comprehend right now but I assure you, all of you have that deep sense in yourselves knowing what you have seen and been told is all true, am I right?"

They all looked at each other nodding.

Stevie did feel a bit of ease like a blindfold was lifted, all was starting to come clear acknowledging the phenomenal of the supernatural that's been hidden under the normal human eye.

Charlie- "you are coming to the understanding of the order, the paradox wouldn't have chosen you for a reason if you could not fathom the idea of another hidden world among us.

Stevie then brought up a very important question, "Those other participates who were escorted out, what happened to them?"

Ashley- "they are very well and ok, they are back to the normal daily routines of their lives with no memory of this recent event. They weren't chosen for specific reasons the paradox looks into the heart, mind, and soul. If you don't have faith what's the purpose of believing?"

Stevie then asks, "what we had witnessed to those people who weren't chosen before they vanished from the library stone table, was that a memory erasure?"

Ashley-"It's a little embarrassing but the reason cascarones confetti eggs were used cause at the time we didn't have any cable guy remotes available for the erasure, their harmless it's one of the oldest tool tricks we've been using all explained in the Seer guide booklet. It's also used as a memory erasure.

"Remember it's not as horrible as it sounds, it replaces the memory with a happy ordinary thoughts of what they weren't supposed to see, and the Cascarones is one of our oldest tools used for centuries disguise as a common festive Easter celebration knowing the colorful eggs has mental healing powers erasing the human's current disruption memories that were not to be. It's made of the very essences of the prism Arc law the Aether the sacred covenant light of this world."

Ashley took a deep breath, "You saw a vibrant multicolor rainbow with fiery confetti colors showered over when the Cascarones was cracked over their heads, but we usually have remotes to use as our erasure but somehow we always end up short around here losing remotes," she said with a gracious smile. "The Aether is a powerful unique celestial prism in every element of matter that flows through this world." She then said in her thick Texan accent, "now tickle me pink yal but we all see the Aether after a rainy day do we not?"

Stevie look up at Ashley and said "Genesis 9:13."

Ashley was taken back, "that's right, your Christian aren't you?" she giggled and went on. "Once again behind that rainbow lays out the divine law that marks the world forever that restrains the supernatural and magic from contact with the mortal world."

Ashley then quoted from the Seer's booklet "all are among us around the world all following the divine order law."

Charlie then tells them there will be some accidents or a few lessers may get out of line and that's where Seers come into play to make sure all is set right and normal.

"Ok, we need to wrap it up." Charlie announced, "All Seers are divided up into four groups all based on your training and qualifications. To start, you all will be classed in the fourth rank called begins, mostly a group of Seers that are newcomers and beginners mostly in training following an over-SEER and learning of the supernatural world as they go, mostly keeping vigil of the elemental lessers, which are Fae folks like pixies, fairies, gnomes, wood elves, and brownies, the list goes on. All began Seers report to Miss Ashley over here." Ashley smiles to bow with a curtsy as her curls bounced with her face turning red.

"The next intermediate Seer groups are known as mediums or as we call them Gamma. They handle over the apparition, spirits, ghosts, and as well over lesser elements. The next advance groups are known as BETA some called enchanters that are over-Seers second command in rank. The over-Seers handle with every element of Archons to giant beasts to minor affairs of other ranks of the supernatural. We Beta's mostly deal with the dark that goes bump in the night."

Valarie was always ahead of the questions, "who's the top class of the highest first rank?"

Ashley was immediate to answer, "That would be the saga, which one hasn't come around since the time of Merlin. What is a saga is one so skilled in which could posse's god-like omnipotent powers. I don't think the heavens would ever allow a mortal in that state of grace of a god, cause the last time in records was a saga known, as Merlin who was known to be the last."

Stevie then said with excitement, "Wow Merlin was a Seer?"

Kris- "what happened to him?"

Ashley answered Kris, "no one knows, the archives records show the saga was taken off the timeline like as he vanished after the great Arthur legion."

"Left to take charge of the order of Seers replacing the Saga who would be next is the Supreme Madam the Librarian," Charlie said as he then gestures his surprised quiet new group, as he was ready to take leave.

"That seems to be all the time we have, we'll go over the basics of the began Seers next few days and file your paperwork to HR but be ready and well rested cause we have lots to go over and we will all meet up here."

Ashley then contributes to her last statement leading her group t the exit, "You were given an employee badge with your name that has been updated that will get you access to the elevator, and here are your company polo shirts and pants with the earliest and finest technology protection with fiber mesh together that can stop a gunshot bullet and inflammable it's the best quality out there. All began Seers will be wearing white this year. I'll be seeing you back here first thing after lunch on Monday."

Stevie and his two companions were all heading back to the elevator feeling mentally exhausted from excitement and still dazed replaying in their thoughts of everything he just heard and witness, wondering if this was all surreal asking himself if he's ever going to wake up from this miraculously dream.

As they all four were in the elevator it was almost as if they all let out of relieved breath air but suddenly Ashley yelled out, "Oh wait!" She barely caught the elevator door from closing. "One most important thing," Ashley catching her breathe from running to rush to reach the elevator door. "A warning reminder…"

Stevie could tell immediately their hearts sank and their adrenaline went up bumping through their veins.

Valarie was the only one that exclaimed out loud, "what'd you mean NOW A WARNING!"

Ashley pasting to catch another breath and said, "Don't forget the paradox magic reveals your sight to see under the Aether. Reveal this to anyone the secrets to any mortal who is not among Seers will lose your sense of powers and your memories as a Seers and will be placed among mortals as if it never happened by your next sunrise the following morning. It is the ultimate test as Seers it's a curse with a blessing and I leave you this, how strong is your faith?"

She smiled and she then let the elevator door shut.

5

Ding Dong
The witch is dead

THAT FOLLOWING MONDAY AFTER LUNCH Stevie and the new bunch were already met up at the library. The new crew had a busy anxious morning taking nonstop cable troubleshooting services calls at their call center above ground located on the first floor even the weekend went by so fast after the Tri-Paradox experience having surreal thoughts still wondering if all these legends and myth of the supernatural was just a conjured dream. Stevie had a reality check in front of the clandestine elevators swiping his cable guy employee badge to grant access as the doors open and from that moment he knew and smiled.

They all meet underground close to only Seers at the magic round stone table that they like to call the library and the only one person missing from newly chosen Seers of the four from the Tri-Paradox was Lisa.

The three were all eager to discuss and share stories following up on each other's rundown of coming across the Supernatural over the weekend.

Stevie asks, "Hey, so any you guys see anything over the weekend?"

Valarie may be European hinted with a unique look that made her wise for looking like in her late teens carrying an accent that you could barely pick up if you paid attention. "Ran into a couple of fairies the other day which was extremely annoying," she said rolling her eyes. Valarie still continued, "Just right outside of Austin's food supermarket off Lamar St. and 5th and no one can tell the difference if you stare enough.

Stevie then answered, "Fairies…! No freaking way."

Valarie's anguish was in her tone of voice, "they would look like anyone else and fairies are promiscuous, such a poisonous race if you ask me, nasty little sprites devil's they are, selfish, gloating fully obsessed with themselves. Always up to no good with their dirty magic tricks, their help is always regretted. Ugh! I can't stand them!"

Stevie replied with curiosity, "Tricks?"

Valarie then was quick to repeat, "Tricks!" She was looking straight at Stevie as if he knew something. "They are nasty chicanery fireflies with their sunshine nature element magic, making treachery pacts with mortals."

Kris sighs and being an introvert he thought to share his judgment and replies, "Picture yourself in the operating room for brain surgery and your doctor and staffs are all good looking straight out of a GQ or sports illustrated magazine with an IQ of a six-year-old."

Stevie interrupted, "ah, that's frightening." Kris continued, "Don't get me wrong fairies are full of surprises and bit vain than usual but miraculously they would eventually succeed the brain surgery and may not be what you excepted but hey they attend to get the job done."

Kris then took comfort and was leaning against the stone table, "I too have seen a few fairies before, even elves, and I believe a troll once but fairies can be of a nuisance."

"Oh wow, I didn't know fairies are capable to be that bad and now you say there are elves and trolls?" Stevie asks who wasn't a one-bit shock.

Valarie took upon herself to examine strolling around the stone table, "if you think fairies are bad wait till you meet the High hills Elves, they are one of the extinct race far worst than fairies not only in vain like their kin Fae's but an arrogant race with their pompous prince they are last of their kind also known as Wooden Hills elves."

"What… the elves' have a prince, and you did just mention a troll right?" Stevie said confirming what he heard quickly before being interrupted by Valarie's amused laugher at Stevie's intrigued questions, "You have lots to learn, it's highborn that is. Highborn's are royal blood, there's one in about every race including ours?" She smiled and continued her sentences. "The fairies also have their own royal families that keep the order of their race. It's known that the highborns are the most supreme to the race of their majestic rare powers. It's why highborn are leaders in charge of their kingdoms."

Kris then changes the subject and took his attention at Stevie and asked, "What did you see?"

"I'm not entirely sure," Stevie answered. "What I usually see are auras and color's of spheres."

"Astral vision," Valarie said who look at Stevie. Stevie complied to ask, "Say what?" Valarie answered, "like a medium you see spirits and ghosts."

Finally, there was an answer and even a name for his delusional vision as it turns out to be a gift all along.

"I think my visions are starting to take vivid shapes," Stevie blurted out who took a seat at the stone table. "Yesterday I meet up with my roommate for a Sunday brunch before she headed out to work who bartends downtown. I'm still new to the Austin area we were off of South Congress Street right over the Congress Bridge."

Kris budded in, "that's SoCo."

Stevie nodded "yeah that what my roommate said and in that area we were eating outside at a restaurant patio when appeared from the corner street was a young homeless free-spirited hippie with no care in the world who was living a trifling life outside on the streets but it never phased her for she was more concern and gave attention to her batch of snapdragon flowers she was selling." Stevie then gave a concerned look reminiscing his thought memories of what he remembered and continued. "There was a glow about her with the brightest purple-pink eyes I've ever seen as if almost like looking into radiant glowing flowers were in her eyes that were lit by a purple fire it was so weird." Valarie and Kris then took attention to Stevie as he continued his story, "The free-spirited girl was selling multiple wildflowers that gave off a sweet aroma smell pushing her wooden cart in the middle of a bike path selling random wildflowers that read, "Persephone's Season flowers. The maiden was so odd she wore white daisies flowers in her pitch-dark ebony hair that was braided back around her head. She also wore farmer's suspenders over her floral tye-dye shirt with gardening gloves in her back pocket with a sunflower gardening hat that was not on her head but hanging from the back of her neck from straw hat lace. Just then a cyclist had accidentally run into her and the wooden flower cart causing somewhat commotion knocking her over to the ground scattering flowers everywhere with her wooden cart snapping one of its wheels off. Surprisingly the young hippie girl stumbles to get up on her own rearranging and patting herself down. The accident crash was rough and looked like it hurt but confounded with not one single scratch or bruise was found on her but her modesty was spent as she then looks at the damage made to her cart. She stood there emotionless staring at the cart broken wheel as if it were her only accommodation to life that she was about to snap in a few seconds. The cyclist in his bike gear uniform with his helmet came over to her with a few rough scrapes and scratches on his elbows with a cut above his eyebrows. "What the heck lady, can't you see where your going this is a bike lane only!" He pulled out a card from his bike gear suit and in condolence, he rudely tossed her his business card as she gathered her crushed wildflowers. The cyclist getting on his bike then said, "call me I'm a lawyer," having a smirk on his face. Suddenly the poor girl's facial expression showed it all and her batch of snapdragon flowers turned into dead flowers of tiny skull heads, she exploded as if she was bottling it all in for years. She began fuming in a bright magenta color aura where ironically my left hand began to freezes icy cold alerting anything supernatural in my surroundings, something I've always picked up as a kid."

Kris replied, "You're tuned to your sixth sense?"

Valarie then asks, " and then what happened?"

Stevie then mentions he didn't know who or what she was but you could tell she was living a hard rough life behind her fake smile that she was dearly holding on to. There wasn't much sympathetic from the bicycle rider who just hop back onto his bike but all in the meanwhile the homeless girl hippie's eyes were glowing a bright magenta color. She began to tremble as the sky above us out of nowhere started changing into a dark eerie display of purple-red clouds rolling over with a few bright purple lighting striking a view across the dark cloudy skies. The wind started to pick up suddenly blowing with such force it seemed to come from the red-purple fuming hippie. She lifted her right hand slowly and what appeared holding in her hand was a bright red-purple metallic ball of energy. Stevie tried to explain his story that everyone there around the scene except the lawyer cyclist was blindly invisible to the extreme magic exposed from the upset hippie as if time was possessed while everyone was in slow motion until time froze itself.

"From that moment on I knew I was looking at an archon, an immortal describe in the very back pages of the cable guy hand booklet, I read she was known as one of the Greek Gods."

Kris then got up from resting on the stone table and surprisingly he crosses his arms and was taking an interest in the story, "so you and the cyclist were able to see under the veil?"

Valarie went to say, "The cyclist was a lawyer, and what sounds like he had it coming."

Stevie just nods and replies, "Not sure if it was all on the hippie goddess's doing but I did realize the cyclist was also the only one able to see through the arc law who wasn't a Seer but the fear on his face never left him."

Stevie continued his story from everything after that moment went wrong and happened so fast he didn't know what to do. The goddess then lifted her fiery purple ball of energy raised above her head aiming it so as if to release it soon upon the cyclist. Stevie tried to explain the upset imminent goddess continues to glow brighter as she then brakes into tears conflicted with emotions while she spoke her words that were true echoing throughout the skies. "Can you see now selfish mortal?" The broke emotional hippie goddess said with such fury a force purple lighting was reflecting from her actions whipping a show across the crimson-clouded sky above her. "I've peeked into your soul, you and all men are all the same running foul stench all over everything like cockroaches that you are with no respect for the world but your own foolish needs."

Arising her threatening violent purple-red sphere resting upon her palm growing rapidly over the cyclist with a cringed disgusted face as the lawyer laid hopelessly in awe upon her foot on the ground shielding from her.

"Millions have worshiped me, but why do I care anymore," The goddess rolling her eyes at the sky she turns to the lawyer cyclist studying him like he was a bug, and continued. "What shall it be a daisy, a fly trap, It doesn't matter I'll waste every last drop of my grace power." The goddess sigh for a moment and began to laugh historically showing a perfect example of what it looks like when a god has a nervous breakdown, "It'll be worth of every last drop of my millennia sunset savings, taking the joy to turn you into what you deserve…"

Stevie tried his best to explain what had happened next in the heat of that moment as he sat there thinking within seconds the lawyer was a goner but suddenly time and space not only slowed down it froze reality as the goddess look around confused and distressed. Momentarily a bright soft angelic light appeared above the mortal and the goddess that illuminated over both of them.

In the sky, the bright heavenly lights began taking shape glittering in white appearing as an angel radiating with unearthly whiteness making everything surrounding the angel seemed dark. The angel was described to have black shiny hair with white olive skin paired with green radiant eyes. The angel was appeared sparkling above them only shown midway below from the angel's torso to the top of its head and could barely see through the angel.

The angelic being then looked gracefully upon over the cyclist with a yellow light emanating from above her head that it appeared to be a shining halo.

The angel smiled with her hands folded together like a prayer and a band of colors appeared to glow over the stress lawyer that was shaking violently. The lawyer's eyes flashed transfixed and confused as if all his worries left him.

Afterward, the graceful angel looks upon the resentful goddess with a stern look appearing above the angel's head the shiny gold ring erupted emitted with white blazing fiery energy.

The impressive image puts the terrified hippie goddess in her place. The goddess laughed nervously lowering her plasma ball in her hands and nods a little bow towards the angel above her and picks up her broken wheel and flowers never lifting her head back up.

The goddess quickly retreated in shame and embarrassment while the angel was then dematerializing. The lawyer cyclist was elated returning to his bike confused as if he lost track of time and went on his way forgotten everything that just happens to him."

Someone then answered from across the library hall, "upholding the Arc law."

They all turned to Ashley who appeared out of nowhere coming from the other side of the corridor hall following behind her was Charlie with his sleeves rolled up revealing the fascinating art of tattoos on his muscular arms. Stevie then repeated asking the first question, "The Arc law?"

Ashley continued and began walking approaching the stone library table including her into the conversation "Call it whatever you like, there are numerous names for the Arc law, the covenant code, the divine law, or even the ark law with a K, and sometimes called the rainbow law which sounds a bit tacky."

Stevie took the tribute to ask another question, "how was the cyclist able to see the goddess through the arc law?"

Charlie then took over to answer, "That's what we're here for, as a Seer, the blind-fold has been lifted from the veil revealing true sight in your third eye to see among the world in its true form revealing magic and creatures of old to the truth of the gods to fairies and monsters that have been living among us. Just another recap we Seers are to take charge of the supernatural that breaks the divine law exposing and harmful to the human world. It's all covered in your cable guy booklet guide as it states Genesis 9:13."

Everyone then pulled out their pocket Seer booklets following Charlie's notion, "The act of divine retribution was the day the Aether was created after the great flood."

Ashley interrupted to clarify her scriptures, "The flood came, and took them all away, (Matthew 24:39) and you know the story of Noah?"

Charlie nodded with a reassuring gesture at Ashley that they were listening and continued, "After the great flood washed up the world a rainbow with a promise was placed among all surviving Supiens that are among the supernatural of our world that was left after the great flood. It's so much more than your bible rainbow tale it's a promise that the world would never flood again. With the light prism of eternal force that is shown as a rainbow is the Aether that is created and exists within every matter atom of this earth that we cannot see with the human eye. Of course in your Seer's pocket guide booklet explains the natural law that compels all that is not human to lose or break contact with the human world. It was then mortal men were given to make their own free will without influences of Supiens of the supernatural world. There will be a few out there who rebel against the Arc law why we cable guys must always be ready."

Ashley placed her left hand on Charlie's shoulders as she walks by him strolling around the stone library table taking over the conversation. "Stevie what you saw is pretty remarkable and dangerous, describe in your Seer's booklet guide explains two types of Archons, the good ones that follow the rules and the bad ones breaking the Arc law. Being a witness of an Archon exposing at will is a serious dangerous matter especially for Seers and why yes it sounds like you saw, was in fact an angel, a light being maintaining the divine law.

"Wow like cops?" Kris erupted.

Stevie then replied, "The goddess did look terrified of the angel as if laser beams were going to blast out of the angel's eyes."

Ashley and Charlie look at each other.

Stevie took their reaction and replied, "No freaking way angels can do that?"

Ashley said, "not sure of the whole eye laser beams but Archons are usually powerless against the divine forces of the heavenly angels who are better known as celestial beings. There have been two major roles of Supiens that have govern our planet throughout time and history, there are your Archons who are ancient deities found in many of your history books that claim themselves as gods believing to be the rightful rulers of this world while the angel's objectives are quite the opposite. Since creation the guardian angels have upheld their responsibilities carrying out divine orders, come and go on this earthly realm protecting its orders."

Charlie got to shine on his proposition, "The heaven celestials usually handle the powerful Supiens like Archons and other dark Imps running muck everywhere, while we Seers are left to handle with lesser Supiens."

Valarie then rolled her eyes and said: "you mean leftovers."

Ashley took attention and broke into her Texan accent, "Hey ya'll we all can't be picky and choosers now, but imps are a handful enough with dark forces like trolls, goblins, dark fairies, sprites, satyrs, the list goes on that interfere against the divine natural law." Ashley got a little excited on the topic with her accent peeking through.

Valarie sigh and interrupted, "sorry but where's Lisa?"

Ashley answered, "she's here, but not with us. She up on the first floor taking trouble calls to fix the cable issues for customers continuing to be of services as a telephone rep now."

Valarie then continued to ask, "She failed didn't she?"

Ashley confirmed by nodding, "to our sources she told one of her family members." Charlie continued the conversation, "all is forgotten for her, and Lisa's memory of being a Seer has been wipe clean replaced with a charming memory that's made up of a regular interview hired as a customer representative supervisor for taking calls. Its all part of the Aether, Seers are unknown to the human world as well. If you tell a single soul you risk losing your mark along with the gift sight of a Seer."

Charlie brushed through his ash sideburns revealing a hint of his frost streak marking his Seer mark. "It's a testimony sacrifice for us all Seers all part of the Aether, it's like a pact contract of being a seer, you can't tell anyone kind of like Batman in a sense."

Then Ashley turns to Stevie and made a sly remark with a grin, "or like Superman."

Charlie then winks at Stevie to say, "well that makes three Seers as newcomers as it should have been in the beginning."

Ashley replied, "You see every year the Tri-Paradox has always picked three Seers for our yearly assessors if needed but this year was different with four and we're still not sure why that is but that now leaves us a total of one hundred forty-four thousand lightworkers."

Charlie then looks upon Stevie and suddenly following all eyes turn onto Stevie like he was now the center of attention.

Ashley broke the awkward dead silent, "so… we had a change of plans today, you were all supposed to be in the modus operandi a chamber where Seers are to be trained and tutored with lessons to fulfill their momentum of your gifts and powers."

Charlie quickly budded in his sentence, "its basically to get you to tap into your most potential power."

Ashley then excused Charlie and continued, "But instead we'll have you split up shadowing one of us Beta that are fully trained Seers that over-sees beginner Seers for the rest of the day since we are behind on our mission charges which are trouble calls for today."

The three responded with little moans feeling thwarted.

"Lessons today were set in plans with the Librarian," Ashley replied with a smirk. The group immediately change their reaction as they all got up agreed and nodded exactly with the plans that did not include the scary Librarian, it seemed they all agreed to be down for anything to avoid the scary Librarian.

The three were split up with Kris and Stevie pairing up hiking into the woods together with Charlie while Valarie went with Ashley.

Charlie took charge leading the way. "All right guys, your probably wondering why I brought you here into the Greenbelt woods, it's well known to be Austin's well-kept secrets."

Anyone could tell Charlie had a passion for Austin Texas excitedly describes the city's magical park as they descended downward hill hiking a trail into the woods. "It's the city's grand backyard with nature hike trails and recreation open to the public." Kris being an Austinite hiking behind Stevie who was following Charlie began sharing his knowledge, "Greenbelt Covers about a little over eight miles known to the public and more of hiking trails stretch land that begins at Zilker Park and stretches North towards the northeast."

Charlie continued Kris's sentence, "Stretches Northeast to the final section commonly referred to as "The Hill of life." Charlie pointed the way and continued signaling the boys to take lead as they hike from a two-split trail.

"Where there's a secret order of enchanted Fae folks reside here and their kingdom lies at the end of the woods of Westlake subdivision spreading throughout the Greenbelt Park."

The boys pulled out their pocket booklet Seer guide to review while hiking as they followed Charlie. "I have been requested for a trouble call here or one might say a mission duty we also call those charges. Unfortunately, this charge is a 2-star rank or higher, it's secretive and classified for only over-seers like Ashley and myself."

They continued hiking the trails as the day began retiring. "Here in these woods, you'll find its home of many supernatural creatures mostly lesser sapiens. The Greenbelt consists of multiple magical creatures hidden from the human world like fairies, elves, and even home to witches among these woods. The Barton Creek Greenbelt consists of three areas: the Lower Greenbelt, the Upper Greenbelt, and the Barton Creek Wilderness Park.

Stevie throwing his hands up and paused "wait, wait, wait, and there are witches here? Whoa!"

Charlie continued and took lead onto the trail, "nothing to worry about all though not all witches are evil there hasn't been any activity or sightings of witches for years in these woods. Considering these parts are some of the world's last magical places left on earth, this place is loaded with fairies and their hidden realms." Charlie turns to the boys signaling with a two thumbs up with a smile "hey keep Austin weird."

The hike was longer than what the boys had anticipated continuing to follow the trail behind Charlie leading the way without rest.

Stevie began to feel unease placing his left cold hand in his pocket feeling a little agitated about the woods believing they were being watched.

Kris decided to lighten the conversation, "Fairies are full of tricks and surprises they're mostly used as pain meds to witches or even more. Fairies are full of magic that can enhance a witch's power or their spells to elevate the playing fields."

They arrived at the end of the trail in front of two giant white rocks on both sides of the end trail that lay west of the woods. Charlie pointed towards the large stones continuing hiking west on the trail. "Alright, guys just past these stones lay a hidden enchanted kingdom called Essence, a realm of the tree Fae folks, one of the few ancient realms left in this new world. There I have a trouble-call with these tree fairies."

Stevie abruptly had to repeat and ask swiftly, "TREE FAIRIES?"

Charlie chuckled and hiked towards his trail, "Yea it's all part of the magic, and tree fairies are found in rural places around cities within their parks in the trees they're everywhere you just couldn't see them until now. These types of fairies are mostly known for element magic and harboring nature. Fairies are harmless but can be playful and tricky at times especially when it comes to fairy magic it can get out of hand. Let's stay on the trail and it is about an hour before sundown, I'll meet you guys both back here at the giant rocks, remember to stay on the trails and stay together. If ever confronted and questioned what do we do?"

Stevie and Kris both said, "cable guy protocol." It's a protocol that we immediately learn when becoming a Seer how to deal with humans that is not to the supernatural world being disguised to ourselves as the cable guy.

Charlie then said, 'that's right and here take this for assurance," as he handed them each a remote.

"Use these bad boys if a problem comes across you guys against any Sups."

They each examined their remotes as if they have never seen one before.

"Since you guys are not fully trained on the cable guy remote just only use the pause button and I do mean only the pause button." Stevie had a sudden burst and shouted out right after Charlie started taking off without them and he paused and turned at Stevie "Ah Charlie! What about the witches in the woods?"

Charlie smirked and continued his hike towards west onto the trail past the two big stones and he turns back again with a big smile and said, "who Kris, he's a witch."

Stevie watches Charlie disappear into the woods as he was taken back what Charlie just revealed to him about Kris who is considered a witch standing only five feet away from him studying Stevie leading against a tree in the middle of the woods. Stevie felt a little concerned about this Kris guy who doesn't look like he talks much looking very pale with black hair waved to the side having dark brown eyes with the scary scar on his right eye he thought it made him look frightening.

Kris didn't look any younger than Stevie. He wore the yellow polo cable company shirt with black skinny jeans and black leather lace boots.

There was a silent awkward moment where we could hear the birds and crickets chirping.

"Wait!" Stevie exclaimed as he saw something that he thought he saw was unusual from the corner of his eye scuttled through the grass ground into the bushes.

"Could be a rabbit or squirrel maybe a snake," Kris said guessing at Stevie's recent surprise jerking around at the ground with tall grass for the moment.

They both began to speak at the same time with a sentence interrupting each other. Stevie said, "I've never met a witch…" as Kris asked, "What special gift do you…?"

It was another awkward silence that Stevie immediately broke and asked, "What sorts of spells or powers can you possess?"

Kris leaned off the tree and started walking southward onto a trail that Stevie followed up after him.

"I know my way around here like the back of my hand, did you know I was born and raised here in Austin."

Stevie replied hiking behind Kris, "aha an Austinite."

Kris just nudges his shoulders, "My mother and I use to hike around here gathering ingredients and herbs for her spells and potions and what not but to answer your question do you believe in evil?"

"This kid already spooks me," Stevie thought, and surprisingly his left hand hasn't frozen up but usually it attends to when supernatural is brewing around close nearby. Stevie then nodded and answered, "ah, yeah."

Kris then asks again without taking a breath. "Do you believe in true consequence soul Tridimensional to a parallel in forces of true darkness?" Stevie nervously stuttered confused about the question and answered, "yeah…"

Kris wasn't finished testing Stevie? "Do you believe in the reaping of souls of one's nature in existents of true pure energy?"

Stevie started to feel doubts and was truly getting creep out by this kid. His only answer was "Sure," but he assisted to give Kris a chance to hear him out and started hiking still walking alongside Kris.

"Witches can smell dismayed emotions, fear, sadness, madness, and even the insane." Kris then paused after he spoke and kept his attention straightforward into the woods looking at Stevie from the corner of his eye.

"I practice goety, and no need to be scared of me I'm not dark, though I can not speak for my powers, I assure you no harm will come to you."

"Wow," Stevie thought even though this kid was younger with smooth clam gestures, he sure was imitating especially with his scar on his eye shape like a moon streak crest on his eyebrow mark by the tri-Paradox.

"I dabble in some dark arts before but mostly for protection. I've obtained to only use binding spells, a force I gain power from the source I conjured to acquire supernatural power. I also know a few charms, blood and bone magic its wicked stuff there, but traditionally witches are capable to be healers even the worst witches out there are capable of healing."

Kris took the turn to ask questions about Stevie. "So you see ghosts, astral visions huh?"

The question was bewildering inside Stevie's head hiking along with Kris feeling completely embarrassed, comparing his unknown powers to Kris's fascinating witch powers.

Stevie took notice that the woods seemed to get denser blocking out the sun as they kept going further southward into the woods.

"It's not much but yea, I always thought I could do so much more instead of being the flock I always wanted to lead instead," Stevie answered sharing within his deep thoughts.

Kris was grateful for how honest Stevie was open to his opinions, "whoa there shepherd boy just asking about your powers?"

Stevie blushed, "I usually do see auras or color spheres but lately I'm starting to see them take shape or forms now."

Kris collected his thoughts and asked, "ghost, spirits, you even mention you saw an Angel and an Archon, your powers are growing and getting stronger by the influences of the tri-Paradox that flourishes and enhances all of our powers and senses."

Kris paused again and turns to Stevie. "Hmm… Ashley must have seen something in you and they don't just pick us for any reason.

"What do you mean?" Stevie asks.

Kris continued onward south on the trail, "I've read through the booklet Seer guide and it states that every once a year nominated Seers are all scouted around the world by overseers who in the end sees potential in their novice anticipating to get chosen by the tri-Paradox. They even say those who stray away are destined to be Seers that are meant to be."

"It was all a coincidence," Stevie scrutinizing in bewilderment of his whole past life up to now. The epiphany came across Stevie acknowledging how it all began intervention of ending up in Austin Texas. Remembering saying a prayer that day heading home from work meeting his first Seer and how amused he was with Charlie that aspired him to make the change and move to Austin.

Stevie then stirred the courage to ask, "How is it that you obtain to know all this?" Kris answered, "my mother being a witch, she would tell me stories of Seers, I use to not believe in the legends until now."

Stevie replied, "sweet so we're like rock stars."

Kris answered, "not quite, more like the boogeyman to the supernatural world never realize this whole time Seers were the cable guys. You see most Supiens have a reason to fear cable guys if legends are true some of the powerful ones would despise all Seers. There's a brief summary in the cable guy pocket booklet that I read about some thousands of years ago after the great flood an order was made to cleanse and exterminate the world of the unnatural Supiens being not holy that survived the great flood. I also learned as time went on Seers were also called the Knights of Templars. What we do know throughout the millennia times has changed in the balance of good vs. evil between Seers and Supiens. Now, these days Seers just maintain the order of the Arc law."

Stevie replied reading off from his Seer guide booklet, "We no longer kill Supiens more so just restrain and protect them if expose or influences to the human world."

Kris still hiking taking the lead on the trail, "After I lost my mom I was lost to the streets getting in trouble by the law sometimes just getting by what I can. Being consumed by the dark arts I had picked up from my mother that I almost ended up losing my life just like my mom until Charlie found me and recruited me."

The boys paused for a moment. "Charlie said I had great potential and strength that my powers can be controlled and he mentions it can be used for the greater good, he basically saved my life."

"Is it me or is it getting darker around here?" Stevie had to ask as he was struggling to bring up the conversation how to ask about how Kris's mother died as they continue onward on the trail that lead them into the edge of unfamiliar dense birch trees.

Kris paused holding up Stevie from going any further was taking notice and fully alarmed of their surroundings. Within that moment Stevie saw Kris's face reaction with concerns all while his left hand began signaling danger, as his hand turns cold.

"Something's not right about these woods, I don't recall any of this. We better head back." Kris applied again, "the sky is getting dark quickly hidden by these deep thick woods it seems to be sunsetting."

Kris was now turning around backtracking their trail rushing to get back before it got dark with Stevie following, as the trees got thicker and thicker pushing branches after branches and thick shrubs to get by while Stevie could sense a coldness in the air of old a warning with his left hand began to freeze up.

They both paused taking a break panting with Kris raising his right hand finger feeling for the air temperature.

Kris wasn't looking too good he was sweating and looked faint. "There's strong dark magic here, something that's trying to drive us out."

The boys kept moving as it was approaching dark right after sunset Stevie could see Kris was holding something black like a compass and muttering what seems to be a spell under his breathe for some time, hopefully, it's some kind of find my way back spell Stevie thought.

Off in the distance, they saw a faint eerie bright green light like eyes peering into the darkness. "Hey, Kris, what's that over there you see it? It looks like a light or a fire." As they got closer following near the lights reaching about a hundred yards away deep in between the woods they could both see clearly there were more visible green fire lights as they got closer.

Kris was breathing heavier and heavier with each step they took. "I can't go any closer, go near the light somewhere and around there look for some sort of pile of rocks smeared in red makings and knock it over."

Stevie left his new friend confused and unsure what he was approaching as the green eerie lights became brighter and the air got colder revealing taunting erratic scenery as he came upon the lights. What Stevie saw surrounded in the middle by thick birch woods was a little terrain on a little uphill basin surrounded with a palisade short rustic fence made of human bones crowned with human skulls and with the gate that had a sharp set of teeth that served as a lock. Night descended as the sky darkened the eyes of the skulls begin to glow their eerie green light illuminated the area of the dark woods. In the middle of the terrain hill, presented a slanted triple stave hut made from black wood and protected surrounded by a fence made out of human bones.

Stevie wanted to run but his legs wouldn't move and it wasn't the fence that startled Stevie it was that the hut which stood forbidding standing on its large chicken feet. At first sight, it was horrendous with its hind legs were nesting lying down as he approached the fence slowly with the giant hut house stood up on its giant chicken legs turning its back facing Stevie with its front door entrance facing the backwoods.

The hut began to shift its back towards Stevie like a large chicken protecting its nest the front door of the hut as he walks around the rustic bone fence searching for a pile of rocks as Kris mentioned describe it to be smeared in red markings.

Within minutes he found a pile of white stones inside hidden behind a large split stump oak tree a few yards from the other side of the eerie fence, being about knee high stacked covered in red paint markings Stevie haven't a clue how Kris knew must be a witch thing he thought.

Momentarily after knocking the hidden displayed creepy stones like Kris asked he felt a huge weight was lifted over him while the chicken hut began to go in a frantic going in circles as Stevie approach the other side of the human bone fence.

There on the other side was Kris dumbfound at the sight of the chicken leg hut house as it rotated with its back of the hut towards them away from the front door as Stevie approached to meet Kris.

"You know what this is!" The witch boy Kris proclaimed excitedly looking better than before. Stevie replied, "ah… shackpoultry?" Kris chuckled, "this is the legendary hut of the Grandmother Crone witch. The Famous Witch of the Eastern world, Baba Yaga."

Recovering from feeling distraught Stevie comically asks, "Baby Gaga who?"

Kris was starting to enjoy his company warming up to Stevie and he continued to chuckle and explained. "The Arch-Crone Witch, she's known to be a legendary witch that the world had thought was just a myth. Baba Yaga is Eastern Slavic a German/Russian witch believed to be cannibalistic and very dangerous. She is famously known to have a fence made of bones, mostly children bones from all ages." They both look around taking turns to study the true tall tale that they happen to stoop upon.

Stevie figured a thought and ask, "I'm guessing that wasn't red paint smeared on those white stones and were placed there to ward off enemies isn't it?" Kris answered back, "Baba Yaga is known for her dark art of powers as you can see but that particular spell is known to ward off any trespassers especially other suspicious witches."

Starring dazed at the glowing disturbing fence Stevie grew more aware of the dark character taking interest to look up the daunting witch in his cable guy guide booklet. As he read, "Also known as The Bone Mother, they say the witch travels perched in a large magical mortar with her knees almost touching her pointy hairy chin, and she pushes herself floating across through the woods with a large pestle." Kris shared his insight on the witch, some stories are told she's wild and untamable with powers of unknown hardly ever to be seen."

Stevie then asks, "She's in hiding?" Kris continued, "Don't you get it, for hundreds of years she's the master of disguise even she's hidden from Death. No one is capable to find or trace Baba Yaga, just only tales of the witch from those who were lucky enough to survive to tell the stories."

Stevie's nerves got the best of him reaching into his back pocket retrieving his cable guy remote stun gun for keepsakes and continue to read into his Seer guide booklet. "Wow, she sounds awfully scary and powerful."

"Very… some say she's a goddess of wisdom and death," Kris said walking past Stevie. "Being that old she must contain powerful old spells, charms, and resourceful books."

Stevie then exclaimed at Kris's sudden reaction, "and where you think you're going!" Kris started to walk towards the entrance of the skeleton fence as the giant chicken hut squat with its back to them protecting its front door entrance.

"Why the reason more to get into that chicken hut plus the witch is not home." Stevie didn't hesitate, "you really think that's a good idea, we better head back before Charlie."

Kris carrying a dull personality oddly interrupts Stevie excitedly whereas Stevie took notice of Kris's interest revealing his talent gift was in magic.

"It's a Servo spell! Its old Celtic magic that guards and protects the possessor's territory as you can see it won't reveal its entrance front door."

Kris laid out his hands in front of him with palms forward eyes closed and began to mutter under his breath again.

Surrounding Stevie, he started to hear creepy dark hidden whispers of multiple voices in strange Latin getting louder and louder as Kris was closing his palms together slowly still chanting. When the whispers got louder the darkness appeared out from the surrounding woods with the whispers turning into a screaming match over their own voices. Quickly disturbed Stevie covered his ears watching Kris's command he finally claps and with that, the loud voices stop with the darkness he conjured fading away.

Stevie was pasting from sudden anxiety but what a surprise he was still calm, "what was that?"

Kris expressed his answer turning to Stevie smiling then turning back looking at the large chicken leg hut house and citied some enchanted words, "Нет мира для нечестивых"

The exotic chicken hut house spun twice dramatically fast for its size and faced front forward towards the boys nested with its hind legs squatting down arching its slanted entrance frontward where the entrance of the bottom door slab meets the ground step.

"That was a spell I came up with to retrieve spells, those voices are part of the cool trick that helps me find hidden secrets like chanted passwords."

Kris looked confident and replied smirking, "She's not all that powerful, I basically crack her protection spell just now."

Stevie was starting to get used to sudden surprises, "what did you just say?"

Kris simply replied, "It's in Russian, No Rest For The Wicked."

Kris didn't wait any longer to open the front door entering the creepy deprived majestic chicken hut house. Taking control of the matter his courage didn't even persuade Stevie, "Just a quick peek in and out ok, plus who knows what we might find could be something useful."

Stevie took the chance to stroll around outside to make sure they were not being watched before he nervously entered the meager hut of the cannibalism's home.

Inside the hut was magically bigger than what it looks like from the outside. It was scantly and poorly dusky patched with grandmotherly draping of a foreigner collecting dust and cobwebs, dark and cold inside with very little gleamed light being lit up giving off some light by radiant spark coming from a high wooden butcher table in the middle size room next to a kitchen. It was a huge single room magically the size of a cottage from the inside divided rooms with hanging old rags with black candles and beeswax's drips everywhere.

There were also bones, cobwebs, and herbs hanging from the top ceiling along dangling garlic and kitchen essentials such as a butcher knifes of all sizes that worried Stevie. What's more terrifying was seeing some sleeping bats hanging from the ceiling. There was also a huge black cauldron displayed in the middle of the floor that could fit three people inside.

There was a corner kitchen with a long cupboard table draped with shelves full of books and mysterious mason jars some with strange items and herbs.

Kris then walks towards the dim storage pantry table where the shiny light was coming from.

Displayed on the middle butcher kitchen table, he found many witchcraft objects but saw one item that drew his attention. Kris grabs onto the only object that was bright enough to light up the witch's hut was a twinkling shiny glass lantern shaped like a box with a handle and a little lock door. It began to shine so brightly it was shiny enough to almost light the whole room it left the corners hidden in the dark.

Kris was fascinated he continued to rumble about ancient scrolls and gold treasures stored in the dark corners made it clear he was comfortable enough with Stevie while running through the shelves pulling books and scrolls in a deep concentration looking for something while holding the shiny lantern.

Across the dark subdued room, there was a dreadful black bookstand shape out of a creepy disfigured hand grasping a black leather book on its stand that was being shown by the moonlight peering through from outside through a high peek window.

Stevie could sense a weird vibe making his hair rise from the back of his neck leaving him to have goosebumps, intrigued as he approached the dark bookstand with the black iron book laced up in decrepit black leather with symbols of what looks like two half-moons. Stevie wasn't getting any weird tingles feelings from his left hand freezing up so assuming it was safe enough to open it.

With caution, Stevie reaches for the black iron book with his left hand as the book opens itself and before Stevie could retrieve his left hand back, then with an invisible force pulls his hand stuck onto its black pages with foreign writing within the pages of the dark book.

Stevie was unable to release his grasp to the pages of the book with a small sting watching his freezing left-hand turn ice cold and absorbing every black dark pigment straight off from the book's pages seeping into his hand.

He quickly frantic then fastened with his right hand to his left wrist and failed to release his left hand again still stuck to the book leaving the pages that were once dark blood black is now left with crisp white pages.

His left hand began to tremble watching his hand frost over his skin he quietly panicked and finally yank to release his cold left hand from the surprised creepy open book that spooks him out.

Astonishingly he realizes he wasn't hurt mending to his left hand warming it to his chest looking onto the open book and magically it appeared on the middle pages written in blood black ink was the word "Obumbratio," that shortly after Stevie read the word it vanished from the pages.

Kris still in conversation walks back towards the middle of the room from the pantry with the radiant shiny glass lantern occupied in his hand. "You ok over there, you found anything unusual cause you look like you've been spooked."

Kris puts aside his quick findings of ancient scrolls on the table as Stevie walks over to the table acting like as nothing happen but his eyes spoke wide open concerned what cold happen next.

"Check out this ancient spell." Kris then picks up an unlit black candle and blew at it and magically the wick lit up. "Pretty cool huh, but wait!" He then blew again at the lit black candle that went out but this time it made all the candles in the hut magically lit up the whole room revealing the horrid of the inside of the witch's hut, even the big pot cauldron lit up with fire.

"Pretty neat huh?" Kris replies again, "A very old spell I found to literally lite your way."

Stevie and Kris took the chance to chuckle as they glance around it was mostly like a creepy grandmother gypsy's attic Stevie thought.

"Look at all this stuff, we probably shouldn't be messing with any of this better yet we shouldn't be here."

Kris convinces Stevie just a few more minutes and places the sparkling glass lantern back on the table while Stevie went towards the lantern reaching for it.

Stevie examined the awkward shiny glass lantern "I wonder what make's it lite up?" He then unlocks and opens the small glass door of the lantern zipping out was the sparkling light of gold and silver glistening light-bug zapping around the boys illuminating around the room circling the kitchen landing on the other side of the middle butcher table taking shape that glimmered into a golden shade topless male.

Kris was alarmed motion Stevie to not move and murmured to Stevie, "that's a fairy."

The fairy then yelled and shouted with its arms stretched out and yelled "Tricks!" Kris and Stevie were both surprised as they took upon themselves to shout back then looking at each other speechless with wide eyes looking back at the cover magazine boy with pretty looks the fairy had a slim muscular tone body with rip abs and a face that could be on a spread cover for top most beautiful people in the world.

"Tricks!" The fairy suddenly said again and vanish flashing into gold silver sparkles of glimmer reappearing surprising the boys again standing in the middle between Kris and Stevie's rejoicing hugging both of them with its arms stretch out over their shoulders. "Saviors, friends of the royal Essences of the Faerie Seelie court. I'm free, I've been kidnap and traps for days, I'm forever in your debt." The fairy's skin was glistening started to glow and took a bow.

All that Stevie and Kris could do was analyze their current situation that they got themselves into starring at one another.

The fairy began to ask Stevie, "Are you a dark Fae or a light Fae?"

Stevie had to put the conversation in check, "I'm no fairy at all?"

The fairy then asks being unfamiliar with the human world, "then are you dark or light?"

Stevie was not sure what the fairy meant. "I'm neither one," Stevie replies, The fairy then agrees, "you are correct about that, I can sense both light and dark complex within you that you are to walk the gray line between dark and light.

"I offer you in return my bond of internal light essences." The fairy runs up to Stevie surprisingly quickly hugs him as Kris shuffled away to defend himself.

Kris tried to be alert but was too late. "NO, don't let him touch you!"

Trap in a bear hug with the fairy Stevie just stood there frozen on spot. The friendly fairy was massively strong for being slim but this time Stevie felt an ease of warmth comfort ease coming over him. The fairy was wearing something that looks very similar to a Tarzan movie wearing only a loincloth green short man-skirt made of two big shiny green leaves lace on both sides of his thigh legs scarcely with smaller leaves covering up the rest of personal area.

"You can stop hugging me now," Stevie politely asks. "I can't," replied the joyful fairy stuck on the spot lock in a bear hug with Stevie.

Kris showed he was clumsy stumbling to get a hold of the cable guy remote aiming at the fairy with a projectile concentrated beam over the fairy. Kris shouted, "It works this pause button on the remote seems to inhibit the majority of its body movement. Stevie then took the opportunity to slip away from under the fairy's hug still paused in an absent bear hug. It was the fairy's outfit that was screaming who likes short shorts, wearing a root leather elegant strap sheath that holds a deadly dagger. It was an elongated strap over across his bare chest tied with a leather satchel pouch by his side. The friendly fairy had the skin of a tone admix with green and gold glitter as if he spread glitter lotion all over his skin.

"I don't think he means to harm," Stevie said. They notice the fairy had pointed shaped ears that were covered by its black wavy hair wearing no shoes but huge shiny green metallic bamboo leaves as shin guards up to his knees, brandish in gold and green wearing a golden headband with an emerald pellet necklace and a golden green right armband shaped in a trailing vine.

Kris unpaused the remote and the fairy drop down on one knee and bowed before Stevie, "You are my kindred, brother of the light now. I am at your will, what shall I call you brother?"

Kris took the approach padding Stevie on the back should standing between him and the fairy, Kris became complex amused at Stevie's dire situation having a quite unusual attitude he too was confused and contrast with excitement, "don't be so gray he's now bound to you shepherd boy and you are now linked to the fairy, you're Stevie the steward and he's now your patron it's old folklore but I didn't think fairies still carry out these ancestral traditions.

Stevie took no pleasure in feeling extremely uncomfortable to close around the naked stranger that he just met in a bear hug who is now bowing at Stevie's feet.

"I didn't ask for this, please get up." The fairy retreated and asked, "Was it something I did wrong, Steward the grey shepherd?"

"No, I just don't know who or what you just did, and what did you just call me?" Stevie answered.

"My name is Trix's emir of Élan of essences," the fairy glowed and bowed again. "You are now brother to the Élan realms, you now share the light."

Kris was astonished examining his buddy up and down. "You've been marked, you and…" Kris then turns to look at the happy fairy, "I believe if I'm correct you are now one sharing a telepathy link that ties to the fairy to know your whereabouts, thoughts, and worst you're like his master kind of like the genie in the bottle but without the wishes."

Kris couldn't get his eyes off the fairy that was a very good-looking dude to look at. "Ok right now is not the time." Stevie continued marching towards the front door, "we have to get out of here!"

Stevie spoke too soon, with his left hand that stung turning numb in coldness the chicken hut house started to shake hearing a clear voice in his head that sounded like Trixs the fairy's voice, "the witch she is coming."

Panic struck Stevie when he looks into Trix's eyes and knew he was warning him. "Did you just say something in my head," Stevie ask Trixs?

Kris picks up on the incoming warning stare from the both of them and knew right away what was coming, "we definitely need to get out of here."

Almost immediately they heard a hideous noise as the earth shook with aches and trees groaned they rushed to step out the witch's front door Stevie followed Kris out as they saw treetops from a distance being push as if something huge was rushing their way.

The wind suddenly picks up blowing ghastly as they knew who was coming.

They scrambled running back into the witch's hut scuttling looking for places to hide.

Stevie saw a view out of the musk dirty peek smudge window of the outside trees tip tops snapping back opening the way with winds blowing up a storm with flashing lighting revealing among in the dark of a horrific view of the old Crone witch.

As the legend says it was true, the old hag crone witch was perch on to what looks to be a giant old mortar that flies through using a large pestle as a rudder and sweeping away the tracks behind her bending back the trees with a broom made out of silver birch.

Baba Yaga the witch crone riding in her mortar she stopped to paused and sniffed the air, "I smell humans," she cried in a croaking voice with a crackle, "who is here for my tasting?"

The front door jolt's open with a loud bang there stood the witch.

Kris went straight to the kitchen pantry hidden behind the dirty covered drape rags.

Trixs the fairy didn't seem too bright as he hid behind the front door as it blasts open with Stevie dropping to the floor crawling quietly as he can behind under a large kitchen table into the cabinet that was also covered by damp drapes shelved with jars, potions, and awkward enough residing there was a creepy tiny wooden doll rested under the table shelves with Stevie there was also a large black goliath frog facing each other face to face with Stevie's that surprised him as he clasps his mouth from shouting from sudden fright to not be caught.

The Description of Baba Yaga is so horrendous the old crone witch appeared as a very ugly woman that would have been taller of about seven feet but crotch over with a hump on its back was standing about almost six feet with long wiry grey hair wearing a red scarf around her head hiding her greenish skin and teeth, jaundiced eyes, and sharpened facial features of almost like a reptile.

She wears a lot of old jewelry exposing her brittle wrinkled body with feathers and bones in her hair. Her long pale purple fingernails were like talon daggers that contained a powerful paralyzing poison that incapacitated any victim she caught. She has a dress on that needs patchwork along with her ragged skirt as she also wears a black crested vest.

The old witch was untying the headscarf that she wore over her grey-white damp hair tied around under her long pointy chin. She looks meek and was thin ready to fool her prey with undeniable strength wearing unclean grody rags under her garment like a beggar with a huge long distorted nose revealing long sharp teeth with a few iron caps while grinning.

Her skin was horrid brittle like tree barks even her elbows revealed bristle tree twigs. Squinting her eyes it would gleam like a predator when she steps into the shadows being blind but she sniffs the air with her crooked nose locating her prey. Immediately she drops her stick broom made out of grass straw hay and rushes inside the hut towards the middle table hissing with a howl picking up her empty lantern having long talon fingers with nails that could be used as daggers.

She continues to smile suddenly from behind her she used her telekinesis as the front door slams closing the door revealing Trixs who froze on the spot.

Outfoxed her prey she turns around facing the fairy with the lantern in her hands opening its tiny glass door.

"Please no, not the fairy trap, not in there again!" Trixs yelled out revealing his hands up palms facing the witch quickly she absorbs all of his living body essences that glimmered into golden silver sparkling dust being sucked back into the lantern. Hearing the footsteps of Kris as he bravely steps outside of the pantry's dirty curtain revealing himself he quickly tosses a spread line of salt from a steel can.

"It's a barrier against maleficent witches." Kris cornered himself between the salt barriers aiming the remote in his other hand directly at the witch that was blocking the exit door.

The old witch slowly looks to Kris not slightly surprised placing the shiny lantern back onto the butcher table tilting her head like a wild animal studying Kris as if she knew he was there all along.

The witch's beady eyes were transfixed gleaming yellow at Kris starring at her prey licking her lips with a slithering tongue.

Taking steps closer to Kris the witch flickered her left claw hand unarming Kris as his remote magically flew out of his hand across the room.

Kris whispering under his breath then bowing his head down already on a spell since the chicken hut started to shake and rattle.

Cold darkness engulfed the room in an unpleasant low moan that echoed bringing shadows from its dark corners of the hut.

Kris slowly lifted his head revealing his face to the witch with his eyes shot blood-red turning into black eyes with his face making distorted images of like a demon. Kris grabs his head and shook violently and fell to the floor and for a split second, but nothing happens.

The witch let out a screeching laugh pulling out a relic pentagram necklace revealing it to Kris who was sweating and panting as he looks up at the witch he was helpless. Unexpectedly she stops laughing and was starring in the direction towards her dark creepy bookstand.

She staggers to the wicked stand in bewilderment of anguish seeing the dark book laid out open with white empty pages absents of its partiality darkness.

The book of shadows immediately shuts on its own close locked as she approaches the book.

Stevie still hid under behind the kitchen table rag curtains while the witch let out a boisterous cry so intense both Kris and Stevie were covering their ears from having their eardrums being busted.

In the reaction to the black book the old witch was bickering throwing and toss things of what she can get her hands on pasting back and forth walking past Stevie a couple of times.

She then paused and draws her attention towards Kris being on the other side of the room behind his protection spell cornered by the line of salt.

Speaking in a foreign language the witch raised her left hand swooshing Kris's whole body with such a force he was lifted into the air pin upside down to the witch's cornered wall.

The old witch walks over to Kris slowly the wooden floorboard creaked as she approached closer to Kris enchanting in tongues revealing her right claw hand covered in green mystic mist.

Baba Yaga took a brief moment inhaling a deep breath before stepping over the line of salt, within seconds the salt engulfed in flames.

The boys had no idea who they were dealing with while Stevie could hear Kris agonizing as he hid underneath the table pantry.

Frighten and scared Stevie had to get over his thoughts of is this really happening.

"Hey!" Stevie shouts as he pops up from under the table revealing his identity to the scary old crone witch as she had Kris pin to the wall with his shirt rip revealing his stomach and chest.

Aside from the old witch being shocked and confused by Stevie's sudden presence, she was about to claw into Kris's stomach with her right talon fingers covered in green mystic mist.

Then out of surprise Baba Yaga let out an echoed cry revealing her nasty mouth with sharp rotted iron teeth with a force from the old hag's cry blasted Stevie across the room with a sonic explosion smashing his body into the kitchen shelves of glasses and witchcraft items falling onto the floor shielding himself covering his ears.

The outcry from the witch had a spellbound incapacitated Stevie from making any movements compelling his body to be stiff with pain close enough for his eardrums to explode he thought.

The pain was so intense for Stevie his first instinct reaction got the best of him with pain aches all over his body pulling himself up off the floor with his right hand grabbing ahold of the corner table to help lift himself up.

The scream from the witch continued still being cast out towards Stevie with glass being shattered and objects being slammed against the wall over Stevie.

Stevie then slumps to the edge of the table holding his resistance getting scratch up by flying items but with exaggerated pain, he still managed to grasp onto the corner of the table and with his left hand grab the closest thing he could reach from underneath the kitchen table pantry.

Then with another surprise, Stevie quickly throws a mason jar at the old witch with all his might smashing the jar at the witch's face shattering the mason glass jar filled with a clear liquid.

Baba Yaga grabs onto her face with her magic force releasing Kris as he fell to the ground landing on his head from being upside down pinned to the wall.

The old crone witch went into a frenzied state with her face buried in her long claw hands going in circles with fumes coming from her face and underneath her rag clothes was emitting black smoke.

Stevie losing his strength fell back onto the floor behind the table pantry with his body still stiff catching his breath unable to move or see the witch but he could hear Baba Yaga wailing and shirking thinking for a moment he thought could she be melting?

After a few seconds, the wailing agony passed away all was silent and still.

Stevie could feel the witch's tight spell warring off as he lay still behind the kitchen table. He could hear Kris moaning, "ouch my head."

Stevie remained still recovering behind the table he could hear Kris dragging himself nearer around towards the kitchen table from the other side of the room. Stevie was just about frantically to ask, "Hey Kris?"

Grabbing the corners of the table leg beside Stevie's foot was a horrific scene Stevie went numb, unable to move a rotted claw hand oozing with its talons snatching up Stevie's leg crawling her way up to Stevie was Baba Yaga.

The ancient Crone witch was no longer the witch she uses to be but a ragged decomposing body of a melting monster screeching gnawing her teeth at Stevie reaching up to him while he was paralyzed and helpless.

She then rips his shirt with her oozing talons claws of what's left of it still covered in green mist clawing below Stevie's sternum.

Screaming with pain and discomfort Stevie felt the monster climbing her way up to him melting away speaking in distorted tongues as she began to disintegrate from underneath her rag cloak. Clawing what she can into Stevie stomach left behind two permanent angle scars from the traumatic attack to his rib cage due to her hand melting away

Stevie was oozed with slime down to his waist left with rags from the witch's garments laying on top of him leaving behind a pentagram necklace with a foul stench of steam coming off from the rags of what's left of the legendary crone witch leaving an odor of burnt hair and dead carcass.

Kris rushed over to Stevie to help his friend up with their new companion at their side was Trixs the happy fairy.

"You ding-dong her!" The fairy exclaimed.

Kris replies, "you what?"

"Ding Dong…" The fairy said with his hands up in the air.

Stevie and Kris both exchange looks realizing it was no pun intended and both said completing the fairy's sentence, "The witch is dead?"

Trixs then replied being a fairy that came with the whole package including with the airhead nimble attitude, "Duh, what did you think I meant?"

Stevie took notice it was the first time to see Kris smile then he asks, "Stevie are you ok?" Trixs pointed out, "ah… buddy, you've been cursed by the witch."

Literally the fairy was pointing to Stevie's fresh new scars.

"Oh no… not a curse mark" Kris replies with worrisome, as his eyes were wide open.

That's when Stevie knew he was in trouble and had the chance to ask before blacking out, "a what, a curse… am I going to be ok?"

6

The red door test

PANIC SLOWLY STRUCK STEVIE WITH tingle feelings all over his body he felt he was being microwaved with his insides burning but was cold on the outside of his skin.

Waking up with a foggy unclear mind and a massive headache he thought he lost his senses when woken up by a loud rumble beneath him very unfamiliar like the earth was breathing.

Lying in a gloomy murky pitch-black room he was blind in the dark with no light as the ground shook feeling for the floor was a flat slab concrete that was cold and damp.

Stevie pulled out his smartphone from his pocket for the flashlight app and still couldn't see through the murky fog that was so tense he could barely see his hand in front of him. Keeping up in collecting his composure he kept telling himself "don't panic, don't panic, everything will be ok."

The mystery gloomy dwelling would echo anything as if he were transported to a vast hall empty darkness chamber thought to himself how did he end up lost in an eerie cavern. Feeling for the ground grasping for a wall, a path, or any sign of a road as another deep rumble shook the dark dwelling that came from within the ground behind him as he ran forward into the immense of nothing.

Stevie started to think what's the last thing he remembered before blacking out was the hideous old crone Russian witch scarring his stomach and remembering his last location was scouting in Greenbelt woods.

Moments before his eyes were adapting into the dark another rumble was let out stirring Stevie to get away from the deep tremble that reminded him of a deep old man's snore.

Out of the clear view in the darkness from a few distances, Stevie saw what look to be a light shade casting its bright shadows before within the dark without having any source of light in the dark dwelling casting bright light shadows that looks like a reflection of an outside scenery shape of trees and boulder rocks.

The light shadows themselves glowed brighter the closer Stevie got to the bright shadows shielding his eyes walking towards into the light shade being so bright he felt a warm breeze overcame his whole body breathing in the fresh air.

Opening his eyes to the sunshine on his face with an aroma filled with nature he transfixes and was lost surrounded by wooden tress noticing he was back at Greenbelt where Stevie and Kris supposed to meet Charlie back before sunset but looking around his surroundings clueless about his location turning in circles asking himself, "what just happen?"

Just then, being surrounded by the outdoors of trees with flashing colorful tiny fireflies zapping through the woods leaving trails of glistening sparkle residue of its pixie dust zipped by and dance around Stevie.

There were cries and shouts afar to Stevie's right side coming into sight, "he's over here!" Charlie appeared out from the shrubs behind one of the rock boulders and Stevie noticed he was approaching carefully.

"There you are, kid, you all right?"

Stevie answered, "What, what… happen?"

Following up right behind Charlie rushing through to pass him was Ashley catching her breath with Kris running behind her.

The glee colorful fireflies magically twinkled manifesting into a selective unique group of people that were very beautiful he thought.

They all resemble what Trixs the fairy was wearing with bright colors having their own shine to themselves as if their skin was not shiny enough.

"We were hoping you would tell us?" Ashley then asks Stevie while helping him off the ground checking for his vital signs as he signals he's ok.

"What's going on… did you guys get a search party for me?" Ashley answered by nodding her bobbly head with her bouncy curls as her short perm hair moves freely while she talks with her hands on her hips "pretty much."

"Kris, what happened?" Stevie asks.

"You really don't remember do you?" Kris then asks Stevie.

Stevie would get distracted looking at the fairies with their good charming looks and their colorful attire almost naked resembling a tropical bouquet with a shiny glistening glow to their skin.

Stevie was keen to notice another magical character separate from the search group unlike the fairies who took cover hiding and peering from behind the trees keeping its distance very mysterious Stevie thought and could tell it lead the search party from afar as it stood out where it's skin was white as powder with blond long hair pulled back wearing a green sock beanie dazed at Stevie starring with its pale metallic green toxic eyes half dress in a greenery vine plant outfit. After Stevie glance away for a second, the mysterious Fae green-white olive creature was gone.

Stevie continued, "All I remember is being attacked by that old scary witch and Kris you were…" Kris then replies, "You don't remember at all do you?"

Stevie answered, "what you mean, I was just with you and that awful witch had you pinned against the wall and Tricks who look a lot more like those guys" pointing to the searching crew fairies who were scrutinizing peering from behind the trees as if frighten of Stevie.

"Hey are they fairies too?" Stevie replied.

Ashley with her hands on her hips and her heavy Texan accent, "sorry to burst your excitement darlin' but it's early noon."

Stevie noted to himself, "wait… it's noon, that means?"

Kris obliges to answer for his confused lost friends, "Stevie you've been missing for almost a day."

Stevie taking a step back feeling dizzy "that can't be…?"

Before blacking out again, Stevie remembered that Charlie and Ashley caught his fall as his vision faded out into darkness passing out in a deep slumber.

Stevie slowly woke up to a bright hazel green four-eyes wearing glasses, all up Stevie's face who found himself lying in a medical patient table chair.

The new stranger wore a white lab coat over his blue jeans, wearing converse sneakers with a white plain V-neck t-shirt and black suspenders. His four eyes were a set of huge square spectacles that fits his oval face, Stevie was being examined with high end technology with a medical laser light scanning Stevie's eyes, "ahh our subject is awake."

Stevie then realizes he was topless with bandages below his sternum over his wounded two scars by the deceased Crone witch Baba Yaga.

Hook to vital machines Stevie laid there on a technology medical-bed occupied in a elaborated white glass cubical lab surrounded by extravagant equipment and tool machineries circling around them.

"Take it easy you'll wear yourself out, you're back at the Seer's Library underground on the third base level this is the trinity room more so of a care unit recovery for you guys, and it's also my office." He nodded then adjusted his glasses that were sliding down on his bridge nose and continued solving his Rubik puzzle within seconds in one hand, "We're just checking your vital scans now." They were in a medical lab below floors in a huge glass square dome warehouse with touchscreen glass technology as cubical glass sees through walls that are state-of-the-art high advance technology that Stevie has ever seen before.

Grabbing his arms pinching himself making sure this wasn't a dream Stevie replies, "I swear I keep dreaming?"

"You've been missing for half a day in the woods, I assume you remember being found about an hour ago before you passed out again from exhaustion and no it's not a dream my friend it's all hundred percent real." The scientist gave two thumbs up at Stevie smiling revealing his deep dimples replacing back his big spectacles on his bridge nose again as it was sliding off.

"Some scouting you guys had at the Greenbelt so I hear, the Greenbelt can be full of surprises." Stevie took cautiously and took notice of his surroundings.

"Everyone is fine in your scouting group, they're all waiting at the library chambers but if your wondering your dark friend with the creepy moon eye scar did ask for you though."

"Hey, you're that guy at the Tri-Paradox library table the IT tech guy?" Stevie's found himself surrounded in a typical mad scientist laboratory shelved with vast advanced technology and many tool equipment in clear crates and boxes.

On one side of the corner was a lair of chemistry and biology with stacks of lab tables set with chemistry tools, test tubes, and graduated cylinders alive with experiments and bubbling with liquid chemicals.

Even the intensive care unit the "trinity room" looks so highly Elite with the newest technology to medical lasers with glassed hologram walls of graphs and info of his vital signs. There was one piece of unique equipment that caught Stevie's eye immediately recognized mounted on a glass corner wall underneath the hologram screen.

"Wow you have every video game console made all into one game star, you even design the console as a star shape that is amazing!"

He smiled at Stevie with amusement of appreciation and gratitude immediately got excited he adjusted his spectacles and said, "Yep Game Star exactly, has your every video game console entertainment ever made all in one single star. See its shape like a star and it modifies," as he began rumbling off in a scientific manner using math equations.

Lost in the translation Stevie was amazed and confused at the scientist's prompt intellectual conversation. Even though the guy was a genius Stevie knew his IQ was well over 190 remembering hearing about their I.T. lab guy was the youngest to have a doctorate in experimental physics and was awarded a PhD by the University of Zürich for his dissertation on Molecular dimensions to have commended Charlie in admiration.

He must be one of the smartest people on the planet Stevie thought seeing multiple degrees Showing he is a Dr. of Immunologist, with a degree in natural resources, environmental science, and a Ph.D. in nuclear chemical engineer.

He quickly mentions to Stevie he graduated from many elite schools one of his favorites is graduating from Ingolstadt University in Germany with an executive masters of leadership in human resources management and degree with a master's and M.D. in Biological Science and medicine.

The genius sighed, "As a black kid growing up in a strict family was hard enough I was never allowed to have a game console and let alone I was even spanked if got caught playing video games." He chuckled, "well I don't have that problem anymore."

Stevie then asks, "So you believe in all this magic stuff huh?"

"There's almost every explanation for every theory on the law of physics into magic and technology. Ever heard the saying, any sufficiently advanced technology is indistinguishable from magic, and I quote," he said.

That's when Stevie took upon and wonder what the Dr.'s thoughts are, "what's this whole ordeal with the Aether and ancient Gods among us," Stevie was then interrupted.

"Ah yes the light-bearing Aether, and you do mean the rainbow veil that composes magic and supernatural beings to compel as non-coexist with the mortal world, in other terms scientifically I call it the Luminiferous. As far as I can consider home native Terrans and extraterrestrials like archons are falling star folks aka the gods that have been here quite sometime even before the great flood but most of them with a pass gene hybrid rhesus blood type (Rh) a protein around the blood cells that's what makes them tick but I can go on and on."

Even though Stevie couldn't quite add up what the Dr. scientist was saying he then asks, "Then what was that at the stone library table the Paradox they call it that makes us Seers?"

The scientist then replied, "The paradox is a neatfy thing, if neatfy isn't a word then I mean isn't it neat?" The Dr. questioned himself and then answered. "It's a chemical unbalance effluvium from a dimensional plane within the library that increase the balance of neurons activating the whole cerebrum of the chosen Seers including the cerebellum to allow its complex sensory and neural functions activating all four of the brain's lobe reaching at its primitive height some to as high as forty-five percent. If you ask me Morphology is more my expertise but your lucky being a Seer comes with longevity, heck we got a three-hundred-year-old walking around here somewhere.

Abruptly walks in interrupted by the Librarian, "Nerd! What's his status report?" Forcefully the Librarian rudely walks in with a dreadful look wearing her black right-hand leather glove clad in an old black mid eight-hundred fashion dress attire.

Nerd handed the Librarian a clipboard she then snatched away as she reviews it going over the report on the clipboard. "His vitals are showing he's fine and stable, no serious wounds or pierce tissue only damage skin scarred of what's left of the contaminated incantation," the scientist doctor answered.

"Any sign of diabolism, presage, legerdemain magnetism?" The Librarian asked. "Check, check, check!" Nerd said.

Then the Librarian asks, "Purified and his vitals?" Nerd the scientist then replies, "Check and all cleanup but it left a scar spell-botch."

Stevie had to ask, "ah a W-what?" Nerd replied to Stevie, "A Scar-mark, in this case, it's what's left of the curse or spell that didn't go right or incomplete though you were lucky to survive such tragedy. I do have to admit that is one nasty scar you got there. Luckily nothing toxic or poison from that old crone Russian witch, just a hero scar from the trauma experience." Stevie traces his finger over his newly fresh scars, "Did that Witch put a spell on me?"

The Librarian was ignoring him steered focus onto Stevie's report reading through the clipboard while the scientist answered, "Usually victims meet their sudden death when exposing to high radiation on a three-level count which you call is magic that caused your scarring."

Stevie was removing the rest of his bandages below his sternum while the Librarian still going over his chart as the young doctor scientists dabbled medical cream onto Stevie's scars rambling on a highly educated speculation explaining the theory laws and complexity of magic to Science. Stevie quickly punches in a sentence before the scientist was able to finish his theory. "I remember the witch's hand was glowing and she clawed at me, was that radiation?" Nerd was intrigued and answer, "It's a highly complex ordeal, they may call it magic but I call it science. I must say you're the first to have found contact with a high dose of diffusion depending on the diffraction of the wavelength of the spontaneous movement emission to the source of its energy which polarizing your skin causing scarring that should of cause fatal incident but your body had no effect as if you were immune or you have some healing factor, Seers usually don't heal that fast."

Solving his tenth Rubik puzzle the doctor scientist then asks, "Are you sure you're not an elf." Stevie repeated, "an elf?"

The Librarian intruded, "Enough, enlighten us what you remember?" Stevie spoke, "I'm sorry everything happened so fast it was a blur. One moment we were saving a fairy I think." Nerd interrupted saying, "ah lite-sprite, sorry an extraterrestrial, a light being on a different third parallel plan existent to our world just hidden from the human eye."

The Librarian interrupted Nerd and again with just a heed hand motions she then motion Stevie to continue and said, "Go on." It seems the scientist has an explanation for every magical myth or legend in a scientific hypothesis form with Stevie able to finish his case. "Ah Mhm right, and then the next minute we were trapped in the witch's hut being carried by huge chicken feet, and then out of nowhere being attack by this hideous witch."

The Librarian mentions the witch's name "Baba Yaga." Stevie continued, "Then the next thing I can remember is passing out and waking up to the void darkness in a massive

82

space that was wet and cold like an old cave maybe but it wasn't and the weird thing is it felt it was grumbling as if it was alive." The scientist interrupted again to ask, "wait I'm sorry did you say alive?"

Stevie replies, "yea, then I saw a light, don't know how to explain that one. It was like a shiny shade of a light shadow and the closer I got to it the brighter the light shadow got. Then after that, I was back at Greenbelt, supposedly passing out again?" Stevie then had their full attention as he notices they both were in serious thought of silence starring at him. The Librarian then ask, "how recent can you remember?" Stevie replied, "I remember waking up back at the greenbelt having a search party rescue team with those fairies and odd green stranger among them." Nerd gave attention to Madam the Librarian, "hmm, I'm going to run these test again just in case I missed something."

The Librarian gazed up and down with such a glare at Stevie as if he was contagious, handing the clipboard back to the scientist daunting away with her one-handed black glove signaling the Nerd doctor scientist to step away giving her space while giving Stevie a fictitious appalled smile. Stevie was baffled at the Librarian's coarseness towards the scientist as she was examining Stevie's scars and was starting to get upset with her admittance earlier, thinking of how rude she came across. Stevie then spoke directly to the Librarian out loud with a glare, "Well I'm a NERD too, having hobbies of my own."

She steps away with a small gesture with no remorse, —"YOU NOW LIVE IN A WORLD WHERE LEGEND AND NIGHTMARES ARE REAL." The librarian said before she walks away darting towards the exit, "When, and if your well, resume your way to the library Modus Operandi chamber in twenty till for your final year tribulation."

Stevie was speechless and then replies, "I just got here… another what?" Then Nerd shots Stevie a straight look being behind the Librarian signaling uh… oh… nodding his head no immediately cuing Stevie to end his sentence.

The Librarian stops halfway out of the door in silence and turns her attention towards Stevie "and if not" she then forces a crude creepy smile at Stevie, "it was a pleasure." She then nods to the scientist doctor Nerd signaling him he is now your responsibility to escort Stevie out. She gave Stevie a dare look and storms off like she had a bad taste in her mouth.

"Gess… what's her problem, acting like she runs the place calling you names. I can't believe you let her call you that!" Stevie said as he unstraps himself off the medical patient bed.

The scientist doctor began to laugh, "who Madam, the Librarian, nah she can be difficult and is known to rub people the wrong way but you forget she does run the place and Nerd is my name by the way."

Stevie felt remorse, "oh I can see that, oops sorry." Nerd chuckled again, "no worries I take it as a compliment probably the smartest Nerd you'll ever know literally."

Nerd sounded sarcastic and he then winks at Stevie helping him unstrap from the vital medical machines. "I must say if my calculations are right the Librarian is a force to be reckoned with and she probably sees you as a threat."

"Why would she see me as a threat?" Stevie asked. Nerd was obliged to reply, "You just slain one of the most omnipotent forces in the world, that ugly Russian granny bone witch you melted was the grand hind witch. I would defiantly stay clear from the Librarian, she always did look down on scientific knowledge but like I always quoted, "Any sufficiently advanced technology is indistinguishable from magic.

Stevie then realized there was multiple Rubik puzzles completed everywhere as he tossed one to Stevie signaling him to twist the cubic puzzle while he began completing his 20th puzzle in one hand. "I am surprised they're running tribulations this early of the year, you guys must be a special bunch for that test.

"What test?" Stevie asked in a surprising accusation.

It's a requirement for all Seers to try the last test of tribulations at least once, but you have nothing to worry about they usually have Charlie or one of the high Seers to run the tribulations. The outcome of this test is Aeons and its reasons are to enlightens or enhances a chance to be a great Seer with help of gifts by other paranormal entities that some are known to be legends, which are bound to help us. The journey to achieve these gifts is called the Aeon bequest.

The Aeon bequest allows every Seer to be pardon or excused if they are pick by the universe it's kind of a special deal cause now they know they have a way to influence the world timeline or to be a curse that would be the worst outcome, but I'll tell you a secret the Tribulation is to search for your sheer will power, it will be a red door tribulation."

Stevie didn't want to feel lost in the conversation removing his bandages slowly, "this grand hind witch Baba Yaga how dangerous was she?"

"One thing for sure you are pulling a lot of attention around here my friend. There are talks of ancient prophecies approaching and all eyes are on you. I don't know how you did it, but if I were you I would stay on the down-low you know staying off the radar. Wouldn't want to spread your business in the known world as a Witch killer. Better yet there are talks about you being the Witch Bane and you're the first sign of the prophecies!"

Stevie then said, "the witch bane... no no it was an accident I didn't mean to kill anybody..."

Nerd comically said, "well my little pretty I can call that accident too... but hey look I don't want to be a burden of news all I know is you just exterminated a legend, an Arc Witch that is."

"What's an Arch Witch?" Stevie asked.

Then Nerd answered, "there are many types of witches but Arc Witches are the worst and most powerful of them all. They hold supreme power and knowledge of great dark and light magic occupied in a higher position in their clan hierarch. That old hag you have slain is the world's ancient myth Baba Yaga. She's Russian folklore just in case you're wondering."

"Kris had mentioned about that," Stevie said.

"She was so mysterious and powerful. She's been unexposed for centuries, many have tried to conjurer or crusade in search of her wisdom and power or to slay her foul ascendancy. Some say she was so powerful she had the source of knowledge that even she was invisible under the eyes of Death himself," Nerd exclaimed and then said, "Pretty powerful stuff I'll say."

Stevie was speechless at what he was hearing dumbfound and reminisce what terrors he experiences with the whole accident with the old crone witch realizing how close they were to be killed and survived through it all. Nerd could sense Stevie was starting to get overwhelmed.

"Hey look Stevie this is the way I see it, man, you're still here buddy, and evil witches would want you dead so that should tell you about the Librarian and we're all here and this life isn't for everyone you know." Nerd was starting to make sense to Stevie, "Don't tell anybody this but my calculations," he then signal with a cough, "excuse me, but I believe we all have a purpose in life, a calling one would say. Even a guy like me who's come to a reason of understanding and concepts of life through numbers and mathematics I've come to a conclusion which took me almost years to figure out my purpose."

Stevie let out a soft sigh and says," I guess your right."

Then Nerd gave another piece of advice, "The universe is under no obligation to make sense to you, and human senses are not the measure of what is or is not true in the universe."

Nerd asks Stevie at the end to come to see him every once a week to check on his status quo.

Nerd walks over to the other side of his glass square dome facility to his right wall was a white two-story drywall board with two ladders reaching its heights on both ends of the board covered in math, chemistry, science equations all over the board.

"We all play a part of this great grand design, the greater plan G.P. I call it." Stevie at ease and was fascinated at Nerd's point of view with a twinkle in his eye that showed much passion for his work as he showed Stevie around his laboratory. "So here we are this is the infirmary/lab/ gadgets weaponry room, and I'm your nurse/geologic/equip guy." Nerd gave a smile adjusting his square spectacles then with his arms stretched out wearing his lab coat claiming his territory.

Under his wall of chemistry and mathematic equations was a corner selected section close off behind secretive curtains. One part of the side curtain was left open exposing its corner.

Quickly Nerd grabbing the red curtains covering up his corner secretive project lab, Stevie only got a glimpse of what looks like an alloy metallic robot with a face shape with angelic features of a woman compiled to be sitting on a steel table mix with tools, nuts, bolts, and screws. "That right there is the grand ultimate design of my final work I call it Project Double Zero." Nerd then claps and folds his arms together capturing his moments mesmerized at his work looking onto his large whiteboard above his secret curtains. "Still long to go but the process has been immediate." Nerd was very excited and anxious discussing his secretive project then he realized he had revealed enough and started to collect himself.

"Excuse me" he coughs. "I believe you better hurry it up and meet the rest of your group at the library before I have to escort you out," he said with a smile.

Stevie taking his exit stepping into the domain elevator Nerd briefly stops Stevie. "Oh hey one more thing Stevie, try to stay clear from Madam the Librarian. Baba Yaga the witch you just killed was Madam's archenemies. Rumors have it some hundred years ago she had vowed to be the one to end the reigning power of Baba Yaga. Don't you get it that Arch-Crone witch was known as a goddess of wisdom and death supposedly had a history with the librarian? That's not even the cherry on top, not only is the Librarian an Arch-witch as well she is now in line to be the next head of the Grand hind witch that controls the supreme council of all witches. The grand hind witch controls and rules over all regions of good and evil witches to their covens all around the world. You have been marked as you can see by the last grand hind witch." Pointing over Stevie's recent scars on his ribs.

"Witches all over the world will want to see you dead, but don't sweat it, just the evil ones let's hope." Nerd just chuckled to get the conversation light-hearted.

Like that made any better for Stevie feeling sentimental about his luck. Just then the elevator door opens and Stevie step inside as it began to close with Nerd send off his last tip to offer. "Luckily for you, the Librarian is over her dark wicked days, just stay out of her way ok."

There wasn't much encouragement right after the moment Stevie departed from Nerd, he was a little distressed thinking of the Librarian having to cross paths with her again soon enough. Just the thought of her gave Stevie the chills making his left hand go cold numb.

It was kind of an awkward moment for Stevie to meet up with the rest of his novice friends at the library's Modus Operandi chamber knowing where he last left off disappearing leaving Kris from the old crone witch's hut.

The chamber was more so like a combat training room with vast space to spare enough room for a small army battle contest.

Kris and Valarie were standing by with Kris's nose into the Seer guide booklet studying while Valerie was examining the weaponries of the vast walls of the Modus Operandi chamber and luckily the Librarian wasn't present.

There was complete silence between the three of them. Stevie gazed at three lit candlewicks that were color red, white, and black on chambersticks place on the roundtable. He could feel the eyes of his comrades staring down at him hoping he knew the answer. Stevie did notice an odd red wooden door standing alone in the middle of the library chamber room.

Valarie was the first to break the silence while Kris gave Stevie a gawking look, " how did you do it?"

Stevie was confused and answered Valerie, "I don't know what you're talking about?"

Valarie approach Stevie scrutinizing in a meddlesome tone, "what are you, a shadow bender? Kris tried to describe to Stevie explaining what he saw as Stevie disappeared into the shadows blacking out from Baba Yaga's hut.

Following Kris, Valerie said in an urgent tone, "You're not telling us something?"

"Telling you what?" Stevie exclaimed but to his relieved Charlie walks in as Stevie was explaining again all that he could remember after being attack by the Russian witch to first waking up in a mysterious rumbling dark cave to remembering waking up again being rescued at the Greenbelt and then the next in Nerd's infirmary recondition room.

Charlie nods to Stevie and started to explain the final test of the tribulation while Valarie snatches the white candle and Kris picked the black wick leaving the red candle to Stevie.

"Our trails of the tribulation are quite simple you are given a task, if you failed the task you do have a chance to redeem yourself again the following year. If succeeded you are offered a chance to claim your Aeons. For those that don't know Aeons are magical tools or weapons, even one might say their gifts to help Seers through their hardship pursuits. Valarie being so dry she wastes no time and cuts through the chase, "what's the task?"

"In this task, you are given a candle with a flame to light your path to finding a way and with this light, it just takes one of you to pass through this red door for your whole team to pass, simple enough right."

Valarie scoff and gave a chuckled, "that's it, that's the test. Pass through that red door with just even one of our three candle's lit, piece of cake."

Kris was quick to ask, "what's the catch?" Charlie stretches his muscular arms and began to roll up his black sleeve on his right arm then they notice Charlie was covered in art tattoos of animals to objects weapons and creatures it was a fascinating sight of art to see. Charlie pop's his neck and smiles to say, "You have to pass through me first."

At that moment Valarie said, "Done" and she wasted no time surprisingly rushing towards Charlie as if she had the attribute of an amazon warrior with her candle still lit.

"Halt!" Valarie was about few feet to approach Charlie while he was ready for her in a defensive stance then they all froze including Charlie.

Stevie had a dreadful feeling creeping upon him as he places his cold left hand in his pocket signaling him of the surrounding supernatural turning ice cold.

Stepping down from the corner of the corridor stairways echoing each step with a click of a heel came to be louder as she came closer heeding Stevie a cold stare was the Librarian.

Stevie couldn't get over the facts of what Nerd just revealed to him that this mystery mistress lady is over a hundred years old and not one to mess with, she was able to steal a bit of grace from anyone but still holds the meanest Librarian look in the world with a strict pose structure that you could tell that it presents her.

"I'll take it from here," she said to Charlie flick him off with her wrist of command.

"Yes, Madam," Charlie nod and looking onto the others exchanging looks wishing them well. Taking his leave hearing the corridor hallway doors closing behind Charlie.

"Now then." The Librarian tilts her head with her awkward right black leather glove rested upon her black walking cane that was top with a black jet jewel with the other hand folded behind her back, "where were we."

Stevie much preferred a race countdown but Valarie was immediately swift wasting no time with a surprise attack towards the Librarian. Amazingly with the chambersticks lit with the white candle still in her hand, Valarie surprised them with a quick tumble of an attack of flips with no remorse. Kris immediately took his place on the ground sitting Indian style with his eyes closed chanting while his black wick candle was placed before him lighting up his face as the room started to get dark.

Everything happens so fast Valarie backtracks her tumbling quickly being caught off guard almost losing her balance as she came close to contacting a dark shadow that eliminated all light into the darkness that was pouring over the ground stretching to every corner from the shadows forecast by the Librarian casting her power reaching over covering the red door that stood behind the Librarian.

Stevie was backed up to the wall as the Librarian's shadows were reaching towards him. Valarie yelled, "don't let her shadows touch you!" Valarie is one of the fascinating gymnasts Stevie has ever seen, dodging and flipping over the Librarian's dark casting shadows sprouting dark black tentacles that were darting after her. She tumbled and flipped into the air and she was so close about three feet away from the Librarian she was then struck in mid-air. Magically frozen in the middle of the air the Librarian lifted her left hand as if she were holding Valarie up stuck in mid-air tossed Valarie like a rag doll pinning her to the walls of the dark shadows.

Valarie yelled before being engulfed up by the darkness of the shadows "Go! Don't let her get your li" then she vanishes into the darkness.

Stevie looks over at Kris who was still chanting and saw the shadows surrounding him like he was holding up his own invisible barrier. Stevie came close around behind Kris feeling hopeless with no special gift or powers to surpass this frightening test.

The darkness was burgeoning over them like they were in a bubble guided by the only lights they had from their candlewicks. There was a sudden menace growlings from the ground that seems to come from beneath Kris as he sat there.

"Oh, somebody's not happy?" The Librarian said with a grim grin standing still resting on her black cane staff.

Kris was looking exhausted and started to sweat above his brow. Whatever force was holding back the Librarian's black magic was weakening. "Stand behind me," Kris said as he bit his thumb and drew blood making a pentagram and symbols mark on the ground. Wasn't something Stevie was prepared to see for being a little squeamish around blood he could feel such forces arising from beneath Kris. The Librarian wasn't one bit amused she irks with a dissatisfied look on her face. "Blood magic, such dirty business."

Before Kris could do anything the Librarian place her hand on her lips and blew causing winds to extinguish Kris's lit candle and was immediately gulp up by her sinister black shadows. Just as terrifying as the first arch-witch Stevie encountered he couldn't even describe how terrified he felt cornered like a prey waiting to be devoured up next.

Stevie's lit red candle was the only light gleaming against all the darkness in the room and stood there was the Librarian with an appeased smile as her dark shadows creeping up slowly onto his leg. At this moment Stevie knew he had nothing to lose, closing his eyes in the thought of darkness seeing how the Librarian overcame his comrades he raised the chambersticks candle from being blown out allowing himself into the darkness conjuring everything he had prepared to become annihilate not giving the Librarian the satisfaction of taking his light.

With the candle still lit with very little light from its tiny flame, his first reaction was lost, but he felt suddenly cold overcome his body hearing a familiar deep loud snoring in the darkness of cold within seconds echoing with the ground rumbling he raised his hand reaching in total darkness and felt a knob in the dark with a door place right in front of him.

Turning the knob opening the door Stevie opens his eyes stepping into the light of the library chambers and there were Charlie and Ashley stunned with others around the stone table. Charlie started clapping congratulating Stevie and with them were also Valarie and Kris.

"No freaking way!" Ashley said observing walking around Stevie with her clipboard dabbling notes. "Unbelievable but your light is out" Stevie confused and feeling dizzy let out a small relieved breathe that surprisingly igniting his candlewick with a tiny flame.

Charlie interrupts "well look at that he walks past through the door from the other side. Charlie then turns to Valarie and Kris, "Luckily for Stevie pulling through your team gets a chance for Aeons bequest." Everyone went silent as the red door opens and walks in from behind Stevie the eerie dark Librarian.

The Librarian walks over to Stevie with strict posture with a calm act who looks like she's ready to bite his head off. She took one look and gazed down and up at him and gave him a cold hard stare as she squinted her eyes telling him "I don't know how you did it but you spew of old magic and I have my eyes on you."

She then looks up at everyone, "Don't we all have other business to attend to?" Looking at all the other Seers in the crowd audience as they all scattered to their positions attending back to their work and business. After the Librarian took her place and storms off as usual Charlie started to explain, "no one has ever opened that door from the other side and no Seer has ever been able to finish or surpass their tribulation on their first try especially passing through the Librarian."

Charlie then looks onto Ashley as she said, "All have failed the test through the Librarian including Charlie." Charlie chuckled and shrugs his shoulders to reply, "Well… the librarian is very grim about who deserves their Aeon gifts, but that doesn't matter, what matters is you all pass and I must say I wasn't expecting that coming from you hotshot" as he raised his hand to high five Stevie.

Ashley walks over to her new alliance, "well I knew this group was special the moment I saw who was appointed as seers each three of you have potential." She looks at Stevie and smiled as if she knew a secret about him that he wasn't aware of. "Tomorrow is an extra special day after completing your test of Tribulations you three are now eligible to seek a journey for your Aeon bequest that each of you is well deserved."

"Seeking Aeons on a bequest what's so extra special about tomorrow?" Kris asks.

Ashley replies, "Aeons are gifts you'll be seeking, and don't you know it's a blue moon tomorrow!"

Valarie then mentions, "So what, there are about four blue moons every year." Ashley then said with excitement, "Yes, but this one is extra special an actual blue moon, it's a millennial moon that is. Charlie began to say, "Why you think you guys were rushed for the tribulations it was Ashley who was so convince you guys would pass.

Ashley continued, "The millennium moon they say is a radiant magical blue moon since the beginning of time and in every historical event it has shaped our world as it is today, it's the mark of a thousand-year reign of power, its kind of a huge deal here." The three all gave each other a blank stare trying to faze what Ashley was revealing to them.

"Guys the great flood as in Noah happens on this exact millennial moon, the burning bush, the sacred crucifixion, the list goes on."

"Wait those guys were Seers?" Stevie asked being surprised

Ashley replied to Stevie, "Every one of them."

Charlie and Ashley were now finishing each other's sentences. "Make sure you get enough rest… eat a good breakfast… make sure you're on time tomorrow, know your special skills and ability that will come in handy when looking for your Aeons."

After the completion of the red door challenge, it was Valerie that showed she didn't care if Stevie won, shutting down Stevie's cheerful excitement, "I just came here to pass a stupid test that's all, I don't care if I beat you or not so give it a rest. You're in my way."

Stevie began to be reflective and wondered to himself what he did wrong knowingly he would try his best to stay out of her way considering in his head was it all him, or was it all just pure luck or coincidence how far he's gotten, is it possible he gain these powers he never knew he had and if so could he manage to pull it off again? Stevie was starting to doubt asking himself if it's even worth the trouble going after an Aeon but kept thinking, what is it that I keep running into the dark hearing loud eerie snoring that makes the ground rumble in the dark, he thought he could be dreaming then? "Am I really fit for this job?" He said to himself and guess time will tell."

7

THE MARK ONES

IT WAS A VERY ANGUISH ride for Stevie that morning arriving at their destination venturing passing through Barton Creek of Austin not knowing the challenges that lay up ahead, Stevie thought a couple of times to himself, "Am I capable of being a Seer and this Aeon gift they have us seeking for what possibly could it be." Stevie even thought was he even qualified in the skills like the rest of his peers, one who can summon dark magic and the other who is set skilled in combat.

Stevie was starting to doubt himself wondering if he could accept the challenges that may lie ahead.

They reached higher into the rolling hills surprised at their arrival as if they were going shopping pulling into the Nordstrom parking lot at Austin's Barton Creek Mall.

"We're here!" Ashley said excitedly getting off the company Hummer vehicles. "We're going shopping?" Valarie almost said it sarcastically.

Kris wasn't too fond, "I hate malls."

They were expecting company credit cards but Ashley pulled out an ancient gold silver slip box that gleamed in rubies and pearls. Standing in the middle of the parking lot in front of the mall entrance they were curious as she opens the mysterious silver golden box inside was a case halfway full of gold silver incense ashes.

Ashley then saying a blessing over the powder box then dubs her thumb into the shiny ashes and asks, "now I aspect you all have read up on the Aeon bequest in your cable guy guide booklet and If you do not accept who you are the blessing will not work and the ancient mark of the Aeon flames will not be able to protect you."

"In your Seer guide booklet, it recalls," as Ashley quoted. "The Aeon bequest is an ascension that leads Seers to a path towards their gifts. Aeons are weapons designs by the divine to give Seers victory throughout the rest of their journeys. The key is to believe in your gifts to help activate your power. Your Aeons are alive and you are its master, it grows stronger as you grow, faith will make you grow to believe in yourself.

Now, remember the incarnation ascension has been passed down for generations its descendants are from the masters before the great flood of Enoch himself who passed down this protection blessing to his grandson that can only be expended by Seers."

Stevie feeling quite guilty who forgot to go over his Seer guide booklet about the Aeon bequest couldn't get the right question to ask, "who was his grandson?" Valarie spoke up and was gladly to revive history from the bible, "Noah, he was the first seer after the great flood."

Ashley then replied, "Yes Noah was the first seer to the new world after the great flood and with the majestic incense passed down from millennium that protects and guides Seers on their spiritual quest for whatever gifts or weapons calls upon them. Some say it's a gift from the universe."

"This mark of the ascension that you're about to journey and to receive must be planted hidden from all eyes just to be safe."

Valarie bowed her head down pulling back her long blonde hair revealing to be marked on the back of her neck to be cover by her hair.

Valarie- "is this what I think that is?" Ashley replies "yep it's Eris, an old enchantment so powerful and could be deadly literally how it works it manifest your soul shielding your body for the remaining ashes of a burning phoenix elixir with unicorn horn root dust."

Ashley has more to say, "long ago since the beginning seers have always been protectors of the human race and with that, we do get a little help that goes against natural law." Charlie handed them each their candlesticks with Ashley explaining.

"With this candle Seers are taken to a path to choose a gifted blessing from their deities or guardians by calling the commands by Creed. It's an ancient blessing only for seers who are marked are taken on the quest, it is your destiny that leads you to your divinity bestowing their gifts upon you."

Charlie then mentions, "These white angel feathers will help you through difficult intimidations."

Kris rolled up his short sleeves, "If this is some powerful old spell that I have heard tales about if I'm correct anything that happens to us happens forever afterlife printed on our souls and to be a myth aren't unicorns extinct?" He was revealing his spot for the mark to be hidden behind his right shoulder.

"This is a very special night where the tetrad blue moon that twilights the skies making the stars come out more bright than usual so we're pulling all the guns on this one," Ashley said as she turns to Stevie for his turn to be marked and smiled at Stevie graciously, "we're all rooting for yal, you will be invincibly protected by our own light yes your soul unless your mark is revealed why it is important to keep it hidden it hidden."

Pulling out his left palm she gave Stevie a concerned look. It wasn't the best place to put a mark but this was the only thing Stevie knew would be secure and placing the mark of Aeon bequest Ashley said, "protect it."

She handed them each three white feathers.

"An angel's feather, when your ready lite your feather on fire and you have exactly twelve hours till the blessing wears off so chose your destiny wisely, and good luck."

Valarie took immediately the first to cast her blessing before entering the mall she lit her feather and it burst and vapored into blue flames engulfing her up as she opens the door and vanished into thin air.

Kris- "Wow, just like that a transcendence physiology spell and my guess it's used by the power of an angel's grace, very clever"

Stevie- "power of angels hmm, can I walk with you?" Kris nod and whispered opening the door entrance for Stevie, "You didn't read over the cable guy booklet didn't you?"

All Stevie could do was shrug his shoulders and just nod. "So all we do is lite our feathers a boom look for something on this bequest, a weapon or some sort?"

Kris-"sure if that's what you want to call it, the Aeon bequest is an old myth-ritual something you don't hear about that rarely ever happens where chosen Seers have given a challenge or task by whomever spirit or entity is appointed to and if pleased you will be rewarded or cursed, but no worries this sacred spell mark of the Aeon bequest should protect you against anything thrown at us.

Kris pulling out his white feather holding it up as they both walk into the mall together.

"See this here is what will protect you once lit you activated the spell and poof you're gone to another dimension being covered and protected by angel's grace a very heavenly powerful protection spell.

Kris did come resourceful being a local witch Austinite he knew his way around, "Supposedly this shopping mall is built on sacred high grounds why it's a perfect conductor covering all four corners of the element dimensions. I don't blame the Librarian trying to halt this Aeon bequest it's the sacred tetrad millennium blue moon tonight. Its witches prophecy since the dark ages that this next millennium moon will raise a witch bane who will inherit the power of the blue millennium and shall make ways of all nations of good and evil."

Stevie was perplexed, "Is that why the Librarian challenges us at the red door tribulation."

Kris replied, "I assume she thinks you're the prophecy to the fall of thirteen high council coven, the end of all witches and magic."

They both stood there in reminiscing for a quick second. Kris being sarcastic, "but no worries, it's not like you just replace a grand hind witch or anything."

Kris stopped in front of a retail gift gag novelty store and walked in lighting his white angelic feather as it burst into blue flames engulfing him and before he vanished walking into the store he said, "I've always like this store."

Stevie strolled around the mall for a couple of minutes, overthinking again being spooked about from the recent news of hearing the witches' prophecies and the delirious reality of being a Seer that he was still trying to cope with?

Stevie knew the alternatives of being a seer is he could always turn back to his normal living lifestyle simply revealing his truth's identity as a seer to the outside world. It's said being a seer is part of the job carrying a heavy burden unable to tell anyone except one who is a Seer unable to share the secrets and knowledge of the supernatural world. By the next sunrise enchanted by the aether, which binds all humanity unable to see its truths hidden from reality and easily all his knowledge would be gone not having to remember any memory of being a Seer. His life would jump be back into the simple boring routine and all would be forgotten with no memory of his adventures nor magic phenomenon's or battling witches and meeting odd folks fairies. Or was it just Kris trying to get into his head, what if it's all just a coincidence, or was it just pure luck at the right time and moment accidentally vanquishing the last grand hind witch?

Stevie knew he was overthinking it while the other two peers wasted no time and had already vanished into their bequest, he remembers he was told they have twelve hours to complete their mission and all he had to do was lite his enchanted white feather in flames that will take him to a journey to find an entity or spirit who is to bless or curse the partaker that will bequeath prosperity to become great Seers.

The whole idea sounded crazy to Stevie but if he had to choose a spot or destiny it would be here he thought. Stopping in front of an apple store pulling out his white feather. Stevie looks around at everyone in the store with employees and shoppers not taking notice of anything unusual taking a deep breath hoping for the best closing his eyes as he lit his feather with a lighter.

Stevie could hear muffling of voices in the background fading "sir, can I help you with…" air was taken out of his breath as he opens his eyes spinning in a blue vortex lasting for six seconds then everything came to a complete stop making his ears pop like someone jerk him from behind.

Everything came to a clear view after he opens his eyes being so bright after his eyes adjusted to the light he was in a bright clear white room with everything was shiny covered in white even the floor became a scene above clouded in white as if looking downward to see the world landscape as if he was on top of a cloud.

Everything seemed calm and happy there was even angelic music in the background with glistening walls and pillars shinning all in white like diamonds, even his clothes were glistening in sparkly white. "Where am I?"

Kris

Kris was awakened by a strong earthy aroma finding himself passed out lying on top of a pile of black gravel, not knowing how long Kris has been there but he could sense strong ancient magic.

Feeling like he was just dropped from midair into a deep aroma of what smelt like a congestive coffee factory mix with a strong scent of hot tar filling the room.

A very dim light from afar Kris could make out fire torches mantled on the charcoal rock wall coming out from a long dark tunnel leading out to what seems to be in a huge vast chamber what looks like the inside of a dead volcano with enormous giant black chains dangling dangerously from the ceiling lavacicles chained tied to the volcanic Magna chamber walls.

Inside the peak of the dead volcano in the center was a crater that was occupied which was hard for Kris to make out noticing a massive huge red dark dirt almost a fly compared to Stevie and the red mountain hill about five hundred feet high hunch into a ball entrap with those huge gigantic black chains strapping down the red mountain dirt with restrains to the volcano walls and seeping onto the dried up magma blocking beneath the lava pressure eruptions. The large red rounded mass looks like a huge topper in the middle plugging up the volcano.

There was a loud heaving that came from the red dirt mountain enslaved uncomfortably in the giant black chains.

For a moment Kris felt a shred of fear panic come over him realizing that the red dirt mountain was alive and obviously was dangerously trap here for a reason.

Kris took caution being light on his feet watching his every step climbing onto the black chains afraid to wake up the red mountain beast that was chained up for whatever reason.

He wondered was this his Aeon bequest the entity to bless or curse him with a gift or maybe he would be its dinner he thought?

Kris took out his candlestick and to his dismay, he was trying to lite the wick but his candle would not stay lit as if some magic was at play.

A loud deep mumble echoed as it came from within the trap colossal red mountain hill, "I. SMELL. YOU."

It spoke rattling the whole volcano mountain and the huge chains that hung above. The dried-up lava mantle around the chained beast in the center of the volcano came to life between the cracks with fiery lava every time it spoke as if the volcano was alive the whole time underneath it.

"THEFT. I. SMELL."

It said vibrating the whole volcano with fiery embers and volcanic ashes that went up from the center of a crater crack floors of the volcano chamber every time it spoke. Kris was breathing heavily taking hiding behind one of the massive giant black torus chains rings that's binding the beast.

Kris started chanting in his meditation posture style conjuring his known dark witch spell to help cast his creed with his candlestick in his right hand.

"YOU. STENCH. FOUL. INCUBUS!" Trembled the volcano with the chains clashing as the giant spoke very loud and slowly.

Kris was now experiencing anxiety pasting his chest trying to calm himself from being shocked by being revealed by the great beast knowing his personal secrets were just read.

"SUMMONING. OBSCURENESS. HAS. NO. POWER. HERE. IN. MY. DOMAIN."

Kris suddenly realizes he was in trouble trap in with an unknown massive great giant confined to a volcano must be great and ancient that it can sense others especially their obscurely hidden powers.

Kris was afraid to conjure up his powers again unknowingly who he was up against, gathering his nerves he began climbing upon the lava chains walking up closer to the beast as it senses Kris's arrival. It breathes out heat waves, "UPON. PRIMAL. FLAME."

As its last word spew fire heat upon Kris within seconds he should have been torched up to ashes but instead, it ignited activating the flames of Aeon that engulfed Kris in bright blue lights of flames enlightening a little clear view of what he can make out of the beast.

It was a humongous red giant that looks to be made of fire-red dirt and shiny clay mud of some sort? Revealing only its mountain back and its side, two-thirds of its body arms, legs, and large face pinned down into the lava mantle crater only revealing half of it's right face with it's fiery eye and half lip exposed.

Kris was the size of its eye pupil, its skin color with dark-red dirt with a bright red beard made of patches of ember red fire. "AWE."

It laughed shaking the mountain, exciting the volcano as if ready to explode.

"YOU. COME. MARKED. OF. OLD. FOUL. ONE." It took another deep breath trying to smell Kris's every pore on his body as Kris tries to stay grounded avoiding to not get engulfed up into its nostril.

Back of Kris's mind, he was worried about his mark hoping it would not be revealed. "TAINTED. THEFT. YOU'RE. HEART. IS. COAL."

It then made a face with Kris hoping it was just a smile.

Kris- "Ancient one, you know who I am and what I came for."

Exploding lava splashed out as it laughed shuffling its embodiment trap black chains.

Immediately Kris was citing his incantation creed spell and to his amazement almost falling off from the huge black chains catching his fall with the angel's grace flame protection spell did seem to owe up to its name, that a few hot lava splashes onto Kris untouchable.

"I. REWARD. YOUR. OBTUSE."

It took another deep hot breath, "FOUL. THEFT. TWO. RIDDLES. YOU. MUST. COMPLETE."

It's breath almost knocking Kris off his feet. Afraid Kris asks softly, "two riddles?"

Kris was interrupted by the red giant, "TWOFOLD. BLACK COAL. FIRE."

Kris muttered repeatedly "twofold, twofold, black coal fire, my fire, what fire?"

Kris immediately reaches into his pocket grabbing his candlestick again trying to chant to light his candlestick and nothing.

Nothing was working neither his spells nor the creed and racing time in a panic of spoiling the riddle Kris grab the end of his candlewick and pulled it straight out of the candlestick tossing his candlestick and leaving the string-wick between his right-hand fingers standing straight.

Kris bit his left thumb enchanting rocking back and forth rubbing his DNA all over the string wick. He then fastens himself and closed his eyes with his white Aeon blue flame shielding him as he magically materializes a black wax candle between his fingers over his string wick. Kris fell to his knees pasting, catching his breath while the beast grins.

Kris got up revealing his black candle raising it towards the beast as it lit up with a shiny black flame.

The black candle disintegrated into particles as the beast laughing inhaling the black particles replacing it in Kris's hand with a black lighter. Kris looks at the black lighter and saw nothing special just holding what looks like an ordinary lighter even light's up like a lighter.

Kris wasn't sure if the lighter was magical or not but it did seem to attract lava as it was slowly crawling up onto his feet unable to move on the spot.

Luckily for the Aeon blue flames, Kris was able to be still alive but was unable to move.

"VERTEX. POINTS. IN. THOU. COAL. HEART. WHAT. GEM. YOU. ARE."

Lava was now reaching up to his knees, "ahh, Ancient one" pointing at his leg as the lava slowly progress up to his stomach. Again, Kris muttering repeating the riddle over and over, scratching his head raising his arms up from the volcano lava engulfing him within minutes.

2

"STAY. HERE. WITH. ME. FOREVER." It echoed and laughed. Kris was in a panic of shock where the lava was now rising to his chest thinking of the riddle repeating the giant creatures' words. "Where his heart was coal" and just then he thought. "Diamonds! Their diamonds!"

The lighter flames radiantly lit up extinguishing all the lava with such a force around him as he covers his eyes from the radiant bright light from his black lighter and vanished.

STEVIE

Stevie peered out from the empty glistening white room he found himself in, looking out into a long stretch hallway of a sky view from left to right enchanted in all pure white with clouds founded in each corner in a palace of place of bliss the atmosphere was soothing and calm.

Stevie found it to be a labyrinth on a cloud with hallways that curved until out of sight on both sides that look to go on forever into the clouds. The long hallway corridors continued to go onward with white pillars set for every ten yards with no doors or exit just open space of clouds. Stevie could hear a faint sound coming closer from a distance at one of the ends of the hallway corridor. It started to sound like rattling keys clashing together getting louder and louder by the seconds it followed to an eminence power of a dark red thundering and lightning ball of clouds gathering and heading in his direction. The ringing was so imminent with intense bright red lights it looked like a train was coming at Stevie. It was coming at him so fast he ran and took shelter behind one of the many pillars stepping into its shadow cast by the eerie red light.

The red light got so bright the closer it got the louder it became. Being so intense in its presence it felt like the pressure was weighing on Stevie crouching down shielding his head and his ears while closing his eyes he could hear his breathing getting deeper he knew he was falling into a trance. As he fainted he could hear the loud ringing fading away.

Everything was calm and he slowly opens his eyes and recognizes he was still crunching over under a shadow but now under a different view shadow with an unfamiliar setting.

Becoming aware he knew he was in a different location not sure how long he was out but found himself leaning behind what looks to be a broken throne that was once grand with its top half blown off.

Being vigilant he got himself up and notice the damaged throne was dazzled in gold and silver ornament with pictures of images with lightning bolts and a half body of an eagle.

This once grand mysterious palace was majestic even though it looks to be mutilation and demolished with debris everywhere it's golden silver throne room floor has a view of the world surrounded by clouds as if the palace were high in the sky looking down below.

Above Stevie there was no ceiling it was an open sky of the cosmos with planets and stars shooting across. Many of the statues and magical pillars that look to be alive with columns having nature elements to their scenery were all broken into rubble and stones scattered everywhere with burnt scorch markings along with ruins.

Stevie was reminding himself to get a glove on his left hand for it goes cold and numb when supernatural is always nearby.

Studying at a corner broken pillar from far behind the broken throne Stevie notice something you couldn't miss hunch over in the corner on the floor was a condemned dark cloak figure that looks to be out of place with long scrawny limbs. It seemed to be hugging one of the edge corner broken pillars trembling in fear.

Stevie couldn't make out clearly from where he was standing what it was he was seeing, it was cloak wearing a dreadful black rundown wet robe with rag holes stuck to its malnourish long body drench all in black smoky mist from the inside of the dark torn cape it was wearing with holes casting dark shadows with images of dreadful dead faces trying to come to life.

Scrambling into his pockets pulling out his candlestick Stevie grasp his creed incantation cheat notes that he had written on the way up here this morning trying to spit out the words that he could tell his nerves got the best of him as he started to stutter.

"I invoke thee…" the discarded figure turns its skeletal head to look towards Stevie as it laid there on the ground still hunch over revealing its sickly gaunt face.

Stevie was taken back petrified with chills running down his back.

The poor creature looked skin-in-bone with high cheekbones and a boney chin with rugous brittle pale light blue skin as if it was frozen dead for thousands of years with its eye socket sunk into its head revealing its beady blue fiery eyes that it also wore a broken black diadem that one could tell it's dark sovereign design use to be royalty majestic but lost all its verve and vitality.

Lost of words Stevie stumbles back tripping onto the broken throne's step stairway. The gloomy monster moved instantly crawling towards Stevie reaching out to him revealing its withered large blue boney hands moving its rawboned mouth gasping to say something but its open lips were silent.

The stares it gave of death it drought Stevie as if he smelt his soul and its glace wanted Stevie's soul-draining his health just by looking at it.

As it got closer almost close enough to touch Stevie they were disrupted by a familiar faint sound.

The gaunt blue creature was greatly appalled by the ringing crawling quickly back to its corner hunch in a ball rocking back and forth shielding its head.

The ringing got louder coming back again the bright red light adjoining to get worst like last time.

Taking shield Stevie hid behind the broken eagle throne expecting what to come next feeling the same reaction a warm tingle inside then a high pitch ringing in his ears, grabbing his head dropping to his knees from the pressure.

Just then Stevie felt a nudge pull grabbing him from behind, as he was yanked backward.

All was a speed of light ending with lights hundred times more clear than day flashes warping to somewhere else as his surroundings changed again. Stevie was no longer hiding behind the eagle throne but under a ray of light that looks to be in a center of another white shiny crystal chamber room all alone with fascinating floors made up of colorful gems of diamonds everywhere surrounded by a view of the universe space itself.

The chamber was vast with silver gold statues and objects that agleam up the room, some were golden weapons of axes and silver swords on mantle displays.

Oddly just looking at the weapons gave Stevie the sudden urge to pick one up and start hacking away must be a charm to the weapons he thought.

Above him at the center of the ceiling were moving galaxy clouds with bright starlight like it had its own small spotlight sunshine that was shining rays of light from the center of the ceiling chamber onto the diamond's floor.

Stepping out of the little sunray light he notices one particular wall dimension into an opening space that had a door cell with bars even the bars on the lock door gate had their own awkwardly platinum shine of power to it.

The opening space looks more to be an asylum cell with odd sculptures inside.

In the middle of the solitary confinement was contemporary art of two captivated life sizes statues that behold elegant beauty within their stature as if they were sisters paused in the wind masquerade in Greek wearing toga dresses and ancient jewelry garments.

It was their ensnaring reptilian eyes that daunted their beauty with piecing pupils ready to strike bringing goosebumps on his arms and chills running down Stevie's back.

The two Greek statues were both fixed onto a glowing blue crystal box that they both posed holding up high over above them, but that wasn't the strangest yet in that room for at the back of the whole wall of the cellblock behind the two statues was a white canvas gray plastered sculptures coming out from the wall that wasn't finished or some type of couture art Stevie thought.

"Stuck to be him," Stevie said gazing through the shiny bars with a lite laughter.

Displayed up above on the back wall was a large white plastered forehead sculpture peeking through with its half top of a face exposing just above from the bridge nose and its left eye closed shut with fingers that were exposed as if the trying to come out of the wall. The rest of the back plaster wall below the halfway large statue had few small uncertainties sculptures revealing out of the plastered wall.

One phenomenon that also caught Stevie's attention was across the interstellar chamber room was a pair of headphone Beats on its own glistening pillar mantle.

To his amazement it was the only item he was most familiar with that had its grand showing light. He thought it was ironic to see such a recognized moderate gizmo displayed here having a pair of his own at home that were just plain white but these headphone Beats he could tell were very special.

The ingenuity headphone Beats are designed with splattered vibrant colors giving it a unique art that looks like squirted paint onto the Beats with light blue lining on the inside of the band to the earpiece.

Unexpectedly a flash lightning appeared behind Stevie revealing a sudden shadow that not of his but a reflection shadow from standing behind him was gigantic wings being spread across behind his own shadow reflection.

Slowly turning around to see standing underneath the spotlight ray sunshine was a celestial being. An angel Stevie thought as it was a magnificent creature to stare upon it being three times the size of Stevie and it was a calm sight to see gracefully garbed with elegant silk pure in white aura.

Its waist down was covered wrap in blue metallic silk, flowing in red, gold, and silver ribbons wrap all around its tone muscular body. Also not to be wearing but it was part of its humanoid shiny body with silver and gold armor attach to its beast chest and arm guards and shiny shoulder body protectors displayed the brute of the angel's strength gleaming in gold, silver, and the color ruby blood red.

It was a type of armor that Stevie's never seen before revealing most of its angelic muscular torso and chiseled body.

At first, Stevie thought it had three faces but it wore a radiant silver metallic head-gear helmet over its head that was intriguing to look at with its long dashing golden hair underneath. The warrior's helmet was remarkable from the front above its nose to the center of the eyes there was a shape form of a cross that laid stretch across the front of the helmet on its face shielding its blue frost glowing eyes.

Both sides of the angel's helmet had their own compelling faces.

Its left side helmet revealed a black cloak dark hooded figure and to its right side of the helmet was a blood-red hooded face wearing a white masquerade mask even more sinister looking with no face behind the white vixen mask.

Stevie knew a little of angelology back from Sunday school when he was a kid always fascinated with angels and their theology but this angel he knew was different and knew nothing about it.

Not only did it had enormous angel wings but it had three pairs of its own set of gigantic wings.

Most of the feathers on the wings were shiny white mixed with metallic feathers of silver, blue, red, gold, and some were lit on fire.

The smaller sets of wings were below behind its back with its folded arms to its chest with its hands tuck under its muscle arms. Another massive set of wings that was bigger than the two were folded behind its strong back shoulders with the second set of wings that were expanded out.

It would tilt its head and tilt to the other side like a bird smiling studying Stevie.

Above the angel's head was a ring it started to glow a shiny gold light as it came closer wanting to communicate with Stevie but it only spoke telepathic, "Kadosh." It said.

It was quick with movements of a strobe light when it moved within seconds it was changing its form turning and spinning so fast for Stevie's eyes to keep up with its transformation.

The huge metallic warrior would freeze for seconds but now in full form its appearance change to what looks to be the full figure of the left side of its helmet.

As frightening as the faces were on the helmet it was now in full form appeared in front of Stevie.

It was even more terrifying, a flowing dark aghast dangling above Stevie matching its appearance of the faces on the helmet. Only a few feet above Stevie in an eerie way starring back studying Stevie as it took form in a cloak dark rob with no life. The dark figure wore a brass black shield chest with faces of monsters. To be honest Stevie was expecting to see another draught face in the hooded figure but it was lifeless, empty, and hallow. Its body leaned forward inches away from Stevie's face as he closes his eyes unable to move standing his ground against the dark figure. At that moment Stevie had the urge to just give up, but a complex of mixed emotions of emptiness was overcoming him it was something he had never encountered before.

It spoke to him again telepathic and it said, "Kadosh."

Stevie felt cold chills running down his whole body like his life force was draining away. The depressing dark character then quickly spun again flashing before Stevie's eyes unable to move he then felt an urge of compassion for madness. The angel's form change again in a blink of an eye this time starring at Stevie inches from his face was the sinister vixen white masquerade mask having an empty face behind it. It's eyes hollow starring into his like looking into a deep black hole, Stevie felt like he was losing it going insane as it was staring into his soul.

Its face white mask was so unreal it was alive and it moved its hands in a fast paste making a menacing grin with its high cheeks abroad and squinting empty eyes.

With its smile gesture and its six long fingers that look like white talons were so shocking he felt like his heart jumped into his throat. The divine creature's hands act like it had a sense of smell of its own while reaching and gliding its hands all over Stevie and again telepathically it spoke to Stevie, "Kadosh."

It all happened so fast it lifted its huge hands as if caught red-handed with its empty mask making a face gesture as it spun around again changing back to its first beatific gentle form with its wings extended out whereas Stevie could feel calm and ease overcoming him.

Spoken too soon the angel surprisingly extended all its six wings as in shock it bowed as Stevie look into his hands and there rested was the exact pair of headphone Beats that were just on the mantle over across the chamber.

The glistening sky sunlight ceiling was startled and began to change colors into a bright glowing familiar red bright lights with a familiar ringing alarm that got louder and louder.

The majestic angel used its three pair of wings before disappearing with the third covers their feet out of modesty and respect. The second set of wings made it fly while the third pair covers its face, as a token of profound reverence, so that they are unable to be seen.

It seems to have vanished when Stevie looks back from the alarming red lights coming from above where it used to be sunrays that were growing rapidly brighter. Stevie finding himself in the same scenarios again unable to concentrate having feelings of anxiety attacks coming upon him with pressure against his body.

Stevie placed his splashy headphones beats over his ears with the tremendous loud ringing from the radiant red light with temperatures rising as if he were in a burning incubator.

Taking shield crouching over covering his head behind another small white mantle that was displaying one of its eccentric objects he thought for sure this time his luck ran out.

Feeling uneasy with endless discomfort throughout every inch of his body closing his eyes waiting for the worst, he felt the intense pressure lifted off him as he felt he was easily free falling backward with his eyes still closed shut hearing and feeling the intense anxiety fading away as his heart was racing back to its normal pace. Suddenly Stevie landed on his back softly laying there hearing birds chirping around him slowly opening his eyes seeing a miraculous view through the top of the trees with the sky sunset view scraped with its fall colors.

Remaining still breathing in the fresh air with a smile on his face and the sunset to his left through scatter trees with a few minutes of what was left of the sunlight. Slowly getting up Stevie thought how crazy a Seer's journey has taken him waiting any moment to be awakened from a dream but was glad to be alive with new headphone Beats around his neck that reassured him his quest was no dream feeling grateful and important having proof of this honor and glad his Aeon gift is a fascinating earphone headset.

Stevie ended up finding himself being transported on top of the west tall hill across from the shopping mall parking lot where they park their Hummers.

Coming down from the hill into the parking lot the lights were coming on as it was getting dark Stevie realizes time here was faster than the place he visited for he was gone for a couple of hours but only felt like less than an hour.

Ther'y're waiting on Stevie was his Seer crew sitting outside on one of the entrance mall benches.

Kris getting up exclaiming to point out, "Look there he is," meeting Stevie halfway through the parking lot following behind Kris was Ashley and Valarie.

Valarie then asks, "you're glowing, and did you get a bronze spray tan on the way back?" Stevie just replied, "I don't know?"

"Well, you took forever at least your in one piece."

Kris was about to ask questions, but Ashley butt in pulling back Kris when she saw how lost and complex Stevie was after confronting him she then studied Stevie and notices his colorful headphones around his neck.

"We all need to be getting back guys it already getting dark and we all had a long day."

On the way back in their Hummer was a quiet ride with Ashley driving behind the wheel they were all a little bit tired and lost in their deep thoughts from their journey.

Kris playing with his new Aeon gift tossing and flipping over his pocket black lighter repeatedly while Valarie was silent staring out her window into the sky playing with her newly possessed pink silk scrunchie wrap around her left risk that Stevie hasn't noticed before wondering if those were her bestowed gifts.

Not much was given in telling each other's destiny of their Aeon bequest respecting each other to decide when they are ready to share.

The whole ride felt like a heavy burden weighing over him or so he thought "could it be my new sweet Beats over my neck?"

8

Ancient ties

FEELING A LITTLE DISTRAUGHT AND confused from their Aeon bequest creed the ride was quick coming from the North Creek mall experiencing the hocus-pocus for being lost in realms with a destiny of weapons choosing who know what were the requirements in becoming a Seer was a bit little too much for the new crew.

They were all silent stirred in their thoughts while the radio was blasted up maybe to avoid discussion. It wasn't something that they were ready to share quite yet and knew Ashley and Charlie were respecting their wishes. Being surprised that the ride didn't last long as they immediately pulled into downtown Austin between 5th and Guadalupe St. "Why are we not heading back to the headquarters at the library?" Ask Kris.

Ashley and Charlie are head chargers who oversees minor Seers that are beginners acting more like their supervisors they were up in the front seat while the three new minor Seers in the back seats of the Company's H3. They were parked in Ashley's perfect parallel parking who kept bragging about her parking saying how hard it is for some to park downtown parallel. Ashley turns back to the three of them and exchanges a serious look to each of them and continues, "This is my exit I have some external work to do a trouble-call with the church but tonight you guys celebrate after you have complete your final charge mission. This is where your Aeon gifts from the bequest are tested and so my friends your tribulation ends here and we're here to see if your bestowed Aeon gifts are meant to favor guidance and protection in heed of your duty."

"Where is Here downtown Austin?" Stevie asks enduring to know what's next?

"Here you'll see if your weapons are blessings or damning Aeons which we don't want, damning are cursed objects or weapons that are made to bring chaos and destruction, problems we don't want adding into this world." Ashley then quickly ending her sentence, "Which ends up in the long run curse Aeons could lead to the wielder's death or worse lose your soul." Charlie apologetic interrupted, "Deities and gods are never to be trusted in some few cases they only like to cast curses." Charlie lifted his shirt not only revealing what a perfect male body specimen he was with rip abs and a strong torso it was his tattoos that grab their attention. They were all in awe, Stevie always admired the artistry of tattoos but Charlie's was magically alive with 3d shapes and animals moving on their own across his chest. "Curses can be used as good tools," Ashley said looking at Charlie with a stern face.

"Down this street", Ashley pointing. "There's a back alley behind china town with a tiny oriental pawnshop just hidden around the corner you can't miss it," Ashley said with exaggeration.

It was hard for them to pull away from Charlie's erogenous masculine attributes with Kris and Valarie still gazing at his muscles, "There you'll meet quite of an ominous character a mystic trader is what they call him now these days? His name is. Mr. Yang is very ancient and wise but kind of stubborn and seems to be not all there if you know what I mean," she points her finger to her head signaling the old man character could be crazy. Ashley then gave them concern looks.

Stevie turns to say as he walks towards the back alley, "Wait wait... It is not some back alley black market now is it?" Stevie being amused gave a little laugh and then ask, "Better yet it's not some creepy Chinese dude like the one-off from Shop of Horrors or off from Gremlins now is it?" Ashley and Charlie's exchange looks with an awkward second pause of silence and chuckled among each other.

Charlie broke the silence, "Whatever you do… DO NOT MAKE DEALS WITH HIM!" Charlie said again to remind them, "You are there to have Mr. Yang inspect your Aeon gifts if he offers you a deal considerately decline his offer. He'll do anything to fulfill his collections of Aeons especially curse objects from across the world." Ashley gave advice of reasoning, "If your gifts happen to be a damning Aeon, cursed, he will excitedly and impatiently want your gifts." You could tell Ashley said this with concern and meant business. "We Seers have the sacred library," she quoted "the cable company, will have to confiscate your curse Aeon gifts if it happens to be so." She then turned to Valarie, "Valarie you got the command rite just in case if he refuses to help?" Valarie nodding yes Charlie said, "We have our own ways within the library of dealing with dark cursed objects. Created by the wise men the first mystics of Seers uses the library being enchanted with dimensional chambers among the sacred cavern grounds the library is a perfect confinement locking away these ill objects. Mr. Yang will probably tell you more than what you need to know, but you'll know the difference." With that Valarie started to storm off heading to the dark back alley." Charlie whistled, tossing Valarie a Golden Coin. "You will need this to get in," handing Stevie and Kris each a golden coin.

"Oh! One more thang," Ashley said in her Lubbock Texan accent rushing around the car with her blonde cut bow curls bouncing over her shoulders quickly handing a gun scanner she pulled from the H3 was a scanner that looks like a grocery price gun and she then said with a smile, "Test this out for Nerd won't-cha, and after you guys finish up you'll meet up with Charlie at the new bar cabaret club. Heard it's stirring some controversy around Austin, supposedly it's run and managed by some new Goddess in town." Charlie looks at Ashley with interest and then said, "A goddess, is she registered?" Ashley responded, "I don't know but I believe the inspection roster said Goddess of chaos and time of some sort like that but what I do know she's originated from India/Asia. So we're checking protocol, it's all part of being a Seer to make sure everything checks out in the regulations inspection contact with the supernatural."

"You know it's all still work-related and be on your best behavior," Charlie said and winks, "It's just down the street from the corner I think it's called the Lone Star Speakeasy, something like it I believe it's a Burlesque cabaret club."

The guys caught up to Valarie in the back alley and to their surprise there was little light and a bit spooky with lighting stirring up in the dark skies with sprinkling rain between the skyscrapers above them. Kris- "looks like a little storm is heading this way, how convenient." Ashley was not kidding just around the corner in the back alley almost hidden was a life-size statue panda look to be almost too real. The panda was wearing a Chinese emperor hat with a shiny pearl on top that looks to be a large marble or knob. The bear was also wearing a short red vest that suits to fit the animal with dragon graphics logos. The panda was sitting on its behind with its paws on its lap waiting for something to fall into its paws. The panda's back was up against the alley wall decorated and painted in red onto the alley's high walls with an entrance to basement shop with low barred up cellar glass colored windows.

The alley's red wall painting contains a short brief section that was painted with red and yellow Chinese symbols next to English reading. "Old Yang's Chinese antiques and magical items shop"

Next to the fuzzy panda was a five-foot little wooden carved door with matching Chinese symbols of dragons that had no doorknob with its own little red Chinese over door canopy. Valarie studies at the panda and said, "Must be the Qing dynasty, see his little red silk vest and the hat says it all. By looking at the door I think we're dealing with royalty here guys, but how the heck do we get in?" The three were looking around for any clues to get inside with Stevie carefully thinking and watching Valarie studying the ancient door, he thought how wise and stern Valarie is like if she was an old soul, wondering if she had military experience? There were dumpsters, crates, and back-alley doors with their door lights gleaming through the thundering lite rain. Then Stevie jolted after he turned to the panda, "hey guys wasn't the panda sitting down?" the panda was now standing on its two hind legs with its paws cup together extend out like it was a circus act. They were looking at each other dumbfound confirming with looks at what they just saw with Kris asking, "Maybe it wants something." Kris reached into his pocket and pulled out his golden coin placing it onto the panda's paw. Kris then said, "Well that didn't work." Then Stevie place his gold coin onto the panda's paw, "maybe it needs all three?" The moment Valarie place the third coin the panda statue came to life while the boys jerk away in shock. Valarie looks at the sprightly panda with calm and ease tilting her head with her platinum blonde hair pulled back tightly in a ponytail studying the bear with her lost stormy grey eyes. "It's a guardian spirit, like a familiar," she said. The panda bowed and the pearl knob that was part of the hat fell out onto the ground rolled to Valarie's feet. "Ah, and here is the key." She picks up the giant pearl knob, "This is old school magic stuff right here guys." The panda started to shuffle side-to-side puffing then it sat up waving its paw towards the dragon wooden door. Kris-"I think it's trying to tell us something." " To open the door," Valarie said as she places the pearl knob in the center of the door and turned the knob with an eerie creak as the door cracks open.

So much for coming in quietly as they were immediately rushed into the door ringing a set of bells hanging above the door being shoved in by a magical panda nudging his head staggering to get in. The three of them tumbled over each other down a couple of steps gathering themselves in a dark shop where else the panda headed to his water bowl.

The crowded room of antique collectibles was engulfed with incense and lit candles lighting up the little shop with a storm brewing lighting would flash through from the shop basement stained windows.

It was like stumbling into an old pop's pawnshop shelved with weird artifacts and also someone was a fan of dragons with multiple pictures and different types of dragons with posters all over the wall some were Chinese dragons.

Stevie caught an eye on an odd silver artifact embedded with black jade diamonds that looks menacing highly decorated with craftsman skills of dreadful skulls patronizing in agony decked around the exposed silver box.

Proceeding towards with bravery Stevie then looks inside the unnerving open silver box with it seeping out black smog peering out from inside the box making out to be screaming anonymous tiny blank faces crying out that astonished Stevie by the horrors as he came closer to the box seeing a tiny mirror within the box with his reflection as the small box suddenly shut closed leaving Stevie mesmerized.

The tinkery silver box was labeled with a note that read, "Pandora's box." At the top of the note, it read in capital letters, "DO NOT TOUCH."

There were few random items they notice hanging around like a cage with sleeping geese resting on a large golden egg that hung over the glass counter loaded with rolled-up carpets that note with a label that read, "magic rugs."

The eerie shop was loaded with strange objects one was mostly covered in dust was a shield made out of bones with a note that read, "bones belong to something powerful why the shield has magic." One item that stood out mostly departed a gold statue covered in cobwebs in the corner with Chinese descriptions but easily read with another note that read, "Midas the king himself sitting on a throne in gold."

One would think how this pops pawn business stays alive but the shop was fascinating loaded with miscellaneous pawn collectibles to jewelry, masks, dolls, flags, stones, and statutes. There were also some strange plants in pots, clothing in wardrobes, weapons, and a few cages with moving hidden creatures.

One crate had a red hen nested inside with a Chinese inscription on the silver cage. Kris testing out the new scan gun created by Nerd and he quickly scans the red hen reading the scanner, "Immortal pet hen of prince Huai-Nanzu." Many dark eerie items such as one in a glass cabinet they saw what looks to be shrunken heads strung up with Stevie tagging the head items and labeled as he reads "Amazon's curse."

Valarie gasp after few seconds of starring around their surroundings, "That can't be?" She then grabs the scan gun from Stevie as she turns to a glass cabinet shelved with gems and diamonds with jewelry.

She was eyeing one particular necklace that bedazzled as a golden pendant with glamorous red and pink gems glistening through the glass.

Reading the scanner gun she then said, "this is the actual necklace of Harmonia, crafted by one of the Twilight gods himself the smith and craftsmen, Hephaestus." Valarie goes on, "This necklace is legendary for its curse, and it will make any woman remain eternally young and beautiful but wearing the necklace also brought great misfortune to all its wearer or owners. There are legends of this curse necklace." All three of them starring at the jinx necklace in awe as Valarie finished up her sentence, " Created by the smith hammer god given to Harmonia as a wedding gift, the daughter of Aphrodite and Ares, a curse on the House of Thebes for Aphrodite's infidelity." Stevie then replies, "Aphrodite goddess of Love was married to Hephaestus and cheated on him with their brother Ares god of war, wow one messed up family I tell ya."

Kris exclaims out still checking out scanning with the high-tech gun, " Hey guys check this one out, the fan of San-Qing a weapon to control the four elements used by the Jade Emperor himself. It is said this fan was the cause of the great hurricane of the seven seas." Stevie immediately chuckled and said looking at the huge fan hung up taking half the whole side of a wall, "that's one big ass fan." Stevie recognizes that his left hand went cold so he was alert to his surroundings.

There was a photo on the wall that captured Stevie's attention. It was an unusual vintage photograph of a little boy in a sailor outfit who seems to be crying but the awkward photo was wrap in a water bubble frame for protection hung up on the wall. Stevie ran the gun against the water bubble photo and reads, "Haunted photo body and soul Hell tears."

Stevie wasn't too mischief about hauntings for his family has a haunted lost portrait given to his father a few years back from an old family friend who was a priest from Rome. Stevie always found the family gift portrait creepy as it hangs on a high wall in the family room a picture of a mysterious saint nun to be a queen of some sort wearing a crown with a golden arch staff where her eyes follow you and penetrate your every step around her painting.

Kris giggled after scanning a pair of pink ballerina slippers locked away in a mystic glass dome. "It's true what they say, don't let looks deceive you." Kris continues, "it says the slippers once belong to a powerful enchantress who once performed before the gods and legend has it when worn it posses potent powers so great its performance could cut grace."

Valarie in a deep thought quietly interrupts to share her emphasis response, "grace gives you the power of a God, if you know its secrets the Waltz of twilight power can protect you against any god in its full grace of power."

She was then surprisingly interrupted by a strange foreign voice that came from behind the purchase counter. "It will only last you thirty seconds."

The three froze on the spot realizing they've been watched the whole time coming from a large character shadow cast behind the backroom counter doorway strung up with Chinese curtain door beads. Above the archway backroom doorway is a clear big sign that read, "You break you buy, now taking eyes, forearms, and all major souls."

The mystic trader was a petite size compared to his scary large shadow stepping out into the view wearing a traditional Chinese red-blood gown with golden trims smoking on a long golden pipe. He also wore small dark round spectacles its frame made out of gold having long white hair tied into a long braided bow with a long white-whiskered beard resembling a kung-Fu master that reminded Stevie of his comic books. The mystic trader's hands were folded together hidden under his golden-red drape long sleeves calmly he began moving to adjusting and shifting random items and objects around while studying them.

"Master of Chi, I sense together you bring unbalance Feng Shui you'll never discover your power that way in which needs harmonizing."

Valarie immediately took her surprise and bowed humbly as the boys followed standing behind her following her lead they bowed as well.

The petite Chinese trader took to his place as they watch him and would then place a stuff black cat into a silver birdcage then placing the cage on a mantle and deciding if rather hang the cage instead.

The mystic trader was throwing off his client's chi energy with everything he touches it disrupts and adjust the three companion's energy force by moving objects affecting their temper or attitude emotions all while with Stevie flabbergasted as he figured out witnessing the mystic little old man's magic talent.

Valarie was losing her temper quickly as the little mystic trader was struggling to settle Valarie's chi still turning over many items and rearranging objects.

With Valarie still being negative and short fumed she continued to be agitated with the little trader who was then going around in circles heading to the front counter at the corner stand and he adjusted some teapot collections stacking them on top another balancing awkwardly high that did change her mood, but it didn't fit well with Kris who was starting to feel bothered and agitated while Stevie was admiring in bewilderment witnessing such irrefutable power in front of him.

The Chinese mystic trader's face look ancient with high cheekbones, his skin color was demoralized with pale white skin blended with an eerie tonic shade of green outlining around his facial hair and around his neck, must be some rare skin condition Stevie thought.

Valarie asks Mr. Yang if he's a royal dynasty objecting to his fine red golden silk robe outfit with Mr. Yang mentioning it's old just ancient stuff pass down from generations. Never really answering Valarie's question as she was distracted at the ballet slippers.

The old man had a stout chin with a white silk beard the Chinese trader looks up revealing his face with a unnerve smile in complete dimples revealing his teeth for a split second that look like fangs with razor teeth, he smiled again for the second time revealing normal human dentures as his patron guest all eased up.

The Chinese mystic trader starred directly at Valarie as she paused from rambling on reciting her Seer order with the pink slipper glass cage in her arms slowly placing it back not leaving her sight off the old Chinese man.

Valarie lowered her head feeling positive chi taking over and she then quickly recited again, "We've come for Mr. Yang we…" and was shortly interrupted again as they were all surprised by the old man's abnormal quickness.

Mr. Ying the old mystic Chinese trader was so fast there was wind with an instant flash of him snatching the gun scanner from Kris who was ten feet away from the old man behind Ashley less than a second the old man was back at instance within the same spot behind the counter analyzing the scanner gun.

Then with a whiff, Mr. Yang made a disgusted face like he smelt rotten eggs and said "Science!"

The old man spits on the floor flashing his fangs once again in a split second relieving the taste from his mouth then tossing back the scanner at Kris who then felt exploited by the old man taking a scan of him.

The scanner was quickly picking up a reading it skyrocketed high levels flashing an omega star before it overheated and fried out.

The threes company weren't too sure whom they were dealing with being alert and remembering to not make deals with Mr. Yang and then he said, "hmm science what a foul taste."

Wobbling to his destination taking baby steps as they watch him walk over to his panda patting its head pulling bamboo treats out his sleeves feeding his friend.

The foreign little guy seemed to be a happy old man with no care of the world but Stevie began to ask himself what kind of magical being were we sent to is he and wondered are we safe?

Valarie started to recite her Seer orders again but only this time was interrupted, "Blah, blah, blah, you mark ones come in here only want procession," he said with a thick foreign accent. "How about a trade for once eh?" Mr. Yang asks.

Valarie marched right up to Mr. Yang following him to the back of the front counter and started to recite again, "the gathering of the sunrise as to the end of collections three Aeons by the order of." Mr. Yang then raised his creepy hand with long talon fingers cutting off Valarie for silence once again. Stevie had to admit he was admiring Valarie's courage that's been the glue holding the team-up.

Mr. Yang inhaled deeply letting tremendous smoke fumes out of his nostrils where he vanished for a split second and then reappeared next to Valarie behind her as she remained still and calm while Kris and Stevie were jumpy by the magical appearances from the old man.

Valarie showed her Aeon gift raised up her pink hair ribbon to Mr. Yang's face as he just looks up and down studying Valarie instead of the aeon object, her eyes then widen as the old trader announced, "enchanted frozen heart will crack, ice will melt, for you hold a trinket belong to the lost god of the North-star that is no more, the old goddess of the underworld death's little sister, Hel."

Mr. Yang then walks past Valerie with no interest signaling her that he was done after she went off again into a rumble of questions about his quote mentioning ice melting.

It's not quite the questions or answers you aspect from a mystic Chinese trader Steve thought. Before Mr. Yang drew interest at Kris as he offered his last remark to Valarie where he drew a creepy reptilian smile and said with a thick accent, "Where your heart lies, no one knows, you're not coming home that's what you know." That shut down Valarie real quick who was ill silent white as a ghost.

Eyeing the mystic trader, Kris was walking back up against the wall with nowhere else to go with Mr. Yang wobbling slowly towards Kris studying him blowing smoke from his pipe. The old man was up at Kris's face with a quick close sniff, "interesting… do you know where you stand boy?" Kris who turned pale white was frozen unwilling to say anything pin to the wall like he saw a ghost. Then the old man said with a scratchy hiss voice, "Let's see it, boy?" Kris pulled out and revealed his black lighter showing it up to the old man's face as he blew smoke onto the black pocket lighter and there behold a mystical invisible force field making the smoke fumes dancing around the lighter. "Aye… The sacred fire of the fallen cursed one," he giggled. "The Fallen archon Prometheus. "Unbelievable you manage to size up to the wise primordial into giving the sacred fire twice?" Kris just blinks with a cold stare unable to move or say a word as Mr. Yang took a step back with his creepy hands behind his back looking away from Kris facing the opposite directions with boredom and then ask, "I can fix that eye of yours boy, release from black stain making you good as new with a clean plate, exchange for the firelighter boy." Mr. Yang smiles back at Kris who was still holding up his Aeon gift lighter hesitated for a brief moment.

Valarie nodding her head no, standing behind Mr. Yang signaling Kris "NO deal." For whatever the old man's offer was Stevie notice it meant a lot to Kris as he paused lowering his lighter and place it back into his pocket. Stevie knew thus for certain about Kris is that ever since the day he was born he's been cursed. What he shared while they were back at the greenbelt was that since the age of eight Kris has always been abandoned lived a troublesome childhood who's mother was a theft who dabbled in the dark arts almost costing his life.

Stevie was flustered with mixed emotions letting his nerves get the best of him knowing he was next grasping onto his Aeon gift headset beats wrap around his neck feeling the dread approaching him. Again Mr. Yang randomly flashing his fangs in split seconds catching himself falter was nowhere to be found with his vanishing trick escaping his slipup but Stevie could creepily feel Mr. Yang behind him with his talon fingers with long nails wearing a pinky gold clever tapping on his Aeon gift resting around Stevie's neck.

Stevie took Valarie's concept to remain calm and still while he blasted his Bluetooth music headset on while it surprised Mr. Yang as he jumped and giggled clapping his hands excitedly, acting like a little kid excited to see a toy for the first time. Stevie freely took off his Beat headset and held it up to the happy little man who was so anxious. "The headset Beats are wireless see no wires," Stevie said but suddenly Mr. Yang went bi-polar opposite reaction. Mr. Yang's grin went into a frown immediately he blew smoke onto Stevie's Aeon gift that funneled around his headset Beats more vivid. Mr. Yang looks directly into Stevie's eyes revealing his true eyes that glowed red with his eyes shape into a reptilian pupil. The ground started to shake as the old little man's shadow started to grow rattling the shelves, speaking in ancient tongue echoing with extreme power radiating from Mr. Yang and he blasted out loud. "Just a mere mortal!"

Then everything snaps back ironically clam with Mr. Yang shrinking back with his hands behind his back wearing his red golden Chinese gown as if nothing just happened minding his business. Out of nowhere Mr. Yang started to file his razor nails leaning over the counter and gave his offer. "Render 500 souls for your gift mortal" Stevie was quick to ask, "So it's not a curse." The old man made a discernible face and made another offer, "for all the gold in the world?" Questions and commotion were immediately blurted out, "ALL THE GOLD IN THE WORLD?" Valarie trying to shout over Kris as he too spoke, "WHO HAS 500 SOULS?"

The three continued asking questions over themselves Mr. Yang retreated to his little self still fix on Stevie filing his dagger nails as the room went silent.

Mr. Yang then simply turned his head to the right facing away from Stevie with his hands hidden behind his long red gown ready to make his final deal.

"For your gift

I offer a falling star."

Kris whispers to Stevie, "he offers you a wish."

Mr. Yin continued,

"Cosmos align the meteorite falls

the path is hard in one's journey like a ball of yarn

Leave the grand design to another, boy, and play with another yarn

Twined tangled you be lost among those twinkling stars

For it will be death that is on this path

It will lead you to it."

Kris and Valarie look at each other waiting for a response from Stevie where they both knew they were thinking the same thing, "He offers you to walk a path of a mortal with fulfilling dreams of any desires, many greatness and heroes have long for this wish," Valarie muttered. Stevie was lost in his thoughts and responded softly then exclaimed out, "Awesomeness!" He smiled "Thanks but no thanks always did like being twisted into the stars." Valarie and Kris were taken back while Mr. Yang was shocked and startled looking confused sporting a little pout on the old man's face at its most. Guessing the trader wasn't expecting his offer to be turned down.

Valarie then turned to Mr. Yang and ask, "You do know what it does don't you?"

Mr. Yang looks up at Valarie with a cold stare squinting his eyes at her and replied, "Whatever it is, it came from the heavens."

They were all headed out the door after thanking Mr. Yang with a head bowed following Valarie who ask once more before stepping out, "What are you?" Mr. Yang replied," just a merely old mystic trader who collects desirables."

Leaving Mr. Yang grinning ear-to-ear Kris following Valarie out with Stevie behind Kris, while the little old man was still trying to convince Stevie to accept his offer. "YOU FOOL, you don't know what this is all about, turn away from it." Right before Stevie could step out of the little pawnshop he patted and rub the fuzzy panda that was beside the door.

Mr. Yang sighing finally gave up with the scare tactics and whistled Stevie's attention smiling tossing Stevie a fortune cookie in a plastic wrapper and told him before he stepped out of his shop. "Take your fortune you go boy, luck might find you."

Turned out to be a guys night out with Charlie afterwards wanting to know the guys a little more at a night out to celebrate asking to come along on a house call check in on the new club/bar passing for Seer inspection as Ashley had other missions all while all while Valarie ditch early right after their tribulation asking to be released and would rather be at home.

Speakeasy burlesque club

It didn't take long for the boys to reach their destiny, which was just a few blocks away meeting back up with their leader Charlie that stayed behind.

Walking downtown enjoying the night view lost in deep thought smiling ear to ear but from a distance, Stevie could see a crowded mix of tourists and paparazzi gathering around a cherry red Lamborghini.

Probably someone famous he thought as some actress steps out and was being escorted by multiple men park in front of Austin's W hotel. She was a fascinating elegant character drawing attention in a silhouette red dress posing for all the cameras taking her photos, male escorts were holding pushing back the crowds wanting a signature or picture.

What happened next could not be explained like time itself slowed downed as Stevie watch the voluptuous celebrity vixen remove her dark red shades flashing her luxurious shine blonde locks of hair all in slow motion while being in a spotlight of camera flashes. It reminded Stevie of watching a sexy ad commercial while she applies red lipstick puckering her lips posing for shots. It was almost being in a trance watching the world's most magnificent creature he thought for a moment, but in a strange way she glowed in such radiant aura it gave off a warm feeling of love that mix with sensual feelings towards the adore character. She was the most beautiful woman Stevie has ever laid eyes on to his knowledge. Stevie shook his head chuckled clearing his thoughts amused at such depravity of a dog in a man we are snapping out of his embarrassing mature thoughts gathering himself and kept walking to his destiny.

Stevie was taken back just a little about the feelings that he just witnesses thinking nothing didn't add up right with mixed emotions of lust like your on cloud nine for a brief moment and then change suddenly like being dropped feeling empty like a hole in your heart waiting to be filled. "Must be some bewitchment or sorcery from that celebrity?" Stevie thought, he'll surely bring it up to Charlie and Ashley's attention.

Stevie feeling a little dazed and confused has lost Kris almost walking past the new cabaret that was stirring up as one of the hottest new clubs in Austin TX. Stevie caught on catching the grand premiere opening with red carpet and spotlights that could be seen through the city night. The front club entrance had its own red velvet rope as well having a covered checklist bouncer holding up a massive line that could be hours to get in. Stevie paused at the front for a moment reading up tonight's entertainment poster next to the entrance door it read, "Meet your Lone Star Girls of A.T.X. Party it up at Speakeasy burlesque club with meet and greet the four wonders of princess fairytales the world's gem to entertain and fulfill your dreams with extraordinary struts of magical talent and dancing... don't forget special Well drinks cover before midnight."

"Hmm..." sounds catchy Stevie thought as he was heading to the end of the line when it was Charlie calling him signaling from the entrance door holding a Well drink in one hand queuing Stevie to come up the entrance checklist to cut in the long line. The bouncer had shimmer appearance of a mortar with bull horns was a muscle meathead who looks to be living off steroids justifying Stevie figuring him out when the club door bouncer asks for thirty-five dollars Stevie was shock asking why the cover charge and was told it's before midnight when the magic is at nigh.

Charlie whispered to the meaty muscle bouncer who then didn't hesitate once he was aware of what they were, Stevie thought being a Seer has its perks wondering if those perks cover drink specials too or it could be a fan of Charlie's.

Immediately Stevie started to explain with Charlie what he just encountered outside with the famous vixen in the red dress while Charlie was too distracted shuffling through the overcrowded club with go-go dancers on single-stage platforms throughout over the dance floor and loud music making it harder for them to hear each other as they entered the club. Stevie following Charlie shouting out over the music explaining his encounter outside, "on the way over here there was this amazing woman all in red parked in front of the W hotel, I swore she wasn't mortal." Charlie- "she wasn't what?"

Stevie- "she wasn't normal, her eyes flash and her eyelashes were magical oh man just then everything seemed to." Stevie was interrupted as the music lights started to fade out into the darkness leaving the table candlelight's and the bar lights only lit up for the show was about to start.

Charlie shouted then lowered his voice as the show was starting, "the girl's ditched, Ashley had an important mission tonight and Valarie requested some rest and went home so it just the guys tonight you, me and Kris," pointing to the upstairs corner balcony above the show dance floor was Kris leaning forward on a rail bar overseeing the dance floor from above.

The three-story club design layout was phenomenal something out of this world with the top floor reserved for elites with millions and gods. Its stairway entrance to the third floor read a sign above that said the halo floor.

The club set was a full stage with two alters stages raised above behind the stage in the background facing over the dance floor with a small balcony from the fourth halo floor above the third floor with its little stage off the side in the corners with a body birdcage. With a stage to the back wall connecting to the dance floor leading with stairs to the stage, the layout was incredibly ready for a cabaret show premiering above and around you as you dance the night away from the dance floor and for those not on the dance floors are being entertained by the show.

Charlie was anxious and very amused smiling ear to ear and had to share, "Hey so I look up this chick goddess in our stat records and you'll never guess, she supposedly has this O.C. disorder." Stevie then replied, "a god having Obsessive-compulsion disorder is that even possible?"

Charlie responded, "yea, there's something on file about this god always starts out with her right foot only, taking off with her left foot is said she becomes berserk a trigger of the dark divine goddess of destruction and chaos. Boy, what I would do to get that goddess's lefty going but hey if you hurry we're upstairs hanging right over there but I'm going to get a few cold ones first at the bar.

Introduction music starts to play out as the club lights dim down gathering everyone's attention and the background MC started to announce. "Ladies and gents boys and girls from all around the world… we welcome you and now we bring you from the corners of the world the most magical wonders of the world. The Speakeasy burlesque club of Lone Star welcomes you our "Austin's Texas Diamond girls your Lone Star princesses."

The three-story venue cabaret club was spectacular with go-go dancers having their corner stage with girls fit for an upscale Vegas show with its event main stage raised above the ground with stair steps leading to a sunk-in dance light-floor that had its separate floor with videos on walls from looking above the dance floor.

Surrounding the dance floor are four stage platform cages in its four corners with fancy lighting fixed with moving laser lights with disco balls to fog machines. The show's lighting was exciting alone with the announcer going on with the routine music in sync with the light show performance, "and now for our main highlight event of the night introducing four of the Lone Star princess." (SC Music/3)

The crowd got silent with Stevie stuck among the audience crowd on the dance floor as the lights went off and started to play the opening theme music, "From an enchanted land far, far, away there is an enchantress princess fairest of them all who can speak the language of animals, whose hair is black as ebony, her skin white as snow, and lips red as blood, but please call her." The curtains lifted up from one of the four small stage corners revealing an extremely attractive girl who was a shiny dark brunette wearing a tiny red-head bow who was in matching fairy tale snow-white character costume in a blue shiny one-piece corset with a yellow bright girdle, "Please call her Chastity, for she is known as Princess Chastity White." Remarkably they were living up to their name, the princess then went with the music graciously moved and raised her hands softly and stunningly blue singing birds flew to her untying the back of her corset while magically tying bows around her carefully not revealing any lady parts finishing up her dancing act and went on stepping onto the main stage. With everyone's attention, the MC went on announcing the other girls in almost the same manner as the curtain went up on each one of them and had their music routine.

"Watch out her family is in the line of a well powerful anesthesia pharmaceutical, specialty in sleep hypnoses." She too was remarkably beautiful in a two-piece flower lin-gerie dancing with glowing stick streamers who was very good that seems to be displaying her enchanted hypnoses with a ray of magical colors from her streamers gathering up a crowd to her cage while performing magically with her flowery streamers that glowed and dazzled in the dark. "Who needs Mr. Sandman when you have princess Rose Dawn."

The third gal they announced was more of a daisy duke country redhead wearing a red cape ready to go on a picnic. "She hot, she's feisty she's Little Red. They say when she posses the red cape it turns your blood so sweet not even one white lie can't get past her." She had an attitude of a hothead who can handle her own when she got rowdy with a guy who tries to get touchy with her while she was approaching her platform on the dance floor during her opening performance. She didn't seem to have any special ability except her chest but she did the show in strength how talented she was on a pole. Stevie ended up spotting his crew upstairs balcony corner above the dance floor watching the show.

"Famous for her redundant sunray golden locks, graciously she's lite on her feet watch her memorize you in her art of hooping." This mesmerize princess had extremely long hair that has a talent with hula-hoops that at one time she had 20 hoops going at the same time while performing her dance and could have sworn her long hair twirled a ring. Enchanted Princess Vibrissa. They were all getting the idea about these performers is somewhat possibly related or kin to the actual princesses in the fairytale stories.

(SC Music/4)

"And now," as the MC announces the crowd gathered around the stage with more men whistling, combing their hair, and dashing cologne. "For our final surprise only in a few moons, she performs the Hindu dark goddess who runs the show… " The lights dim's down, "she is known many names, a mother goddess to many, the black Goddess of time, and Destruction." With loud dramatic music rolling into an open beat they did save the best for last as the goddess appeared on stage magically with pyro tricks having her own sparkling fire stage curtain behind her, the four princesses announced "Mother, Kali the destroyer, the dark goddess." She was an interesting vibrant colorful seductress bonded with golden arm cuffs, a Hindu goddess demise by her dark tone beautiful skin, ravished in a shiny two-piece whose waist is a beautiful golden girdle with numbers of shiny red ruby gems as dead men arms and multiple small skull diamond heads covering her lady parts. The whole venue mostly men were shouting, cheering, and whistling at the goddess as her dark hair was flowing with her eyes beaming bloody red as she was dancing magically in a three-dimension plane for everyone to see. The dark goddess grew two more pairs of arms and hands, she then started to float gliding through the air from the stage stopping midway middle above the dance floor as she echoed with the ground vibrating, "Time has come, Time is present, Time is coming."

The Seers could see how this performance breaks all covenant codes 9:12-17 the natural law has guidelines that go against any supernatural forces exposing magic to human contact, from gods to monsters to witches and fairies even the smallest of the supernatural are all better known as "Supes" for short in the Seer's booklet. Breaking the natural law interference with or exposing magic to the human public eye causes problematic consequences for which most mortal's mind and soul could not comprehend in their ordinary daily lives.

The show had magic stunt tricks in their music routine performance that was part of their act but the Seer's among the audience knew better, their duties are to protect the human world against the supernatural forces breaking the natural law that protects the mortal world called the veil aka the Aether.

Stevie's left hand started to distract him sensing major supernatural activity placing his cold tingle numb hand in his pocket to keep the warmth. A sudden rush of force swoop over Stevie from the dark goddess as everyone in the venue evaporated into flames then ashes around him until he was the only one left alone with the dark goddess who started to float towards above Stevie landing gently on the dance floor. The dark goddess paused starring at Stevie, as he was puzzled and stunned at the direct stare from the goddess's beauty remembering what Charlie had mentioned about the goddess as he studied her wondering which step she would take.

Surprisingly, Kali the dark goddess's eyes went bloodshot red after she took a step with her left foot ringing her ankle bracelet charms.

For it rumbled with fiery cracks beneath the floor every step she took leaving fire crack craters sprouting fiery hell from it.

Stevie was horrified at the transformation that was obscured with fiery lava growing behind her, as the dark Hindu goddess was temporarily possessed twitching and turning manifesting into something formidable with her open mouth exposing terrifying fangs with a bloody red drooling tongue.

The daunting goddess went violent with her unbridled lively growing matted hair that would flutter and whipped from a distance at Stevie from his chair tossing him across the dance floor.

"You dare challenge a goddess of doomsday and time in my own domains minion!" The goddess exclaimed out charging after Stevie who was lying on the ground from his recent attack rolling over to get up quickly. The second attack was so quick from the goddess who was already upon Stevie with a blink of an eye where her left foot was pressed upon Stevie's chest as he laid their helpless. The goddess was restless hunch overprotective of her prey swing her six arms equip with weapons and items like a trident and a bow. In her other two hands holding a sword and a bright light disc swirling with her bloody red distend tongue reaching around for Stevie's neck.

Stevie was trying to shout over the goddess's fiery chaos being trap beneath her left foot pressing against his chest as she raised her sword over Stevie. "Wait, wait, I'm not a minion! I'm a seer, I'm a seer!" Kali paused with the sword still in her grip ready to thrust her weapon into her minion prey.

Kali then calls Stevie out after feeling her goddess grace of power

"Oh my Brahman, look at what you made me do, unleash my Shakti revealing my godly might shame on you god lover," Kali the dark goddess was unequivocally embarrassed. "Pure energy form is divine energy, bless it be from beyond the cosmos. Tell anyone what you witness about my divinity form I'll eat you," with her demon-like tongue licking her red lips."

Stevie was hoping the eating part was an inside joke.

Soon enough the dark goddess realized her actions lowering her sword as her immense god-like powers gathered and cease to exist changing back into her previous normal form of beauty with her weapons and extra arms disintegrated into thin air.

"A seer?" The goddess asks after becoming a monstrous entity being calm and collective reaching softly for Stevie's face gently with the side of her hand brushing his white peach fuzz on his chin. "God-lover you are one of the mark one's, a Seer, upholding the laws of the veil rainbow son of aw-dawn."

With Stevie pasting catching his breath felt calm and ease overcome him thinking for a moment he thought he was a goner but the goddess help Stevie get up from the dance floor. "You do mean Adam, son of Adam?" Stevie asks rectifying the irony of the bi-polar goddess with a third eye peeking through her forehead appearing as she flashed with a bright light and within seconds the goddess was up on stage taking a bow with everyone appearing back alive clapping and cheering as if nothing ever happened like time itself was rewind.

Every audience insight was engaged to the show in awe except for Kris and Charlie who kept looking up like they were expecting someone or something to happen when they notice Stevie among the audience on the music dance floor looking ill. Charlie shouted over the applause to Kris "well, nothing out of the ordinary looks good to me," taking a sip of his drink.

Similar charm magic to the enigmatic woman in the elegant red dress from earlier outside of the W hotel that Stevie saw on the way over to the club, the vibrant dark goddess Kali had everyone reverent to her giving off an aura that made you felt at home with ease and comfort.

The performance was phenomenal the princesses were synchronized in their dance with the goddess Kali to a routine that was sweeping the crowds away it was something magical that the world has never seen before. Even though it was borderline amateur they found a way to express their magic with the entertainment business informed by art, music, and dance through elegant class cabaret performers who were now being lavish with bills of money for their splendid entertainment, it was a pure genius with new revenue for the entertainment business.

The dark goddess approaches the dance floor from the stage fix on Stevie for a moment squinting her eyes at him analyzing Stevie's group mix within the crowd on the ground floor at a table. The goddess gracefully smiled walking towards them and behind her followed her kickass foursome princesses.

"Enjoying the show Enlighten ones, who is cursed to see all but is one with all?"

The goddess said clearing up her tribal India accent as Charlie and Kris arrived showing up behind Stevie before the dance floor where Kali reached for Charlie coming off from the stage and slowly brushed his frosted sideway hair.

Charlie didn't mind the flirtation his hair faded in with white frost pepper right above the short sideburns that mark him as a Seer who can see under the veil, a symbol of or a mark for Seers.

"Can't catch your tongue god lover?" The goddess asks Stevie to embarrass him by his catch calling a name that she calls him echoing her words, "God-lover?"

All cable guy Seers were all marked unexpectedly where they least want it, but Stevie did started to part take in liking his Seer mark it was simple with his frost peach fuzz on his chin, Stevie thought it made him look wiser it started to grow on him.

Kris's enlightened mark was his right-scarred eye that is about half an inch above his brow curved to below his eye that he got from an accident with his mother when he was eight. A shape of a crescent moon his scar was enlightened with the Seer mark frosted onto his right scar eyebrow. Kris has the whole Goth silent dark urban look going for him who stood out after the tribulation bequests him with the new look making his eye scar pop out more real of a crescent moon not sure if he was pleased about it.

The four princesses came around exceedingly cordial to greet their Seer guest but only Chastity stood back behind the other princesses.

"SNOW is what she likes to be named she does have a soft voice that can sing like a bird and talk to animals but she only has chosen certain animals to be with her a deer and bluebirds. Everyone thinks she snobbish just shy and not too fond of strangers, at first."

"Ladies you were a charm tonight" Charlie swooning the princesses with his charms, "oh I like this one, he's a flirt." Princess Vibrissa said who was blushing leaning over Charlie's shoulder fondling her long dramatic blond hair over Charlie's chest. "Mother Kali," Charlie bowed towards her escorting the goddess gently guiding her hand helping the goddess to her seat at their table sitting down to be introduced.

"Please call me Kali," she said to her guest. "Girls please give us some room," she signals the girls to go on back to entertaining the club.

"Let us know if you need back up," the redhead daisy duke with the red cape said with a tempered tone. "Or if this one gets out of hand," princess Vibrissa said towards Charlie whipping her hair exotically taking interest flirting with a wink at Charlie.

Stevie was in a state of shock lost of words not sure what is surreal of what he had just experienced earlier alone with the dark goddess afraid she might go chaos possessed again.

"You're wondering why I'm here in Texas, the capital of the great Lone Star state, reaching all four corners of the new world folding its path to everything that leads here in Austin Texas where everything is possible." The goddess continues to preach, "I am gold and beneath my feet is silver."

"Literally she meant the club is coins, "Charlie then snaps in a sophisticated gesture and said with a smile, "and where everything is bigger in Texas."

"Can't you just feel it," the dark goddess said stretched her arms reaching for the sky laughing, "all the cosmos and stars are aligned and connected and it's all happening here!"

They were all in awe but you could tell Charlie being the crew leader a charger supervisor of his group had a look that was intimidating swooning the goddess while the rest of the boys were in awe. Charlie continued to ask, "With no disrespect let's cut to the chase." Kali turns to glance at Stevie and look onto the cross necklace and the red pendant he wore with the white dove and said, "I admire your faith god-lover, it's strength within you, must have an old soul."

Stevie grins and tucks away his necklace underneath his shirt collar. The goddess then asks little red to get with Charlie to review the Seer's application that registers holy license permit to look over the magic protocol that's being mix with business, making sure the veil code checks out.

Kali claps with arms above her head in rejoicing "It's here Austin Texas, a new awakening of magic is changing closing in together towards this city, it all connects where this city is slapped in the middle of everything can't you feel it?

The chaos goddess continued laughing but it was Kris losing his temper and patience quickly then ask, "feel what?"

"Don't you know, Austin Texas is smack in the middle of multiple ley ways, pathways of realities... but anywho."

Then the goddess replies again, "Something major is coming to a change and it's closer than you think, oh you know being a goddess of time, change, and destruction and all." Kali gazing at her red nails, "you better believe love, that I got front row seats!"

You're a god? Kris snaps at the dark goddess.

Kali then looks to Kris engaging him with a smile. The goddess quickly added, "wouldn't want to miss it for the world, isn't that right Black licorice, I can smell you a mile away knowing what you're all about just know this that it will be me to end it all."

With Kali gazing the whole room with her arms conquered outward reaching above. With Stevie and Charlie eyeing each other Kris shot a quick reply, "I find myself more useful now in these days."

Everyone knew at the table that the goddess had the upper hand who knew what else she knows about each one of them being a deity she just aired out Kris's secrets.

Kali was laughing delightfully and ask Kris, "oh really what's that being a Seer."

"If your goddess of time, what's going to happen?" Kris asks the goddess Kali who was then smiling at Stevie who was compelled by her ancient beauty for Stevie saw swirls of ember fire through the dark goddess eyes feeling dismayed and confused from asking his previous question being watchful.

"She wouldn't be able to tell you," Charlie finished to say, "and even if she knew she still wouldn't be able to tell you or any living soul, gods and their riddles, it goes against their natural law for they may lose their grace." Kali laughed and then said, "I own time, cable boy," the dark goddess chuckled.

Kali then mentions to the Seer crew taking interest in her new guest's curiosity exposing them to the truth.

"Mostly invisible to man your world has always called us many names Jinn or genies, aliens, extraterrestrial, parasites and like angels but we have free will some making decision for yourselves, and long ago we the gods were left as watchers descended to the lower world of your kind sealing our godly powers away was a sacrifice to live happily, to live like mortals surrounded by discomfort and inconvenience. But Texas magic is here now this city Austin has energy like no other than before cant you feel it, many will come and reserve to take orders I mean... residence here in your lone star state.

Stevie then went on to ask, "So the gods never left."

"Bingo god lover!" The goddess said with Stevie feeling uncomfortable being called god lover from a goddess he then asks, "I'm not much of a lover, but what are we here for?"

The goddess didn't take consideration and continues to explain walking around their table gazing up and down at each one of her guests.

"Earth is a very young planet it reminds me of your human curriculum called school. Its all energy it is all experiences, did you learn anything from it? You all came here to learn lessons. Earth is a challenging planet you come here with free will in depths of emotions and limitations."

Charlie then asks the goddess, "so we're all being tested?"

"It wouldn't be a test if you knew the answers." The goddess smirks and winks at Charlie admiring his shrewdness, "What a greater test than to live a life thinking you're living all alone. What greater test is there than that to have your own free will?"

Kris didn't understand and was cohesive in sticking to his gloomy character, "So we're alone."

The Hindu goddess respectfully informed to correct and snapped Kris out of his imprudent attitude to his thoughtless suggestion, "You're never alone!

That is part of the test thinking you're all by yourself."

Stevie with a sudden realization on his face in awe, "so life is the greatest show all part of a test thinking we're all alone!"

Kali stood behind Stevie teasing to be a little mellow flirtatious playing with his hair, "Who can blame them god-lover, its a free enterprise front row seats to a once of a life-time, kind like the end of times but I'm here just to be a club owner and an entrepreneur." She then winks graciously.

Charlie's round cheeks with dimples got cherry red coughs then nods a little bow kissing Kali's right hand.

"Well thank you for your time ladies the show was spectacular you got something going here, welcome to Texas." Charlie said bowing to the goddess then replied, "Guys I'll see you outside," Charlie followed after Kris.

"God-lover can't catch his tongue patron of the Essence light, one with many names so I hear." Stevie was lost and then he had to ask politely, "if you don't mind not calling me that anymore and who Tricks?"

The dark goddess laughs, "Slayer of the Arch-Crone witch, scarred by the witch her self," as the goddess, pointed at his ribs, "It's told the Crone's power marks swift changes it's been prophesied." Stevie lifted his shirt allowing the goddess to explain revealing his scars upon his ribs that he got when he encountering the ancient witch Baba Yaga. "They're calling you a curse to all the witches, known as the Witches Bane."

Stevie was thinking great that was the last thing he needed was a title especially a curse one. "Your firefly fairy buddy Trixs hung around here earlier filling me in with everything shouting to the high mountains all the way down to the next block to congress street that you are now light brothers, he too came to me had questions about opening a bar of his own a fairy club down the street can you imagine off on third called blue light district just dirty boys in undies dancing on poles imagine that, but who knew that this new world would stir up into commerce with this goddess and the prince of Fay what a mix." Then at that moment Stevie look baffled he understood Trixs was a fairy he saved a few days earlier from the old crone Slavic witch Baba Yaga and realized he's bound to a fairy Prince?"

9

Case of the Mondays

WEEKS WENT BY AND A number of days counted Stevie was well around getting the hang of being Seer disguise as a cable guy touring around Austin Texas filled with hidden supernatural he was never alone with a colleague he considers a friend named Kris who knew his way around the city and neighborhoods.

A few things Stevie learned about the unique job it was always handed on handwork and knew to never question its outcome. For one thing, he knew humans were never alone among society and never have been, you could be walking next to harpies bird-like people that are known to be sincere and kind but are masked as normal people among the average human eye.

Stevie did run into a few harpies at work on the first floor of his call center taking tech support calls for the cable company, as they were fully aware of each other of who they were in secrecy. There was also aware that is half wolf-dog human that Stevie did come across once at his work among humans disguised that respected everyone and each other.

There were times where Stevie was mandatory to take actual trouble calls over the phones on the first floor at the beginning of his shift in the morning till noon he would hop onto the Seers exploration to carry out his job patrolling the city limits and at times their Seer charge orders for the trouble-call would just be visits on sites to investigate on going supernatural events.

There was one other character Stevie desperately tries to avoid who ironically was not of the supernatural but a big conspiracy theorist that was always on to Stevie since he got access to the mysterious elevator.

"Ah Stevie, STEVIE…" Crazy Al would call out waving down with a chase down after Stevie across the floor as they use to be cubical neighbors taking calls side by side but recently since new involvements and high recommends Stevie ask to be moved elsewhere but could never seem to escape his investigator.

"Hey, buddy you've been out for a couple of days I notice?" Crazy Al stride along by Stevie escorting him to his workstation lingered onto his cubical.

"I had paring meetings with human resources and leadership," Stevie smiled at his curious associate turning on his computer making way on purpose to began his shift and, thought to himself as he made up not believing his excuse, "What the heck did I just say?"

It was the beginning of his shift in the morning and it was protocol for all Seers to have an alternate disguise as an employee checking in and out of being an actual cable repairman among the population of the normies aka an average human.

It wasn't Stevie's favorite part of the job especially having a gumshoe wanna-be chum as your neighbor co-worker vaguely and annoyingly having Stevie under his magnifying glass metaphorically speaking.

"Psss… Hey, you going on that secret elevator after lunch aren't you? Seems like it's a thing you do never returning back to your desk after lunch before the day is over, so what is it long interviews?" Crazy Al said disgustingly licking his greasy lips.

It wasn't the first time being ridiculed by questions by crazy Al but must he always lick his lips wet before or sometimes after every time he would say the word secret as it were a hunger word that made him hungry or was he on to Stevie, could he possibly know Stevie's secret life?

All that Stevie could say to a surprise question out of nowhere, "yea something like that?" Retreating away from his desk walking quickly towards the exit into the hallway leading towards the mysterious elevator that was so-called "hardly ever being used," Stevie was being chased off with conspiracy questions and random accusations as if he was being investigated.

Today was the Monday that Crazy Al found the animosity and the courage to confront his proclaim even further before following Stevie throughout the hallway floor to the elevator steel doors.

"There's a hidden secret society underground isn't there?" With his hands, Crazy Al manages to abruptly bring about his last questioning holding back the elevator door into staying open catching Stevie off guard demanding answers.

"You don't think I don't know your secrets, I know what's happening around here, do you?"

Stevie gave a relief look gesture giving crazy Al a chance to acknowledge him trying to avoid the thought looking like crazy Al just finish eating a whole bucket of chicken all by himself as it was refreshing at first until Stevie allowed him to finish his conspiracy, "visitors from other dimensions, another world besides ours underneath our noses, you keep humanity in line from the things that we hear in tales and stories that go bumping in the night, native terrain extraterrestrials.

Stevie's quick response to his last statement, "What are you're talking about?"

"I'm talking about reptilians and I know what you are, and I will expose the men in black."

Just shortly after crazy Al's sporadic allegation he was interfere and disrupted by the mysterious charming old quiet security man who usually sit majority of the time in his security desk beside the front entrance door in his janitor blue overalls wearing his original Hawaiian vacation shirt with a batch of keys to his side and his odd long white Viking breaded beard sweeping away with his push broom whistling to his charming tune as he excuses crazy Al to move along with his long broom.

Stevie barely catching his breathe many thoughts went through his mind as the elevator door closes he knew he was thankful for that old mystery janitor.

The elevator door suddenly opens to the recognizable whistling echoing with keys rattling as he stepped out onto the underground library floor entrance to the main Seers interconnections but was caught off guard unexpectedly finding the stretch long corridor halls that relate to being empty castle seeing a familiar shadow figure of the mysterious janitor sweeping down the primeval corridor halls of the ancient underground temple with pillars and marble stone floors along with cavern walls and rocks that illuminated the area with medieval-style torch flames address throughout attach to the pillars also with multiple TV's reviewing world news events.

Stevie continues trying to follow the old man janitor's shadow sweeping off quickly to the next long corner of the corridor hallways casting only its reflection of his shadow disappearing only a ghost could manage the cleverness but it was the old man's informal whistle so recognizable that it always echoed with Stevie managing to follow it's harmony.

Stevie just thought what he just saw in the gaze of the dark corners Stevie would catch a small glimpse of a small straw figure from the corner of his eye run by so quickly in the dark corners nothing else would be there after he turns around to look what was following him. Could it be he thought, thinking about what he might of have seen his left-hand go numb very cold, it was Stevie's personal alert of the supernatural of a sixth sense that Stevie develop ever since as a kid sometimes it was sometimes it was a blessing and at times it was overwhelming.

Stubborn but certain Stevie followed through the dark enigmatic chambers through empty halls catching the shadowy figure at the end of every turned corner it disappeared but Stevie ended up at the central library of the underground maze sanctuary castle ironically the room was gathered and collected with gentle snowflakes flowing through with the warm air dancing to the tune by the whistling of the mystery gentle old janitor's enchanting music.

The Seer's library stone table with the huge majestic color rock tainted in blue aura glowing majestically right in the center of the rock stone table occupied with a strange wooden straw doll he most certainly recognized back at baba Yaga's hut and knew what he thought he just recently saw it from the dark corners a few minutes ago thinking was he being followed by a creepy old doll.

It was a peddler's doll more like a haunted doll Stevie thought with nailed in huge black buttons for its eyes that would begin to shine like-glow worms for it gave it life awkwardly starring into your soul, it gave Stevie the chills with a creepy vibe approaching the sitting doll afraid the worst thinking it would get up and start running off the Seer's library stone table.

It was the shuffle and the sudden shock of a rude awakening by a heavy stomp from a black walnut staff slammed a few feet behind Stevie that made him jump it was Madame the Librarian the last person Stevie ever wanted to see, distracted with a double-take looking back behind him at the stone table realizing the wooden doll disappeared instantly almost forgetting what Kris advise him about witches being raised by a witch his mother was one and remembers Kris saying the powers of dark witches includes deadly covertness and stealth which gives them intimidation to be the best kidnappers in the world.

All Stevie could muster to say to the Librarian the headmistress as he lost focus turning around in circles expecting to see the wooden doll pop up again out of nowhere, "ah.. Hello."

Madame the Librarian may be strict old fashion but she rides highly in decorum always coming off bitter towards Stevie like a personal grudge he thought being a cynical person could never sit right with an arcane witch or any other grand hind witch, to be honest thinking she was always making him out to be an asinine acting a front towards him as if she's been hiding a vendetta or an agenda against him. It was something about Stevie that bugged her showing to be so mysterious herself around Stevie.

"Charm of the jester in my sight, what are you up to?" The Librarian said coldly heartily, her pose was even a threat of neatness folding her hands waiting for a clear answer like a strict old Victorian Librarian in an old fashion library that caught a clown in the middle of its act without permission in her library.

"Ah, I lost my way, oopsies pop goes the weasel." Stevie gave a slight sigh with a made-up laugh forcing a chuckle to her displeased. "Ahm.. You haven't happened to see a wooden doll popping out of nowhere would you?"

Madame replied, "A stale joke, I'm not impressed."

Stevie took the effort to consider it as a compliment with generosity, "I tell ya, it gets harder and harder to keep the secret of grand deception about the supernatural once you are loaded with so much vast acquaintance."

"Shall it be a shame to lose another Seer one can only subdual so much I don't blame you child if you must but don't blemish your life away if you are dismay?"

The Librarian prestige her accusations already casting out doubts towards Stevie to give up to rid of him and go on to tell his secrets of being a Seer to make fast going back of living a normal life.

It is known to tell anyone besides a Seer or of the supernatural will automatically cause the Seer to lose all ability to see under the veil and forfeit any memory thought of being a Seer will be changed to yesterday's dreams. Stevie learned it was some universal law for all Seers to abide secrecy of all supernatural to be hidden among mortal men also another name for mortal humans is known as "Normies" among supernatural.

"Are you kidding?" Stevie asks and then said, "miss out on the adventure of the suspense knowing how hard to keep a secret life of being a Seer and the responsibilities are so surreal it brings me to hope about purpose in life with faith to believe in our future. It's an honor to be here."

Madame didn't stray too long on his answer very much knowing how to respond to such commendation you can tell she's not used to endearment compliments around her.

"Flattering can only get you so far that's why your ambition and initiative will always be judged."

Stevie's moral conciseness only responded with a gleeful smile and he said, "sure thanks for the tip."

There was no crack through her stringent defiance approach Madame suggest a little stroll to her astray to accompany her as she began to walk escorting him to the exit. "Now these antics of yours are over and that it is settled our path keeps meeting our acquaintances."

Stevie following the Librarian walking out behind her as if he wasn't good enough to be beside her leading to the exiting steel elevator doors through the halls corridor library he was troubled by the strict tone of voice from the Librarian, he was bothered by the lavish proper manner she always carried about her but Stevie was caught off guard and slipped into saying, "You can say that again."

The Librarian paused for a brief moment from strolling collecting her thoughts swiftly excusing Stevie's remark under his breathe permitting with just a look pretending she heard nothing as the steel doors closed.

Throughout the rest of the day for Stevie, it didn't turn out to be a typical Monday after all as exhausting the day began he was aware of an investigation that might have fairies involved but ended a Monday with a surprise.

Meeting up with Charlie and Kris in the afternoon settling up their cable guy equipment and ladder for their first investigation training at a residential home front yard installing services at a cable post as the boys were still learning how to disguise themselves when undercover among the human eye that is non-magical are called normies.

"All right guys just so you know that Valerie is with Ashley since she revealed she's not too fond with fairies and surprises she has every right so we figured Valerie could be some of use with sticking to Ashley's field."

Stevie then asks, "Which is?"

Charlie answered back to Stevie's question. "Ashley is anointed by the archbishop of the dioceses of the Catholic Church, she's known to be an expert in demonology and exorcism."

Stevie was surprised at the recent news in the depth serenity of his supervisor's valor but notice Kris was standing awkwardly quiet looking down at his shoes that Stevie found it to be oddly normal that Kris would put his two-cent about the dark.

"Were in for another trouble-call mission but an investigation of supernatural requisitions more so than just inspecting cable in saving someone's TV."

Charlie said suggesting Stevie and Kris act accordingly along as a cable repairman in their uniforms untangling cable wires setting up equipment props in front of a friendly neighborhood near shoal creek downtown.

Charlie notices something was off about Stevie not being himself dozing off into his thoughts. "You're awfully quiet today, got something on your mind?"

Stevie barely had the spirit to give in but he didn't mind to share, "I've been doubting myself lately, it feels I keep getting myself in trouble with a mess everywhere I go I tend to make situations worst."

Now one would think only an apologetic empathy could be reasoning or some comeback after that one, but it was Charlie who had something different to say about that, "One of the many things I like about you is you have faith."

Kris just glances in slight awe at Stevie refusing to look at Charlie and possibility agrees. "Isn't why you're still here?"

Just like that, the conversation was dropped leaving Stevie with a smile both boys were grateful to have a leader that know their moral compass and the value of others.

"Miraculously because of you Stevie there's a rumor going around among the Fae community with tales of rapid changes of the supernatural worlds with speculations and suspicious growing about around an obsolete lore supposedly lost to the human world is making its way back and as Seer's that's what we're here to find out what is this lost lore."

Kris also mentions the witches around the world are concerned and aware of the dramatically changes among the witch community, "The witches are also hearing there's stirs among the animal kingdom as the rest of the world awaits for the change that's supposedly coming that's overdue could this be it?"

Charlie immediately responded with double assurance, "I doubt it, but we need to know what we're up against, and that's why we are told to meet here cause we have somebody that has an ear for animals.

Appeared as the special guest honor to the boys seeing Snow a star cabaret show name goes by Princess Chastity White carrying the last name of an actual descendant enchanted legendary princess White as snow with red lips as cherry looking similar to the fairy tale character told in today's stories wearing the day of age outfits fairing with her character persona performing at Kali's club Texas's Lone Star Speakeasy located downtown is becoming a hot highly event every weekend.

"Hello, boys,' holding them witches down for me lately?" She said softly in an unusual urban slang like she was from the north then realizes she missed Kris coming back from around the truck with cable supplies around his arms that struck her princess manner. "Oh what a pleasant surprise, at least the bad witches, right?"

The princess winks at Kris with a role affection of royalty charm posing like a fairy tale princess giving in on the joke.

Charlie was no player but he knew he had ladies line up for him while he was the only one that got a gracious hug from a glee princess.

"Charlie, I came as soon as I got information for you." She giggled as she continued to flirt with Charlie as he struggled to politely put her down from climbing on top of him while Stevie smirks at Charlie's complication and Kris rolling his eyes holding in his air barf.

"We really appreciate you coming out of your way Snow," Charlie said as he shrugged off the princess's desperate hug and then became to be serious.

"In times of matter of your precise safety, especially your kind who can talk to animals, we have found a lead that could be at high places of investigation to know who could be following you, and Ashley and I will take care of it."

The boys had no clue what that was all about not questioning but then it was Snow who became serious and changed the dialogue looking up at Charlie with a trustworthy nod.

Everyone knows a true princess with royalty heritage sometimes can possess the power of speak charms that can communicate with animals.

There's a friend of mine a wise owl of the trees that I know that hears all and knows all and says this unexpectedly lost lore you are looking for has a moving passage that relocates to stay hidden and is enthrall to be a host of underground trolls and like any animal, it is wise to steer away from its chambers if you value your life." Snow caught on and caught the smirk off from Charlie's face, "this isn't really why you called me out here isn't it Charlie?

Charlie was appreciative of his well keen sophisticated ally to have a princess that was quick on her toes.

Charlie then points at a cute little lodged tiny house after thanking kindly to Snow for her assistance contribution and instantly enlightens his party of the furtive conspire delinquency that's been hanging over the community neighborhood lately.

There's has been reporting's of a thief around the neighborhood for forks and spoons that have gone missing in the area and fairies are suspiciously fond with silver utensils and to our calculations, this tiny house is the only one that hasn't been raided and there I think you'll find Mrs. Hubbard quite interesting with her rhymes along with her dancing dog occupied in the backyard that service that tiny old lady in that tiny old house

"A dog, how unexpectedly graciously delightful." Said the princess excitedly flattering with her charms as her cheeks began to blush.

"An enchanted magic dog I presume in the collection of forks and spoons?" Kris said who was not amused.

"Wait you mean to tell me the dog is the thief, how is that possible?" Stevie asks recalling the question.

"Don't you know by now anything is possible silly," The princess eagerly charmed in to answer for Charlie?

Charlie gave the boys a doggie bone and recommended it would come in handy looking at his watch quickly before scouting off into a search of the discovery of the underground troll dungeon lairs mentioning close nearby he again explained to the boy's protocol to keep well aware hidden from under the human eye of any contact with supernatural, "Well I gotta run, and knew you boys would make a good match team with Snow."

With that Charlie let it to Kris and Stevie to make out their first Seer charge mission trouble-call to investigate the conspire transgression committed that could be against the natural order that doesn't comply under the covenant codes of 9:12-17.

Every supernatural has to submit to the law of the covenant that must have no interference with human contact or crimes that comply against humanity. As Seers disguise as cable guys are to keep the order of the Arc law better known as the covenant codes of 9:12-7 that patrols the supernatural among the human world.

Charlie left the boys believing in them to complete the mission they scuttled and hurried off with their equip cable gear wearing a tool belt with a cable-bag hanging around their hip in their disguise uniform as they went around behind the tiny house back yard to the back house door entrance with Snow following behind staying back in the tiny backyard.

"Knock, knock, it's the cable guy," Stevie announce before entering the tiny little home. "Is anyone home?" Kris said as they gradually invited themselves before they heard a little old lady's voice ask them to come on in.

Stevie began reading off from his Seer's clipboard citation review papers, "Mrs. Hubbard we're here to install cable through your backyard to provide you better services for your cable TV."

He read a quick intro supernatural bio about the mysterious old tiny lady known as Mrs. Hubbard that has no family contacts but all she does is sleeps taking long naps sitting in her rocking chair and crochets everything and anything if possible.

Stevie tried to put everything in explanatory in his mind at what he saw from the inside of the tiny old lady's house-rocking quietly dozing into her sleep taking notice everything was crocheted in white with crocheted countertops to crocheted coasters in her wrinkly hands as if nothing out of the unusual until realizing ironically the odd tiny old lady Mrs. Hubbard overdid it with crocheting as her walls were even crocheted with patterns as wallpaper to her lamps shades were also crocheted as her phone stand to her recliner rocking chair and her picture frames including the flowerpot to everything was crocheted in white linen in her bedroom room.

Stevie and Kris didn't bother to ask letting the tiny old lady Mrs. Hubbard dozing off into taking her nap in her rocking chair but rather they look into their Seer's Handbook booklet.

The cable guy booklets are becoming useful in handy describes Mrs. Hubbard as an extraordinarily wondrous character in the marvelous nursery rhymes from Mother Goose.

They were clueless to what they were finding out with no one taking care of the over age-old widow who looks well over ninety-eight years old alone in the tiny house that can barely take care by her self but can manage to spare toiling with a rowdy mysterious dancing dog that ran off in dismay from its new guest visitors into the backyard that the old lady took no amused looking to the recent surprise displayed before them as they handed her a doggie biscuit bone.

The tiny old lady Mrs. Hubbard then bust her sleep bubble sitting straight up from her rocking chair and said before dozing off again,

"None for my poor little doggie"

The cupboard was bare

When I got there

A bone to get for my poor doggie

Went to the cupboard

For I 'am Old Mother Hubbard."

The tiny old lady was jaded sitting in her rocking chair already losing interest to her new coming guest mindlessly twiddling with her crochet knitting up a storm with her ball of yarn beside her rocking chair before quickly falling into her late afternoon slumber naps.

"I think she said that rhyme backward?" Kris muttered into Stevie's ear keeping close standing behind him.

Stevie wondered but never asks, speculating how it never phases who cooks, cleans, and picks up after the tiny old lady.

"Maybe we should investigate the dog?" Stevie states scratching out the pink citing ticket as he writes in his clipboard.

"Well, give it a go, lets see what happens with the dog?" Kris wasn't remotely interested but only ignoring his eagerness or hiding his anticipation for the fact of matter he was just as curious as Stevie was.

Taking his few steps forward inside Snow as she peeks politely from outside to see who was inside while Stevie was putting on his white Aeon weapon wireless headphones there in front of them running inside were dozens of dancing silver spoons with forks and plates as he was startled while starring at his reflection through the silver utensils and knew it was safe while his left hand would have warned him.

"Hey, Diddle Diddle,
The cat and the fiddle,
the cow jumped over the moon.
The little dog laughed,
to see such sport,
and the dish ran away with the spoon."

Snow references and quoted the familiar nursery rhyme and she pleaded to fill them in with gathered material of what she found out to help them further their investigation.

"I believe you have someone that broke their funny bone alarming tidings, a charm gone wrong where nothing can't be funny nor laugh at anything it sounds all depressing which makes sense of all the mishaps of the missing silverware around the neighborhood but don't go hard on the doggie."

Kris articulates his thoughts, "You mean the dog is responsible for all this?"

Before Snow departed wishing the boys fair well and good luck after saying goodbye with her run-off plugin promoting her cabaret club she keeps them posted with her new discovery investigation for them.

Snow- "The doggie says he's not from here but from the seventh brightest star a small constellation from the northern hemisphere following a star called Orion, in search for the cat and its fiddle who took flight from Egypt to the medieval times belonging to Catherine la Fidèle lost since the Reformation only one that knows his way back home with the right pair of dish and spoon that would lead him to the cow name Taurus that can jump over the moon can take him back home after he finds a funny bone for Mrs. Hubbard, but if you ask me something doesn't sit right, and he's no ordinary talking dog that I've never encountered before.

Snow with her descendant royalty is a Speaker, one that can talk to animals that can speak over twenty languages including animals, which she is considered a Babel descendants very ancient and rare power to possesss ties to old families when the Whites had kingdoms.

They meet the dog outside in the tiny backyard there in the back corner was a red doghouse wagging its tail with the brown doggie sitting up wagging its tail waiting to greet his guest strangers expecting a pat on the head or scratch behind the ears.

"You must be the doggie that's causing trouble around here?" Stevie felt awkward talking to a dog but suddenly it barks at Stevie and surprisingly understanding what it said while wearing his white colorful splash design Aeon headphones over his ears.

"Hope that's a funny bone you have cause I can sniff it on you?"

Stevie was uncertain of the dog being just a few feet away from it and replied, "You can talk and unfortunately it's not a funny bone but a milky bone I got for you."

Kris was entertained at the extract settings before him and was puzzled, "Stevie you can understand the dog?"

The brown dog sniffs the air once or twice then hid its snouted nose under its paws and told Stevie, "I can smell dark in you and the other one don't smell nice either, you're not like the other Seers around here."

Stevie repeated cautiously, "not like other Seers?"

Kris felt he was alarmed and immediately asks Stevie, "What did it say, what's the dog telling you?"

Then the dog said barking back with Stevie not knowing how he could understand the dog in its language, "That wasn't a question."

Stevie comment replying to Kris, "the dog didn't say much."

Stevie took out the milky bone from his pockets and waved it in the air offering the little doggie of its prize with its tail coming alive with its paws in the air standing on its little hind legs, "If you promise to never steal again I'll let you have this milky bone."

A deal agreement was made between the doggie that couldn't resist saying no to a bone and with its gratitude for not convicting the little doggie that the little mutt has already set up a surprise.

The dog wasn't the only one with a hindsight smell Stevie took a whiff from the air, "You smell that?" He asks Kris, "It smells like gingerbread?"

Kris's next repose had them curious, "then who's cooking?"

A loud racket could be heard through the tiny house kitchen window as well the back open door drawing their attention they took warning following the clamor noises of the cooking and cleaning commotion coming from the tiny kitchen they step inside through the back screen open door that was left open.

Not even bothered the tiny old lady of the tiny house continued crocheting her coaster not concerned fell in a deep sleep but in the next room to a jam-pack kitchen of a mad poltergeist of dancing spoons and plates with forks in command with the tiny house being helpers in cooking with the dancing dog wearing now a kitchen apron being the maid chief storming up a chaos mess with pastry goods, there was ginger, cloves, cinnamon, cardamom, nutmeg, anise and is sweetened with molasses that were tossed through the kitchen the air with flour and eggs floating into a stirring bowl in the air like a coarse bakery running amuck.

Catch by a sore eye they could tell there was something amidst behind the dog's mischievous toil in the kitchen some type of sorcery. Kris at hand first thought it was a ghost but oddly saw the dancing dog constructing incantations standing on its two hind legs.

Pop-out of the oven after it rang jump out a gingerbread man that sprang to life.

The boys were taken back in disbelief but understand the possibilities were far-fetch to try to comprehend of understanding lure magic especially from a magic dog.

The dog continue to bark and spoke as Stevie could understand the dog, "for your generosity and thoughtfulness this gingerbread man will lead you to treasures and desire destiny, better catch it before it goes."

Stevie would repeat back to Kris what the dog was saying and before Kris could speak to ask the dog to bark the answer as if it could read minds.

"A troll lair you will find the cookie will lead you if it doesn't get caught, better go now before you lose sight."

Kris sped off after the gingerbread man wasting no time once explain as Stevie quickly ran after Kris after he humbly obliged and thank the magic dog and never had a second thought about the odd unparticular event.

10

A little bit of fortune

LATELY ABOUT ALMOST EVERY MORNING for a couple of days Stevie would catch himself smiling back at his reflection in his bathroom mirror, but at times he thought he would catch a shimmering figure staring back at him from the mirror wasn't sure what to make out of it. He did bring up these incidents about the mirrors to his friends but it was Valerie that was more cautious to let Stevie know to stay away from mirrors as much as possible without any explanation but the thrilling excitement he couldn't help smiling being distracted from his thoughts comparing about the times coming home in his pickup from his boring causal labor position when working at a grocery store then after with his truck windows down driving home in the west Texas wind, thinking how grateful he couldn't see it then but now it couldn't be clearer.

Today was their first-day training with their special Aeons they were given personal time to figure out their gifts that they deservedly earned on their Tribulation journey mission.

Ever since after the incident with the ancient witch Baba Yaga his dreams from last night and many other nights Stevie has been having the same recurring nightmares. Always awaken up dumfound and lost in a massive engulf dark foggy cave with high tensions in his dreams that weren't from being lost in the darkness it came from a dark enormous presence that he could always sense the huge being having to be alone with it in the dark vast void chambers.

The dream always starts with Stevie waking up feeling for a cold stonewall in the dark fog pulling out his smartphone to use as a flashlight. The ground floor would always shake where there's an immense rumble within every forty seconds in the vast cold dark chamber. Stevie started to recognize that the deep rumble had a pattern of having the nightmare multiple times he would always end up running away from the loud eerie rumble waking up drench in sweat.

"So you two manage to lose the little gingerbread man cause it ran too fast for your skinny and stout legs I see, such a shame." Valerie took pleasure to laugh, as she was making a game to mock the boys. "If it were me there we would be basking in our rewards exploring the troll's hidden lair by now."

Stevie and his crew which included Kris and Valarie have been anxious since they were instructed a day before to go over Performance w/ Tools & Weapons in their Seer's guide booklet and were advised to have their Aeon weapons for their lessons. Stevie wore his Aeon headset wrap around his neck that was struck with colorful art with splattered paint. Stevie would wonder how his Aeon gift can be used instead of just playing music as a weapon as each Aeon is special to its owner as its protector or used as a weapon.

The three were restless and anxious to train on their first day with their Aeon weapons.

Kris with his magic black pocket lighter who says he's learned one or two pyro tricks already adapting to learn with his Aeon gifts and Valarie was wearing her Aeon charm scrunchie around her hair pulled back with a ponytail that seems to change colors from time to time from mellow pink to hot pink when death is near.

Training today was going to be different while their chairman and Beta leaders are their over-seers are away on their own important mission house call, while the rest of the group waited impatiently in the Library training room for a different Beta over-seer instructor from another class who leads their team substituting for Ashley and Charlie.

While waiting Stevie began to hear a familiar whistling he's heard before. The whistling started to echo ghastly with an intense high ringing pitch for a whistle that got closer and closer to the exit door right outside of a corridor hallway.

Valarie broke Stevie's thoughts of concentration, "already ten minutes late, and supposedly it's one of the Beta overseers who command's team four."

Stevie then replied relating to the whistle, "You guys don't hear that?"

Kris shot a look at Stevie not understanding Stevie's question then turn to Valarie and said, "So I hear this instructor from team four is some kind of a queen of some sort and they say her magic is well known in the mediumship community best known for divination and specializes in herbology in the healing arts."

Stevie was still feeling lost and confused at the mystery whistle that got louder and thought could he be hearing things.

What walked by that only caught Stevie's eyes suddenly sweeping the hall with a push broom whistling was the janitor Stevie first remembers running into before getting onto the elevator. The snow-haired bearded janitor with the one-eyed patch was a short man wearing overalls with the same Hawaiian blue and white stars aloha shirt under his outfit.

The uncanny character then lifted his eye patch to get a good glimpse of Stevie revealing his extraordinary glowing sparkling blue eye leaking with a murky blue smug in the air. Within seconds the mysterious blue janitor sweeps away and vanishes causing Stevie some commotion peeking out the hallway hearing the usual eerie whistling fading away.

"Did you guys not see that I swear I keep running into him."

Kris replies to ask Stevie, "What are you talking about?"

Stevie brought a concerning matter to their attention, "you guys didn't hear his whistling?" Then Valarie studying Stevie with a straight face started to ask descriptive questions leading Stevie on a guessing game and started to laugh with Kris.

Momentarily walk-in fashionably late snug in a colorful stood-out hot pink two-piece business outfit with a customary pink jacket something that came out of an eighties catalog stuffed with shoulder pads wearing white pantyhose with yellow heels. The instructor looks like a dramatic vixen actress from a retro TV soap wearing a red and blue headscarf bedazzled with a red jewel flower design with blue emerald petals. She wore multiple accessories wearing huge golden loop earrings, her fingers garb with golden rings, and having layers of enchanted necklaces and pearls exposed dangling over her pink blouse.

She was a very odd character with a hot mess wearing too much blush and has on screaming pink lipstick matching her hot pink nails to her outfit carrying an expensive designer bag it being half the size of her hung over her right shoulder.

In the training room among the library, there was only a desk table with three remotes and a white dry-erase board hung on the wall behind the desk like a classroom. The over-Seer trainer spoke with a strong Romanian accent as she places her heavy belongings on the table, "Here begin your first certification lessons incantations one-o-one safeguard to protect yourself using your disguise cable remote better known in your booklet as the Seer's tool."

She then held up one of the three remotes displayed in front of her new students, "This Seer tool was designed by one and only Nerd himself, a profound known Seer whose intelligence was the first to sway magic components into a compute magnitude of technology, he can easily be known as one of the smartest scientists on the planet. I do wonder though big as his brains must, ahem…" She then realized and started blushing to continuing the conversation, "Isn't it hot in here, where were we." It was obvious to the group that the Beta instructor had a thing for the scientist, having hot flashes and continuing to fix herself while she pulls out a fan from her bag began fanning herself with the other hand.

"With your special abilities and skills, the Seer's tool is the remote that is programmed to help and guide you on your house calls and missions against the supernatural better known as we call them Sups. Now for the introduction, my name is Ezell Sana Matuska Athalia I am the Gypsy Queen of my people, I have been asked by your over-seer mentors to substitute today's lessons as they are out on their important trouble call mission. For you may already know I am the senior Beta over-seer leader of team four but you all can call me Esma," She said smiling in a thick accent. "Some alone around the world can sustain the powers of wizardry and witch magic that are used for the good and evil for some." Esma was a dramatic speaker walking back and forth using her hands and body language as she spoke.

"There are three classes of magic with three stages of progression to full wizardry magik status, and that's magic with the letter k.

Today you'll be covered and be going over just the first stage of wizardry magik, incantations, which are now distributed into your profound remotes. Again she went on glorifying on her crush Nerd the scientist, "The second stage is hand incantations' whose magic is performed by gestures by the hands, fingers, motions or magical components such as tools like your distribution Aeon gifts. The gypsy queen then reflected by flashing her special Aeon gift was her personal large handbag adoring her brand name accessory.

The third and highest stages of wizardry are the supreme exponents' wizards of pure thought, who need neither words nor gestures but by their own will alone pierce the heavens." The Gypsy Queen claps snapping Kris and Stevie who was in deep thought daydreaming of one day what power they could possibly possess a chance to have.

"You can forget achieving the third stage of wizardry it's impossible and quite dangerous only a few have been capable to produce such power since the time of Merlin himself."

She then opens her Aeon huge brand bag pulling out a small booklet and oddly a colorful pottery pot filled with red dirt. "As you were all instructed to go over your seer's guide manual booklet over the weekend covering which selection of power source to use for each classification monster you're dealing with having your safeguard remotes." She started to giggle and said with an accent, "we don't want you pressing the wrong keys that might double your problem or worse blowing yourself up."

Kris exclaimed out, "you mean these remotes can do that?" The instructor nodded at Kris and continued, "You should know by now your instructions, in order, to move on to the next tier level of being a seer, you must be certified to use these seer's tools before you can use your Aeon gifts from your Tribulation. So if you did review going over your seer's guide booklet then you know all Seers must pass their lessons to use your Seer's tools aka remotes for this will be a test of your knowledge, skills, and teamwork. If all goes well and you do pass I do have a little surprise for you, now any questions before you may proceed?"

With that thought, Stevie had a look on his face in dismay trying to recall looking at his other peers shrugging his shoulders if they remember they were told about any pop quiz test.

"Now to get started with a little bit of fortune you were also told to carry loose change were you not?" Again Stevie shot a look at Kris and Valarie clueing them he had no coins of change on him. Esma then advances to the three of them with a serious look on her face as she looks over at the group to her watch in dismay at the group taking forever as they look confused with one another with concern features on their faces.

Valerie quickly pulled out a beaten-up bent quarter from her jean pocket with dents and scratches snatched up by the gypsy queen who then immediately scrutinized and studies the coin pinned between her two skinny fingers up to her face.

Kris secretly handed Stevie a coin from his loose change while the instructor was distracted by Valarie's quarter looking away.

"Ah yes, the problem solver... How valiant and mystical she is so incomprehensible and shielded," said the gypsy queen handed back her coin.

Valarie nudged Kris, as he was startled interrupting the gypsy queen he handed his shiny dime having one side of the silver coin with gunk accumulation on the dime. She stood there in silence her cheeks turning red who eyed Kris looking back at the dime handing it back to him and replied, "I have nothing to say for I believe you are well known of your dark curse," she then turns away with no more notice returning his dime back to him.

Kris shot back as if he was used to cold suggestions, "gees thanks."

Then it was Stevie's fortune that she was dead on with Stevie giving her his borrowed penny.

"But this one, a borrowed copper!" Kris and Stevie look at each other reading each other's thoughts, "How could she know?"

The gypsy queen was astonished holding the coin gleefully as if she won the lottery studying the coin she then states, "old and ancient with anew, I see great power, no this can't be!" She then mutters softly to herself making conversations as if she was talking to herself in a tongue.

Making out from what they could hear from the foreign language she spoke, "The Millennial," the gypsy queen then snaps out from her trance and pauses to look at Stevie then looking back at the penny in her fingers then frowns as if she just suggested her predictions were wrong. "For one thing I got right, you'll need your friends. Ok on with it now give me your coins." She clapped with making her gold rings and bracelets cling noises and reached for the other coins from Kris and Valarie.

It took a minute for Stevie to pop the question still trying to get over to his recent sudden prediction while he had the gypsy queen's full attention, "Excuse me, your majesty, with no disrespect, but being a queen to a clan in all wouldn't that make you suitable to be the grand hind witch?"

The gypsy queen quickly grasp her pearls with admiration and began blushing started to laugh historically catching her breath she then replied with a Romani accent that almost sounded to be sarcastic, "titled to be the grand hind witch, me as the high ruler magi of magic known around the world summoning all about witches of whatever country thy into my bidding." She continued to laugh converse to a delusional behavior, "To reign all magic to order and to give congratulations or punishments according to the all witches' successes in their witchcraft trade and delegations." She then snaps back at Stevie, "Because of your decorative highly regards of me Esma will tell you your answer."

The gypsy queen then started to whisper to her colorful pot, while Kris was alarmed by her actions he spoke up to tell Stevie and Valarie, "she's using an enchantment spell."

The Gypsy queen then drops the coins into her pot as they witness the coins magically seeping into the red dirt. She then replied to Stevie sarcastically fluttering her eyelids puckering her lips, "While you complete your task noble one."

She was so quick surprisingly she then pushed the pot off the table breaking it onto the floor and sprouting out of the broken pot rolled out three alive tiny man plants with green ovate leaves arranged in a rosette for its head.

"Aha, they came out to play!" Esma said clapping with glee.

The walking little man plants had thick upright long dark roots used as a tiny arm with hands and legs for walking that stood about twelve inches tall. "Mandrakes!" Valarie said dashing with a flip over the table to grab the remotes tossing the other remotes to the boys ready for the next test.

Valarie being two steps ahead of the game and was already programming her remote yelling the classification levels to the boys who were still in awe at Valarie's guile stigma and acrobats. "Mandrakes are classification magical pants that are class B, their better off in stun mode."

The walking odd plants were approaching Stevie and Kris who were still disarmed and confused about all the commotion as the gypsy queen was observing she stood back and started to proclaim her accord. Valarie's mandrake went after her as she ran towards the wall and flipped off the wall over the little man plant as she zaps it with her remote stunning the mandrake frozen on the spot.

"For I am Ezell Sana Matuska Athalia the third generation of my clan, great-granddaughter of the legendary gypsy queen Taliba Athalia of Libra the impel silver tongue."

Kris was quick to identify who murmured to Stevie and Valarie, "her family was the first to cast the monstrous silverback curse."

Stevie suddenly yelled back, "Silverback what?" While pacing back and forth shaking his leg struggling with the little man plant climbing up his leg reaching for his tool remote in his pants pocket.

Kris was already in a stunned mode with his remote quickly putting back his seer guidebook in his back pocket yelling back to Stevie, "The first werewolf is the silverback, the gypsy queen's great-grandma was responsible for oh never mind!" Just then Kris had his mandrake stunned by his cable remote tool having just one more plant left which was Stevie's magical mandrake.

"Stevie the code for the stunning ray on your remote tool is source 011," Kris shouted again "press the source button then punch 011!"

Esma's punctuation in her sentences wasn't always accurate in her thick foreign accent. "It's a death wish to be incredibly powerful, all was better off when Iagabikha Baba Yaga was grand hind even she was hidden from the world until you killed her."

Stevie shouted in panic as the third mandrake ran up cornering him up against a corner wall. "How do I unlock the remote?" Stevie was rushed pressing multiple buttons on his clicker remote stumbling as he pulls out his seer's guide booklet.

"Esma is queen to her people knows her role not to take thy grand hind witch that takes the will of extreme power to sovereign all the witches of this earth." She spoke with her hands being dramatic with her arms stretch upward as her antique jewelry bristled in gold with bracelets dangled and jingled within every movement as she spoke.

Kris continued and shouted, "Enter your PIN number to unlock your remote it's assigned in your booklet!"

Just then Stevie's mandrake stretches its little plant arms sprouting its root vines that shot out at Stevie wrapping its stretched vines around his arms as Stevie drops his booklet and his cable remote tool.

Standing back watching over the assessment was the gypsy queen who then continues, "For the grand hind witch is bestowed a blessing with a curse for every solace moon is known to be the witches hour that's every third full moon of the month."

Stevie was having a struggle against the mandrake plant tugging on his arm as he barely unlocks his remote picking it up suddenly zapping the tiny Mandrake as it blew up into little pieces making it look like a zucchini was in a blender splattered all over one of the corner floor.

"Ah, I don't think those were the right codes but I think that work."

The gypsy queen gave a dismissive look on her face at the messy green explosion and continued with using her dramatic hand motions. "Upon the full moon at the witches hour, any witch or wizard is legal to rise and challenge the grand hind witch for order summon to the death for supreme control."

"You just made matters worst look!" Valarie pointed, as she was the only one focus on the lessons.

Leaving nightshade scraps of what's left of the third mandrake blasted away with pieces all over the corner floor that began to move, twitching and suddenly developing into growing little mandrakes that were multiplying springing to life. Immediately within seconds, there were a handful of mandrakes growing in their little sizes scrambling all across the room.

Esma then explains, "Now the tables are flip and never has there been a malevolent as ever to evolve for hope on this planet with forces of uncertainly even though the new Grand Hind Witch is the martyr of darkness when it comes to power oh… there always comes a time when all changes with magic bind rules when one is replaced, and that will stir the witches' cauldron. Having to look over your shoulder is no blessing."

Kris was able to reply trying to stay focus on aiming his remote paralyzing his mandrake, "You're talking about the Librarian aren't you?" Esma answered, "she plans to end this tycoon matriarchy evil rule once and for all by not executing their ceremonial spill for the queen of witches, a hideous blood ritual sanctified the grand hind witch it's traditions requires a life of a royalty prefer princesses that must be consecrate to carry on its legacy of power."

Just then two mandrakes went after Stevie as another one jump on his back almost dropping the remote as other mandrakes jump's onto his hand gaining control of the remote blasting other mandrakes into pieces all being scattered forming into multiple mandrakes. Ashley and Kris were focusing on stabling their mandrakes as theirs were frozen under control by their remote beams.

Everything happened so fast one Mandrake manages to sneak up behind Kris attaching itself to his remote disabling Kris's frozen mandrake as it rushes at Valarie jumping into her face, as her mandrake was release.

It was mayhem suddenly as if the mandrakes had a plan all along knowing what they were capable of blasting each other to create an army full of growing marching nightshade root as they were zapping away with Stevie's remote while he was being wrestled with four other mandrakes climbing up all over him.

They weren't too sure if their foreign instructor was helping them or attacking them as the gypsy queen spoke standing back from the chaos watching them in despair with calm and ease, Visualize sitting in an empty theater in front of a blank screen and letting that screen fill your mind."

Stevie shouted back sarcastically struggling to stay on top of the little plant invasion surprise attack, "That's kinda hard to do right now!"

Their substitute mentor continued, "Tools to create the mind can help your gift into a powerful weapon. Mostly everyone taps into Precognition and Clairvoyance and doesn't even realize they're already in control."

It was an awkward situation for Stevie feeling confused and at the same time, he was lost at being amused, frighten, and excited, the whole thought reminded Stevie of a flashback children's classic animated film as he shut his eyes just momentarily. Just then music began to play out loud through Stevie's Aeon headset Beats set rested around his neck.

It began to play out loud a remix to the music from the Sorcerer's Apprentice from the film Fantasia but ironically it had a hip-hop EDM mix.

Everything and everyone paused for a quick second then out of nowhere it was blasted out loud as if the training room had installed invisible stereos walls surrounding them with music playing from his Aeon headphones and Stevie shouting, "you got be kidding me, that's it that's my power, AWESOME!" Suddenly Stevie was rushed and fell over by a numberless of mandrakes being piled up wrestled to the bottom of the pit with the music ringing from his gift intriguing the mandrakes drawing most of them to Stevie.

The team seems to be losing the struggle between the masses of walking shrubs, as things were about to get worst.

Sarcastically Esma said, "Ah oh my little walking shrubberies are full of surprises today I think they like you."

"They're sprouting!" exclaimed Kris struggling with one rigged around his neck as he notices all the mandrakes were beginning to bloom purple flowers opening their petals releasing yellow pollens. "Not good!" Valarie said announcing quickly, "it produces toxins that can put you in sleep paralysis." Everything went slow and heavy for Stevie figuring it was the effect of the surprise pollens from the mandrakes.

Being shuffled and roughly handled under a dog pile of walking plants Stevie was getting drowsy could barely make out from a gaping hole underneath the green plant dog pile watching Valarie taking action kicking the last Mandrake off her grabbing her ponytail and twisting her pink Aeon charm yanking one of the few pendants off her pink scrunchie taking a knee bowing down and started to chant.

"Russia winds from afar we heed your frostbite from summer winds to ice-land spar!"

The room temperature started to drop, then the music died out, within seconds the room was just as cold as a freezer with rapidly growing icicles and ice throughout the whole room.

"Clever witch, someone's been doing their homework," Esma said in amazement as she was studying Valarie putting a wool sweater jacket on that she pulled out of her large brand purse.

All the living green-brown mandrakes went motionless and drop into a ball where its roots shriveled up looking like dead green potatoes with bushy celery tops. Stevie was gross-out, "eew they look like deformed Brussel sprouts." Valarie wasn't having any of it as she walks past Kris who was laughing helping Stevie up from being under a pile of lifeless balls of mandrakes. "Mandrakes can't survive with temperatures under forty degrees Fahrenheit it then goes into hibernation mode and I'm just about anything else but I'm no witch."

Valerie then without any hesitation demanded Kris to fry the attacking Brussel sprouts continuing to say, "since we all know Stevie is just in the music department." She said coldly with her arms crossed over her chest with her back leaning onto the exit door. Esma murmured, "valiant and mystical."

Kicking with their feet, Kris and Stevie managed to shovel all the mandrakes to a corner burning to a crisp using Kris's pyro skills from his Aeon gift as he learned on his own around safety surroundings possessing to control his fire with his lighter that was just an average black lighter you could purchase at a convenience gas store he received from his ascension from the ancient fallen entity Prometheus.

"MARVELOUS!" The gypsy queen clapped in glee, "just marvelous, bravo, Splendid, well done, one draws its enemies, while the other's execute its plan. Stevie what marvelous strategy improvising with your Aeon weapon."

Valarie who was still leaning on the exit door resting her motions gave off a vibe that she was ready to go rolling with her eyes and replied, "really?"

The gypsy queen began to speak in the third person,

"Remote tools are now yours to keep, and now for Esma's last surprise, it has come to my attention, Esma is in need of a team tonight as mine are away on vacation attending to their house call missions some few are across the country while others see it to pass this great opportunity. She pulled out a bright red metallic envelope sealed with wax symbolizes an apple to a crown.

"Substituting as headmaster while our chairman is away."

They knew the gypsy queen was second at command as she meant to highlight the librarian's absences. The gypsy queen said excitedly, "And with tonight's faction I have been cordially summoned with high regards to a rare invitation, it will be announce the title event of the surprise party when your presence is required." She exulted.

Valerie then response to fill in the blank sharing with her vast knowledge of the supernatural world, "Cordial summons high regards are calling knights old traditions so old it is dated back when animals and humans freely communicated one another, it is a very rare explicit revelry that we don't see these types of invitations of these days in age. Also, these are summons used back in the ages to take orders from the crown tallest pinnacle of the land mostly royals like kings or queens would beckoning the highest grand guards of the kingdom."

Kris in a response knew already the adjective, "let me guess, they want us to chaperone the party?"

The gypsy queen ignored Kris and continued, "Oh how huge this is, the only special guests with grand powers of clairvoyants of all ages have been invited around the world from fortune tellers to prophets, I wonder which gods would show up." The gypsy queen took a pause from her excitement and began to be serious, "They are saying among the supernatural community the fabled grand foresee party is hosted by a surprising celebrity supposedly with returning old power in the coming of a new era of magic, a well-known artist in the music industry I hear and overseas who is new to the Americas and very fortunate to come across a summon like this, it's going to be a lifetime experience to foresee the fortunes among our greatest peers all under one roof."

Valarie snaps back being all of sudden interested in the conversation still has her arms crossed leaning to the exit door, "It sure does sounds like a party."

"Since I'll be attending the great event tonight," the gypsy queen stated adjusting to look at her necklace clutching her pearls from her other old necklace relics. Esma was staring deep into her necklace of pearls, "Within the invite, I will be hosting the watchman of the grand guard for the party needing a team of Seers on duty a one in a lifetime to a magical event for invites only."

Valarie immediately interrupted, "we'll be there." The boys look at each other as if they had any say in it.

"Excellent, ah where did she go?" Esma the gypsy queen stirred in dismay shaking her head clicking her tongue.

Alerting Stevie before Kris went after Valarie who then stormed off out of the training room, "the lessons are up it's 6 o'clock I have to jet out too."

Esma then fingered at Stevie signaling him to come closer, "ok little guy you and me will have a little talk." Asking Stevie to stand by she gave the boys the location address to the Surprise Party so Kris can pass it along to Valarie.

Before Kris left he paused right outside the doorway of the training room and asked, "200 Congress ave, that's at the top of one of the tallest building in Austin."

The gypsy queen gladly nodded to agree with Stevie and was delighted to share her thoughts.

"If I may, the Librarian should be the last of your concerns boy but it's wise to not make your concerns the last."

Stevie couldn't help think past how everyone is terrified of the Librarian who he sees their Madame as very boorish and rigorous she could be towards him.

Stevie replied, "You trust her the Librarian, but don't double-cross her." Esma then gave a grave look preparing to ask a deadly question.

"Tell me, when you defeated her test at the red door, is it something about this Aeon tool you possess here, she desperately tried to stop you did you not notice? What did her face look like when you defeated her?"

Somehow she had a split personality that had managed to be in Stevie's personal space being face-to-face waiting for his answer while Stevie was alarmed taking steps backward gradually grasping his beat headset hung around his neck.

"Why is everyone making her out to be this big boss?"

Stevie quickly figured out Esma was definitely special in her own way maybe with bipolar disorder showing multiple personalities but her reaction got him scared and the gypsy queen put a serious face and she replies, "the Librarian is over three hundred years old."

11

The Millennial party

STEVIE AND KRIS MEET EACH other both starring up at the Austonian skyscraper underneath a calm storm with a view of silent purple-blue lightning.

Kris spoke to Stevie "Valarie said she'd meet us here."

"You think the party will have food," Stevie replied back.

"So Esma told you the Librarian is over three hundred years old?" Kris asked Stevie then he answered, "yeah, and she hates me."

Kris chuckled, "I wouldn't sweat it and I overheard the Librarian has been busy ever since rumors been going around about missing princesses and so I hear there's only one missing that performs at Speakeasy the goddess Kali's cabaret club, and ever since then the Librarian hasn't been seen."

They both knew they were thinking about Snow it was first news to Stevie who responded, "Missing princesses? I thought the Librarian was different? What makes you think it was the Librarian?"

"Kris interrupted Stevie, "think about it, what witch would dare to pass up unlimited power plus who wants to challenge a three hundred-year-old witch."

Stevie then asks Kris, "But why a princess?"

Kris responded, "Royalties seem to have special properties for witches to distribute a special ingredient for their dark magic." Kris didn't want to elaborate so much on the topic.

When they both meet up with Valarie at the Austonian lobby before heading to the event on the very top floor she caught Stevie starring complex into one of the lobby's body mirrors. "I thought I told you to stay away from mirrors!"

Stevie was aware of Valerie's stern concern as he explained once again he thought he saw a shimmering figure starring at him from behind his mirror reflection but it was Stevie that changed the subject suggesting it was a good idea for Valarie to volunteer the team to escort the party with Valarie always showing up out of nowhere as she replied. "I thought our team could use some future sightseeing maybe we can see what's clear in front of us." She turned to look at Stevie.

Stevie felt discouraged after that, trying not to concentrate on himself too much thinking about Valarie having doubts about him being capable to hold his own for the team, those were self issues he tried to not think so much about.

Arriving at the front entrance lobby elevators one of the end single elevators was labeled the Austonian Club.

Valarie then pulled out a card in front of a guy built in a black suit with an earpiece a white invite card that read "Austonian Club presents the event," it said, "will announce the title event of the party when your presences are required." It was marked, "Grand Foresee for three" and on the back, it read in gold lettering "the 56th floor."

The elevator door then opens and blocking the entrance was the elevator doorman in his suite tux extending his hand gesturing invitation, please.

"I don't think we're dressed for the occasion?" The team was in their polo company shirts wearing khakis jeans with light brown work boots with Valarie who looks serious was the only one wearing her compete set with a cable tool belt around her waist.

"Remember what we're here for we have a job and no time for social hour I think we're going to need all the luck we need."

She handed the doorman their invitations stepping into the elevator.

Kris gave a remark to follow up with Valerie's statement, "I think we're going to need more than luck."

Stevie felt a sudden dread overcome him like it felt sudden death was looming around, as usual, his left-hand goes icy cold from within his bones through his skin sensing unnatural paranormal in his surroundings having him put on his blue fingerless gloves to keep warm.

Stevie pulled out a fortune cookie from his pocket tossing it to Kris, "brought a little fortune of my own." Kris then tosses back the fortune cookie back to Stevie, "is that from the mystic trader Mr. Yang?" Stevie stuffed the wrapped cookie back in his pocket, "It sure is, and the mystic trader told me to take my fortune everywhere I go." Kris then answers, "I don't think he meant that literally." Stevie just shrugged and they went on through the open elevator door.

At the very top of the Austonian of the fifty-six floor, everything was grand and majestic like from an inside of a medieval castle from the entrance to an enormous throne room an assembly hall with a long stretch diner party table settled with a magnificent golden throne shape like a peacock fit for a queen at the end of the party diner table, it was a sight to see something from another parallel fairytale dimension of impossible huge vast space of a palace sitting right on top of one of the tallest buildings in Austin.

The top floor was like a luxury grand castle hall that looks to be the decor of a dark twisted fairy tale with unique tall black mirror pillars shape into glistening glass marble red apple trees. There was even an elevated bright light runway with a path above ground surrounded by dark water leading to the end of the diner party table of the grand hall displayed in front of the monumental gold throne that resembled a familiar peacock one from Stevie's memory from a childhood fairytale movie he recalls. The party table is seated with a thirty-foot conference dinner table occupied with the odd ineffable guest.

The grand dinner party table was loaded with plenty of catering food it was a feast of gourmet apples contrasted in every paring dish decorated with enchanted candelabra that look like wicked hands gripping a glittering shiny wax red apples in its grasp, it was such a formidable décor even the table was already loaded with eldritch guests of grand foreseers.

From one of the many guests, they immediately recognize Esma the gypsy queen at the corner table saving them each a sit by her side at the edge of the party diner table.

Being seated without being questioned had its perks known to be Seer recognize among the supernatural as a cable guy Valarie sat next to the gypsy queen with Stevie sitting next to Valarie and Kris sat across from them sitting next to a delighted heavily plump pink grandmother charmed in a strawberry fleece cardigan who looks like she's capable of feeding a class full of children carrying a collection of teacups set on a push tray already serving Kris a brewed tea.

Stevie asks Esma, "I thought we were on patrol watch tonight?"

The gypsy queen answered Stevie, "why dear, monitoring is your field of work, didn't you know," she then winks.

I could get used to this occupation Stevie thought and with that, she smiled at Stevie and told him to enjoy the rest of the night and to keep observant.

Stevie being a Christian was asked countless times but found a way to excuse himself to not involve with reading into his future even though they all offered and insists but he still denied and thank them as they all respected his wishes. "I only speak accordingly in my prayers mostly in the mornings you know the word is the light of dawn is what I hear." Stevie implied almost by quoting the bible repeatedly where half the table took interest in him.

(SC Music/5)

The night was starting grand sharing each others company Stevie enjoyed the event so much he was even impressed with the strawberry tea lady's reading on people's next day meals but momentarily theatric music began to summon all lights magically dim down and faded leaving candle lights glimmering as an astonishing theatrical opening surprising their party guests beginning with a number song performance of raining topless men who wore straps in black leather gear came out of nowhere in sync to their routine wearing black latex skinny pants parading in black dazzled high heels. Some of the male performers wore black masks covering just their mouths looking athletic and very entertaining some carrying baton sticks looking like dominatrix policemen wearing aviators with police hats on.

Making a grand entrance there appeared walking on the runway was a ladyboy but rather of gender fluidity was an amateur queen strutting in silver black high heels walking between the performers that the topless males in their strutted stilettos made a path entrance to the diner party table synchronizing to a number of their dance performance as cross-dressers with the production on point performing an adult art entertainment with alluring routine. He had on a similar outfit as the dancers also wearing aviators but with a mixed clash of a tight latex diva wearing a head garment as a queen with an exotic pointy crown around his head with a hook around his neck wearing a high collar heavy dramatic cape.

Stevie was drawn took notice of how the host looks startling familiar but he couldn't put his finger on it.

The amateur queen had old money overseas inheritance everyone could tell and is known to be of a mischief raconteur more on the line of naughty behavior with flaming intendancies making derogatory jokes at every chance that can be made.

She was also very insufferable in vain and fidgety as she commanded her topless male escorts handing her a mirror, "she needs her fix, her fame, her power!"

In one hand holding up a face mirror knowingly mirrors surrounded him seeing a reflecting of his narcissism gloating with pride. He made his way performing around the table giving everyone their satisfaction he then ended up on top of the diner party table ending his performance to let everyone know his presence and announcing a title to call him, "the evil queen."

Nobody as a guest didn't know how to react to such a diner party just having a performance that was sensually unusual except for Stevie who was the only one that awkwardly applauds clapping out of innocent with enjoyment gestures and he quickly joined the other guests who dare not. After the entertainment performance, it left guests speechless with the European host the evil queen who then looks away from Stevie after giving him a smile who drew his attention throwing himself back from the table onto the enchanted peacock throne.

The evil queen would constantly forget her party being self-accolade with admiration towards her selfies on Instagram displaying accompanying conceited attributes of one's self reflect.

Not everyone could tell if the party host was just sobering up or just plain batty.

"N,' another land, far far away, many, many years ago," he quickly then chugged the whole bottle of deep eddy vodka straight that was left in an ice bucket brought beside his throne sitting at the diner party table and continued. "About the time of fairy tales of charming princes and princesses, fair maidens, romance, castles, magic, and witches." He spoke with his hands, as he would play up and down with his emotions, everyone then knew he was a hot mess.

"What shall the title be of this event huh? Soothsayer extravaganza party?"

Such a great performer he was but could show that his stature was very poor of a host that he just couldn't make up his mind.

"Like my mysterious great, great, great, great, grand auntie Grimhilde that bestowed me her inherit property and she had a luscious taste but don't get me wrong, I've learned she was a riot, a wicked queen icily beautiful woman with knowledge of dark magical powers. I suppose the one right out of the story was somewhat accurate of my auntie's vanity, ageless and cold as ice it was her sixteen year old stepdaughter that cost her life leaving her fortune and magic for fourteen generations straight to my blasted cuckoo family still idolizing those northern mountain Harz in Germany but gurl... I got out of there REAL quick, gotta love the taste of heirlooms there to die for!

He then was showing off his crown and scepter. "Sure did had to pry it out of my uncle's lawyers hands they don't call me evil queen for nothing but having the career of a star does pay its due. The evil queen was startled to laugh in mockery.

Stevie blurb out calling their host, "you mean the evil party queen?"

"And how about were you able to summon the high regards ultimatum?" The gypsy queen immediately asks with her fellow Seers besides her hoping everyone forgot Stevie's last silly remark but were also curious for the answer for their purpose of being here.

"Within my heirloom knowledge came to know about this exact sweet spot the ley lines of its power and found it to be whoever resides the tallest pinnacle rules over the land. One of the tallest buildings occupies this residential power to be rulers over this city Austin Texas and its land that commodities the sweet fairies and your dashing elves and its monsters etc. The highest pinnacle power was lost to mankind after the great fall to the last highest pinnacle a time when mortals walk beside the gods but no more with its throne and power to be shut down. But this queenie was able to discover its secret power location and it is well known to the Seers of this grand residential power beholds all Seers to treat seated power as if royalty that can't be rejected any invites can not be passed up it is summoned regards for it forces I'm mean commands you all to be here."

"If I may," the gypsy queen quickly meddled, "we serve upon the invitation, we use to be your servant till all that changed after the fall of the great tower Babel."

Unable to respond but it was Stevie that lost patience for a second time when recognized the same creepy wooden doll he ran into before at the Seer's command center in the library grounds on the stone table last time when the librarian was around. Stevie didn't want to make a scene trying to not take his eyes off the mysterious wooden doll knowingly he may lose sight of it again as he repeatedly tried to get Kris's attention across the diner party table where he was the only one that could notice the creepy doll that sat above the evil queen on top of the golden throne.

Then randomly someone down the table was quick to ask? "Who is he?"

Finally getting Kris's attention Stevie pointed out the direction of the creepy wooden doll but he was too late as it once again disappeared leaving Stevie to look like a fool.

The Evil queen smeared her latex body lunging on her golden throne with a bi-polar reaction responding abruptly throwing an empty glass bottle scattering it across the hall. "Never mind that, ah...! My guest what a pleasure to have you this evening." Everyone could see the host was hostilely ill or was just over too dramatic and began his course around the table.

"Let's began with doomsday, prophetess of Neseborow." The evil queen called out his attention towards the middle person of the diner table few seats away from Kris wearing middle age clothing with an undergarment monastery gown that covered her head with its straw scarf but was terrifying to look at as her face stayed hidden facing down with her straw dirty hair covering her face. "Foreknow," it said in a slithering voice as you can make out she had a large crooked nose and her back was bend with her legs twisted she held onto her walking stick.

Esma showing courage spoke out and whispered to Stevie and Valerie in alarm as she slowly reached to her Seer remote pulling it out from her Aeon gift brand bag left by her side, "That's Mother Shipton."

Stevie whispered to Valerie as she whispered to respond back.

"Who is that?"

"Her alone can separate power from the church for what she sees she foretells she the nemesis of Madame the Librarian arch enemies for centuries, she's an English witch that is the daughter of Agatha Southeil who conceived with the fiend itself and bared a child."

Stevie was horrid of the thought and realized, "You mean her father is the?"

The evil queen stole the show back broadcasting to boast out loud to his guest with unhinging unworthy remarks, "oh your always ahead of the game you bastard of a devil you!"

The English scary soothsayer being a unique witch stood up with a threat and slammed her wrinkly stone fist onto the table and callously turns on to attack Stevie with rants and curses as her straw mop hair flying everywhere she spoke and then spit to the floor.

"Curse you pet, Bane of Witches!"

She spat with her flying spit as she spoke with her voice so hoarse that it sounded like a hair in her throat but it was the reveal of her hag-face that was terrifying.

"All were stupefy by her grotesque charms the twisted witch screech from across the table with Esma standing her ground reaching over to guard Stevie with her arms as her rings began to glow with her eyes wide open with a warning.

"The befoul Librarian's pet doesn't scare me, gypsy, binding the Librarian's deeds we witches contribute to the dark will never pledge to your Librarian's mediocre pushovers nor her infirm books she will never reign to heed power of order as the grand hind witch!"

Esma the gypsy queen then caution the English's dark prophetess, "Hold your tongue witch you have no power here!"

The evil queen took amused at the entertaining threats thrown across the table acting like a gossipy vapid woman overly obsessed by her elegance still glaring into her hand mirror. "Eeeww looks like we have a catfight."

Mother Shipton was chanting in dark tongue opening her arms wide but it was the evil queen that mutually agreed to a cessation of fighting after Esma yelled, "Do not let her speak!"

"Now ladies, these are mutual grounds for the party event if intentions are elsewhere, you might as well bottled it all out and leave now!" The evil queen flashed her eyes after her sly remark popping with a dramatic slap of opening of her long silver metallic fan in her hand that came out of nowhere whipping it out covering half the evil queen's face flamboyantly waiting for the drama to be unstill lounging on her golden throne.

"Curses!" The English witch pointed her crooked skinny black molded finger at Stevie.

"The dark was lost," the witch crackled and began to sniff the air from Stevie's direction. "But now it's found you and don't be fooled... pet! The witch then spit at the ground few feet from Stevie casting a quickly curse, "love will be your greatest demise waltz's in the air masquerade slippers, this will be the fall of your last dance, death to your heart you will never find love from another soul!"

Kris being a male witch rather not be called warlock showed himself with his dark black witch eyes appearing coming up from behind Stevie to show his friend support and asks with a demanded tone, "Ursula Southeil what curse did you say?" Mother Shipton then sneered and hissed at Kris recognizing his dark score enclave loneliness.

As the English witch spoke her last words forcing her grotesque head from turning sideways cracking a wicked demonic smile before vanishing into thin air.

"That wasn't for you dearie."

The evil queen made a look from her peacock throne chair stirring from the recent accusations began to say and to Stevie picking her party from where they left off.

"What a party pooper, and from the looks of it someone is after you." The evil queen turns her attention towards the party guest changing the subject at a complete three-sixty. "Now it's so good to see the famous painters sight twins all the way from Poland, love your golden locks and what do we have here, greatness before us."

Esma mistakenly took the pleasure to speak first proudly getting up from her chair just then the oracle of Delphi interrupted who was blindfold and said, "It is pleasure to foresee for the stars are ripe for seeing."

Then the three frightening hideous slime grey-hair blind crone witches covered in languish old slime called the Graeae from the edge of time were reserved at the other edge of the long party table all three ignoring everyone and everything deeply with no interest just snickering and chattering among themselves taking turns sharing one eye ball to see and one tooth among the three to say each word after one another in a sentence, "anything for the bloodline of the blight vanity."

The Graeae crones ended up crackling paying attention to their knitting with the evil queen replying, "Yeah whatever that means…" The topless bare man chest evil queen rolled up to her black leg spandex up into the air while sitting clapping her silver heels laughing historically, "Lets party!!"

"For this room is full of foreseers you shouldn't have any problems knowing whose next performer!" Still lounge on his heirloom golden peacock throne he raised his silver heels up again and gave a kick into the air. "You know what's in stored for the winner." Topless men model escorts in high heels rolling out a chest full of treasure was one of her topless use ale boy servant slipping the evil queen a martini drink.

"Roll call…!" The evil queen yelled out in command and immediately her game was on, the first was the Oracle who proudly spoke out "oracular." Shouting out next was the guest that was the blind homeless bearded man who can be smelt like dirt and bread bakery was holding a cane like a wizard and said, "farseeing!"

Then a monk in Tibet clothing with a shaved head in sheer white garments bowed and spoke "clear-sighted." There was an Indian shaman that was next who got away smoking with his long pipe performing smoke magic in the building called out "Visionary." The three grey crones spoke at the same time crackling, "prophetic!"

Esma had her huge crystal ball laid out on the table knowing now why she carrying a large handbag but who knows what that bag can hold, "spiritualistic!"

"Forecast," said a sea hag with a net draping as a blouse wearing a sea pirate's hat having bluish-green color to her skin reading from fish bones and seashells.

Stevie gave a little giggle trying to be silent as he can be and nods at Kris getting his attention, "look it" pulling out the fortune cookie from his pocket waving it to his team.

Valarie nudges Stevie with her elbow signaling him to cut it out but It was already too late that he had gain attention again from the evil queen while the other fore sightseers were finishing on announcing their roll call.

Esma, however, had a distraught look on her face with a gaping mouth that couldn't be closed gazing madly into her magical crystal ball double glaring at Stevie eyeing him looking back and forth to the fortune cookie. Stevie took notice and replied with concern to Esma "What's wrong?"

The pleasant strawberry plump tea lady was the last to announce the roll call game who looks too busy taking pleasure in drinking her tea slurping "new age."

Then Stevie shortly laughs and sarcastically innocently says, "fortune cookie" waving the cookie again at his team and was trying to get his new friend Kris across the table to smile but it wasn't working.

The evil queen was quick to turn on Stevie and said "YOU!" "Will be the first to perform."

His team of Seers looks at Stevie shock and confused while everyone else was looking back at the Oracle to Stevie.

"Ahem, I'm sorry I didn't mean to interrupt it's just I've had this cookie" Stevie was quickly cut off by the evil queen, "fortune cookie is my last word. Everyone took the right turn including you. You did foresee this didn't you?"

The evil queen erupted with a burst of hysterical laughter with everyone else laughing.

All eyes were on Stevie, "Ok..." is all he could say.

Just that fast Stevie couldn't realize what he just got himself into seeing the blind bearded man that smelt like bread might have mental illness as he began rocking back and forth was excited about something that was coming while the three scary Graeaes paused from attention and were cackling among themselves whispering to each other in a dark trance.

"Isn't that right Oracle, didn't you see something?" The evil queen commanded rather than asking. The Oracle was silent for a moment and then answered, "I will reserve my gracious for a coming uncertain event."

Esma then yelled answered back at the Oracle "amateur!" The Oracle snaps back "fake!" Esma slammed her hands on the party diner table, "whom you calling fake where's your sun god, hasn't he been missing for over a millennia now!"

As for the evil queen, everyone could tell the unfortunate host was starting to get discouraged and bored of the drama taking another gulp from a bottle.

"There wasn't any enthusiasm into these readings, is that all you have to foresee... what about the last meals of your life instead, hmm? Suggested the evil queen and continued, "and I'm not talking about predictions of next week's weather, or reading's of your past pets. The best we could get so far is the oracle prophesying the doorman's two weeks schedule. Is magic dying? Is your magic deluded or tainted and what has happened to the destined future sights, is the old world of magic really fading…" Everyone was speechless like the truth was deaf fallen within their ears as the evil queen was moping on her golden throne slugging another drink down his throat.

"You boy, your turn!" Calling out Stevie once again not letting him off the hook.

The evil queen's topless male escorts showed Stevie the end of the party diner table stepping onto the top of the diner table was a made away long runway turning back to face the entire guests that started to whisper and some began to rocking back and forth with swaying, while others were starting to rejoicing, and a few were trembling. Whispers were going around, "it's the millennial…" While others were calling Stevie some word he had heard before that drew into his ear, "the Nexus." Over and over and the more steps Stevie took closer to the middle diner table a few more were saying "coming of the awakening."

The evil queen then encourages Stevie to come forth as he was escorted to walk over on top of the dinner party table.

"What's your name boy?" The evil queen said being the directive host of her event for once.

All tried to guess and began to wonder the evil queen's question but Stevie always wanted to be called a certain name and said proudly, "They call me Starman."

The evil queen rebutted her laughs as Kris tighten his lips closing his eyes looking downward while Valarie took her right palm to her forehead not afraid to show the shame.

"Well then Starman, do you have a hidden talent we can sense it?" The evil queen said very sincerely in her demanding's couldn't tell if she was condescending pulling Stevie's strings.

Stevie walking on top towards the middle of the diner party table pulling out the fortune cookie from the wrapper while the closer Stevie approach the peacock throne at the other end things started to go berserk.

After that, a lot couldn't be explained with the bearded blind man prophesying out of control in tongue having a bright light aura shinning out of his eyes.

There was also an American clairvoyant in a gentleman's suit carrying a briefcase with a company tag logo that said Cayce holistic medicine, who was already entering a state of a hypnotic trance.

At the diner table, there was also a presage jungle chieftain in the arts and started to mimic the spirits with a shaman from the deserts that praising with his hands upwards towards the sky with electrified fingertips studying the astrology skies. While the blonde twins from Poland were storming up a magnificent portrait painting over and over of shapes, objects, and stars. Even the white witch scryer with her crystals went haywire but what stood out the most was the Oracle being lifted up from the ground floating like she was underwater with smoke funneling around her.

All were saying including Esma with her hands upon her shiny globe that began to glow in a trance, "All will be revealed all gates will be open."

Then everyone stops and took a seat with the entire guests paused in an awkward seated position like time had stopped itself starring ajar at Stevie standing above on top of the diner table as if they were all puppets.

Stevie found himself satirically standing on top of the diner party table of the runway with the fortune cookie crack in his hand. "Go ahead read it!" The evil queen said waiting impatiently fanning dramatically who parades with a metallic fan.

Stevie began to read his fortune, "You are kind-hearted by nature."

Then all at once surprisingly the entire foreseer's guest party all stood up together echoing and spoke at the same time while they were blazing lights out of their eyes and mouths while others were glowing.

PROPHECIES
Spoken by all
"SEASONS OF THE WITCH CRONE HAS COMES TO AN END
"One last time" (chorus)
STARS WILL ALIGN BY RUIN'S OF THE WITCHES BANE
"One last time"
THE ANCIENT ONES WILL AWAKENING REVENGE THE OLD ONES
SHALL WALK AGAIN ONCE MORE CHALLENGE THE TWILIGHT STARS
"One last time"
UNLEASHING THE DAMNS THROUGH THE CURSES MIRRORS
"One last time"
HAND OF GOD WILL HOLD THE MOONFLOWER TILL IT BLOOMS HIGH
BLEED RED IN THE SKIES
"One last time"
AFTER FIRE AND DARKNESS OVER THE RAINBOW THE WICKED CRIES
"One last time"
NIGHT AND DAY DARK TO LIGHT
A MILLENNIAL WILL HEED
THE COMING OF AWAKENING."

After the epic unexpected prophecies ended the evil queen was very amused and entertained at the mockery of her guest laughing her head off, frocking with her silver large fan of hers. "YES! YES!" Catching her breath from still laughing while the other guests were all caught off guard they were all stunned from being mesmerized as others were crying.

"Did you feel that I haven't felt that power in ages!" The Oracle asks the Shaman who was on his knees praying to the ground shaking.

Esma was misplace pretending she wasn't lost like she just woke up from being unconscious gathering her crystal ball and personal things quickly into her Aeon brand bag confused and was startled to see Stevie on the party diner table helping him get off while the twins were crying over their masterpiece viewing their splendid art that looks like the cosmos laid over the table.

"Must've been some party?" Esma mustered to say with Stevie helping her walk out while his friends ran up to check on him, "I'm fine but is everyone ok?"

Esma sharply replied, "don't you worry about the others you gave all of us a chance to remember what power felt like. The majority of the people in this room have lost their spunk and you return it back to them!"

The pleasantly strawberry plump charm tea lady spoke out first at Stevie as they were all taking their exit, "Starman, who are you, Millennial?"

Esma gypsy queen did shot back clapping her hands together in glee making her heavy jewelry jingle and was just about to say something but was cut off shortly.

"The Nexus is what you are!"

Abrupt the Oracle causing the gypsy queen Esma to sigh, not ever catching a break giving the Oracle go to hell look missing again her chance to say her premonition.

"You will bring peril and destruction… you will be the ill of this… WORLD!" After that, the Oracle went nuts reciting the prophecy causing a fiasco while the gypsy queen looks away settling in changing her sour attitude to slyly ignoring the outburst from the oracle's theomancy assertion.

The Evil queen twinkled her fingers intensely alerting her male dancer's servants to escort the Oracle out as she was still rumbling on and on quoting, "the coming of the awakening it's the Nexus I saw it!"

Still pointing at Stevie shouting as she was being dragged away escorted out of the party event. "Know what's next? The Millennial who will lead the coming of the awakening?"

Valarie was fasten to the scene and assured Stevie they were high on magic and would forget the absurd nonsense the very next day.

"I'm sorry I'm not feeling too well," Stevie said holding his stomach from slightly fainting. The evil queen was self-centered playing with her large fan and continued to look at her personal hand mirror, "what's the rush love, or should I say the witches bane!"

Valarie shouted out, "that's enough!"

The evil queen was very brash and nagged on Stevie parading with her fan, "I see everyone's frost mark but yours Seer, where is it?"

The evil queen then pretends to reach over for Stevie's crouch, "is yours down under?"

Stevie replied politely quickly pushing away the loudly extroverted evil queen, "May I go ahead excuse myself."

Valarie dismisses Stevie threatening the evil queen giving her a final nasty look that could kill.

Everyone was leaving by then some had left the party leaving the evil queen laughing historically maddeningly with booze and her metallic large silver fan.

"I didn't think Seers were real till now I had to see it for myself wasting my time inviting that miserable old hag when it should have been the Librarian that should have graced her presences but I've already got everything I need to see and I saw nothing impressive!" Snapping her silver fan pouting her lips like a goldfish over her mirror reflection.

Valarie and Kris's help escorted poor Esma out who was feeling tired and foggy from the after effect but the gypsy queen managed to get her last say that boost her spirit before she exited laughed her way out, "mirror mirror on the wall."

"We all carry beauty marks use them!" The evil queen yelled anticipating to any audience wasting no time gently reaching over to catch Kris's face with her forefingers brushing lightly over his brow moon scar mark on his left eye as Kris exited out escorting the gypsy queen as she was possible laying curses in her gypsy language laughed all the way out.

The evil queen began to drivel carelessly shading unnecessary observation spilling the truth unapologetic about Valerie knowingly it would break Stevie's heart. "Such sweet aroma I smell around you boy, HA! She doesn't care who you are and love will be a waste of your time sweet boy."

Valerie turns to look straight forward to the exit and warned the boys, "ignore it, that witch is a nobody."

Before they could leave the evil queen shouted out from across the palace hall, "You're nothing impressive you know you Seers are all just overrated!

Valarie was so contempt she never did look back ignoring all the maligning nonsense from the dramatic evil queen that lounge back on her golden throne as Valerie kept marching forward with Kris exiting the palace hall.

"Ah, a sorceress not a witch!"

Valarie paused for a split second and refuses to acknowledge the evil queen and kept moving forward.

While the evil queen intentionally getting on everyone's nerves lost all her guests and continued to laugh historically, "And what kind of Seer is that? Hahaha! Oh, come on lets cheers to that and call this the Millennial Party!!!!!"

12

House call

IT WAS ALMOST PAST TWO in the afternoon Stevie couldn't tell if he was just excited to be on a house call or could it be all three are hanging out with Charlie today with Kris and Valerie tagging along while Ashley is away at her important house call involving with the church. Stevie always knew Ashley was religious but never knew to a degree where it involves her work so much with the church.

They hung out around the castle hill neighborhood after a stroll check just the west side of downtown a few blocks from the capital meeting up at a plaza with various stores.

"Have you thought any much of the millennial prophesy?"

His friends ask Stevie dwindling on the question it was evident it had been on their minds.

"All I got from it was whispers and mutters but I do remember the part about darkness turns to light." Stevie didn't bother to linger on the question but mentions how crazy attending such parties gives him more room to grow, learning to adapt that he'd never forget.

Turns out Charlie was asked a favor back when they were at the greenbelt by the boulders to the entrance of Seelie fairy court there he was assigned and approved by the Librarian to save a troublesome Fae and investigate furthermore before from being discovered to human contact.

It shows that Faes and elves do comply under circumstances with the human race submit to Seers under conditions that support any impartiality for the living."

Charlie continues to let them on what trouble-call case that they are about to get themselves into.

"Supposedly there's a suspicious white witch rather a hippie witch well known and liked in these local areas, Ms. Kat running a business for a couple of years started out in her hippie van well known for her crystal works with retailers of rocks and healing stones that there are claims of her recent retailer of rocks and healing stones that there are claims of her an allegation of a criminal act of selling and distributing illegal substance that was reported and witness anonymously just a few days ago.

Charlie already clarifying with just a few details laying out the plan before strolling into the store about what they are there to do.

Storming into the store with their pink slip citations in their hands except for Charlie that was less aggressive with a high positive attitude wearing his sunshades over his face graciously introduce himself revealing his mass arms famously tattooed short sleeves rolled up showing his Seer identification badge to the hippie witch stating his number rights tucking it back into his back wallet pocket like a recruiter agent hidden in disguise just asking moral questions about her business and day all while he was looking around the store with his comrades Kris exchange serious looks at Valerie and his team leader not to leave Stevie out of the loop Charlie asking Kris by picking up a batch of white wildflowers for sale studying the silver-blue hair witch. "Ms. Kat, it's deadly to sell hemlock best known as the plant that ended the life of Socrates, needs no other introduction."

The nice hippie lady didn't retaliate describing the next item they found was prohibited noticing the witch has empty eyes with blue opaque color the store clerk in her late sixties was out of character like a zombie possess under a spell fixed with a smile.

Pulling out a couple of old receipts from a basket nearby the cash register Valerie found the one that matters and handed it over to Charlie.

"Now Katherine it's to our recollection you sold a dangerous item a storm glass to a client along with silver oxide and dragon scales?" Charlie talks to her and from the sound of it he knows her, while picking up a dark jet blue citrine crystal from a shelf with other crystal gems and next to a basket collection of healing crystals, rocks, and stones. With the blue citrine in his palm hands and the white hemlocks in the other hand suggesting to his store owner friend, "Do you know what ingredients those items can create?"

The oddly hippie witch again wasn't phased adjoin on her face was the same befuddled look starring at Charlie with high spirits.

"A perfect storm literally and that could land you with a big pick slip that may lose rights to sell magical merchandise."

Kris alerted Charlie finding a back passageway leading to a room with Valerie examining the store witch disclosing with Charlie as she snaps her fingers in front of the innocent lady's face, "this lady is not herself."

Charlie already had the answer for her, "Troll magic, dark fairy stuff makes its victim like a comatose state a sleepwalking slave more like."

Charlie took attention to the dragging sleep store clerk who was spent, "we've been alerted by a few witnesses of suspicious activity coming in and out from your store and we like to know what's going on?"

Passed out onto Charlie's arms he easily caught the clerk lady after using his Seer remote to release few codes relieving her from the troll dark spell laying her onto the floor sleeping behind the sales counter Charlie calling Nerd in for backup with the seer medic crew. "She'll be ok here, after that kind spell that wears out makes you sleep like a baby and she won't remember a thing."

"Wait a second I know that voice!" Charlie said taking charge leading his Seer team on entering the back building byre walking slowly with remote in hand ready located behind at the back of the store that connected to the passageway was laughing and tittering in the corners could be heard from the gruagach taking bets with other fairy minions doing illegal gambling setting up backdoor fights among Faes.

"There's a few of them mostly they're benign, but there's one odd creature I don't know yet about." Indeed there was a hidden oddly creature wearing overly size hobo clothes with a fedora too large for its head covering its face hidden well from escaping eyes.

Showing his crew through the small crack windows and we have them surrounded with the back door being chained up with a lock. Causing such a nuisance back there never against the code conduct of the supernatural interfering with mortal affairs is forbidden but this illegal fighting activity going on is unacceptable!"

Charlie weighs in from peeking through the entrance back door keeping quiet as possible hidden behind the other side of the store backroom doorway letting his team know just so little they'll figure out the rest once raid the area following Charlie's command in their cable guy gear uniform with remote stun mode set in ready.

Fachans are the lesser fairies place in the ring to fight among each other one was just a giant eyeball on its face with petite wings barely afloat are creatures that appeared so monstrously hideous that the mere sight of them could allegedly stop a man's heart or be seen in one's nightmare. The other Fachans fighter is a head-to-toe literally just a toe in chain gear possessed in a singular body part for just a toe, which was placed in a ring centerline beneath their bodies.

Unlike other fairies, the Fachans could not evaluate a complete self-thought and so resented those who could. Prone to violence and highly territorial, they also always carried a weapon or chain that they used against people who dared to trespass into their lands. This is not a fairy character you could show to your kids at night.

"It's the Gruagach."

Beyond this diversion, the gruagach seemed to have been generally harmless Charlie quickly explains before charging in, "He sometimes walked along the side of people disguise as humans but are never known to speak in public. Usually, naughty fairies uses glamor to look beautiful when it's truly an ugly creature. Once a human sees the fairy's ugliness, he or she can never 'unseen' it as anything other than ugly. In other words, once you know the fairy is bad and ugly, it can never use glamor against you again."

The gruagach is a longhaired one a brownie to be exact who haunted farms and byres and was never seen its true face except for its shadow on the wall as it flitted about. A well-dressed fairy exposed with a face of a pig with tusk hiding its sturdy snout under its long dirty yellow hair, in the attire of a gentleman of a bygone period. He has a *slatag*, a little switch in his hand. This *gruagach* was attentive to his fachans minions commanding a dozen to its demands smoking a cigar acting like a mob-boss in front of his spectators accommodating two grundels, a large tortoise wearing a sleeping cap, and a hare presence in on the illegal betting tossing American cash and unfamiliar gold coins with ruby jewels stash over their cruel game across the fighting ring.

With a big smile on his face staying low Charlie gave out a little whisper letting in on a rumor to his friends trying not to be heard, "spsss… so I hear the turtle's name is Cururipur!" No one took it that seriously at the time except for Charlie who was kiddy over the top excited about the bust that's about to proceed or was it the walking talking turtle but these guys were bad news.

They still waited for Charlie's command he alone only knew what the outcomes are with his experience over the years in the supernatural dealing with Faes and monsters is his expertise he then signals a thumb up.

"Leave the big one to me." Charlie said letting everyone know with Valerie asking suddenly for rectification, "How do you know which one is the big one?"

Stevie had his Aeon headphone on wearing them over his head during his trouble-call mission and it being magical began to play a classical overture piece "ride of the Valkyries" on its playlist going off with loud surrounding audio the whole place was charmed by music like in an amphitheater was abroad.

It was the music that made the bigger fairies twitch revealing their abnormal disfigure size as the troll keep stretching taking hiding in a trench coat with a hat disguising itself as a homeless person in tight hobo clothes was having difficulty trying to coup itself together restraining to stay in human form with the music confiding the fairies to act into their true natural form.

Riled up by the surprise and the music quickly losing control of its sensibility and nobility the gruagach grew vastly six times its size into a hulking monster charging with rage at Charlie it was a monstrous boar beast its head scraping the ceiling with its slatag stick turning into a giant club.

Stevie then took Valerie's reputable question and made it a decisive answer while pointing at the giant beast, "I think that one is the big one?"

Charlie was quick, being a southern boy using his tattoo rope spell wrap around his arm he had some experience with roping lessons pulled out of nowhere having his left arm tattooed being one of his power quirks manage to have a rope in hand fastening down wrestling with the beast tied with a right, right, left one hand hooking the rope in the air tying a knot around the monster's broad neck testing each others strength.

Valerie scoops up half a dozen of fairies already in her cable guy bag by her hip with the turtle in her arms as she yelled out, "that troll is trying to escape the back door!"

Charlie and Valerie have left to restraint the fairies while Stevie and Kris went after the escape troll breaking the chain locks on the door.

"I and Valerie will stay here to collect the other fairies till help arrives so follow the troll and find out where it leads then report back to us and that's no if's and but's," Charlie said before the boys scuffle out the back door.

Charlie was impressive back there able to hold down a mortar monster on his own with a collective power he could summon almost anything out of thin air from his artistry body suit of tattoos of his liking. Stevie wonders if one day he too can be just a quick and powerful Charlie was.

"Changelings," Kris said jogging side by side with Stevie following the lost heed trail of the troll as they lost sight of it.

"I didn't know this before we started researching this topic, but changelings are most likely to be trolls." Kris said and continued, "Trolls like how humans coddled their children, so a troll would take a human child and replace it as a baby troll."

Save by their push luck Kris nudged at Stevie to look there in the corner bush hidden was the little gingerbread man alerting the boys to follow as it began to run down from the streets leading them onto a trail. "Look it there, it seems this little cookie wants to be caught?" Stevie told Kris as they both got the same idea.

"This cookie will lead us in the right direction to where we need to go, we can't afford to lose it sight," Kris said that started to run behind following the gingerbread man.

Stevie had to stretch the troll topic as they ran together, "So trolls are fairies and this one was the size of a small kid didn't turn out to be good looking, but it would be strong and protective of its home and community!"

Kris almost had every answer to every logic of the supernatural social living in today's era, "it merely common every changeling troll ends up in the streets living like a bum under a bridge, its what they prefer left alone but it's those that possess dark magic are the problem."

So the whole time the crystal hippie witch who was possessed by troll magic hosting an illegal gamble against her will to concierge for trolls and fairies consorting with other mystical creatures while running a business selling illegal magic dangerous property substance patrol to keep from harm is one of the standard professions of a Seer.

It was explained and mapped out in their Seer pocket booklet the supernatural territory of Austin Texas. The city is a map like an oval from east to west is Mopac Expy and I-35, north to south is 183 and 360 to Ben White. Seer's library headquarters is located above the northwest of the map also elaborating north of Austin shows a bridge of monsters. A highway bridge that holds a concealed lair of confinement monsters located north of 183 with heavy commercialization concrete corridor underneath its highway. It describes that the bridge of monsters is an elevated structure freeway with the main lanes positioned over the service roads with visually pleasing support beams and the roadway structure is a prime segmental structure built to stockade colossus creatures. Stevie always wonders how the monster bridge was possible or knowing the fact that monsters are stirring underneath a commercial road.

The Elves territory and their hidden realm are located making up two major districts neighborhoods in Austin, which are Clarksville Historic District and the Old West Austin neighborhood. The Elevens quarters are located in the castle hills neighborhood and their domain consists west of downtown Austin near Lady Bird Lake and mostly dwell by shoal creek past 13th street north to 35th Street.

South Austin remains to the Fae folks like Zilker Park and mainly the royal fairies are habited in Greenbelt Park.

Kris mentions to Stevie it's never been heard or seen an actual full-size troll sighting since over hundreds of years ago especially here in elves domains knowing elves despise humans but they hate Trolls.

They were lead following the gingerbread man to a park along the east banks of the shoal creek trail a popular area there were a few pro artistic athletes covered in skate gear that was on extreme bikes and skateboards, for one, in particular, stood out graced in rollerblades bouncing with flips off the rails and jumping impossible tricks off park ramps.

It was very entertaining as if the skaters were part of some talent show drawing a crowd among them suddenly they stop when they notice a crowd and only one or two were just left biking while the other just skateboarding off ramps as normal. Just then Stevie realized he recognizes one of the eyes back at Green Belt when the search party found him after the Baba Yaga witch incident remembering the mystery anonymous tailor in green mercenary attire a pale creature with metallic green eyes.

Kris was also drawn to the unnatural athleticism as they watched across the street from the trail of shoal creek, "well that's something you don't see every day."

Stevie was silent as he stared at another odd stranger among the athelic skaters cloaked was a stout giant figure maybe a bodyguard or monster in hiding Stevie thought, standing behind comparison to the professional star skater on the rollerblades with the metallic green pale eyes.

The boys also notice the other skaters have pale skin with pale eyes that glowed every time once under a shadow some with blue some bright green that stood out as their faces were covered with skate gear.

Stevie began to ask Kris, "You don't see that, it's huge standing behind that skater." Kris replied, "What are you talking about I don't see anything?" Stevie began to answer, "It's huge like a hooded warrior with tree branches sprouting out of its head with green skin and dark brown bark for shielding as clothing it has giant branch antlers piercing out on top of its guard helmet with its face hidden."

The skater with roller blades notices that Stevie could see their giant bodyguard and immediately took a whisper to his other skater companions where they paused to glace at Stevie and Kris.

Stevie saw the keen skaters as they notice Stevie's attention, drawing the skaters to close in on them, "Looks like we better get going."

Kris responds, "that sounds like a good idea."

Momentarily the boys were ambushed like ninjas skilled appearing suddenly out of nowhere surrounded and then bombarded with the young star skater removing its face gear on it's rollerblades beginning to ask questions starring directly at Stevie. "Who are you?"

Kris tried to speak but was shut down by other ongoing unrefined questions of their rollerblade star leader being ignored giving Stevie full attention instead with full direct eye contact. "What commands order do you have here? Who is your league? Have we not met? Ye have a purpose?" Demanded the elf on roller blades that was the only one in his group revealing his face that spoke.

The elf was very intimidating having eerie eyes with blue-green colors, pale skin, high cheekbones standing out complex with smooth olive skin revealing pointed elf ears.

Stevie was still transfixed at the stout giant tree figure behind the elf skater with one of its other companions whispering to the star elf.

The elf then asks, "Seers before my courtship?"

Kris grasping his tool remote and murmured to Stevie, "wood elves."

Unlike Kris, Stevie was very fond of the magical stronghold company they were confronted and his first reaction was sticking his right hand out for a friendly introduction with a comical twist. "I'm Stevie and that's Kris, now you wouldn't be like your cousin Fairy Trixs running around opening bars now would ya?"

The elf was rudely stone cold with no reaction but just a curious look on its face with his hands behind his back studying Stevie's hand and then began to laugh.

Kris interrupted the elves' ridicule games cutting to the chase pulling his tool remote in his right hand for the elves to see. "Yea and you guys better back off."

The elf chuckled and replied, "Easy stain mortal, our interest is no quarrel with you but lies upon your friend here who can see Tukus."

Kris wasn't just only outraged but was confused at the reaction between the elf and Stevie who kept starring behind the star elf at nothing who Kris could not see Tukus. "Only high royalty blood can see Tukus, my royal servant he is one of the few that is last of his kind." The star elf said studying Stevie squinting his glowing light washout eyes.

Stevie was quick to reply in his defense but it was Kris that alerted Stevie of the gingerbread man waving them down hidden among the bushes by the trail pasture, "I'm a nobody, but you, however, are in the limelight, you know instead of lemons you're just like lime and you know what to do with the rest." The elves were a briefly silent stirred in a confusion of the comeback and began to laugh with sheer mockery.

"They obviously don't drink limeade." Stevie motion Kris forward continuing towards the little gingerbread man heading south of shoal creek trail showing how he avoids sour occasions.

"If you excuse us we have house call matters at hand," Kris replies. The elves continued to laugh and ridicule pointing at their backs while the boys were walking away with the skater elf yelling back, "house call is what you call troll hunting, don't go any further than West Sixth Street Bridge if its Trolls you want."

The star elf on his rollerblades had his arms crossed watching them leave as they disappeared while the elf has a sly smirk on his face.

"I CAN'T STAND ELVES!" Kris continued. "So arrogant and egotistic assuming to be above everyone or everything, just because they're wooden elves one of the first and oldest clans since the beginning could have still survived all this time."

Stevie responds with such interest he was pleased to have met an elf. "Wooden Elves are fascinating people aren't they?"

Kris's sarcasm would reminisce Stevie's commentary. "Never conceited," Kris said jokingly rolling his eyes.

Stevie began to read off elves bio from the Seer's booklet, "Athletic and sharp with agility skills having keen balance and reflexes including their strength, theres' a list of magnitude powers the elves possess is phenomenal."

Kris replies, "More like high and mighty la-de-da think they know it all."

Stevie finishes up reading on elves from his guide booklet, "elves are highly potential in skills of combat and controlling certain abilities through will and that too many others considered it magic. Elves of all races have special abilities with some being more powerful than others (Especially between High Elves and Half-Breeds.)"

Stevie continued, "The elf on rollerblades must be royal having an invisible giant as a bodyguard, how else would he have known about our house call?" Kris then replies,

"I don't know how it is that you were able to see the giant but we better get on that trail before we lose the gingerbread man?"

Suddenly Stevie and Kris were interrupted by a commotion of joggers and a biker down along the path on shoal creek trail. A jogging couple was helping a biker get up while another jogger who was startled as well gets up and exclaims, "What was that a running cookie?"

The other joggers said, "It looks like a gingerbread man came to life running after a homeless person but it ran through here and the homeless person looks like a bear dog in clothing or looks like some sort of wild animal, it was huge and fast all covered in dried mud running that way towards under that bridge!"

Around the corner along the creek was another witness, the petrified victim pointed towards under a bridge, Kris ran towards after the homeless person while Stevie made advances to make sure everyone was ok ensuring with the Seers Seers protocol using his remote erasure to erase their sudden memory.

Stevie meets up with Kris searching for clues studying tracks of cookie crumbs leading to a brick stonewall under a bridge called the West Sixth Street Bridge as the elf said.

"It was just here, I saw it and then it disappeared," Kris said.

Then Stevie asked Kris, " well what did it look like?" Kris was focused on his common spells tracing entrance to unlock trap hidden passage doors by a spell taught by his mother that use to be a witch dabbled in the dark arts with his eyes closed facing the stonewall trying to stay focus and then he replies to Stevie. "It looks like someone who sleeps under a bridge."

Stevie smiles scratch his head confused with mixed emotions still reading through the Seer's booklet knowing they have been on this path before with exploring by themselves that would almost cost their lives.

"Well I've should have known that since it is told in tales of trolls habitat under bridges in all but shouldn't we be notifying Charlie since you know this is a level 3 clearance situation and he did say report back."

Momentarily a hidden rectangular stone rock perch out in the open on the flat brick stonewall surface under the bridge surprising Stevie as he watched behind Kris who kept his eyes closed finishing his is locator entrance spell. "You found a door?"

Kris push into the stone rock opening a dark small way into the wall.

Quietly Stevie nervously follows Kris's lead heeding no danger warning signs from his hand with supernatural senses he was lost in excitement forgetting the repetitive scenario encountering last time into the supernatural alone with Kris didn't turn too pleasant for the boys.

Walking into a vast dark tunnel that quickly curved into a chamber room shape like a dome covered in dirt strewn with mud and gunk mold conquering ancient items in disguise to hide a hidden old lost civilization underneath the ground.

"Look here, these were the halls of the dwarves extinct for over a millennium!" Kris spoke holding his black lighter that magically lit up the whole chamber studying hidden artifacts, broken statues, and lost painting from the old stone walls and pillars.

"It's ironic all this is under a bridge huh?" Kris says as he turns to Stevie exchanging the same thoughts when they both grinned at each other and said, "treasure!"

"Just so we know what we're up against?" Stevie began to read straight out from the Seer's pocket booklet. "Trolls are a level 3 monsters that can create realms portals under mountain and bridges, creatures of the Earth only meant to be dealt with squadron leaders who are trained with high-level compliance of magic and brute physical attacks. Caution trolls are physically dangerous and extremely temperament." Stevie looks at Kris waiting for a reaction and paused to go any further to finish reading up on the trolls. Most Troll magic derives much of its power from the Earth, its magic is very powerful, can use magic instinctively without incantations and their power is terrible and destructive. Troll magic is decisively more potent than the magic that comes from the Old Religion used by the average sorcerer. Trolls are very resistant to other creatures' magic along allies with the dragons that dwell under mountains in empty vast caves and chambers inhabiting mostly deep into its archenemies lost abandoned sanctuaries of the dwarfs.

Kris replies, "and?"

It didn't surprise Stevie knowing Kris feeling no remorse for the threats that lie before them.

"Right…." Stevie said turning to the opposite direction where they came from realizing the entrance is gone and disappeared. They soon found themselves stuck with chains dangling and decorated hanging from the ceiling throughout the dungeon is a trap that magically makes their entrance disappears with no tunnels leading to a round throne chamber room with multiple black chains hanging from above but one particular chain was noticeable it being pure silver was dangling in the middle of the muddy space and walls covered in black mud gunk.

"This is a troll lair that use to be some type of an abandoned dungeon dwarf throne," Kris mentions noticing running water with rustic old ore chute leading into other dark deep vast holes from the ground explaining the multiple tunnels use to be dwarves mining.

A little too late but now putting on his left hand glove from his pockets Stevie's left-hand was giving off warning signs as it went cold. "Be ready for anything?" Stevie told Kris walking behind him trying to see in the dark through Kris's black Aeon lighter.

They both had their tool remotes at hand ready in stun mode staying quiet as ever with Kris's lighter aeon weapon in the other hand lighting the room with his flame. Kris was able to lite up wall torches that haven't been touch by fire over millennia Kris mentions as they found a dark chamber. Stevie was still clueless about how his Aeon white headphones would work or its power still strap over his head naïve about his quirk power. Stevie then pointed out to a dark corner, "What's that over there?"

Squatting hunch over consuming with crunch sounds gobbling to scarf down the gingerbread man with its back towards the boys was a homeless person dress in large poor garments wearing a trench coat looking quite little big out of portion for an average person from far away.

They were in the middle of an underground dirt ditch hole so vast it was a mud chamber an eerie lost throne room could be made out in the massive mud hole with a little steep hill sprang in the middle with the homeless person standing there with its back towards them guarding over the small steep hill.

The closer they got to it with Kris's firelight the appearance of the homeless person was changing and for comfort, Stevie place on his Aeon beats headphones over his head and ears. Standing right before them over the little hill ditch the homeless person turns around was changeling into a little, fat, then big, short, skinny tall man with a disfigured huge nose and gawk deep baggy eyes. "What you lads doing down here…" it said with an intense accent.

Kris looks at Stevie in awe shock and was clueless to speak.

"Troll hunting sir!" Stevie replied quickly and smiled nervously at the odd sickly old man. The tiny, tall, fat, short little homeless old man began to sniff the air and inhaled a deep breath smiling back with rotten odd distorted teeth having visible cavity holes, "No trolls here lad…" it extended its long disproportionate arms revealing its hands as it deformed into huge claw troll hands.

Stevie still wearing the beat headphones looks at Kris noticing Kris starring back and forth at Stevie and the Troll. "You can understand it?" Kris asks exclaiming at Stevie looking confused at what he just witness.

"WHAT?" Stevie impatiently asks Kris clueless about his question.

Kris then tells Stevie both starring at the manifesting changeling troll, "It spoke to you, the troll, and you talk to it?" Stevie then replies asking the question keeping his eyes on the troll gearing their tool remotes in stun mode ready, "what do you mean?"

Then suddenly the man- troll attack and jump from the hill ditch at Stevie as the Seers both stunned the homeless man-toll with their tool remotes and it began to morph fully transformed into a troll before them.

The troll was a huge hairy beast with rough skin that looked human-like with a big stretch nose having rotten huge teeth peering through under his long nose and spoke in troll dark tongue with Kris being baffled pointing out that Stevie is communicating with the troll. "What do you mean your king?" Stevie responds to the troll aiming his remote ready for another stun if needed.

Kris exclaimed at Stevie while the troll was speaking gibberish "what did the ugly troll say, what did it say?" Meanwhile, the mud floor was shifting like quicksand, "It said, they know what we are and we were sent to go after their jewel, to kill the king of the mountain their Jontar."

After the Troll yelled out and howl, three more earth trolls appeared growing from the ground and rock walls having multiple heads and hideous features. Stevie sighed, "great," and Kris replies, "They're even uglier!".

Mud earth trolls manipulating the mud surrounded the boys, as it magically appeared forming mud-balls in their deformed hands ready to throw at their enemies. It turned into an aim-dodging war between trolls mudslinging to exchanging the cable guy's stunning rays with their remotes.

The boys were lucky to get two trolls stunned as they fell to the floor. "They're protecting their jewel," Kris yells out covering behind a stone dirt pillar to Stevie who was hiding behind a small boulder. Stevie yells back crouching taking cover, "I think they're guarding what's behind the homeless troll hovering over something on that short hill in that middle ditch."

With guts and glory Kris took charge running at the troll with his magic black lighter he was able to control pyro magic an Aeon gift weapon from the ancient one Prometheus exhausting fire flames circling the one last troll that was protecting its treasure. With remotes still geared in their hand, Kris made their way into the ring of fire with Stevie behind him. Stunning the homeless troll falling backward and the boys walk over to the small steep dry dirt hill in middle round mud-terrain ditch and there on the mud ground was an awkward display of a yellow flower.

"What!" Kris proclaimed at ready with his remote.

A sudden deep hum was heard with Kris's magic fire circle was weakening dying down arose from the mud grounds like quicksand appearing dozens of earth trolls surrounding their intruders.

"They're troll magic is strong." The faces of the trolls were gaunt of shock every time the boys got close to the yellow flower. "Wait notice the trolls aren't attacking," showing Kris threatening to step over the yellow weed plant but without any damage, the trolls froze petrified eyeing their precious yellow dandelion.

"Wait look, they're so cautious of this yellow flower this is their jewel," Stevie announced.

In the spare moment, Kris felt liberated scorn for revenge he brings his lit black lighter to the flower warning the trolls. "Or maybe we should torch this weed," Kris equipped his black lighter.

An earth troll with rough rock hands was quick enough to snatch Kris's wrist before commanding his black lighter to sprout forth its fire surprising the boys coming from the ground emerging of mud liquid taking its shape grasping grasping onto the boys and was immediately jumped by surrounding trolls.

"Well, that didn't go as planned?" Stevie exhorted as being rough handled by two short mud earth trolls after able to zap two more before being confiscated of their tool remotes.

Before Kris could get a chance to blast away with his pyro skills the troll's earth magic overcame their subordination, as the troll's mud from the ground floor was magically alive restraining the boys to hold still.

With the Seers captured and surrounded by dozens of earth trolls that were discussing and arguing among themselves all while Stevie tried to interpret being lock-in mud confused about how he could understand Troll tongue.

"What!? Oh, my glob, were not here to slay your king and you don't need to eat us." Stevie yelled at the mud trolls troublesome to understanding the multiple dispute troll conversations that were displayed before him earth fairies are a very foul disregard for one another and literally trolling each other with no respect of their kind arguing how to cook their captured diner.

"It was a trapped all along, this is how they do it!" Kris realizes they missed evident clues these were cannibal trolls seeing bones and skulls hidden among the mud corners from the troll's victims as they were stuck and trap in these dark troll chambers.

Some of the trolls began to hum in a synchronize tune, "I can't get my hands free!" Kris struggled to notice there was no way out as their bodies were slowly sinking into the mud in the ground. A short panic struck Stevie deep within his feelings and immediately in return with a short warmth of rush washed over within his body tingling and then he smiled.

One of the trolls yelled and condemned that Stevie was for diner wondering what Seers taste like laughing among each other but it was Stevie who laughed and said to them, "oh you know us Seer's we're just full of Trixs."

Right before the trolls voluntarily chose to attack and shred them up to pieces on the spot a familiar sparkling golden light leaving a trail of glistening sparkles appeared like a ball of sunshine zipping around from the dark corners of the mud chamber then quickly zapping through and around the mud trolls in circles.

The trolls were very disdain towards the flashy tiny golden ball of light hollering and using their stone huge clubs as weapons swinging into the air missing the fiery ball knocking each other out cold. Before one of the trolls could clobber Stevie's head with a rock club the golden fiery ball sparkled and flashed into sunlight radiating the whole chamber like sunshine relieving the boys free as the trolls and mud were turned into brimstone. Suddenly among their presences taking form in the bright light surprising Kris who broke from the crumble dried up mud with the ground turning into a stone floor as their recent new companion insight was Trixs the golden fairy boy prince they ran into at the Greenbelt saved from the witch Baba Yaga. "Trixs is the name and don't wear it out."

The friendly shiny golden glittery fairy began patronizing and didn't even realize the situation of the scenario. "See that, scratch my back and I'll scratch yours!" Trixs the fairy chuckled showing Stevie his back literally. Stevie mentions with a big smile across his face while scratching the fairy's back, "fairies are very unexpected."

Trixs had to respond, "It's nothing biggie for any prince fairy to conjure a ball of sunshine it's the right medicine for these kin mud-doodoos." Stevie gave in to the fairy's comical response and laughed. "Wait, you're a prince?" Stevie asked. Kris pointed out the pact between Trixs and Stevie when they hug after the fairy was saved from the witch Baba Yaga. "It's the pact you and the fairy made back at the witch's chicken hut?"

"I' am a prince escort of the Seelie faerie Court of Essence and the light bond is what unites us close brother," Trixs explains what all comes with the package when making a pact with a fairy while Stevie didn't even mind. "Since now we're one I'm able to sense you when your near and I wasn't too far just down the street from Whole Foods and I sense you were in danger, so I flew as fast as I could and don't even ask me how I got in here."

They began to look around for any exit with the golden fairy still proclaiming his heroic stats describing how nasty and old trolls are. "I felt you nearby and I could hear you in my thoughts," Stevie asks Trixs. The prince fairy pointed at his forehead, "It's all part of the light bond that links us telepathy." Kris rolled his eyes and looked at Stevie mummed under his breath, "be prepared to have lots of headaches."

"HEY!" The fairy shouted, then Kris raised his hands and replied being innocent, "what?"

The fairy was out of the context that was being side-track and began pointing towards the middle ditch on the ground. "Is that a Texas yellow dandelion that can protect the bearer from all dark magic and brings them good luck? I thought it was a legend among the Fae and rumored it was the Troll king that possesses the Texas yellow dandelion?"

"Let's not rush into things, let's not," Stevie said, and was then interrupted by Kris who demanded and yelled at the fairy, "Don't pick it!" Trixs quickly got up from bending down to the dandelion pluck it from the dirt ground place in his fingertips and said, "oops."

The rough ditch ground was dried up mud that began to shake and crack shuffling before their feet like quicksand rising from the ground from where the dandelion was pluck was a huge peak of a Troll head wearing a spiral stalagmite needle crown made out of limestone rock appearing out from the ground.

It was massive and distorted with bizarre anatomical features it was the ugliest rock troll they have ever seen as it raised its obese face lifting itself from the ground like sand with pebbles stones falling off the King Troll's deformed body revealing multiple limbs three times the size of an average troll. The massive troll began to shift twirling around swing its three arms with rock hands half wide the size of a full person barely missing the boys as they duck and tucking into the air taking cover in the corners of the dark chamber behind dusty treasures.

"Who dares to disturb my chambers!"

With its giant claw monster hands snatch and pulled the anomalous silver chain line that was dangling beside the troll king's head wasn't aware of his new guest intruders were watching him. Coming forth from the ground in command to the silver chain was a displayed trophy of a giant birdcage that could fit a person inside was cloaked and shielded over by a red cover blanket.

The troll king yelled but was gibberish to Kris and began to sniff the earth's aroma air. The troll king's loud voice crackled, "I smell a nasty firefly, a tainted mortal and… and…?" The fairy had a concerned look stirring in his eyes, he turns to look at Stevie and cautiously asked, "Brother, are you a believer of the one?" Stevie was confused and short of the moment and replied, "what?" The troll king continued his guess taking a deeper sniff of the air while the boys took a breathe as well in a panic of shock of what to do. The fairy again quickly muttered softly to ask Stevie, "Do you follow the shepherd lord?"

The troll king beamed out and continued to guess, "oatmeal?" The fairy then again asking the third time trying to murmur under his breathe but spoke out loud, "please don't tell me please don't tell me you're a?" After that moment finishing the fairy's sentence, the troll king yelled, "A CHRISTIAN!" Everything went insane in a split second having quakes with boulders and rocks tumbling falling from overhead above from every direction with commotion coming from the troll king losing it's mind banging and slamming his huge rock fists into the ground making gap craters. "The troll king may lack in eyesight blind as a bat but makes up with having a highly sensitive smell, especially the smell of a Christian to a troll is like a raging bull that just sees red driving the troll into an enraged frenzy." Trix's alerted Stevie while ducking from flying rocks.

The earth Troll King had a large face unfair face with beady eyes and its deformed massive earth body was twice the size of a raging bull with having burly stone rock disproportion limbs and having a back like a shell made up of rocks and dirt was gnarling with wet mud dripping from its hanging largemouth it looks like a bucket filled with razor rock teeth and a heavy chin being half of its face equip with having enormous tusks out of its distorted rock jaw-brake mouth.

It was anomaly armored by its unique rock features having rocky spikes as a mane trailing behind its rock back. It pounded the ground with its giant fists cracking the floor shifting rock debris towards the intruders while holding a large stalactite rock as a weapon in its third hand shouting out for its prey. They hid from troll king behind lost gold treasure artifacts mount and shoved in the dark corners of the damp chamber.

Trixs was told to blast the troll with his sunshine ball and the fairy unwisely exposed itself out of the open targeting before the king troll replied at Kris exposing where they were, "fairy magic doesn't work on the Jontar."

At the spare moment, Stevie conjured a plan peeping from behind a large deserted muddle facade treasure chest seeping within mud seeing a cubbyhole on the other side behind the troll king considering it's their exit.

Their entrance magically disappeared behind them trap in a dome mudstone chamber alone with the boss monster. Stevie explains under pressure being older than Kris who looks lost and confused mentioning their way out through the cubbyhole, "ok it's us three now or never, here's the plan… we'll attack first to distract…" then in the heat of the moment, Trix's snapped and started to glow and began shouting charging at the troll king pulling out his flashy daggers. "Wait! I didn't even finish?" Stevie shouted, sighed shaking his head with Kris replying, "what do you expect he's a fairy."

The fairy swiftly confronted the troll with a jab stab at its lower flab overweigh belly with its flashy gold dagger and quickly transformed into a tiny sparkle sunshine ball agitating the king troll like a pest firefly mosquito sparkling zapping through and around the troll king.

Kris took charge and emits a pyro circle of fire surrounding the troll king from his magical lighter having to expense what they have losing their Seer remote weapons. Stevie followed Kris going around the giant king troll silently then running into the hidden cubbyhole on the other side of the chamber. The troll king finally swatted the diversion pixie fairy after clapping with its big hands with such a force it slams the fairy onto a stone wall transformed back into its full body before Trixs could fall to the ground with a glistening fairy unconscious out in the open.

The king troll's attention was now then on Kris pounding the ground evaporating Kris's magical entrap ring fire. Kris got the wind knock out of him after being knocked down by a short boulder surfing through the ground summoned by the troll king knocking Kris off his feet.

The troll king with its engulf nostrils with its high senses of smell sniff three times in the air and rage, the troll king started screaming charging towards Stevie's direction hidden nearing the exit cubbyhole.

Just by the nick of time, Stevie lunges out of the berserk troll's attack like a wrecking ball imploding into the stonewall behind Stevie with the troll disappearing into the rock wall rubble on the other side of the wall leaving a huge exit gap it made while Stevie on the ground rolls next towards to Trixs.

Kris met up with Stevie who was tending to Trixs that was still unconscious laying on the debris crumbled ground.

Two large grotesque troll hands appeared out from the recent fresh newly made passage walkway hole through the stonewall reaching to pull itself out of the huge rumble of the giant gap hole.

Kris was ready with his magical black lighter that can manipulate fire at will taking aiming when Stevie still beside his companion fairy looking around for anything to take armed. The troll king took forth stepping forward reaching out with its hideous stretch face having a wide jaw full of rotten sharp teeth revealing with unknown aliment stuck in some its teeth peering from the gaping hole, with Kris halting the threat the best he can immediately torching the troll king as much as he could withstanding his own heat of the fire.

"The troll is fire resistant, I can't hold him back any longer," Kris said being pushed back by the troll that came forth closer with its reaching long steps and closer to its meddlers. After the troll king grumbled Kris shuffled out of the troll's way taking cover with Stevie sheltering the unconscious fairy from afar. "What did it say, what did it say?" Kris exclaimed shouting at Stevie. Still wearing his Aeon white headphone gear over his head he then now could understand dark troll language, "something about catching us draining our blood and grinning our bones." Kris replies with a dull look, "forget that I asked."

Stevie never forgot the nonentity gold giant birdcage standing alone hidden underneath the red drape cover with movement rousing behind its lock cage.

Shortly after a quick silence attending the fairy that didn't last long an explosion underneath them erupted with a small crater with Stevie caught in the middle was too late tucking in to take cover with small ground rumbles surrounding him.

Stevie saw it was a blast summon by the troll king having the earth elements burst at its command did not harm Stevie but Kris and Trixs were nowhere seen from the impact of the earth element explosion with dirt and grime in the air from the blast. The Troll king took Stevie into consideration being few yards away noticing a dreadful gaze from the terrible troll king made it ten times worst through the haze dirt in the dirty air looking at troll coming closer with its beady eyes shot red there placed was the yellow dandelion flower exposed in Stevie's pant pocket revealing to the monstrous troll king.

Now Stevie was dreading to have met the sly fairy that would have knowingly place the flower in Stevie's pocket on purpose. Stevie was petrified at the gleaming murderous stare he got from the troll king with beady eyes that are now exposed wide open with horror revealing its maliciously dark green veiny red eyes, hyperventilating opening with its drooling grotesque mouth before chomping Stevie's head off.

Instead of the troll king eating Stevie in one gulp it howls and shriek at Stevie while Stevie took cover shielding his face and body there was Trixs underneath below the troll's fat gorge leg quickly before getting smash by the troll's bottom bum with a pure silver dagger stab into the troll's deformed foot and yelled, "silver and gold alloy harms it!" The fairy prince once again gave one hell of a fight only blinding the troll for a brief moment with its sunlight flash from the fairy letting the boys get away chasing their chance going around the troll once again to their newly opening gaping hole exit in the stonewall.

Stevie was the first to escape the muddy chamber following behind was Kris barely halfway into the exit snatch by his left leg the troll dangled Kris in the air like a twig.

It was a huge shock and lively awoke Stevie it gave him such adrenaline apprehensively got back into the troll chamber found the nearest long-forgotten weapon he could find was a time-worn golden axe from an ancient corpse draped in cobwebs of a dwarf that was no more but a warrior skeleton cloak in its last battle gear.

Stevie chasing around the corners of the underground dungeon of the troll lair with a surprise attack from behind the troll king. With its third odd hand, the troll king blindly snatch the golden axe from Stevie's aim surprise attack from behind the troll king revealing its hidden razor back carrying its name for having sharp hidden teeth with a monster mouth on its back, the backside of the troll king has a mutated mouth ready to devour Stevie being horrified, Stevie paced backwards immediately from being today's troll's back diner literally he thought.

Having the troll king's full attention turning around to face Stevie holding onto Kris's leg dangling like a rag doll. The fairy tried it's best continuing to flash and zip around the troll king's face in its pixie form but nothing phased or distracted the troll that began slowly charging at Stevie at a long pace, then with such rage like rabies upon the troll's face it gather momentum speed like a raging bull surprising Stevie as he fidgety tripped over on his own feet knowingly in seconds Stevie would be troll dropping tomorrow.

Laid out in stalemate on the ground from the corner of Stevie's eye distracting with a blinking shiny object, in seconds he rolled over and snatched the closest silver object a tip spear covered in gunk and mud made out of fine dark wood bark.

It was the right time at the right moment it all happens so fast Stevie shut his eyes adjusted his grave weapon as fast and best he can with the spear being so heavy and sturdy the broken spear was mounted in the ground lift at an angle with a broken bottom shaft with its silver-gold alloy spearhead in the air.

With Stevie huddled on the ground into a ball holding on to dear life to the broken spear holding his breathe he could feel the heat breathing and smelling toxic fumes from above him the heathen's monstrous mouth is now upholding the tip of the spear stabbed overhead into the troll king's razor mouth through its head. The broken wooden spear was jolted into the ground upward standing on its own supported with the troll's weight pierce through it stabbing itself as it tried to attack Stevie.

Right after Stevie was slimed with troll's droll from being underneath the monster's mouth in a near death experiencing again this time being a troll's treat hustled and rolled from under the large mouth of the paralyzed troll king with the spear stuck it being alive still using its three limbs to pull out the weapon, came surprised charging Kris with another silver axe spear piercing the troll on its side then another one coming from another side was the fairy prince Trixs that also stabbed the troll on its other side. The troll king constipated in pain grumbled and mumbled out loud unable to shift his whole heavy body it being pierced turning sideways and looks to Stevie letting out its last breath and began to decompose into a pile of mud-rocks into a puddle with just the spike crown left.

Whimpering could be heard from the giant birdcage with its cover half drape over the cage as it fell off revealing what's inside the cage.

"My lady!" Trixs took to his knee and humbly bowed to an elven child who looks no more than twelve years old bearing the light of having a shiny gold aura surrounding her wearing a tiny golden tiara.

Stevie let out a cry, "that's an elf child as a prisoner?"

Shock in awe when he thought he saw it all Kris responded, "It's not just any elf that's an elf princess...."

13

Arena

The Tower of Babel

"CHARLIE DID MENTION MISSING PEOPLE now come and go along the shoal creek could be the many reasons the cannibal trolls are at fault but I bet that will be the last troll activity we'll hear for a while." Stevie brings up the conversation at a local restaurant preparing his ramen bowl soup.

At diner Valarie had to mention, "you have a full house meaning, witches, trolls, saving royal fairies and princess elves, all in one week that's a full house only high lead Seer ranks get house calls like that with near-death consequence and survive to tell about.

"So it was a Razor-rock back troll?" Valarie then asks in a discussion at a late-night diner table that same day meeting with Kris and Stevie covered in sores and scratches with one or two band-aids from their recent battle with the troll king eating at Austin's local 888 Pan Asians restaurant.

"Besides getting a tetanus shot at the lab Charlie did mention he managed a team to confiscate the lost dwarf chambers." Kris slurping his ramen soup budded in to say, "he also said the earth troll king is a unique creature that leads a large group of mudrock trolls being the largest, ugliest, dumbest, and most powerful creatures in the troll family." Being cut off short with no interest in their heroic deeds Valarie went to say, But it was a Razorback troll very unusual hardy ever seen even by the Gods they say." She took a little bite from her plate and continued, "The troll king you guys killed is known as Jontar heir to multiple lairs hidden among the world it just so happens you find him at the right time at his underground estates and probably surprise him at his fine resort vacation home." Stevie let out after explaining his side of the story, "they don't call it a razorback for no reason." She then chuckled and glad to see her training peers were safe seeing already how mature they've grown so fast to impetuous situations and became amused to what some interest towards Stevie.

"And what of the elven princess shining in gold?" Valerie asks the question that was held in the air regards to the boys in hoping it was never asked as they look upon each other knowingly they did not tell Valerie being told to keep it a secret for purpose reasons by Charlie.

"How did you know about that?" Stevie was quick in response then Valerie answered.

"No worries the secret is safe with me, I overheard Charlie outside the area on the phone with Ashley making a report talking about the troll's underground estates returning its prize from the troll is an alive captive princess caged just for a trophy display for at least over seven hundred years a royal elf rescued and she's return back to her rightfully kingdom is mighty chivalrous of you two working as a team."

Stevie was shock to hear how long she was a prisoner but was fervent in describing the elven princess "She was very mystical with hair glimmering in silver and gold with a shine to her aura. Kris began to share his part of the testimony, "she even looks so young but wiser than any and I hear the royalty lives forever from the looks her wisdom increased with the long years."

Valerie was thrown off loathing over the boy's distinctive recount experience at the troll lair incident flipping the conversation.

"So you still don't know what that thing does besides trance music that leads a bunch of mandrakes?" Valarie smiled asking Stevie about his Aeon weapon being that they are beats with a white headphone position around his neck. "Well, for one thing, I had to make a report with Nerd about with this ear headphone set I could understand the troll's language and what it was saying." Stevie replied with Kris asking after, "Anything unusual it said." Stevie then answered, " it was a lot of gibberish having nothing good to say being literally trolls." Then the table busted out laughing.

"What was it that the troll king said to you before it disintegrated into a puddle of rocks." Kris curiously asked. Stevie gave a grave look, then looking up from the table he said, "Charlie advised me it'll be wise not to say anything but I can tell you, and from what I got is the troll said something on the line like." Stevie took a pause reminiscing his thoughts or was he contempt debating to share, while Kris and Valarie waited impatiently exchanging each other looks.

Then Stevie continued with a dopey reaction pawning his trust in his new friends, "The Dawning Stewarts," then the table abruptly laughed again.

After they paid for their meal Kris ordered for the table an Italian cream sorbet as they celebrated together.

"Wasn't it Trixs suppose to have met us here?" Stevie asks before gulping down his ice cream, "wasn't he's the one that called the shots to meet us here?"

Stevie had mentioned that Trixs told him about a new bar he's opening on the corner of Fourth Street, and Lavaca.

"How far the world has changed so much, Gods, monsters, and now we have a fairy running its own bar among humans downtown Austin Texas, I'm sorry did I miss something?" Valarie said with no comical gestures. Stevie then replied, "What's next the Gods running the city council?" Giving each other a serious brief moment then Valarie let out a laugh following the whole table laughing again.

Ironically speaking of the devil Stevie sitting next to the front window of the restaurant caught notice of Trixs his fairy prince friend outside gesturing him to be quiet and come out and follow.

Valarie was mentioning how special tonight would be under a rare blue star in alignment with the planets Saturn and Venus. Intrigued in the conversation Kris briefly mentions and said, "like the star of Bethlehem."

"Hey, guys I'm going to run out real quick something came up, so I'll see you guys then."

Dashing out like that was a bit odd leaving the scenario Stevie thought chasing after Trixs through the parking lot must be some fairy game and thinking he could just be at home kicking back in his comfy bed after his late diner.

Just then he saw the golden fairy got suck into the side of a steep hilltop next to the 888 Pan Asians restaurant. It always was an awkward hill with an abandoned building that comes and goes with chain business plaza on the 2400 E. Oltorf St. Stevie still in the parking lot took cautious approaching the hillside massive stone block wall when suddenly his Aeon wireless headphone went off with music wrap around his neck there an opening entrance from the hillside stone blocks slowly opens allowing Stevie to disappear stepping through to follow after his new friend Trixs the fairy.

It was just as magical as it was a mystery walking into a realm of unknown possibilities but nothing unusual after following through a dark tunnel through the hill reaching to the end of the light that glistered his eyes adjusting his sight into an abroad scenery that appeared to be a classic old Hollywood tinsel town glamor. Stevie found his surroundings to be instantaneously grand with a reception arena foyer lobby, and a red carpet filled with paparazzi and tumult lighting but nowhere could be found his fairy friend Trixs.

It wouldn't be glamorous without headliners being ushered in, as the stars dress in their in their lineage decorated to the best escorted by their entourage being these were not your average movie stars and actresses they were immortal gods.

This was one super exciting extravaganza with fashion avant-garde but the one thing that threw Stevie off the loop was the paparazzi and the concierge serving their divinity gods and guest nectar champagne with all having no faces.

Feeling out of place it was so consuming not one to bother to notice Stevie who stood there pondering words can't describe what he's witnessing when all the gods that walk on the earth are in one place of all parallel time of the planet earth with one god having an estranged massive elephant head walking past by him and must have read Stevie's mind and answered him politely with a bow and such a gentle tone from an enormous top head of a talking animal, "acquaintance is my solitude dear boy, this place you stumbled upon is an arena full of dungeons and monsters of its own its the tower of babel where a humanoid cosmic race of extra-dimensional beings known as gods that hale from our realities worlds all gather to meet at a place of a small pocket- dimension adjacent to earth."

The kind Hindu God with the huge Elephant head wore a tux showing Stevie the way and took haste as it walks slowly away mostly gathering to an entrance waiting to be seated at what was to be a coliseum arena concert with hearing cheers and shouting from large audiences in the background of the entranceway. Stevie overheard the commotion through the strung crowds in the lobby about scourging commemorative about to happen to a set of abandoned earth trolls.

A tribal god wearing a Bumba of Bushongo mask from the Congo came near to Stevie taking liking and glance with its beady eyes behind its huge mask glittered with colors and spun around to a short dance and shocking Stevie it threw up tiny cosmos of lights walking past through its vomit lighting up like little planets following in circles around the god as it walks away.

It was the faceless servants of the tower that caught on and notice Stevie alerting their god with loud whispers to a daemon an immortal wearing an obnoxious retro knock-off white fluffy windbreaker jumpsuit that he looks like a mafia guido character more-like carelessly knowing his size isn't so slim fit with a stomach barging out revealing its peach belly popping out luckily covered mostly by wearing a purple sash and in one hand holding a golden pinecone staff rippled with purple ribbons band around it.

The wine God was the stereotype regarded as vain, aggressively masculine as a front when he's knowingly socially unsophisticated came around to Stevie flashing his golden accessories wearing golden chains and a green wreath around its round baldhead. "Humans are not welcome here you know." The god said from looking back over his shoulder at a stellar star deity just arriving in a captivating business suit attire which features him to be a fit silver fox bachelor a muscle daddy sporting with a silver ash-white warrior beard with a dark golden brown tan looks to be in his late fifties wearing black shades with his entourage a much bigger fan base and shine brighter than any other divine in the entire room.

"I... said... Yo," the sleazy god again asks Stevie as he was losing attention leaning onto a side of a wall in a crude exchange behavior slapping the bottom behind of a faceless cocktail waitress passing by first then consulting Stevie once more. "A Seer boy, you mortals aren't welcome here even for your kind."

The annoyingly macho mannered god introduce himself unleashing his crossed arms over his chest resting on his immense gut extending his godly fidget fingers populated with golden rings signaling a kiss on the godly hand for respect from a mortal, "I'm lord Bacchus mostly known as Dionysus to your primitive kind."

With such appealing innocently Stevie replies and instead valuing in kissing the god's hand he kindly shook it, "oh you mean like the grapefruit god!" Stevie clueless offending the God his reaction replied in a fanciful sneer behind his façade smile, "Dear boy you have no idea who you're talking to and that's wine god to you unlucky one." The faceted God began to fume in a glow purple aura with its eyes radiating in purple sparks in its iris pupil.

"Do you know what I can do to you in a split second morphifiy your being in a comatose state of shock ten times folds in a parallel dimension that will feast upon your soul?"

Stevie wasn't even compelled once or showed any confliction towards the grape deity but wore the necklace that flashed he was a Christian, and with confidence, he said, "If God is before you who can be against you?" Stevie told the wine god effortlessly that it made it so angry other gods had to restraint Dionysus disintegrating their faceless servants while there was another divinity admired that she reign in and ironically Stevie was precipitously blessed and abruptly saved by the nick of time it was the Hindu divine goddess herself Kali, the Black One that came over to Stevie that was back to a corner. "God-lover!" The dark goddess maintains in a black silhouette one piece that defines her jewel body possessing a soothing dark complexion, as perfectly beautiful with her hair unrestrained, body firm and youthful.

The dark goddess called out to Stevie at the sight of peril for he had no clue how serious his life for being a mortal was on the line for just being in a place full of ravenous Gods saved by Kali from almost being blasted to oblivion victim to their unfamiliar customs around here Stevie was blind in seeing the foreshadowing divine threats from the Greek god Dionysus shouting from the background, "Who Does He Think He Is!"

"I thought I told you not to call me that?" Stevie said to the Hindu goddess innocently sighed looking down at his shoes blushing from being seen but happy to see someone he recognizes.

The Greek lord of grapes began to snap fanatically and quickly pounced back, "The mortal is forbidden on sacred grounds!" Then Kali snaps back to inform, "neutral grounds."

"The mortal martyr is up for takings he's mine!" Dionysus shouted causing a scene with an uncontrollable rage but the dark goddess Kali retaliated and then she didn't hesitate to bother to persist any longer with the overheated macho grape entity.

"Oh please… how unattractive must you have fallen since the cannibalism era is so outdated like who does that any more?" Holding her ground with her fist in flames she looks at Stevie once more and then turns back to look at her syndicates of gods and immortals to say, "The mark ones are no more or lesser than you and you know it," Dionysus then said, "one does love the old ways it's a memorable artistic customary, but Seer or not, deemed by the sacred universal laws, who will want to stain their hands escorting a mere mortal?"

She then interrupted the obnoxious god wearing the fluffy purple white windbreaker clothing that chimes to of an annoyance when he moves to indulge, she announced summoning a command in a vibrant voice that rang and echoed throughout all to hear in her authority riding a lion that came out of nowhere having four-armed, holding a sword and blue lotuses.

"I Kali, mother goddess watchmen of the fierce black tongue, one of seven belonging to Agni, I' am the god of fourth fire scorching red star of destruction and Chaos come before you as the Dakshinamarga."

While Dionysus took to his seat at a place in the Greek audience box as he had a lot to say around his peers, "you have got to be kidding me?"

"I redeem this mortal body and soul!" The dark goddess finishing her chanting spell, but the wine god began goading her by multiple illicit responses. "You really want to do that…?"

As she chanted the last words laying a sacred law she marks her tutelary granting Stevie protection so he may enter the sacred ground without any harm showing Dionysus as she secretly knows his secret to be cannibalistic and the other threatening gods she granted Stevie safely body and soul passage on the sacred ground of the tower, placing a disappearing red Bindi spot on his forehead.

She explains to Stevie, these are sacred ground there is rules that must be followed, abide, and obeyed. You are now a guest of mine, and you are part of me here. Anything that happens to you reflects on me, I 'am here to escort you got that."

All the gods around them look down at her while they walk in the arena main stage entrance with Stevie by her side together passing by her fellow divine compeers unsympathetic to their biased gestures and stares.

Stevie was thankful for Kali but it was the goddess that thank him, "hey kid thanks for the Moksha it's a Hindu thing god of state, it felt good to get that out."

That's when Stevie asks, "you're what?" And then KALI explains, "it what the gods get off of pure energy, sustaining our divine grace. It's a power of a force that makes a god in its fullest momentum, in its true state that forms god-like powers as it should be, but all that has been changed now since the one God's hippie son came into play and change the game upside down. If you ask me it was genius for the better course for you mortals, it leads to having decisive rights to your own souls. I too believe inequality."

Stevie made reassurance penetrating the question, "So in terms back then before Christ, these gods used the souls of humans for food to power their energy, until law over the gods was forced and restricted from overtaking the mortals?"

Kali agreed and said, "Giving the mortal free-light in meaning free soul, unless they willingly give their soul to them even the angels would descend down and punish those and would never allow it!" Then Kali mentions the most important lesson, "The goal for everyone is to transcend rebirth and to attain a state of eternal pure energy and that is called Moksha, the god-state."

Stevie was cautious to ask, "Was he really going to eat me back there?" The dark goddess replied, "Oh those gods are always tied up to their silly rituals, more like eating your essence." She then said pointing at Stevie's heart then next to his forehead cueing his brain leaving him dumbfounded, "souls of mortals are like batteries with energy, and you're like that pink energize bunny from the TV commercials."

She then asks Stevie, "I don't know how or why you're here but you shouldn't be here." Stevie had a chance to answer swiftly, "I followed Trixs here."

She rolled her eyes and sighed, "Whatever you do stay at my side at all times please!"

"What is this place and what happened to Trixs, I followed him here?"

The arena wasn't anything seen before by any human eyes since millennia with a structure of a cathedral-like playhouse with red carpeting and gold lining fixtures held multiple divergent gods seated in black box theaters of past and existing culture of the world among most familiar titles and face throughout the history of mankind were all here under one roof a sky open roof that is with the cosmos dancing above. The Tower of Babel the stories from your bible it is a star-gate to the gods or gates to the gods per say is no place for a mere mortal.

"Gods tend to have their tendencies an appetite for fun and pleasure in a place to be themselves for we are not all perfect it's also a place to dispute and magistrate among us deities and for the supernatural."

Kali the goddess lead the way like a Shepherd as Stevie like to think following her like lost chap sheep in a field of wolves, the realm of the gods, and these gods don't simply exist in people's mind they are personified physical characters.

"The Tower of Babel the one in your bible, is now an existing court of the gods hidden our strife on earth in a realm where divine vie their conflicts and disputes with either by a champion or by their own choice grace divine."

It wasn't dismay but a pure shock that Stevie then realizes it never gets old by the many recurring surprises that lead his way ever since chastise of being a Seer.

Stevie had a reluctant question he just had to ask, " but how do you know which god is perfect?" Kali simply responded in an odd mannerism, "There are almost five thousand gods being worshipped by humanity on this planet but don't worry, only yours is right?"

She let Stevie in on some insights, "All the gods came to see a slaughter of the last of its species of their kind and if today will be always remembered as there will be another lineage in line to be extinct."

Stevie wonders as always, he then asks, "why does it have to be today?" The goddess liked the mortal's fox senses and answered him back, "why does it have to be at all?"

Stevie understood the grounding situations that even the gods have their limits to freedom of choice."

Kali then replied with an unpleasant side look of dismay, "the fairy tree folks up against their relative distant cousins the tree elves such dirty sadness... fairies has no match up against tribal tree elves for why the gods came to say their tribute and condolences." Later she tells him it was you who broke the green treaty that upset Stevie knowing now the after effect of being a hero.

"If you didn't know your buddy charming prince fairy is up next for a royal bout trail, something to do about upsetting the elves so now your fairy friend Trixs is challenged to an honor of affair more like a combat duel against the champion of the high elves their heir prince."

Just Stevie's presence alone he could feel such radiant power ringing through the air with his left hand alerting the highly supernatural forces surrounding him.

He felt like a fly among a sea of tremendous waves of aura with such radiant power that he never felt before in his entire life. Stevie was thankful he had on his left glove to keep warmth as his hand continues to sting and tingles with cold alarming him again the surrounding supernatural nova god-like events a no place for a mortal.

Among the social elite crowd of the gods, Stevie also saw Hermes a young man with sharp features, a flashy aura around him with silver bright eyes, and long silver hair that spikes up backward was someone Stevie recognized the mailman he ran into back at the library when he had first arrived before being a seer.

Stevie then spotted a goddess mingling among other gods and goddess recognizing her beautiful face that lit up the whole arena as the goddess of such opulent aura would leave a sweet taste in your mouth if made eye contact with the goddess that she couldn't be missed in the crowd as he once remembers running into the goddess and would never forget an appealing woman so headstrong in a stimulating red dress with luscious red lips with a portion of her body that was shaped and define like an hourglass her body was just like art that would have been known through out all the art museums of love as she stands behind the large golden throne, a chair seated was the boss, a businessman with great stature that shows strength and masculinity upon his features wearing a fine expensive topline blue suit.

The Kali the dark goddess told Stevie never to look into a god's eyes and warned him to stay close and do not stray putting on his head wireless Aeon white headphone and she told him to listen to something patriotic to keep his mind tamed.

The play-house arena from the inside of the tower of babel it looks like a massive beehive around the inside tower with massive court ground with a rough ground, a grid-iron field displayed with mosaic tile pavements through out the field some areas the tiles have cracks with grass and sand exposed underneath with leftover rock boulders from past debris contest it was the arena checkered marble floor that symbolizes the universe of good and evil.

The Tower of Babel can hold a huge oval sports venue, with over 1500-2000 honey-comb stands that seat 5 to 10 per comb stand.

The tower has different levels with floors spiraling upward above over the audience entertainment venue with each comb box stand having its decorative decor matching its deity lordship and godhood personalities.

It was the details of the inside arena tower that drew anyone's eyes at the three gigantic stone figures of titanic giants tall as sky scrappers displaying to be holding up the cosmos as three base support beams that angle's to hold the whole tower resting on one's shoulders the other stone giant raised in its hands over its head on its knees while the last third stone giant had the tower resting on its back looking downward at the arena hippodrome with their faces hidden by their long dirty hair. Everything in the tower arena was twice its average size for a human.

There was one particular stone statue that grasps Stevie's gaze with curiosity looking at the white stones of the life-size rocks drawn to deep history involving mystery por-traying what looks like a fear of huddled men taking cover shielding each holding one another closely draped in toga flowing through air stuck in time.

"Ah you found the triplet Gods of the Muse, they are Literature, Dance and Music are the knowledge of the Arts. Originally there were 13 Muses but alas now 3 were left and here they are before us!"

It was a commentary from the fishy Guido god Dionysus who couldn't leave Stevie alone. "How did they turned into," Stevie asks who didn't finish his sentence while then Dionysus continued for Stevie completing his sentence for him, "into Stone?" The god then started his disgusting habits belching and womanizing the next nearest victim the

Morrigan is mistaken for one of the faceless cocktail waitress wearing similar black attire but how could you miss the phantom demon crows putting away himself in short strife feud with the crow goddess swatting away her huge black demon birds attacking over the head of the absurd grape god.

"Foolish cousins of mine they went up and challenge my father's rule of power, the King of the Gods Zeus summon them to a primordial oath and they lost badly." Dionysus utter with a sigh to finish while being irritated swatting the last provoking phantom crow in the air, "They had it coming." And with that, before he walks away leaving Stevie dry with doubts he told him, "The Muses punishment are forever statues that are a remembrance to any whom mess with me or my father!"

Stevie was baffled at the fanatical glory of one being a god who took pride in his family portraying it to look like an inside family occult that the interest bored Stevie stirred the grape god in a silent rage only the gods could sense the coming of Dionysus's dark atmosphere. "You know Zeus is my father! He is the lord of the elements. Father of the gods and humanity once, a figure to everyone whether mortal or divine and that all owes obedience!"

Stevie just nods at Dionysus clearly missing all the warning signs tells the irrational god before having a short-fused one coming close to an epileptic episode and tells the irrational god, "right, you keep mentioning that Zeus is your father."

Kali the dark goddess began to critic Zeus the king of gods while swooshing the pestering Wine God to go away as he left the scene, "Ugh I can't stand that grape pig and his father is no better yet the worst, such a demagogue whose jock straps are always tight in a wad!"

Stevie figured he would ask later about the tale of the Muses and felt somewhat sympathy compassion towards the sad statues seeing them cower huddle upon each other in fear before turning into their judgment eternal damnation.

After all the goddess did explain leaving minor details clues looking at the sad memorialize statues. "Zeus left barely enough life in them to suffer their consciences for all to see them in shame losing their glory and honor, all would be dust into ashes for we are nothing but stars Immortals living off energy are just sources for us from all types of levels."

After Kali finish her paparazzi interviews advertising her new club she was profound in finding Stevie sharing his music towards the curse Muses statue sharing his Aeon headphones over one of the heads of the Muses statue.

"What are you doing?" the dark goddess commanded?

Stevie smiled and replied, "It's the anthem to my county but in key minor, I figured the gods of art wouldn't mind a little bit of patriot music that wouldn't hurt."

Kali nod allowing the empathy amusement and smiled at Stevie's uniqueness for she knew in his heart he meant well and began telling the tale.

Kali explained between the catastrophic of the Muses having only one sister was Metis goddess of cunning and tune who stood against her uncle and was swallowed by Zeus cause not only was it forbidden to teach mortal men divine gifts fairing them with tune Metis was also destined to produce an unruly son, the future King of Gods and men. Like his father Cronus and his grandfather Ouranos or Uranus same grandpa Kali says in a figure of speech, Zeus was destined to fall before his nephew. So he swallowed the pregnant Metis. Stuck inside Zeus's belly, she continued to provide him with knowledge of good and evil.

The main event show was about to begin with the atmosphere of the arena changing Kali continued, "Something about the Muses Gods having a brother's revenge on Zeus for sacrificing their sister by taking what was left of their sister making her into a gift for the mortals with voices that sing to the world giving it a tune."

Stevie more said so then asking, "So then Zeus tricks the muse into a trap that lead them into being stones forever."

Kali then replies to only being sarcastic, "The muse gods indeed loved their sister and they all say around here the punishment is fit to be stoned in shame as an example of retaliation against the King of the Gods."

Ganesha is the Hindu deity depicted with the head of an elephant stood tall taking guard for Kali's seated box section but the goddess settled him with a dismiss before disputing with any other gods.

Stevie tries scavenging into the vast extraordinary crowds of supernatural beings looking for particular gods in the box stands of the crowds as it was being mentioned by Kali, "if you're looking for the Egyptians they were all annihilated long ago by the holy grace war, a terrible lost such a price to pay for war and many us gods suffered as you can see of what's left and many were also killed or died off."

Stevie was in abundant of wonder in awe of sight grasping the view of it's guest host the tower of babel as he was still searching for someone or something out in the crowd having Kali suspicious retorting to Stevie's thoughts, "You won't see him here one of the coolest guys though giving mankind freewill, after life you know, oh you weren't talking about the Hebrew hippie?

The goddess took from relaxing stretching her arms studying Stevie then suggesting saving Stevie time and continues to linger downward towards her question revealing to Stevie, "Wait till you Christians find out whom the Middle Eastern god really is."

They saw a ritual take place in the middle of the arena court grounds walking into the end of a battle between trolls clashing among their own kind, it was gladiator style the gods announcing to release the Beast, the Demogorgon.

The crowd cracks a cheer once the strange name the Demogorgon was called out with the checkered marble court floor began to be mysteriously foggy with a mystic dark blue fog conjuring among the ground floor.

The intention was so high towards the arena event, this surprises Kali allowing to introduce her mortal guest recipient of hospitality, "This beast is a pit monster an ancient force born before the dawn of time one of the first and is at the very top of the food chain of everything that ever once lived under the light of the sun."

It lives to appear only among the scattered blue fog unable to see the floor manifesting turning the ground solid to liquid beneath below the fog, a name so terrible its history is not known to mortals and what makes it deadly is not knowing what's below even on solid ground."

In the arena on the grounds were three trolls climbing and fighting another to be on top of the tallest boulder that was left to survive after its contest trail for multiple crimes of treason against their kind and exposing themselves to mortals Stevie recognize one of the trolls being disguised as the homeless that he ran into back at the underground troll estates.

Stevie could see why the trolls weren't fighting one another they were saving themselves from the Demogorgon with its pink-purple monster tentacles impaled onto its prey a troll grabbing it down under coming from underground of the eerie blue fog.

"The Demogorgon is the consumer of time and space it's the eater of moons and stars use to be a godlike creature that became a monster ruler of nearly a hundred alternate universes the god monster being immortally nigh-invincible it took all of us to stop it and since we can't kill it we trap it here in the Babel tower."

It got crazy and then it got really crazy, real fast with its slimy pink blue vein tentacles purple suction cups snaps outreaching at the black box seating grabs the guards of the gods, it ate one of Zeus's armed guardsmen as the King of the Gods laugh taking the pleasure in sporting his thunderbolt restraining the monstrous pink god creature the mighty king god showing off his manly charisma power.

The arms of the Demogorgon's tentacles were just right down dirty and dangerous with a hidden ability supporting a shape shift goat decoy on a rock boulder deceiving the last troll with its dirty bait switch trick.

"So no god or living beast can tame this God monster for alone it consumes not only moons and stars but also gods and well-living beings are known to be depleted or devoured by the Demogorgon even eats time and space itself."

It was the pleasure of the goddess to share a forbidden tale history to mortal ears let alone only known among the gods. The Tower of Babel was once made by the gods and humankind together in harmony thinking to communicate with the gods wanting to unite and link with the gods. For long ago they try to reach the one God of the first but instead they got the wrong deity the eater of Gods that brought assaults to the builders and touches the minds of the people corrupting their spirits to fight among each other so they lost their way to reach the gods.

It made our people confuse and hate one another lost to words of their language was easily devoured by one another it was a tragic time for all back then. It is also known to be one of the worst ways to ever go in this world to be eaten and erased from ever being existed, that is why the monster is forbidden."

The crowd cheered on as they watch the last troll get gorge by the Demogorgon revealing it to be a huge giant eyeball it is a monster iris gapping in the center opening into a mouth from a giant colossal monster that looks like the tower was built over its face revealing the eye with its pupil loaded with surprise razor blades of teeth ingesting the earth troll.

"It is somewhat a black hole that consumes everything but it can be contained here till the end of time." The dark goddess was serious in this matter staring down at the ancient monster evoking old memories of the lost time of the battles with the eerie monster that haunted the goddess.

Momentarily after the event was done and the legendary monster vanished with the blue fog clearing up it was Trixs the prince fairy that appeared in the pit arena floor on a platform at one end of the gridiron arena filled with broken boulders and a familiar pale face was the skater elf prince Stevie remembers running into at the shoal creek skate park that informed him which bridge earlier on that day about the hidden trolls where about underground.

"The Seelie Fae Court representative of the royal high fairies their prince is hung on trial for three counts challenge by the circle of the High wooden Elves of exposing on neutral grounds in breaching of the Green pact treaty between the elves and fairies by opening a human stationary tavern with full contact to the mortal world behalf of his own pleasure on southern region elven territory, and thirdly it is forbidden revealing the sacred grounds leading astray a mortal!" Dionysus announced who sneered at Stevie talking through his golden acorn staff that converted sound out loud.

Being hold down from getting up from his seat by the goddess Stevie was then forced to hold his brief temper listening to his fairy companion's accusations.

"Whoa… whoa… Wait a minute now, my fairy clan has been exposed since 1989 poisoning of the treaty oak tree, and mind you that is our sacred fairy tree. Secondly, the fairies are free to roam since the pact has been broken, the Crone witch lost her power and the Troll king is no more leaving eleven territories a free cap an escape without any more fears." The fairy prince also didn't want to leave out at the end of his sentence, "oh and my new brother to the Seelie Faerie court of Essences now companion and bounded by the light he is also a Seer complex but he walks a grey line. HI STEVIE!"

The fairy shouted waving child-like pointing out Stevie among the deities crowd where the attention was now drawn to Stevie feeling the weight of the eyes of cosmos on him.

"To settle the discord summoning champion of combat duel will compromise the alliance," Dionysus exclaimed pounding his staff signal the duel to begin.

The high elf prince was in his dark green assassin gear with a green shine covering its face revealing his pale blue daunting eyes he stood his ground empty handed watching the fairy make his first move.

"Come on, don't you think its time for the world to flip a new leaf its ready for the new coming, you know what I speak is true and look at all the signs around us, the old ways are returning and there's nothing you can do about."

The golden fairy set ready his royal knife that was sash tied around his bare shiny chest steadily he thought of his first next move taking a deep breathe closing his eyes about to unleash his dagger when a familiar hand reached and toppled his sheath dagger from being drawn and exposed sharing the same resemblance of the opposite gender was his twin sister princess fairy Ivy.

"What are you doing?"

It was quite a shock to the whole audience, not the response you would get from a sister at a time of crisis.

"You can't even fight, so typical of you risking the whole fairy court kingdom for what some run up down prophecy you keep claiming a smidgen dream reuniting with humans in a contact reality between both worlds under the veil, all this fairy liking favoring human customs ready to expose us to the world?"

Trixs was in dismay and disappointed in her twin sister, "I just wanted to open…" The distinct fairy twin sister was very similar to her brother same color hair and eyes but very headstrong and was half naked with silver olive skin contrast in purple glistening like glitter wearing female tree Fae apparel covering her lady parts.

"It's never going to happen!" Everyone could tell which one was the oldest sibling between them bickering having not the slightest idea they were laundering all over their royal family personal rivalry necessities in front of everyone. "If it weren't for you, we would have full control over the Seelie Court of Faes!" Trixs respond back to his twin sister, "We do!" Then the silver-purple fairy with purple glitter hair replied, "that might be more convenient for you, but I'm afraid it simply isn't going to work for me!"

The green elf prince exhausted its patients and began playing the wooden flute it pulled out from its side pocket with a beautiful melody so eerie it captivated everyone to its elf magic that compels earth powers.

Sprouted out magically were three full-grown wooden shrubberies cloned as a copy elf with the same features as its flute conjure by the high-end Elf known to be a prince.

The twin fairies began to fight, being serious to their conflict with one another was over like a switch focusing their anger at their opponent gearing up their combatant skills. "Plus you can't fight him alone," The fairy twin sister said strapping on knee and elbow gear as everyone from the tower spectators took notice and were very weary.

Being supervised Kali would check on her mortal guest, "Fairies are weakest at fighting with no comparison cause their magic is limited only purposes for the good and their combat skills don't allow their attributes to flourish, well cause they turn into pixies."

Stevie then understood what the goddess meant that being a fairy you turn into a sprite pixie no bigger than a firefly when in motion to fight. Their pixie magic made no difference to the elf's assassin shrubs except making a few thorns and blooming roses.

"We can do this!" Exclaimed Trixs emulating a plan telepathic to his sister and she responded to him out loud. "It's too risky we've only done it once and you know how that went?" Ivy's response to her brother's plans was conflicting then skipping to plan B was their only option.

"Ok, and stay on beat!" The fierce fairy twin sister said cracking her neck by shifting her head left to right adjusting her shoulders ready for the cue to fight.

It was her fairy brother Trixs captivating everyone's attention as curiosity stirred in the scene Trixs began fairy magic summoning his grass garden of flowers springing up a drum set out of huge sunflowers with Shirley bellflowers and a giant allium flower for the bass.

Trixs yelled out clapping his cattails plants as drumsticks he recently pulled out from his little patch of greenery, "ONE, TWO, ONE, TWO, THREE!"

Taking everyone by surprise including the silent sparring elf prince the pair of sibling fairies had a duo in combining music with their combat skills the fairies were able to manage to hold onto their full human form while in combat.

(SC Music/6)

The retro music rips to "whip it" by Devo, sprung out from Trix's garden drum set as he beats his drum.

It happened so fast the other purple twin fairy Ivy tuned into her brother's music as he began to roll the drums she flew synchronizing to the fast beat. Running so fast she was on beat flying on the side of the arena walls and she would emit quick attacks far quicker than the eye it being block and shield as she comes around flying at the skilled elf prince still charming with his flute she then targeting a surprise charge attack from behind weed-whacking the three duplicate shrubbery clones that then attack back.

It was on the ninth attack revealing she possessed a flaring whip made out of green ivy lashing coming out from her guard strap attire wrap around her waist to her top torso. The deities crowd and their chief servant creatures and entourage audience were loud with over-flowing booing and cheering with almost equal fervor for their favorite amateur contestants concluding the fairies had the larger crowd on their side as they continued to square off.

Ivy then followed the pop music cracking slapping her green ivy whip matching every tune her twin brother played out loud. "Shaping it up, moving forward," the music played as she got closer and closer finishing off every last magical shrubbery opponent she faces off before finally reaching the elf.

The music was suddenly enhanced it felt like invisible stereos were flying everywhere fulfilling the whole tower arena with Stevie's Aeon white headphones blasting to the popular retro music, "whip it."

Slashing through the elf's last magical shrubbery flew in Trixs held his dagger at hand with a frontal surprise attack towards the elf prince who was able to block and skilled in close melee combat with a wooden sharp spear lance grip in its hand holding back another tumble surprise attack from behind counterattacking the purple twin fairy's surprise double threat attack.

The fight was so intense the whole crowd explode with cheers having the tower arena at its maximum occupancy the event was so high intense Stevie didn't want to miss a thing couldn't keep his eyes off the twin fairies.

Magically disappearing and reappearing with disarray tumble attacks jumping into shrink size pixies fireflies with surprise attacks in full-size human form flying over and around the mute elf standing still keeping his guard at reaching to their endpoint whereas the elf showed his endurance he could keep the fight up all night long.

The elf prince manages to block all attacks then he snapped back at one of the attacks from Ivy's green whips holding onto the poison ivy sting weapon wrap around his arm. Elves being immune he claps back fast enough to knock both fairies off balance. The twin royal fairies being full of surprises bounced back so quickly from defensive to offensive flipping over each other from the fall showing their practice paid off pushing back the skilled elf that was beginning to lose his touch as the divine audiences were up to the edges of their seats.

Just like that the music stops and everyone in the arena took the chance to gasp holding their breath then the silence was fulfilled but a few melee ringing clashing direct contact it being too late for the fairies Trixs inhaled his last breath while his twin sister was kick on the side of her ribcage she flew across the room turning back into a tiny firefly pixie from the hard kicked almost missed their target Trixs was on the ground about to be killed speared into the chest by the elf when Stevie realized this is a competition to the death.

"SLING, SWOOSH!" A chime ringing was atoned from Stevie's slash with a majestic white sword in his grasp with both hands.

It was the sound that alarmed and confused the audience of whole Tower of Babel arena with a perfection ring sound slicing through a big chunk of air with a brief echo ringing reminding of the sound.

Blood was drawn running down leaving no more than a paper cut wound on the elf's left cheek with a single blood droplet from its chin about to drop with all the gods and creatures carefully watching to see as the mysterious elf spontaneously quickly nabs his own blood droplet as it falls before touching the ground with the tip of his second silver sword and flips off back ward's away and landed kneeling on one knee to the ground.

Stevie regarded everyone's observant towards the freshly cut given to the High elf prince cognizance about his blood touching the ground.

Then after everyone coincided, Trixs was left unharmed and baffled but was saved by an aimed unseen force with a direct slice so fierce it cut straight through the ground drawing a line between the fairy and the elf all the way from where the stands Stevie stood.

An enormous drawn slice came all the way through was recognized the other side of the circle tower barely missing the audience box from across the stands but certainly slice through the encrypted large red seal coming from the other side of a metal gate away from Stevie's direction in his hands held the same cultivated colored splash glowing white enchanted sword with an innocent unsettled look on Stevie's face with his mouth open he then drops his latest marvel weapon it modified back into thin air as Stevie wore his white color splash Aeon headphone beats with the same matching decorative colors.

The battling duel was over as the elf prince laid down his broken staff spear dagger from Stevie's fanatic intrude blow attack and started playing a repentance melody carrying a sorrow tune to his wooden windpipe having no care of the world.

The twin fairies commuted by hugging each other grieving from their almost lost battle if it weren't for Stevie the outcome could have been different.

The uproar came abroad among the crowds of the Gods stirring in questions about the new guest intruder interference from the divine crowds with his newly surprising weapon that raised concerns mentioning out loud of who is Stevie and what is this mere mortal capable of amongst the Gods they demanded, questioning their guest's hospitality!

There was a force that was commanded for settle attention by MC presenter Dionysus pounding his golden acorn rod staff whispering up a storm mockery of Stevie carelessly in one of the boxes stands of the gods decorated with exceptional fine taste draped with silk and marble pillars he stood behind his father Zeus the King of the Gods sitting in a golden throne chair shape of an eagle studying everything as it lays out.

When being singled out in the arena the dark goddess Kali then says personally speaking to herself, "I didn't see this one coming."

She places her ground from her seat stand box for all to see, "He is a mortal pardon by fire, brother to the royal fairies by bounded to light fellowship to the prince, Trixs."

Ivy the purple fairy twin sister exchanges looks with her fairy brother with a rage look hearing for the first time. "He is the mortal champion that slew Baba Yaga."

The dark goddess then said addressing her elite spectators for Stevie still dress in the cable guy company polo shirt uniform from a long day of work.

"Mark by the Crone witch herself witness by death." Kali announcing and tells Stevie to show them his scars, "he carries the witches mark the bane of witches, the executioner of the forbidden witch the one unrevealed to all eyes even such as ours."

Stevie was unease at the words the goddess displayed him before such divinities idols Dionysus just sat there sighing of boredom assuming Kali was just delaying the inevitable.

Zeus carried a dominate masculinity persona strong jawbone with a full set of grey ash white beard with a hard body and a stout tan always gesturing with a slight grin on his face with peering dimples turning into a flaccid smile, the silver fox sugar daddy was in a dark classic fitted blue suit wearing reflective avatars shielding his eyes. The crowds of the gods were obviously following the King of the Gods they all began laughing at cue right after Zeus clapped for bereavement pause among the divine audience.

The silver lighting bolt king of the sky stood up and extended his arms offering a greeting and said, "Createix."

Zeus called out to the dark goddess Kali, "oh look, isn't it the Goddess Createix," he said sounding purposely announced incorrectly.

"Oh, I FORGOT you were there sky one." Kali said sarcastically with a slight half nod careless to show respect to the king of the gods displaying by their actions you could tell there was a brief history untold feud between them two and Kali begins to tell Zeus, "don't Forget it was the dogmatic headship that made your fall seeing you so senile one would FORGET who is the king around here."

When Kali laughs mentions the word "FORGOT," that word drives Zeus crazy in an irate state keeping his cool showing a lining of his strong jaw biting down his teeth mouth close but it made his eyes glow bright blue like a fiery rod through his shades.

Rolling her eyes the dark goddess placed her hands on her hips and responded, "That's Creatrix."

Then Kali snapped back again," I'm sorry I FORGOT where I was going"

And she then tries to escort Stevie safely back to her chamber audience box seats cause Stevie was lost amidst a whole lot of trouble he's just now in, the Hindu goddess was desperately trying to seal Stevie away as fast a possible.

Kali was very elegant wearing a golden sari revealing a two-piece evening gown for a goddess with killer legs to show off covered in dangled red ruby jewels and gold cufflinks matching her bedazzled necklace string with skulls out of diamonds.

When kali confronted Zeus and his Olympian family she was a given back a crude salutation, it was the wine god that had to share his prejudiced comment with just his father and said, "that woman needs to be put in her box, then Zeus said in reply to only his son, "all in time."

Zeus belches out, after sipping from his gold chalice, "Bond or not your mortal ant broke the sacred ground laws."

Kali retaliated, "he's a Seer!" Then Zeus snapback with thunder rolling in from the background up above, "with no TITLE!"

She murmurs under her breath to hold her restraint, "Gods and their titles."

She then proclaimed again for Stevie, "The mortal son of men guided underneath the northern blue Star when Jupiter and Venus collide protected by I the watcher of the fourth star of the Ember chaos light and destruction grants authority…"

The sleazy wine god reminded Stevie of a mad bulldog taking the opportunity to retaliate for payback with a bit dash of white foam forming at the corner of his mouth Dionysus shouted, "YOU HAVE NO AUTHORITY!"

Zeus signaled his right hand to calm his obnoxious son, "He has governed his rights by interfering, therefore he is titled." Kali gave a gravely concerned look at Stevie, as she had no power to protect him now for he was on his own among the Gods.

Zeus then points towards the gridiron arena field and said with no questions

"Your mortal to the pits he goes." Zeus was lead on by his surrounding appeasers securing to validate his retribution he then smiled and said to Stevie, "You have no title."

"I fight for mortal men sons of Adam." They all look among at each other cause Stevie knew the son of Adam got all their attention. Dionysus murmur to himself, "Barn Animal."

Stevie riled up and collected everyone's attention announcing, "I 'am Stevie the Seer, mortal man son of Adam descendent of Seth under the house of Abraham follower of the lamb."

Just only among Zeus's court could they only hear their father rumble the word, "Peon, "that was uttered under his breath. It is a disgraceful word to call a human goes against the law of one mighty god, and when the hand of god gets called out against Stevie that made all the other gods trembled to look up above ready to be strike but it was Zeus who laughed and showed all the gods.

"Jehovah!" Zeus shouted in mockery and they all laughed making a sport of Stevie then the great sky god let out a sly remark to give a lesson, "it was your Lord hath made this Babel Tower common grounds sacred."

With all the laughter and heckles made towards him some shouted and called Stevie names from the crowds, "charlatan, faker," Stevie strayed onward by the will of his heart and he continued.

"Guided underneath the northern blue Star protected by the 4th star of the Ember light chaos and destruction, I am brother and fairy-bound to the royal fairy Essence, I' am the bearer of the witches' bane, slayer of the troll king, foes to the rocks and friends to the woods that they called me," Stevie went silent and was proud to say who he was, "I am the grey Shepherd or just call me Starman."

The gods weren't settled didn't know to take Stevie serious or not but it was Dionysus that couldn't control his temper and began to mock Stevie, "Starman!" Standing behind his father Zeus the king of the gods still seated in his gold eagle throne with his son the grape god spew out shouting shaking violently before he grabs someone else's goblet drink and split it on purpose to show remorse of a dramatic tantrum that can be shown how similar passion can throw with emotions even by the gods, "Who does he think he is? Kneel before us Gods, for your petulance snollygoster boast is wasteful in the presences before the king of the gods!"

Twattling and insults were hurled amongst the gods from in the crowds.

Stevie kindly took amused and smiled, "I do not follow other gods, the gods of the peoples are you; I only know of Yahweh the living God, our God, who is amongst everything, I do know he's a jealous God and his anger will burn against you, and He will destroy you from the face of the land."

It was the fire that spoke from his tongue in the heat of passion deep within Stevie that riled in him as he spoke the truth from his heart.

All were in a state of shock and a stir of commotions consist among the elite power of the gods that stood behind Zeus stirring the whole Babel Tower arena, some gasps in a comatose frozen with jaws drop mouths open there on the spot was even a faint shriek in the background as if Stevie had said something terrifying even to the gods.

Stevie swayed over and was escorted to the grounds to meet his fellow fairy friends upon greeting Trixs the fairy had a smirk on his face sneering flamboyantly at his friend composing Stevie into asking Trixs, "What?"

Stevie wasn't sure about Trix's response was meant to be funny but Trixs replied, "Someone's got hidden power!"

Stevie took his hand out for a shake but the fairy went in for a hug and was thankful, "you saved us again."

The twin fairy sister took no introduction and sought to say, "I'm surprised they didn't have you singing?"

There was an order to be announced and quickly Stevie had to ask, "What do you mean singing?" Trixs explained as fast as he could, "With every entitlement to your amnesty you must have an honorary hymn!"

Slyly announced, "And your recognition melody?" Asked Zeus the King of Gods who revealed his glistening white shiny grill, upholding his preys to an entrapment.

"Ahm, anything would be good right about now!" Ivy the silver purple fairy exclaimed.

Trixs began to panic and asked Stevie, "Any chance you got music up your sleeves would be the right time right about now, deejay?"

The brief silence was intensely discomfited even a cricket could hinder the dead air putting Stevie in a blind spot with his pants down.

"I… ah I… Oh, say can you see… by the…" Stevie said failing to get a pitch in with a tune.

"WE CAN'T HEAR YOU! One deity shouted from the crowd.

The gods disrupt into amusement cheers following after Zeus's belch of laughter signaling his court guards and the crowd a thumbs down. Erupted a wave of cheers in the amphitheater from the enthusiastic audience, frankly, Stevie started to ask, "Wait, wait, what does that mean?"

The two distressed twin fairies detached themselves from hugging and were fastening to conjure their weapons facing their coming death observant of the blue fog beginning to transpire on the grounds.

"We cant pixie transformed?" Trixs asked his sister whom she then replies conjuring her weapon, "It's the Demogorgon hindering our powers."

The ground became soggy wet hidden beneath the blue fog sprung up to their ankles spreading throughout the ground arena were some sporadic movement that would linger under the blue fog catching up to the hapless gang.

"We need to get to higher grounds, there's that boulder!" Exclaimed the twin sister fairy shouting and pointing at a nearby rock standing alone being their only refuge off grounds.

Climbing onto the height of ten-foot rock that use to be part of some ancient structure, Trixs was the last to climb reaching to the top of the rock exaggerating how he almost finally reach safe high ground then all of sudden a pink with blue vein tentacles sprang forth attach to the golden fairy wrap around his high leg ankle boots. Trixs Summoning his solar sunshine-ball with a flash bright light having no effect on the monster but blinding Stevie momentarily who then staggered witnessing his fairy friend's boot disintegrating in the god-eating monster's pink-blue tentacles.

Stevie scuttled to the top edge of the rock viewing the god-eating monster standing directly underneath the blue fog was a huge gaping mouth almost the size of the arena floor with multi-razor sharp teeth and multiple lashing tongues with a set of tentacles attach to the graving beast.

It was the scariest thing Stevie has ever witness petrified still with sudden fear washing over his sympathy for the loss of his fairy friend just out of the random he quickly thought, "is this soggy blue fog water or it's saliva."

Stevie was pulled back from falling off the rock ledge it was Trixs who reach for Stevie from behind. "You don't want to be Demogorgon food do you?" Stevie revealed his companionship towards his friend fairy immediately hug him in front of Trix's twin sister that is aghast at the newfound friendship between morals.

Instantly Ivy reacted pulling out a small dagger summoning a melee combo with purple light charm attacks knowingly fairies can't use magic for harm, "One thousand years paper cuts!" The purple fairy hurled her light charm ray from her dagger slicing with a counter surprise attack just above behind Stevie chopping one of the Demogorgon's tentacles from attacking them from behind.

Gasps with beguilement trifle stirred among the deities witnessing the unexpected attacks Stevie was in an august company for staying alive with the god-eater this long. "Using your weapon would be nice, Seer!" The twin fairy Ivy demanded to Stevie. Without any time to explain Stevie had no idea how to use his Aeon weapon or summoning its power back now knowing just now how his headphones can morph a rad white sword with angelic powers but now it only just wants to plays music when it wants to being wireless headphone around his neck.

Red slithering tongues with purple dots lash out from the God-eater monster that is known to eat moons snatched outward almost managing to get wrap around ahold of its three victims standing free for all on high grounds the tallest broken large stone pillar staple into the arena grounds resting on the tallest broken boulder.

The fairies were quick enough to dodge the unexpected swift attacks by flipping over each other and shifting around flexing Stevie from being caught by the tentacles flipping his body away from being snatch jumping from boulder to boulder spread across the grounds, as he stood there floored like he was in a ride while they all escape the monster's trenches.

Ivy taking the lead with her whip holding off the monster as many attacks as she can while Trixs took the rest from behind her with Stevie guarded in between the fairies. They felt gratitude for one another at this particular moment the stubborn fairy girl was already letting go and opening to Stevie a little piece of her.

"For long ago when they build the babel tower they try to reach the one God but instead they got the wrong God the eater God. It made everyone confuse with the loss of words to their language." Huffed the purple fairy hurdling over the monster's feeler tentacles grasps.

The blue fog was just a cover-up blanket over the grotesque titanic captive monster made out of hungry mouths with ferocious mouths having a sharp set of teethes in its pink tentacles and its monstrous mouths loaded with another set of a larger set of sharp monster teethes with other sets of razor teeth latch onto its tongues.

The crowd was louder than ever applauding with clamor cheers shouting from the audacity audience with their bold judgments satisfying the Lord of thunder's persona of his posture sitting on his might golden throne Zeus thunderbolt eyes could be seen lighting up behind the black shades he wore to cover his eyes.

"Behold the mediocre with titles," belching out in retribution it was the esquire wine god that shouted collecting each laughter after ridiculing. "A mere mortal who broke the Green pact treaty among Faes to keep elves and fairies hidden from the mortal world by grounding the Jontar the troll King and the same mortal that disintegrating the grand crone witch Baba Yaga in keeping the order of the Faes to their liberation world, and alas he intervenes in OUR affairs again this is his decree!"

The audience assemblies were chained to the edge of their seats mongering to their entertainment with much contempt towards their martyr, except Kali who was helpless under heel bound and guarded by a gentlemen of the temple tower's faceless servant butlers standing next to her escorting her left arm playing out looking onward to Kali in restraint of acting cordial like a lady having an fiery rage accelerating through the dark goddess's eyes with flames fuming from her sockets as she watches on helpless.

The monster whips its tongues finally snatching Trixs by his ankle Stevie saw the fairy's eyes go empty like a hollow shell from the inside.

The Demogorgon opened its gigantic monstrous mouth revealing how possible it is for mouths to have mouths in another mouth before devouring its appetizer, Ivy hacking off the pink tentacles of the monster's grip to her twin brother with another surprise attack using a dagger boomerang that came out of her back pocket if she had pockets Stevie thought.

The falling victim from the Demogorgon's grip Ivy tended to her comatose brother zapping Trix's life force the god-eater monster left him with red burn marks around his ankles. Scurry in circles lost in motion and confused Stevie stood there at the tip end edge of the boulder against the pink eater-god monster closing his eyes slowly awaiting as it peered and arose above the sheltering boulder with its tentacles beginning to open in the center of its multiple mouths that look like a starfish mouth revealing a set of dire multiple razor blade mouths it had several razor canals with pinholes canals assuming where everything goes to get digested.

Everything happens so fast leaving Stevie hopeless finally zapping out the second twin fairy into a coma from an attack behind Ivy with its toxic pink blue vein slimy tentacles feeler then the monster's limbs went after Stevie from behind unalarmed of the attack but knowingly by his senses detecting immediate danger it went off the chart never before with his left hand stung so cold taking off his left glove to tub his hands with ringing sensation going off in his ears.

Just inches away angled in all directions surrounding Stevie trapping him with the Demogorgon's tentacles stretching to reach him upset ready for its last vicious attack it sprung right after Stevie gave out a loud cry and yelled into the air.

While screaming Stevie looks straight up above him with striking bright neon blue eyes that it was glowing out from his mouth and eyes Stevie began to speak in an unfamiliar ancient foreign tongue.

Zeus took displease and discomfort from his posture of this recent surprise and said under his breath with his language, "the old words." (Angel language)

With one swing of his arm there appeared in Stevie's hand was the mighty awesome weapon that turned into the white glowing sword once more, again matching its art color from his wireless headphones that were still on his head he spoke in Angel's tongue everyone could tell that the monster known to eat gods and moons was confused holding still, using the Babel spell knowledge from the moon monster telepathically Stevie could read its thoughts not knowing the monster's tongue Stevie spoke its words in a command that would release the muse gods that were once punishment consume by the Demogorgon and cast into stones.

(SC Music/ 7) Chase Holfelder/The Star- Spangled Banner Minor Key Version -

It's already a known power Stevie's Aeon headphone's music can play out loud in any surroundings at any volume measurement in any place and began playing the anthem out loud among the gods in a giant amphitheater tower there was music appearing from everywhere from nowhere.

There were three separate entrances gates now open leading to the battleground floor a magical theatric spotlight was shown before three immortal gods appearing out from each gate flashing with such omnipotent power it shocks the whole Babel arena tower.

The muses see life as a poem, a theater act of adventures and drama that always transcends to feel in accord with the universe of the cosmic galaxies. It was the muses that bless Stevie with the art of attribution.

The gods of the muse were triplets, decorative in their selective style supporting a color, with one drape in red, the other in blue and the third was in white.

Walking on air with each step taking elevated higher heights with immense grace power they continued singing the anthem matching the tune to its music playing out-loud for Stevie as it is the Muses stature of the arena that favors the innocents overcoming the sacred ground rules taking the honor in pardoning Stevie's honorary hymn.

Was saved by the muse gods Stevie have delighted them and they favored him. They revealed the star spangle banner from his smartphone music list recharge them giving them their grace, to perform the power they once had again.

As the Muses first sang, it froze the arena monster into stone while everyone stood there in one place in their stands even the gods were frozen in shock as the Muses continued to sing the Star Spangled Banner.

"Impossible!" Exclaimed Zeus terrifying everyone and some of the gods around him as he was radiating ozone making the airdrop a hundred times heavier from his electrifying blue silver eyes peering through his dark shades roaring with rolling thunder in the background and with a strike of lighting as he slams his fist onto his golden arm throne chair.

The other gods were taking leads after their leader king of the gods feeling cheated and violated with reaping remorse the Olympian gods reflected with each other's selfish vanity pleasures.

The gods after they saw Stevie's scars some were in disbelief mistaken for he is the forsaken one, with rage Zeus calling it blasphemy.

Kali revealed the scars to them as she escorts Stevie off the boulder onto sacred grounds she showed them the attacks from the ancient witch Baba Yaga.

Stevie did find out through the stories all hear say about those scars were meant to be a sacrifice to rise an old powerful nemesis to this realm she alone could bring chaos bringing this world upside down into her domain known as the black queen. It was supposed to be the supreme witch for the witches but the gods knew better. The dark Hindu goddess showed the mark for those who can and for saw the future now knowing what Kali had meant but Zeus is the father of the sky king among their gods he gets the say at the end, and could not see the future to it.

Athena look disturbs and as well for those few other gods' that are known to see the future were also distraught.

Two Greek goddesses, one with eyes glistering in shiny brown gold glitter a wheat baron in a dress wearing a settled petite fall wreath over her head and the other was Persephone the familiar flower hippie goddess Stevie remembered a while back with the lawyer bicycle incident and began weeping holding tight to one another while Athena daughter of Zeus goddess of wisdom was dressed in a lawyer silhouette outfit wearing oval spectacles with a wise owl on her right shoulder and cried out, "And the second shall be the Millennial, the grey steward arising he is the shepherd for mortal men that walks among the Gods, the grey shepherd has met its destiny." Athena said rising her incongruous shield mentioning the shield like it was a person she then says, "look even my Aegis agrees and shines it warning" raising her shield to cover her face as if to protect from the damned. "This is foretold before our watchers' eyes, is it shall is the end near?"

Not showing any shear reaction Zeus mentions under his breath that had him questioning taking trustful notes from his wisdom daughter and said, "The millennial."

Another goddess of the sun from the Japanese's clan shone brightly dressed in a Shinto dress a red white kimono with her entourage high court myriads behind her chastising withholding her garments to her elaborated dress shining brightly reserving their outburst allowing their celestial queen to ask a question with a demeanor tone. "Is this alas the for coming of the end of creation for all that we are told about?"

Next to the Olympian's podium box seated on a cloud was a popular bald-headed solitary deity known to be jolly with a belly was no longer giggling that would laugh at everything but his happy bubble was pop short sat there with arms cross pouting his lips while it's neighbor was a black demonic bat-like god Chernobog the Slavic god of darkness being with crystallized hands, feet, and horns crushing a stone head chalice in its claw hands that took to his objection rumbling out loud spewing lava out of its mouth onto his black chest plate, "This can not happen!"

"We can not compete against the divine powers of free will" Orisha the Yoruba spirit African storm goddess proposed to ask immediately with rainwater pouring around her under a black cloud.

Mostly all the gods took their stance opposing against Stevie following the King of the Gods summoning a thunderbolt Zeus strike the first of his magnificent power as all the gods began to strike with their emit powers of cosmic ray blast and beams at cue to the words while the music continued out loud, "and the rockets red glare the bombs bursting in air gave proof through the night." It was a beautiful spontaneous sight glorifying the arena sky view of the never ever lasting tower above Stevie with dashing colors of multiple cosmic lights entwine with such radiant power bouncing off like fireworks from a glowing shielded dome projection summoned by the muse God triplets sponsoring their mortal millennial.

The twin fairies awoke from their poisonous slumber healed and arising standing with Stevie amazed at witnessing each of the three last Muses free, now singing with each one of the muses gods was facing in three directions with their right hand raised above holding up their glowing powerful dome shielded from the splendid exasperating light works of the threatening attack powers from the gods.

Once Stevie was able to catch his breathe relief from the god-monster the song star spangled banner as Trixs ask what's going on, Ivy the princess twin fairy told her brother, "your mortal men friend anthem is beautiful. Trix then asks, "What's a anthem?" Then Stevie still breathing a little hard catching his last breath and says, "Freedom."

Then it was with a demanding look at no ease did one of the main Muses exchanged with a dire look of serious revenge at their father Zeus without having to look up directly at the stand box podium eyeing their King of the Gods as they sang.

"Oh Say Does That Star Spangled Banner Yet Wave!" At the last word of "wave," the two gods of the muses look upon each other smiling before vanishing upward into a radiant light. The last third Muses look at Stevie with a with a gracious smile when he sang the word "Land," and place his palm over his head when he said the word, "free," and disappeared at "home of the brave."

14

Home sweet home Gnomes

"Blasphemy!"

ZEUS SHOUTED AFTER A COMPLETE fall of silence that following after the gods finished their retaliation surprise attack of unstoppable cosmic powers blasts at Stevie block and protected by a defense dome of a force field made up from the triplet gods of Muses but it was the angels that drop by like missile comets from above coming down so heavy and hot it looks like acme anvils on fire revealing to be angels with spreading wings crashing a firework party acting like hot raid squads busting an illegal festivity joint Stevie explains to his fellow peers.

"Heaven just intruded falling downward from grace kneeling on their knees as they landed they were angels in shiny gear already in combat formation that started clearing the tower arena busting up the party gathering of the elite gods that made everyone scattered and disappeared as some deities were being restraint and held back by a few guard angels.

It was the Slavic black god with its demonic wings being pin down chastise to the ground by chastity gold silver chains that emitted out from the angels acting like a patrol force."

It was already the next day back at the library Stevie was already check-in by Nerd and his Beta leaders reporting in and out of the library from interviews earlier by the librarian as he explains the rest of the story again to his squadron leaders Charlie and Ashley his two Seer commanders while Kris and Valarie are his colleague Seers in training were also around listening.

"The angels came down like the law with such a force it left everyone scattering away and they sensed my soul cause I'm a Christian. It felt as if the angels had a sense I was there, searching for me through the crowd, it was their leader of the angels that walks straight towards me through the confusion and exploding crowds but it was Kali at the end the Hindu Goddess that snatch me before the angel could reach me and she brought me back."

Ashley is known to work with the church with supernatural then asks, "what color rank was the drape of this arch warrior angel?" Stevie explains its saint Raphael when mentioning it spoke its name in Stevie's mind telling Ashley he saw sparkles of Emerald Green Light around this archangel wearing a green mantle strap around his breastplate with golden adornments. Stevie describes the angel having shoulder-length golden curly hair and explaining the angel's energy was different from any other being of deities it being drawn to as a warm healing power, like a blanket radiating healing with soothing calmness overcame Stevie's body tingling over his wombs as his body healed. Stevie then suggested, "This grace energy was thick and emerald green and it took a minutes after the raid when I saw him walk over towards us holding a long gold spear embroidered with silver-green flags and held in its left hand carrying a green flame mace probably a signature of his in the other hand."

It was recommended by the goddess Kali to not tell the whole truth of the story keeping his personal entitlements to himself especially to witches, the dark goddess explained to Stevie after they escaped the arena. "Dark witches always take advantage of prophecies especially involving destinies."

"After that, I ended back here, in Nerd's laboratory," Stevie said ending his story.

Ashley began to recite bits of pieces of Genesis 11:1-9, "Lord came down to see the city and the tower that people were building, If as one people speaking the same language they have begun to do this, then nothing they plan to do will be impossible for them." Charlie exchanged his thoughts by sharing to end Ashley's recite, "So the Lord scattered them from there over all the earth, and they stopped building the city."

"So this monster eats gods, moons, and stars, is entrap under the tower of babel, unbelievable?" Kris remarked while studying the manual to his cable guy tool remote.

Charlie then said, " Well whatever it is glad its lock away under a legendary tower guarded by Gods, and place on top of this cage is described like a tower gladiator arena who knew, wow wish I could be a contestant!"

Ashley- "The alarming of the angels suddenly dropping by must have sensed your presence, a mortal soul in peril among Gods is forbidden and they'll never allow it!"

Charlie cut in and exclaimed asking in favor of sport, "Buddy what's up with your Aeon weapon…. Morphing… a rad melee holy sword out of nowhere? Who's the dog in the HOUSE! Charlie cheering on changing the whole aspect of things with a positive attitude meant a big deal for the gang, "But on a serious note, we got to talk about that surprise Aeon weapon later, can't wait to spare a one on one with ya."

Stevie was told to level up with titlements as you progress has shown immediate results you are a fast learner, Charlie told Stevie

Stevie was recommended to go home and take a few days off, but before he could run outside clocking out for the rest of the day it was Valarie and Kris that stayed behind to see him leave.

"Guys something I got to get off my chest," Stevie explained to Kris and Valerie how obsessed Nerd was towards the Tower of Babel how he was rather very interested in the god-monster as he kept looking back at his new secret machine bot creation hidden behind that curtain of his, that everyone knows about but he was rather intrigued by the essences of the monster.

Valarie asking what did the Librarian say after what Stevie has told them remembering what the dark Goddess Kali had mentioned to never tell about his entitlements, explaining everything else about what all went down not leaving any details out.

Stevie's unfolds and replies when ask by Valarie what did the Librarian say, "nothing much really but it was Nerd while examining my health was more anticipated about the legends and tales about the tower of Babel describing like he's been there before. He was so intrigued with the arena pit-monster he wanted to know more about the Demogorgon. Stevie then mentions what Nerd had said something on the line linking somehow to his Aeon weapon triggering a reaction or response to when Stevie is in danger.

"It made you speak the old tongue, the angel language?" It gave Stevie a new suggestion when Valarie immediately asked without holding back. Stevie mentions the angel parts to Valarie and Kris and tells them what was told by Kali to not tell anyone about his uncertain powers especially to dark witches, with uncertainly he explains how he spoke the old tongue. That's when Valarie agreed with the Hindu goddess and started to roll the ball pejorative about witches not wanting Stevie or anyone promoting any good deeds that pre-set destiny for the better good, with Kris agreeing knowingly how the dark art's work.

So it was why Valarie says a plan is always a safe start, to begin with when dealing with witches and she also said after talking about Madame the Librarian, "it is also so suspicious of Madam who is over three hundred years old used to belong to the dark arts and suddenly begins interrogating you, the Librarian must know something about you."

HOME-

On the way home, it was known to be a four-hour drive to San Angelo Texas he was able to manage a little over three-hour drive and with that Stevie got the chance to recollect and think through his recent adventures thinking what a lifetime experience of being a Seer has already brought him.

He knew the consequences if things got tough for any Seer they have the choice to opt-out and quit will automatically pull you to lose the ability to possess second sight to perform your everyday supernatural patrolling by just revealing your secrets of seer's identity you will then turn back normal the next day at sunrise into a Normie aka regular person back to their average Joe job eight to five with no memory or recollection of being a Mystic Seer.

Stevie thought what a waste of a dream to have to never remember, looking back how Lisa at the trails there were four selected to be Seers in the beginning as newcomers and she failed to keep her secret of being a Seer and she never came back the next day.

Stevie was excited coming home to a surprise home cook meal and was always happy to see his parents raised as middle class Hispanic Americans being taught that, "you have to work to get what you want around here." Is something Stevie's father would always say being the 2nd generation as well as Stevie's mother.

His father was raised on a dirt-poor farm with five brothers somewhere in west Texas, while his mother was born in San Angelo Texas.

"How's Austin treating you?" Stevie's father asks at the dinner table cutting his meal taking a drink while his mother took her seat after setting the table. But it's always the mothers that can cut through a son's poker face, "You doing ok, cause you look different like you lost weight?" His father pointed out his son's new features, "See you got the white peach fuzz under that chin?" Stevie was quick in responding, "I like to call it wisdom." Being Latino his mother chats back instead of clutching pearls she clutched her gold jewelry necklace with her saints and asks, "Honey you're not stressing now are you?"

The town's got a military base, historic sites, a couple of lakes and rivers, local downtown pubs, they even have a great University placing among top the fifteen percent nationwide for its academics and that seems to sum it up. Stevie ended up dropping out of his hometown's University but always had a hard time staying focused in school.

Then the dad decided to charm in, "When are you going back to school?" Stevie's father was a hardworking, very logical man who was tight with his money for reasoning.

Stevie was caught off guard with bombarded questions coming simultaneously as he desperately tries to answer his parents. "My cable job has taught me a lot, and I did look at online classes," Stevie budded in to answer.

"Honey, did you find a doctor there?" His mother asks then his father continued, "You know there are a dozen of community colleges?"

His mother now referring to ask about Stevie's job, "You are not climbing high poles are you, cause you know how dangerous?" His father then cuts in to ask Stevie, "I bet your job can pay for your school have you check?" It was his father that wouldn't let it go, "it's been a year now and you haven't gone back to college, that's something you might want to consider for your future."

His mother sighed gladly to see his son back home smiling back at him with Stevie eating his plate of diner listening to another lecture of dads' theory of life, worst is comparisons to his siblings as his father has a Masters degree in Business and finance degree in Business and finance. Stevie always felt like he had big shoes to fill in looking over his older sibling's shadows being just an average kid that stood out of trouble and never really won anything. Being an honor roll student with few friends and was very active at school but never like his siblings his sister achieving homecoming queen and his older brother was prom king during their school curriculum. Being the black sheep of the family graduated from only high school with no plan or future career, unlike Stevie's older siblings where they both accomplish many through their lives having their own family and goal careers.

"Without that paper with your education slap on it son your life won't be easy, look at all the doctors, lawyers, the astronauts and most of all the real heroes that change this world all have degrees!" His father slammed his hand out of frustration onto the diner table that made Stevie stare straight at his father with a blank stare with his green eyes asking to be excused for not feeling too well. "Mijo, you look tired, why don't you go to bed?" His mother demanded as she wraps up the dinner table with a dreaded look towards her husband as the father replied to his wife by shrugging his shoulders reading the newspaper with the remote in his hand with the TV on the news station, "what?"

Compared to his sibling and let alone his father all graduated with degrees having high expectations it was an unsettled direction for Stevie feeling like he cant grow up he doesn't feel like an adult struggling to impress his father.

Sleeping comfortably in his old bedroom it hasn't been a full year since he moved out yet was turn into a guest room already with Stevie laying there thinking about all the possibilities of dreams that could come true with the choices he made becoming Seers before falling asleep.

Making progress reports and having test study appointments with Nerd about the same recurring repetitive dark dreams in his sleep ever since his journey near-death encountering Baba Yaga and that mysterious book of shadows his dark dreams started to happen once a week but lately its gotten worst to having a few a week waking up to being in the same usual cold dark place again, always alone with a monumental eerie sound of a deep rumble beneath the ground he continued to run into the vast dark places of the total void so dark it eats up the light from Stevie's flashlight from his phone while running from something but there was nothing that seems like miles of running that he felt something massive was watching him in the total darkness. For when he dreams feels like it lasts for a few minutes before waking up from his deep sleep but tonight's dreams it felt like forever.

Coldness stung the air in his dream with the frigid temperature creeping into his bones Stevie was calm and collect knowing the outcome of this dreadful dream he continued running along a cold stale stone gray wall who knows how far up it goes as he just continues to run forward till finally for the first time he ran into a dead end.

With the only light from his phone, everything was grey and Stevie lost his breath petrified catching himself at an end of a ledge cliff from falling into a nightmare forbid who knows what's down there into the dark pit wondering when he would awake from this dream.

Everything moved the wall, the ground, Stevie could tell through the dark his surrounding environment would shift and change catching his balance one would think is he in a mouth?

Then coming from dark pits down below was a foul blow of gust hot wind it shudders Stevie moving back away from the edge of the ledge shielding his face from the hot air and before waking up from his dream he thought he heard low mumble echoes through the hot wind it shook Stevie and said, "I... SEE... YOU...!"

It was Charlie that asks Stevie to keep checking the cable line behind his house once or twice more often specifically asking to check between Stevie's storm cellar and the old windmill but had no clue what he meant knowingly there is no cable in his backyard but always did notice his left hand would strongly go warmly numb.

That next morning behind his parent's old house he took the advantage to check out his backyard rearranging the basement storm cellar across from the old windmill with a stone water tower pump house with its original worn-out old septic tank. Listening to music sweeping cobwebs and dust from corners has always been one of Stevie's favorite chores to do since a kid that needed spring-cleaning twice a year. At times like cleaning Stevie would use music to escape from the reality of the real world always putting him on a spiritual level that always gives him an upbeat mood.

To give you more feel of Stevie's home his family lives in an old Victorian farmhouse off of Montague Street in San Angelo Texas; the story goes that two cowboys were shot in a gunfight over a game of poker on the front porch of Stevie's house in 1915. Another mishap happens in that home while a snowstorm in 1932, an old dame who carried a cane Mrs. Johnson who lived by herself, who died alone at the front end of the house from burns to her body from a sad accident with a space heater catching her bath rob on fire but promising this old house off Montague Street gets weirder as waning time passes on.

With spring-cleaning in a Hispanic family always comes with music while Stevie was jamming to his white Aeon ear-headphone over his head sweeping with a broom in the ground cellar outside in the backyard.

Surrounded in by country mesquite tress a vast secluded neighborhood area with a community park next to his parent's property jamming through his headphones the music took a silent break going to next song he recently just heard a faint unfamiliar screeching cry, figuring he chases down the wailing to calm his suspicious nerves.

When Stevie found the screeching and whimpering sound he saw an intriguing scene of a hawk in an entangled battle with a huge rattlesnake curled up around the bird, but it wasn't the live animal planet playing out before him that struck Stevie it was what's in the giant bird's claw grasp onto a tiny awkward small living humanoid in red and blue tiny garment clothing.

Like any person would Stevie settled the animals' attack with a nearby long stick, breaking up the fight tangled animals with a hard bump on the rattler's big head and another wack at the hawk to release its prey.

It was a big snake slithering away with some cut and scratches, the hawk releases its prey flying away after being knock by a poking stick there laid on the grounds was a tiny little mythical creature that can be measured by human hand distance from the tip of the thumb to the top of the little finger about six inches height long was passed out cold a tiny little mythical creature wearing a red cone hat.

It was a tiny grey-bearded man wearing a bright-colored tunic tiny blue jacket jumper over tiny brown trouser leggings with a tiny bag of tiny tools hung around at his side with his wide belt and light-colored brown tiny pelt boots.

That's when Stevie realizes with his new profound Seer eyes counting the benefits of having second sight it was an actual gnome in his backyard very tiny a lot smaller than the average displayed plastic gnome in people's garden yards.

The small gnome has a button nose with rosy-cheeks and friendly smiles that make their cheeks puff out having a full grey beard wearing a dunce cap, which is usually bright red to complete its wardrobe.

The little tiny small man with its small tiny beard was grey as smoky ash the tiny fellow slowly convalescing on getting up rolling over on its own from being restless on the ground from its recent forayed attack by animal predators while Stevie perceived to research the tiny small man from his secretive guy booklet guide recognize it to be Gnome.

Stevie read, ("Gnomes are known to be adequate mysterious creatures known to be legends and hardly ever seen even in the superstitious world but only told in tales possessing earth element magic and treasures"). Stevie also read, ("Gnomes are very vulnerable to animal attacks but are seven times stronger than the average human by strength and they speak no words but only with beeps conceivably they could be telepathic.")

"You ok buddy?" Said Stevie slowly approaching the small gnome that was motionless sitting on its little bottom lying on its back with its tiny knees up and small feet to the ground looking upward with its tiny eyes facing Stevie.

It was a squeak beep that came from the gnome that made Stevie giggle but a calm voice could be heard in Stevie's head telling him to look up at the old windmill that he was standing next to holding on to the windmill resting his posture.

Stevie looks up the Gnome disappeared from the ground but reappeared immediately within height place up above eye level with Stevie's eyes sitting on the ledge of the windmill lever.

Stevie asks, "You speak English?" The Gnome beeps at Stevie and Stevie tells it like a monolog, "No, you said you're using my mind to speak to me and thoughts have no language."

Stevie then asks suddenly, "You know my name?"

The tiny Gnome beeps again at Stevie as he replies to repeat what he was told, "you said, we know everything."

Then Stevie applies, "You mean there's more of you?"

Gnome explains that Stevie's backyard host two gnome kingdoms since half of millennia and then asks Stevie a random question ignoring the fact there are kingdoms in Stevie's back yard.

"No... I'm not an angel." Stevie said to the tiny gnome with it beeping back at Stevie he question the gnome's accusation? "you smell holy magic on me?"

The gnome was a strange little figure resemblance of a tiny Santa clause with his solid bright conical red hat and having a feral appearance of white bushy beard with a button rosy nose matching his puffy rosy cheeks revealing tiny dimples with a stained smile.

"I' am a Seer, glad to see your ok," Stevie replied to the telepathic Gnome that thanked Stevie.

Stevie notices the resemblances in height of the Gnomes towards its Fae cousins the Brownies being a half-foot taller but is more comparable with elves being tiny, with which they shared pointed ears and high cheekbones being on the chubbier side made them jollier ever so.

Stevie also read from the Seer's guide booklet, Gnomes only appear to be the most kind creatures being that they are highly influential mystic very intelligent and mysterious sometimes were said to have magical powers that gnome can sense kindness sincerity from anyone by peering into their soul.

They are an innately curious race and had a strong affinity for all things magical, particularly the arcane.

Gnomes have sensitive hearing and were often capable of hearing things that other races might miss. Gnomish eyes were also suited for seeing in low-light conditions, to a degree comparable with elves.

"I did witness the great god-eater monster," Stevie told the small tiny gnome.

It beeps asking Stevie and he replies, "power of the all-tongue, huh, that's how I know the lost tongue of your people cause is the result of witnessing the god-eater the Demogorgon and you can't believe I was able to live to tell about it?"

It made Stevie confused at first but then he picks up on the gnome being a jokester starting to enjoy his new company, "Oh, I get it you're funny mister."

The tiny gnome beeps laughing together finishing breaking each other's jokes then Stevie seriously had to ask, "so in confronting with the power of the All-Tongue monster, shall speak any witness of creatures with the will to hear any native language, that is interesting."

Its gnomish eyes were often compared to look like puppy eyes glittering in black or blue and having reddish brown tan skin with the degree features of an old jolly man however, gnomes showed a greater degree of aging as they grew older and once a gnome had passed his or her first century, their hair began to gray, if it was not already white, and their skin began to wrinkle as in humans it also says in his seer booklet even the oldest gnome retained a vitality that would be extraordinarily unusual among many of the younger races.

"The pleasure is mine, little fellow," Stevie replied as the tiny Gnome bowed towards Stevie in gratitude for saving his little life after explaining to Stevie animal predator's senses turn into killer instincts towards gnomes and to never blame an animal for its reasoning.

"You do know there's a culture about you and your kind everywhere throughout our world, I use to watch you on a cartoon television show in the mornings." The gnome beeps back explaining as Stevie replies to reframe what he heard from the little guy, "So gnomes avoid interaction with humans not so fond of our world but you tiny fellows maintain good relation-ships with deer's, birds, rabbits, foxes, armadillo, and squirrels.

The little Gnome beeps back with Stevie replying, "You've been living here behind my house, and you're over nine hundred years old?" Stevie builds a unique friendship within minutes sharing salutations with little gnome regarding to their unexpected greeting and height.

"So you're saying you are one of the few last gnome clans right here in Texas on the planet earth known as the kingdom Anemos mill located in my backyard beyond in my windmill brick water pump tower house and yet there's another underground neighborhood gnome kingdom below my basement cellar?"

Gnomes might have lacked the drive and ambition of other races, particularly humans, but their creativity gave them a strong ability for ingenuity.

The tiny Gnome beeped in communication with Stevie making him laugh as he was trying to hold his laughter giggles but it would talk through telepathic sharing their tales and history. "So there's a civil rivalry between the gnome clans, and I just made friends with a troublesome renegade Gnome asking a favor for who is in love with a maiden from a rivalry Gnome kingdom underneath ground beyond my basement cellar and you're asking me for help?" The tiny Gnome beep nodding blushing red portraying itself it felt silly for asking then Stevie replied, "Far out! Count me in!"

Stevie was told there's a charm strung in the air for centuries that have cursed the Gnomes to never fall in love for death is always inches near that falls upon close by predators that is always near even if the gnome doesn't reveal their love it's tainted with smells, the gnome says falling in love turns a gnome into a prey attracting to animal predators.

Stevie replies about the Gnome tale, "That's horrible it all began with a small folk myth about a legendary Gnome king that guards dangerous treasures under my house!" The little tiny gnome couldn't say much about the small folk myth but mentions their great one the gnome king resides to be living in Stevie's house all this time under his family's nose in his old pantry under the stairs with his parents changing it to a storage room closet.

A lot of thoughts went through Stevie's mind both creepy and mesmerizing knowingly something legendary has been sitting in his house ever since they moved in guarding legendary treasure supposedly under his house.

Stevie turned into an intrigued geek standing to sit next to the tornado cellar for once he felt relevant to share his potency of dating skills even though he had no experience.

There he was placed on top of the cellar was the friendly Gnome sitting on his bottom comfortably swing his tiny legs off the edge of the cellar taking interest to learn human instincts watching his human friend while Stevie took the pleasure to give a tip of advice on how to charm or win a girl when he never had a girlfriend before.

"Now, what I do know…" Stevie tentatively took a brief moment and thought for a while as he froze and then he exclaimed, "Music is the key that we can all speak no matter whom or what and where you're from we all understand rhythm, and girls like it when guys can dance!"

The Gnome was jolly at Stevie's reaction giggling at the gnome and his beeps while clapping at Stevie as he practices his dance moves to take a spin then doing the Pee-Wee Herman dance move right after he did the moonwalk.

The Gnome tilt its head observing his human friend then resting his tiny head on its little hands with his elbow on its lap watching Stevie as he wore his white Aeon headphones dancing away listening to music. "First you need music, here I learned a cool trick." Stevie took his white headphones pushing the left side button releasing the music to be played out loud. The music was loud enough Stevie's Aeon headphones could play sound bytes as if surrounded by stereos.

"Then you need rhythm." Stevie's Aeon picks up from his favorite playlist of spring-cleaning jams and the music rips to "Selena Biddi Biddi bom bom."

(SC Music/8)

Stevie may be a Hispanic Mexican-American that didn't speak Spanish fluently, but he sure did know the whole words to the song. "Now watch this move," Stevie said showing his move doing slow rotation hip movements then picking up the pace shaking his bottom behind in circles, "and they call this the washing machine."

Dancing in circles with a waltzing beat of Tejano music moves originated from local folks dancing from Columbia beats mix in with many regional cultures like reggeaton and salsa that shuffled its way across Texas.

"If your inner circle isn't hip to the steps, you don't need to worry, any move will work!" Stevie said as he shows his cumbia moves then singing the lyrics at cue beats of the song.

The tiny Gnome stood up beside Stevie and began to coy around building up the courage to copycat Stevie with its eyes so puffy it looks like a puppy ready to play fetch. "The moves can be quite simple." Cranking up Selena's Biddi Biddi Bom Bom Cumbia mix.

"Stand with both feet together, and listen for the one-two-three beats. Then, on each beat, shift your right foot forward in front of you then your left foot at an angle, take a small step in place forward with your feet and bounce your hip to the beat." Stevie confidently keeps his composure from laughing at the cuteness of a tiny humanoid known for its eccentric sense of humor, it squatted like a tiny duck with inquisitiveness, it was quickly engineering the prowess dance moves oddly like a baby shaking its little bottom with Stevie continuing. "Move your right foot back to the starting position and then repeat the sequence on the other side, starting with your left foot. If you have a partner they complete the steps on the opposite feet. Once you master these basics, add some hip bumps and a spin, girls love that, and you'll soon be swooning your maiden."

The two acquaintances immediately hit it off with a shakedown competition to double beats of the washer machine move to the music. Stevie encouraging his tiny friend to take it to the end with the music dancing and singing to the famous lyrics to Selena, "Cuando escucho esta canción mi corazón quiere cantar asi!"

It was just what Stevie needed heading back to Austin at the end of the weekend the next day retiring from his home-town from his mini-break was a boost of prosperity and peace of mind to collect from his high exhilarating rapid adventures of being a cable guy making unusual friends everywhere he goes.

A couple of thoughts strung in the back of Stevie's head looking back at the impetuous responsibilities of being a Seer cable guy. On the road again a Sunday night to Austin on state 71, it felt odd to Stevie not having his Aeon earphone headset weapon put away in his bag normally would be around his neck he wondered how intent it was with his new tiny acquaintance sup friend in terms supernatural, wondering how the tiny Gnome friend fair with his Gnome maiden with the dating tips but it was meeting the gnomes telling Stevie what the magical creatures think of him the chosen path to change things. Stevie was extremely excited to come back home next time to encounter the tiny gnome again, It told him legends among the supernatural deaf to human ears they say that the next Apotheosis mortal man of Adam will walk the line with Gods and mark their territory. You control the outcome the tiny gnome said to Stevie, the gnome believes Stevie will free the land that once was before when humans among the magical creatures together defying the natural order splitting multiple dimensions. Stevie didn't know what the gnome meant explaining to Stevie afterward in a simplistic as can be for Stevie the little gnome meant, "to live in a world with humans." The tiny old gnomes think it's impossible but say's the younger gnomes believe there will be a time when magical creature can coexist with mortal men.

Stevie thought and thought with all the possibilities on his long drive back to Austin and just now he thought to himself why the Gnome never did reveal its name.

15

House Of the elevens

STEVIE SUDDENLY FOUND HIMSELF WAKING up in his truck in Central Austin, parked in the elves territory, sitting in his truck dazed and confused finding to be in front of Castle Hill on Baylor Street a popular urban spot for the locals an entrance to the elf kingdom, the graffiti park.

"How did I get here?" Stevie murmured, as he awkwardly looks over at his Seer booklet and remembering seeing a few selections reviewing the local elves that said something on the line about tree elves are Cloudians they live in trees that are in the clouds, the last of their kind.

It was late at Sunday night Stevie began warming up his left frozen hand with his ears ringing, unexpectedly there was a familiar stranger beside him with a wooden flute in its hand sitting in the passenger seat clad in greenery. "I swore I was driving to my place?" Stevie quickly diagnoses the mysterious green character, he recognized it was the fairy's opponent the elf prince from the tower of Babel arena.

Stevie took his next approach very calmly try not to show affection of astonishment or remorse by the unexpected guest being not surprised or remorse by the unexpected guest as Stevie sat there thinking of hundred concept ideas of what just could have happened with no recollection of how he got there. "I'm going to assume it was you somehow with that wood flute and your hypnotic elf magic that brought me here?" The elf sneered with a sly smile and replied, "you are wiser than your quick tongue Seer."

Stevie followed the tree elf without questioning up a steep hill also use to be known as a local spot for open art-pop graffiti for the public placing his white Aeon earphones over his head, following upward towards a wall concrete slab covered with graffiti art. The elf then placed his hand onto the graffiti wall and blew a tune with his wooden flute. The graphic spray paint art began to swirl changing into a forbidden gate taking formidable shapes appearing into a wooden enchanted silver tree door. "Starman, Seer of the cable guy." That tickled Stevie from the inside grinning ear-to-ear trying to not turn red allowing himself to hear the rest of what the tree elf has to say.

"Also known as Stevie who shares the light brotherhood bound to my rival the fairy prince of Essence violated an offense in charge of breaking the green treaty among Faes." Stevie innocently intruded briefly to say looking up to the elf prince before Stevie was cut off, "The green treaty, I didn't know, I was just standing there and then…" The prince Elf then gave off an advance glare warning meeting eye contact with Stevie as if he would be killed next time if he interrupted.

"A challenged by ritual combat is sacred among the Gods and creatures of your fable tales, and you interfered therefore you are hereby adjudicated summoned by the Elven silver court Avallon of Tartaria. You are to be a guess and escorted immediately with no repercussion." The prince then gave a chance for Stevie to reply.

"Well I was looking forward to my bed night rest, but I can spare a few energy left, were adults it's past our bedtime, I don't mind a late elf tour." Stevie wink and the elf responded coldly, "I don't play mortal games, you are to be trialed."

Stevie then scoffed with a little laugh to lighten the heavy scene, "aren't you guys home welcoming?"

Stevie was led through the eleven magical silver wooden doors transported suddenly slipping into a brighter light atmosphere a different realm that holds its skies filled with bioluminescent iridescent colors.

The view was breathtaking best described to be like on a floating island in the air of ever greenery plateau that seemed afloat among the clouds in high evaluation escape background.

Standing in awe before the vast forest's gates, marveling at the cedar trees' height, breathing in their incense there in the middle view among the forest with miles of the plateau was of a giant enchanted silver crystal green tree beholding a silver castle infused within the gigantic tree.

Stevie was mesmerized by the chrome scenery of countless multiple greenery maze before him with unique radiant plants, among most were mainly magnolias flowers reflecting and shinning throughout the greenery. The whole enchanted eleven realms was an out of this world experience Stevie was an alien to the environment it had gleaming silver lined crystals on everything that looks like beads of water droplets bringing out the light reflecting mirage its glistening crystal scenery throughout the whole eleven plateaux.

"What is this place, utopia?" Stevie asks sarcastically with all respect with everything glowing reflecting from the atmosphere calmly and motionlessly with peeking bright stars so close up above confusing the changing skies not knowing if it was sunrise or sunset.

The seer booklet in Stevie's hand as he read following and listening to the elf it explains the tree elves were the original native Texans that are a Nomadic tribe, living above the clouds in a different realm hidden from all human eyes it was basically elves living on floating islands of mystical trees in comparison it was the size of Hawaii except there was no ocean but the air free-fall and gathering clouds.

"This is the last colossal tree from the old world internal to the ancient giants that are no more a sacred ground that has no limits to its foundation, there have been no records of any human that has ever set foot here since after the great flood. This is home of my people we call ourselves Cloudians the high hills, the tree of ages last of its kind before the old world died, Avallon of Tartaria the silver cloud land of the air we are the lost tree people of my tribe."

The elf prince escorted Stevie who is holding his excitement composure lost secret history absorbed his interest got Stevie quickly forgotten he is to be persecuted and was happily oblige to follow the eleven princes leading a path into the extraordinary giant tree that is the largest tree he has ever seen.

The giant tree trunks were approximately 2.5 miles across the sky with the tree sprouted full length a spectacular sight about reaching 10 miles upward into the sky.

"We call the elven realm Avallon also known from the old world as the four walls of Tartaria surrounded by masses of tall trees and very high hills the deeper you go among the middle of the floating plateau within the giant tree escape with four distinctive top levels grounds making a formidable tree castle.

We were the quello known to be the first civilization before your kind, we are the remaining elves of this free world, and Tartaria is the name of our ancestral realm." With fair complex white skin with pointed up ears that resemble the fairies ears the elf continues. "Tartaria is lost history to your humankind, look it up sometime," the elf said boorishly with a hidden grimace of its face.

You couldn't even describe how to elaborated the ancient giant tree is doesn't do justice it being so surreal even the smallest trees were so large you could not see the top of the trees reflecting light from the magical gentle colorful frozen sky filled with giant stars among the time set sky background with a set view of the sunrise to the left behind the plateau view and a sunset to the right side of the floating giant tree island with stars ripping across the sky.

With the elf leading the way chimed in to let Stevie in on a history secret of his soaring chrome world, "It's there in your human documents your stories known as the Bible we are mention in Daniel 4:11 ("the tree grew and was strong, and the height thereof reached unto heaven, and the sight thereof to the ends of the earth.")"

The royal prince elf continues to surprise Stevie, "We reside from the Cedars of Lebanon an Island of cypress in your human world that there was once used to be a one great giant cedar tree in your world before your time its acorn is to our mother tree. The last giant tree survived from the great war of the fallen." It was so enormous the tree goes above the clouds so when you travel up the everlasting stairway path spiraling throughout the giant tree landscape castle you would be looking down from clouds.

Traveling onward the elf spoke up, "What makes you Seers believe you can trust your supreme leader the grand hind witches are known to be evil? The elf prince asks Stevie as he led the trail path and Stevie replying, "The Librarian does look scary but I don't think she's evil."

The drifting giant floating tree upon a crystal castle on top of mountain plateau giant tree upon the clouds looked treacherous from high atop from a cliff there they followed through an old goat path hidden within the rocks only the eyes of an elf could see its confusing trail directions. "We follow it till we could go no further into coming upon an unnatural upstream creek going upward on a hill against gravity following the flowing gentle glowing illuminated waters mixed in with glowing blue-green pebbles lighting up the freshwater stream guiding the way into a majestic small glowing fluorescent dye lake fascinating enough the glowing lake had it's constant small two feet waves that were unexplainable.

Perch at the end above the glowing lake lead a woven tunnel made out of chrome shiny branches there was an entrance to a hall with jungle pillars of silver trees decorated with greenery and banners of the royalty elven silver court Avallon of Tartaria.

While Stevie was being led into a large garden expo with the silver court manor of the elves fanfare playing its music could be heard of heavenly voices of mystery singers vocalizing to soft tunes of medley throughout their elven halls of the elven court the elf prince escort then explains to Stevie the royal rules, "Here's everything you must need to know Starman to make yourself etiquette among my people as you are summoned hereby the high court to greet the royal elven lord king Oberion. In our precedent traditions make sure you always receive and give the glass with two hands to show sign of respect." It didn't help Stevie one bit as the elf inconsiderately rapidly brushes through the royal customary rules of the elves customs and requirements expectations but the next part took Stevie into a trip after when he was explained if the glasses are empty you are obligated to fill it especially when you're the lowest accompaniment than the company you apply to a banquet among with you will a be servant to the royal party. Stevie didn't think any much of it but it never phased the elf prince how degrading to make one serve a party as a guest let alone because he was human. "Elves tend to see humans as bottom class commoners below dwarfs they are third-class unfortunately extinct long ago."

Stevie then asks, "Who's above the dwarfs?" The elf responded back, "fairies."

Stevie was quite fond of the supernatural's own distinctive diverse cultures and their traditions especially involving obscurity magical creatures of the supernatural.

The elf retorted to say, "that means things can get out of hand pretty quickly so if you don't want to drink a lot make sure you leave your glass half full. In addition to this again if the host guest you drink with is older when you sip from the glass turn your head slightly away from them as another sign of respect to have no eye contact. You have to be careful drinking among elves especially royalty because refusing to drink with them basically means classless manners stating you don't societal especially when they want to be friends and they may take it personally."

The kidnapping to be trailed may have come off too soon as a funny comical issue for such request but for Stevie he was gladly entertained with curiosity getting the best of him.

Throughout the elven halls built inside from the giant tree, everything was made of silver wood willow trees surrounded by silver glowing ponds standing in the middle upon a giant Lilly pad in all the parts of this majestic land there was an uncalamity of chorus voices could be heard with a gentle tune carried through the air that mystically touches Stevie with a heartfelt of emotions as he began to feel light-headed a feeling he was floating on air. "What is this music, the harmony is something I've never heard of before, it's so enchanting." Stevie innocently spoke out of line and said with an action of unrepentant formality.

The elf prince slyly smirks back at Stevie and replies, "Our sacred waters is old magic, the enchanted water reflects sirens tunes foreshadowing deep into the perceiver's hearts." The elf paused and continued to raise his right arm signaling to listen to tunes of chime bells from water dwells lighting up the halls with woodwind remix contrast, "This melody that embraces you, it has never been heard before in our halls it's the tune is what concerns me." Stevie happily obliges to answer the tune melody clapping as he won on a game show sharing his opinion, "What a wonderful world is the music song that concerns you, it's not my favorite but it is a classic!"

(SC Music/9)

Leading into an entrance of a grand court oval hall with glowing luminous greenery revealing shiny silver weeping willow trees glistening surrounding a giant magnolia flower bud attach to the ancient giant silver tree that stood out of place behind upon a high throne floor embroiled with large twisted silver tree bark glistening as it was collaborating with enchanted elven drapery that swings closed around the giant white magnolia flower with silver weeping willows and royal green silver curtains.

Among the elven halls were a few selective aristocrats characters that stood out among the fulfilled crowd of the elven royal guards, most in shiny armory stealth with gear weapons. They all carried elven features like their kin cousin's the fairies with eyes of metallic color and pointy ears that some are bared hidden by their headgears having olive light skin complexion with others some are fair bronze tan.

The entranced elven hall was just as elegant as it was to its people dress in royalty erotic gear while the narcissistic and arrogant resemble in the Seer guide booklet but their manners were less clothing for the royals and more skin was the elves trademark. The elves are very distinctive in affluent royalty their clothes give off their opulence with some elves having a leaf embroidered that some are colored in chrome emerald, gold, and green, the warriors wore red fern leaves embroidered on their shiny shields. The elven lord has multi colors and his royal colors are green chrome and silver some gold. It was a culture of the fittest bodies to be known that were the elves flashing themselves among the supernatural community.

Gossips and talks with rumors were stirred among the aristocracy families of elven crowds pointing out strongly their characteristics in Stevie's Seer guide booklet as he read on into his booklet it was given obviously to Stevie again he was the center of the attention.

Left alone with the chamberlains of the elves to the silver court Stevie took interest in their traditions as they dressed up Stevie quickly and steadily with haste he never felt one touch but the garment dressed in a silver-white overhead clothing settled in by the elf courtier of the high stool rolling up a lavish foliage service tray decorated with silver art foliage leaves occupied with royal shape flower chalices and grand design of honeysuckle vase with everlasting shiny sweet nectar.

Stevie meets his capture the elven prince shortly again among his royal domains with the elf prince smiling ear to ear revealing he was charmed this time seeing a different side of the elf to have seen Stevie among his home palace to make amends but the elf had hidden his intentions very well till now.

The elves chamberlains immediately escorted Stevie direly to the service tray equipped him to be the royal servant but it was the elf prince that commanded his servants to stop.

It was the reflection that Stevie understood the elf prince sticking his hand out confused by the mix up last time encountering Stevie in the past when they met for the first time disregarding Stevie's handshake but this time the elf prince had his hand sticking out with a limeade glass in his other hand as a peace offering explaining for saving his elven sister smiling ear to ear.

Stevie accepted the kind gesture taking the elven prince's hand and shook but witnessing this new found friendship was there their Lord the elf king looking down from his high pedestal throne stage among the escalade of his people taking notice and was very displeased making his way towards the edge of his throne court with his elven vizier in bizarre greenery glossy silver-green attire almost trying to steal everyone's attention whispering to his lord's ear as the eleven king proclaim out loud to let known his presences, "It broke the lot territory laws, destroying govern rulings by slaughtering troll kings are Elves not free to roam as where ever with no fear of consequences." The Elf King was holding endearment to his people from the harm of the outside world by means finding out only letting the royal elves roam free among the human earth realm.

The royals were very aristocracy among their subordinate's elves, followers in their shiny armors, and chrome guard pads that glisten sheer emerald green with shine silver having an eerie effect glow.

The elf prince hinted at Stevie with just looks incautious to know his place queuing Stevie to the silver trey hopeful of reminding him what he was told about the traditions of servicing royalty elves as their Elf Lord King yelled.

"Commoner, where is my drink!"

Stevie acted frantic being queued shuffling his feet playing the servant that he didn't mind being a butler with his eyes wide and mouth shut with too much gratitude he was trying to grasp everything stopping himself from grinning so much putting on a sour face piercing his lips together as Stevie began blushing red holding his breath while pushing the silver tray having formidable luck bound to make fool complex scenarios without knowingly Stevie struggled by annoyances of accidents how he was able to pull everyone's attention throughout the hall chambers by making the tray squeal awkwardly across the court as it's ironically known to every elf that the eleven transportable serving dish made out of pure silver is so precise in steering it has never made a screeching sound before as Stevie makes a face pushing the silver eleven salvers on its wheels.

Approaching the light bright silver throne court Stevie's capture the elf prince taking attention to his king and bowed, "King Oberion, monarchs of the light realm, father May I present you, Starman, the see..."

Stevie will always take enjoyment being finally known to his dream fantasy hero name among the supernatural but it was their elf lord king that robbed Stevie's compulsion glory of naming titles interrupting the prince the king grabbing his goblet silver chalice from the white silver tray without any notice at Stevie holding out his goblet to be served as Stevie began to pour into the king's white silver chalice, "Dare to bring a commoner mortal, especially it being a time-waster in my domains before our presences, you know the consequences Ezra. I don't want to hear anything of it!

The Elf Lord took a sip from his silver chalice, as it was ordained in elves culture the commonalty server must drink aside with allegiance if among higher rank must look away from royalty while drinking was a sign of respect but the crowd was paralyzed at the suddenness of the clumsy unawareness from Stevie as he sips from his cup with much difficulty with making a slurping sound as if it were soup bowl holding his large chalice awkwardly forward towards the elf lord trying to drink from the side of his lip with his head tilt to the side looking away trying not to spill a drip taking big gulps holding the liquid in his mouth striving to recognize the flavor of his mysterious drink.

The elf lord king then looks at Stevie aghast in disgust all while their elf prince enjoyed every moment trying to hold back his giggles as he was trying to maintain a calm gesture without smiling.

"Toss the waster into the barrows of Agog shall the ancient deep roots feast on his flesh!" Then Stevie spit out his mouthful drink of sweet nectar, "WHAT?" Stevie exclaimed.

The elven king never even bothered again to address nor look at Stevie as Stevie was so focus and drawn to the attention of the giant tall creature that stood out among the elves standing there silent it was hooded the mysterious warrior monster with its antlers sprouting standing guard and tall behind their elf lord king that served the prince once awhile back at the skate park, Stevie was remembering.

The Elven Lord King of all elves regarded with such a disdain taste in his mouth it set the tone in the light throne room hall that made the prince doubt his special guest even more. The elven lord's attire was secluded in a tight royal chrome garment with a round silver gold chest plate encrusted with diamonds and emeralds designed to portray ancient roots of the silver tree, addressing his elf prince son Ezra, who then bowed his head again like a sad puppy towards his father while escorting Stevie along their standing grounds before the throne and their party with his silver eleven trays in the middle of the court oval throne room surrounded by very luxurious quorum quidnuncs elves some tattooed in silver and gold and wore gold green emerald and mostly silver jewelry that glistens.

"Sire," said the annoying eleven clad the lord king's second command vizier standing beside him and continued. "The complication is this mere mortal commoner is the intruder of the sacred ritual combat shaming our people and champion over the troll king, alas breaking the green treaty peace among folks."

Their elven lord king took immediately with a displease snob look studying up and down at Stevie as if he missed something replying in a demise forceful facial smile looking at Stevie questioning his features with just his stare.

There among every crowd everyone took bowed by surprise except Stevie to an elven child princess came out of nowhere having a light glow that lingers to her intruding her family royal affairs by coming forth near her father's court to culminate her reasoning, "this mere complication is no ordinary mortal, he is my savior father." The eleven-girl child then giggled out her personal last revenge of redemption.

Stevie was reasoning towards the elven child remembering saving her from the Jontar the troll king being drawn to her perfectionist innocence's he took his turn to fill up his chalice after serving the elven child princess as they both took sips together with Stevie slurping again following the elves culture with his face away from the elven child clueless of her age but keep eye contact as the elven child giggled at Stevie.

There was only one in the room who dares challenge to speak before their elven lord king was the elven child princess Ayeran among royal elven parties she was pardoning her brother the elf prince to arise from bowing.

The child was glowing with a glimmer in a silver shade with Stevie remembering a flashback of running into her underground back from the troll cave after the skate park quarrel with her prince brother that gave the tip leading them to the Troll king's lair at the beginning that ended up saving her.

"Why father, Starman is no intruder he is the treaty breaker, the Troll King slayer," the elven child chuckled and continued holding everyone's attention. "It's with fresh air he is the witches' bane, a mortal seer among men of Adam, who dared broke sacred oath and treaties of my people but most of all shamed the elven clan before the gods." The elven child chuckled again as if she was a rebel of her clan and said, "How amusing."

Stevie then understood even out of this world of royal families of elves has complications between son, father and daughter were displayed in public with the elven lord looking distraught and confused and asked his daughter confusingly, "but Ayeran this mere mortal is our complication?"

"Whoa... whoa...," Stevie intervene to excuse himself and confronted innocently immediately with his palms in the air. "I'm not who you think I 'am, I'm just a farm dude raised out of west Texas with a city heart."

Ezra the elf prince suddenly flips a new leaf and began to favor his hostage friend validating to excusing himself before his father and announced, "Starman is guided by the one eye underneath the great blue Star protected by the watcher of the fourth star of the Ember light of chaos and destruction, fairy bond-ship to the fairy prince and is loyal with the royal fairy Essences, he is the bearer of the witches' bane, slayer of the king troll the watchers call him the grey steward arising."

Everyone still and silent as the elf prince continue to voucher for Stevie,

"He is known as Stevie Ruiz a recent Seer added to their addition, already known for many titles, and a great asset to their team as they once lead a search group that I help to recover him."

"Ah, yea, isn't that what a team family does for each other?" Stevie exclaimed having no excuse speaking out of turn he had already step over the line with the elves unknowingly the royalties rules striking every elf soldier to take arm in command pointing their spear weapons and agile elven swords towards Stevie for ill speaking before ahead their king elven lord.

Stevie couldn't be shocked anymore and relinquish to kept silent not knowing his place the Elven Lord signaled a halt to his soldier cavalries astonishing everyone at Stevie's behavior for this was the first time a mortal was ever allowed in their realm with Stevie perusing his justice he was allowed to plea.

"My attentions I swear was not intentional," Stevie said. "My actions took me by surprise not knowing the powers I possess back at the babel tower arena and not knowing the powers of my Aeon it posses like it has a mind of its own."

The elven lord king then snaps back and asks, "That's an Aeon, a weapon?" The elven lord starred and sneered directly at the white Aeon ear headphones decorated in the splash art paint placed over Stevie's head. "Space color special edition, they are headphones by great design and it plays music." Said the elf prince staring hopelessly looking for recovery from his father the Lord of the Elves as he said proudly.

Stevie was confused and tried to hide his confliction at the dysfunction of the royal family how they treat one another and to describe the dilettantes of the royal family has the elf son prince longer for his father's appreciation whereas the elven child sibling princess defies her father in rebellious all awhile the father strives for his daughter's affection.

"Trixs is my fairy friend, and he was in danger," Stevie said in a statement to rectify his justice.

Many emotions ran high among the elven halls of their hearers filled with whispers obtaining rumors about Stevie to be a slave or bounded to fairy control strung in the air teasing Stevie's ear.

The elven child misspoke in eleven tongued, "Aelic Dämon," while Stevie wore his Aeon wireless headphone on his head he then could understand the language of the elves through his headphones.

"He carries the mark, no doubt he's the one."

"The one?" Stevie murmured under his breath that he suddenly caught on and interrupted with an alibi. "Look all these titles are nice but I'm just a guy who's a proud Hispanic-Texan that loves chips and salsa," Stevie said with his hands innocently in the air.

As Stevie was trying to weasel his way out of the conversation the elf lord king commanded Stevie at a halt to stand still, "I shall accept your cheap provocation." The elf lord king then signaled with a nod and the elves vizier announced a swiftly unfair trail with a bias-rudeness towards Stevie charging him of contentment of interfering ritual combat.

"Blameworthy of the elves to losing all creditability before a mortal in front of the gods to interfere for the elven clan has never lost once thus why our kind has survived through millennia!"

Stevie replies quickly with his response, "So is this payback?"

Then the elven lord king announced, "The Seer Stevie Ruiz known as the Aelic Dämon is hereby sentenced to the giant cedar tree the Abog of Humbaba."

Stevie query their judgment and shouted through the erupt masquerade cheers and shouts from the corresponded elven crowd taking up for their king as Stevie was suddenly confiscated magically by lively mountain leaf laurels in silver wreaths strapping his hands together in cuffs summoned by the elf lord king.

"The Abog Humbaba, what's the Abog?"

The little elf princess giggled ironically with a sense of humor that was out of place and began calling Stevie a poor clueless martyr as she answered his question.

"To be hung upside down redeemer, the Abog will slowly feast upon you by the deep cedar forest tendril roots of the ancient tree for hundred years."

Stevie- "Eeww… So I would slowly be decomposed for hundred years by a big old ancient tree sapping all my nutrients?"

Just then the elf prince snubbed Stevie from behind released him from the silver wreath wrath letting loose and lifted his shirt, "reveal the Starman's two scars from the cursed old hag." There on each side of Stevie's stomach stretch downward onto his rib-cage showed evidence attacks of two scars from the liquefied grand hind witch Baba Yaga.

Gasps and whimpers were strong among the houses of elves as they understood what this meant and among their crowd with the gleaming golden elven child taking her turn to announce, "This chosen one, and his many prophecies before us is the Aelic Dämon."

The elven lord's vizier murmured under his breath to his lord king Oberion father of both elven children but the words feel keen to all elven ears, "Behold she sees the future."

Silence mutiny was up at hands seen through the elven child standing her silence accompanies by her entourage as their apparels fashion in gold holding their ground to her authority was golden as her reputation.

The elf prince charmed his indebted took his sword and drop it bowing to Stevie and so then his sister elf princess took leisure of bowing to Stevie for seeing his future as doing so the domino effect of all others elves bowed following suite of the golden elven child princess as their chrome lord elf king yelled and shouted out loud, "No!!!!!"

The princess child took only a half bowed towards Stevie as she tried to kneel but the princess was immediately stopped from kneeling with an aggressive fury grip from her father the elf lord grasping onto his child's arm from taking a knee with the whole throne room filled with elven speculator kneeling clans gasping at the royalty family drama again with the audience in shock but there was some entourage that did consider to follow behind their eleven golden princess child and took the respect to bow on one knee to honor the redeemer.

The elven king was horrified and disgust with the matter presented before him disrupting the powers of his eleven kingdom. The shiny chrome elf Lord yelled in rebellion not honoring his guest, "No!!!!! No one bows or pays tribute to the intruder under the house of Avallon! Arise! Arise!" The elven lord commanded with his voice in such fury it echoed and stirred the chambers.

The Eleven King furiously points to the giant magnolia bulb flower set upon the stage throne and continue to say softly displaying a split bipolar disorder personality as he softens his tone and quietly remembers his place as an elf king and constructed himself in fear, "It disturbs her…" Then the giant flower bulb began to sprout open with dread on the elven king's face.

The grand hall was over shine by the blooming radiant white flower bulb of the magnolia springing to open forth a warmth light shining so bright for a second everyone shields their eyes even the sight was so intense for the elves eyes.

It was then the eccentric golden elven child spoke, "captured and taken before the eleven councils such a threat you host it violated our sacred flower that stirs as the balance has been disturbed she will demand to have you here forever Starman, for where the world is titled to your safety, be haste novel hero one, for my grandmother will have you."

The elves also have their elf goddess being as the highest honor in their presence their highness the adjudicator of her realm as their eleven mystical halls played reverent sacred music to their heir supreme and with the chord playing its last note that fades away.

Standing before them sprouting out from the giant magnolia bulb opening its perfectionist white blooming flower was an enchanted elven goddess that seemed to be floating and gliding from the ground with her bare feet hidden gleaming blissfully in white flowing garment with her age has no power over her. A smile from the elven goddess is gracious enough to greet anyone, "Titania." The glowing elf goddess spoke greetings with tranquility putting anyone in a trance holding still while dressed in white free-flowing garment looking like a glistening alive ghost in the flesh with the whole floor of the elves clan on their knees still kneeling bowing with their heads low onto the ground.

"Your highness," the Elven lord king bowed with everyone following except for Stevie standing out from the crowd as their white glowing elf goddess was cloven in a sparkling gown glistening as she moved embroidered as magnolias from the inside her white garment she took notice a foreigner was standing still among her elves the only one that did not heed to her power.

Stevie was enthralled by the goddess's light bright aura like a trance mosquito drawn to the light appearing within few steps away being below from the stairway steps looking up at the elven goddess as she stands glorious upon the throne stage.

"A hopeless knave with such palaver tidings you bring with your presences in my Dominion, come to me mortal, let me hold you for your heart holds contempt."

Compelled Stevie walks up the throne steps into the soft light settling rest with permission insight of awe overwhelmed she made him drop the servicing chalices by the sight of their elven goddess still shining radiantly.

It was the lord elven king still on his knees bowing to his elven goddess who quickly shared his assumption while Stevie took comfort like a child resting his head onto the elven goddess chest while she holds him with a gentle hug.

"He is treason and inflected our order and has already changed our world the way of living, he is to be restrained here till."

Then the elven goddess showed the lord of elves with a kind smile putting him in his place by just a look from her face reminding him he is not much but a concubine to her matter.

The goddess interrupted and was suddenly in a fictitious role of a grandmother calling out from the crowd, "ah is that my lovely antecedent, how thoughtful for you to save my granddaughter."

The elven child took rise standing out from the bowed crowd of elves and with respect, a curtsey to speak again, "Grandmother it has been over half a millennia since we've seen you, the one is known as Stevie Ruiz the Aelic Dämon is trailed to be hung upside down in the abyss of the great tree of Ug for saving it's kingdom's predecessor for our future is still endure to the prophecies of the coming of the new world, is why it is highly recommended the mortal should not be delayed."

Stevie was confined and confused realizing he was snugged and held up against by a stranger with sweet memories coming back from his past a flashback of being held by his grandmother as a child.

It was an awkward situation fraught with danger that Stevie didn't realize what he tumbled into being between two of the elven legendary royalties and their family's calamity.

Being keen and sharp was his specialty Stevie was aware he could pick up on the family's quall among powers of old and new. Everyone knew as well that Stevie could see through the intentions between the elven goddess and the elven grandchild soon to be a goddess began prophesying again and was suddenly cut off short by her grand elven goddess before she could finish.

"Peg puff," the older elven goddess said with a peal of silent canned laughter, "no mortal sin here but a venial accident, and let's not fudgel any longer with prophecies you and I know its arbitrary so let us not keep our mortal guest linger much longer."

Turns out the elf lord and their elf goddess came upon Stevie seeing that her granddaughter is alive the acting of being facile was obvious praising her granddaughter because it so happens revealing secrets matters between the eldest goddess and her son the king elf lord that mentions their made pact trade with the dark trolls Stevie wearing his Aeon headset could overhear their forethoughts binding evil.

The elf lord king whispered to his mother, "We gave away our progeny to be left alone our future value possession, and your elf granddaughter as a sacrificial prize!"

Cause the elf goddess felt threaten by her grandchild all-seeing powers and the child seeing her grandmother for who she really is but after all behind that family's turmoil the elven princess child still loves her grandmother as it shows how sly and manipulating the two faces they are with one another, it's the power that is greedy, it submits to selfishness and it shows.

"The suited mortal chosen one is well protected I see, smug with darkness cover by ember fire."

The elven goddess said with such eager curiosity she then glazed upon Stevie reaching softly unguarding Stevie's Aeon earphone sliding it off from his head resting over his neck. "A soft tender heart with such dark recollection of trails, I offer you the right of asylum saving you from your despair and troublesome, I alone can pardon your demeanor actions interfering into our royal affairs before the ethereal gods, you'll honor your company at by my side for there will never be darkness."

The elven goddess was luminous standing before Stevie mesmerize under her spell with his jaw open in awe, as the clans of the royal elves watch their leader provoke her power to take control. "I sense lost and great black clouds surrounds you?" Her voice then echoed throughout his head, "Let me guide you."

Stevie just found out he was profoundly soaked in his sweat and was confused to find out he was an illustration show to display an observations to the elves as the elven goddess explains in front of her faction elves worshippers, "see there my family cohorts that there is the darkness escaping its depths from mortal flesh."

When all hope of independent thought was to be lost with Stevie, he didn't realize he was drawn having no control being hypnotize following the elven goddess's lead taking her left hand with ease comfort, and to be smitten away hidden from his world but it was then an ominous shadow that suddenly pierces into the luminous light.

Every shiny chrome elven soldier took arms with their quorum royalties taking notice of their surroundings in distress as they were the second besides the elven goddess being the first could sense a change in the air of forthcoming, but calm as she ever was it was the elven goddess that knew they have just been invaded.

The elves having keen senses took alert alarming themselves scanning the coming darkness around the throne chambers as deep bells rung announcing their unexpected guest as soon after a gust of fierce freezing winds blew into the great halls of the elves everyone holding onto their garments while cold darkness stirring winds crept among the tight seal corners with gasping from the elven crowds at an appearance coming from darkness walking with great stride across the great hall carrying a black wooden acorn staff wearing her single black glove in the other hand.

It was the veneration of the Librarian who carries no name but is known as Madame to her close cohorts with such recognition among supernatural both light and dark that sees her confidence that demised the exaltations of the elves' pride ceremony, with every step she took was a blow from her staff echoing the great halls announcing her disturbing unsolicited welcome.

Such a force came off the dark Librarian demanding a reclaiming sequestration charging her own way towards the front of the throne hall uninvited with all elven weapons pointing at her but no one dared to testify her capability for they knew of her as the new grand hind witch.

"Dare to defy my sanctions, do you new dark queen of witches?"

Madam the grand hind witch then replies, "such irritable cacoethes I just got myself into playing with ethereal gazelles like creatures yourself will give you misfortune." She then turns to Stevie as she was only speaking to him.

When Madam found Stevie she immediately grabs her black handkerchief and brushes his forehead, Stevie thought was because of the sweat and was confused about her sudden intrude dark arrival and then became alert to his senses like coming out from a mellow daydream.

Madam reserving to her century old vocabulary in atone that was with an oddly delightful pleasant manner, "Dear boy, fondling with contrive witches and playing with the ultracrepidarians and their monarch requisitions will have you grufeling in their travesty."

When that happens the elven goddess said something in elven towards the library witch marking her territory.

Stepping up the stairs to the throne, Madam was always restrained in a posture of stoic affection even when it comes to threats. It's almost like she can run to winning the most scariest Librarian in a discipline school or prison of inimical misfits who don't mind letting loose her battles if it ceases to be important.

Madam tilts her head and said mocking the gloss elven goddess revealing her power by using her name, "Titania and they say you look younger one that matches the summer approach evening but instead with the fall wilts fall wilts around you with such reputation of your silly seasons what little tittle you presented known to be equally match, its perhaps you who has broken the covenant law 19:12-17 violated with human contact and to the looks of it, its without consent, white queen?"

The Librarian took charged in motion at the eleven cases against Stevie to be dismissed and he to be released, as she demanded.

"This is your commoner?" The Elf Lord King asks with the elven goddess interrupting him as she then raised her hand motioning their elf lord king to say no more as he shouted back, "He's our slave!" And just like that the goddess was revealed of a split personality with high pitch command it ringed with her tone of voice as she yelled out her son's first name in eleven tongues to dismay one in such power, "EUNUCH!" The goddess called to her son Elf King and then within seconds the goddess changed into a radiant intimidation of power glowing white light blossoming to shine around the elven goddess as she chuckled softly, "you dare to challenge me with my name dark book worm with your second class tainted substitute magic you forget your place you have no power here, you have already lost the boy's will and your power will always be black."

The Librarian quickly response back in a manner with retaliation by taking another step forward up the throne floor steps even head to head, eye to eye with the elven goddess, "Futile," the librarian said fearlessly of the elves rising threats as she dishonors their eleven white goddess queen the librarian then said, "what is mine shall weep with me."

A sudden radiant aura of power between the two enchantresses clashed in battle, with such prestigious with one another enabling their powers was emitted with forces of dark and light of superb power equally match as their aura took reign for power over one another as one was pure light the other was dark cold black shadows mix into the warm light fighting for capacity filled above the chambers as everybody look up and watch their sovereign's grace abilities.

The librarian abstrusely released Stevie from the elven trance by compressing her black-gloved left hand from the slumber spell that Madam telepathically spoke to Stevie to put back on his Aeon headphones passing him a discerning look as if he were being loud and destructive in her library caught off guarded by the Librarian.

While the Goddess and Madam exchange passive introductions, madam exclaims, "You have negligently perendinate a pupil of mine unconsciously passing away his time." Stevie was profound by the enormous tensions from the two notable great adversaries among the paranormal worlds disturb seeing his highest commander fighting for his life as the librarian appeared very ashen skin colored with a deadly look to her face with her eyes sunk in a divulge of pure black having such dark aura Stevie was startled a little by the revealing features of the dark witch.

With every elf still bowing with their heads down avoiding to look at the scene confrontation, the odd elven child princess naively then explains and spoke directly at Stevie who alone with Stevie stood standing up next to him, "you've been here already for more than three days outside of your mortal world where it is only been a few hours in my world, the ethereal world is so vast you silly white rabbit... yes... I see the white rabbit."

Unyielding the Librarian continued, "You hinder the great rule?"

The elven goddess laughed, "In my realm? I recall his actions were not of earth but is of the ethereal realm." The elven goddess exclaim as principles and powers were relentless exchanging among the rivalries.

The librarian proceeded to fair her presentation. "Allow me to indulge, it's your power receives your precedent from the past that creates the present look now what do you see?"

The Librarian confessed while the elven goddess took sight her eye began to glow returning with an unembellished look. "Your powers have gained in strength Madame and you have worn out your welcome," the elf goddess warns the Librarian.

Then the Librarian responded back with a gesture manner, "My goodness the feeling you instill is terribly strong, shall we retire?"

It was done the elf goddess let Stevie go, foreseeing was her gift returning with a favorable smile she then said gently with amusement, "adjourn, thou shall be done."

It was then the Librarian that grasp Stevie's risk with utterly ashamed, like a misbehaved child embarrassed of his improper manners and about to get a proper lesson storming quickly into the corner shadows dragging him along with the flick of her risk the grand hind supreme witch wasted no time showed her power with such a force making her way towards her blocked exit as the soldier guard elves were shoved into the air. Before they could vanish into the shadows it was the elven goddess that called out to Stevie as he was escaping following behind the Librarian, "You would soon then realize it was I trying to save you from your despair, you will come back son of Adam man of mortal."

16

Monsters, Stars and A Birthday Bash

IT WAS STEVIE WAKING UP slowly finding himself back at Nerd's Trinity room a genius league Seer Stevie works with that runs his very own medical infirmary and test labs, "running test scans for dynamic dreams you've been having." Stevie was served in a medical science lab with state of the art tech laboratory located below ground floors from the sanctuary library in its below level massive cave with a huge glass see-through warehouse cubical with touchscreen technology walls that were displaying measurements of Stevie's body vitals.

Nerd sighed, "good morning sunshine or I should say good evening, third time should be a charm finding you here again." Nerd smiled having scanning probes over Stevie. "You've been missing for five days since you've been in the otherworld till you got back in our world on a Friday night slipping into the elf realm the days will get you quick here," with a controlled remote shape in an egg in his hand checking Stevie's vital x-ray structure of his head as Stevie laid flat onto a white tech lab table that manifests into a sitting chair while in place. "Do remember spending time in the Fae world is a lot quicker than our earth realm."

Stevie then replied while getting up from the lab tech table, "why don't you ever go on a trouble-calls, you know, a charge mission of your own?"

"I 'am a Seer but I like to play it smart trying not to get myself involved in the action so much, not my style wanting to be on the front lines plus ever see a black man with common sense say, sure sign me up for danger?"

Stevie replies, "And that's why you're the smartest." Nerd simply replied to Stevie, "Bingo!"

Stevie let out a little moan rubbing his forehead adjusting his body off from the lab medical chair, "I can remember but why does it feel like a ton of bricks just fell over me, waking up not remembering how I ended up here on this chair?"

His short peaceful aroused awakening was quickly ended by the presence of Madam the librarian who never spoke much signaling Stevie a command to escort him out with a quick stroll.

They continued to walk along the side on a great arch moon bridge one of many of Stevie's favorite places located below the bellows that look over an empty abyss of the dark void he always wondered how deep it could go trying to avoid looking downward from the stone bridge.

"As above so below, is the way of looking at things." She shared randomly with Stevie allowing him to take a peek down the abyss below from standing on the arch moon bridge.

Stevie took the advantage of asking open ending questions in the spare moment while alone with the Librarian he was responsible after all at the beginning of making her the new grand-hind-witch.

"No hard feelings with changes happening around here lately huh, must be a big pay raise with loads of responsibilities taking on the role of the grand hind witch in all while on top of that you're the leader of SEERS making orders, and charges commands, controlling and holding down the supernatural which also makes you the Supreme grand hind witch? Isn't that right, it kind of sounds like a burrito to me?"

Stevie was hoping to crack a smile as being escorted or even loosen the topic with his run-up dry jokes but notice his situation became dire complex and was desperate for answers getting cold stone looks from the Librarian.

"So this black grimoire is some importance to all witches community of the world, so at least that's what Kris told me, some dark times are telling that it begins with that book with the rise of an apocalypse and with some dark curse that comes along with it?" Stevie gave an innocent look to let her know no more jokes are coming from him as he meant it knowing this was seriously getting nod permission from the Librarian to continue.

"Asking for a friend could this book have some dark possession or entity of an infection of some sort dark power that could be absorbed through one if touch the book?"

The Librarian asks after her eyebrow rose in an arch with interest, "What's your intent boy? Who is this about?"

Stevie responded with hesitation to his answer, "No, it's just been… an alarming learning experience being around the dark arts… and… all, drawing my attentions thought I just want to know what we came across and what we were up against in that old witch's chicken hut."

"You proceeded to be doing well after annihilating truces of the Faes you have allowed the fairies to roam free beyond boundaries with no control and no fear." Then Stevie quickly responded, "You mean Baba Yaga?" Stevie knew fully aware informed by his new friendship with the fairy prince that it was the crone old witch Baba Yaga that kept fairies in line.

The Librarian continued, "unwelcoming your presences to unpleasant gods proceeds yourself as a force target, breaking the Green Treaty pacts among Faes and trolls from results in consciences allowing fairies to run a muck having elves with no order is very dangerous business."

Stevie was astounded and lost but had to clarify, "to be honest I was escorted, I didn't know I was walking into the gods' arena, the Tower of Babel and that Troll King had the elve's princess captive for hundreds of years?"

The Librarian shut down the topic so hasty Stevie took understanding the other side's point of view just realizing the depth of danger he was just in.

"Everything has its reasons boy, since our recent confrontation you were a slave to the elves for they wanted eternity from you provoking an entire civilization having high regards known among to be deadly totalitarians to all living things despising mortal men the most, revolting against myself in an unpleasant puck environment with no heed for humans is no place for the wicked especially for just one to save."

Stevie was baffled and embarrassed but thankful for the Librarian pulling him out of the elves nest trying not to over apologize for the situation. "About that, I'm truly sorry, and thanks I didn't mean."

The Librarian snapped back at Stevie unable to finish his apology picking up where they left the conversation of the grimoire, "The black book of the first grimoire is also known as the book of shadows to thwart creation itself with powers of one that can only can only imagine and many more such as necromancy, alchemist and potions. It said the book was there before time existed, and known by many forces of witches if one possesses the book can possess such dark power that gives the ability of shadowing."

"Wow, shadowing… huh?" Stevie in awe but holding with animosity or was it fear stirring deep inside him that he felt.

Stevie was profound finding that Madam the Librarian began to open up like a book sharing to explain the power of shadowing—"there are numerous universes so pay attention young chap, space in between there and here is what's holds the universes that is the nexus, and between each universe is a portal."

Stevie gathering his mind as he was in conclusion following the Librarian "wait, wait, so this power that allowed you to travel through shadows is the nexus?"

The Librarian confirms with a nod and continued, "A portal that can open to any location across the distance any moment in time, past or future, to control the shadows if one can possess such power but can be deadly to the soul."

Stevie was still in awe, "shadow bending with such power is cable to do that?"

The Librarian gave a sturdy warning breaking Stevie's wonder astonishment, "A single change can devastate all reality if not careful, why its only known darks gods were only capable of such power."

Such a big load of info was dropped onto Stevie the only thing he could excessively ask as the words spilled out of his mouth, "you said the "were" word?"

She then also warns to be careful using shadowing power ignoring Stevie's past comment, explaining such power as Shadowing is known to span any life-force of its processor and may lose your soul." She gave examples of past anomaly entities that pose such power, "Why such power suites a god and these favorable dark god lords that possess such power were known as Death, Hades, Hel and the devil himself were the few collective known to use such power and look at them now cost them eternal."

Madame the Librarian out of the blue took the liberty of changing subjects and began asking about Stevie's dreams while he barely was getting over his silent daydreaming in deep thoughts of his recent self-discovery that may have concerned him.

He thought they were just going to talk about the book, the black grimoire, and his excuses but then Stevie was asked about his lucid dreams as Madame the Librarian mentioning his dreams his left-hand goes cold numb.

"Any reconcile complex in your dreams that could be some of the repetitive position in a state of disorder or confusion?" She asks strictly in a demand tone manner being excused as if he spoke out loud in her library.

"Yes, Mam. I have." Stevie wasn't surprised that she knew of his repetitive personal conflicts and replied but it was Madame that then asks sincerely in her last tone that gave Stevie the effort to coincide with another witch beside Kris, "go ahead I'll listen."

Stevie went on unfolding the details of his dreams recurring in the same odd dwelling of some void describing how depressingly cold the environment was carrying itself as if it was alive how the dark would eat the light.

"Sometimes I would run and run for miles going nowhere with huge eyes watching over me." Stevie got chills and goosebumps every time he thinks about being alone with something huge in a dark cold vast place. "Waking up to some mornings in sweat pasting for air just doesn't seem right. I just don't know it feels like a nightmare but in the end, I seem to always find my way out."

In an instance Madame the Librarian snaps back to her prone posture showing Stevie the way out back to Nerd's Trinity medical lab, "and I resume once more you will continue to find your exit knowing your way out again, Nerd will be summoning you outside you should be well-rested by now for a late night after hours trouble-call and don't keep him waiting."

Just like that shutting down the conversation Stevie took the first impression she cared finally opening up taking the end of her sentence and flip it, most people would call it bi-polar but Stevie knew better it was something else about her that was off that made her very prone with tight socials that made her be the Librarian, the book witch and Stevie accepted it for what it is.

Stevie took notice when his senses went off the chart earlier with his hand going cold as he expected it to be, she then gave him a least of advice that he considered, "keep your warnings seriously I suspect you get cold when you are in grave danger." Then Stevie realized his hand went very cold whenever he encountered Madame, is she a threat?

Stevie spun around coming back to his conversation that already ended remembering an important million-dollar question that flew by in his head that he had to let out loud and ask before missing the Librarian, "by the way who's the janitor that's always popping up around here?"

Relatively Stevie wasn't surprised to see the librarian disappeared and replaced was Nerd with his gadgets wearing a headgear over his eyes replying to Stevie, "huh?"

Seeing the Librarian his supreme leader disappearing impolitely at crucial moments being wicked of her own after all she is the grand hind witch leader of all witches of the world and that would never be an under statement.

"Hey thanks for looking into these dreams for me Nerd it's been bothersome for some time." Stevie took his thoughts to himself in a deep concern concentrating remembering his problems started when he touches the book of shadows.

Nerd asks Stevie, "Still groggy from your dreams I see?"

Stevie answered the doctor, "it's the same dream over and over almost every time lost among the dark fog in this vast void that feels empty, cold and sad it feels like I'm not alone and there's something huge in there just watching me."

Nerd could feel discontent from Stevie seeing he was unease about something and it wasn't about his eerie dreams.

"She's known for her titular antagonist renowned to be dark among the Supernatural community, but it was our Librarian Madame who found you and rescued you, it's the side effects that will wear off shortly of her witchery stealth magic that allowed you to escape the elf realm it demises your sleep dreams for a while but you'll be fine, and traveling in magic will do that to you. I heard about the whole fiasco between you and the Fae folks aka the elven tree people, I'm just grateful that the Librarian is on our side."

Nerd persists with certainly and Stevie quickly replied, "you're the second person to tell me that." Stevie reflected with a concerned look that Nerd pick up on it, "You don't like the Librarian do you?" Nerd asks genuinely taking a break from his whiteboard occupied on one of his many hundred Rubik toys in one hand when he took time to pay attention to Stevie, staying still for a brief moment giving Stevie full attention being a Brainiac with a high IQ, had a habit of scribbling work on his clipboard or his post notes scattered across his wall.

What intrigued Stevie the most about Nerd was not just his intelligence but also his silly compulsive behavior habit of dismantling Rubik cubes puzzles throughout his laboratory always in his trance of deep thought never giving his mind a rest and sometimes you may catch that Nerd talks to himself.

"I don't trust her and I don't blame her she's a witch." Stevie confines in his comment while Nerd then asking Stevie, "Isn't Kris a witch?" Stevie replies, "It's different, the Librarian is the grand hind witch now and it feels as she holds resentment towards me like she hates me."

Nerd- "Ah the usual silent scolding treatment, the Librarian tends to come off that way with everyone but remember it was you that out street her at her own game at the final red door test. Let's not forget she is over three hundred years old."

Nerd replied with a giggle, "and to think they say she was responsible for the great black plague, famously known for the Great Plague of London.

There was silence for a minute with Stevie in deep thought to a conclusion he didn't have doubts.

Things got to wrap up and it was Nerd who began to pack up his gear bag, "It's already past seven on a Friday night and we're late to our trouble-call by the way our charges is to meet up with Charlie as they made some plans for you hope you don't mind tonight?"

Stevie took the interest to ignore his push charge command and began to ask, "These elves, witches, gods, and dimension portals, with other worlds, is just so fascinating that's all right here in our backyard!" Nerd answered calmly, "take it with a grain of salt, at least you now know we're not alone and let's keep it a secret shall we."

Stevie confusingly got sidetrack lost in the conversation and then asked, "wait we're late for what?"

It suddenly dawns on Nerd that Stevie has been gone for a couple of days being held within the otherworld of the elves' ethereal realm for only a few hours but it could be days past compared on earth. "While you were missing again, Madam the Librarian took the liberation and insists on relocating and rescuing you herself while we planned a little get together more of soiree surprised birthday for Charlie and that were late for that started a Charlie that was late for that started a few minutes ago and you're coming with me.

"I didn't know Charlie lives uptown north of Austin?" Nerd was walking ahead Stevie following behind carrying a wrapped birthday gift walking among residential hallway. "Yeah, a bachelor living at the Domain has its perch, but Charlie mainly resides here to be close by off the 183 Monster Bridge, that's what he patrols the bridge 183 and research Blvd." Stevie replies, "Monster Bridge?"

Nerd then taps three times at front door apt #77 and the door open to greet their invited guest in, "well… look who finally showed up, come on in boys." Ashley said with her Texas accent welcoming the boys to join in Charlie's home to the small birthday gathering. Charlie's eyes lit up from across the room from unwrapping his gifts when he saw Nerd and Stevie come through his door and exclaimed signaling Stevie with his finger to come here, "Dude! What happen?" Charlie asked with Nerd and everyone in the room starring at Stevie.

Nerd cut in the conversation quickly looking at his watch, "hate to be a short circuit but you know me I got a few things running up in my lab that requires my attention." Stevie stood there with the gift in his hand with Ashley's thoughtful brisk as she was about to take the gift, " awe you brought a gift?" Stevie replied, "oh no, I carried this for Nerd." Ashley and everyone at the party gathered close around to Stevie took a few steps back with caution gearing away from the gift that could explode any moment in his hands.

"Oh come on!" Nerd exclaimed rushing by with a served plate of food to go in one hand and a bag of birthday goodies and treats in the other greeting everyone then saying good-bye before he left.

"Awesome it's a push-button" Charlie expresses, as a humble character with much gratitude towards life about making everything better and everyone saw this charm about him.

Nerd excitedly began to procrastinate his gift very casually with a drumstick in his mouth, "It's a magic nullifier first of its kind, its basically, are those grilled poppers over there by the way?" With everyone's attention towards Nerd waiting for his sentence as he focuses impudently on serving seconds he reaches across the table to fulfill his plate again but not only reaching for the jalapeno poppers but going the extra mile for the mash potatoes holding everyone upon his answer.

"It nullifies any magic within room range and I think it only works once if it does work."

Charlie was ecstatic, "How did you know I needed something like this?"

Before leaving Nerd then winks at Charlie tossing the unwrap paper in the disposal shaking his nullifier button gift before placing it on the table it was Nerd that said, "still working on the kinks but happy birthday big boy." Nerd walkout and left the birthday party knowingly Stevie was among friends that he would be able to hitch a ride back home with everyone taking Nerd's hints leaving his gift left alone aside on the table.

Stevie notices there were a few odd secluded visitors at the birthday party but few Stevie did recognize all being Seers in one room.

Ashley patted Stevie on the back letting him know there was always support, "you don't have to say anything, we're just glad you're ok."

Out from the corner were Kris and Valarie smiling back at Stevie waving at him and getting up from the breakfast table to gather near Stevie.

It wasn't long till Stevie spilled the beans telling his story of his adventures he encountered mistook for a short vacay from work.

"Gods and arena battles?" Charlie exclaimed then Kris said, "witches and elves?" It was Valarie finishing the trending galling sentence, "Prejudice tribunal, Stevie your life was in jeopardy in every step of the way."

It was the trip on the way over to the birthday party riding in a two door silver Hummer SUV HX, that Stevie was reminiscing his last conversation with Nerd sitting in the passenger seat, "why the Hummers for our wheels," Stevie asked? Nerd simply replied, "it's a tank in a form of a truck-car in a tank but with style, it can drive over anything, up anything, and through anything, it was built for war." Nerd chuckled while Stevie sat there deemed at the road conjuring the nerves to ask the next question.

"What does Aelic Dämon in elven tongue mean?" Asking Nerd being a pure genius knowing almost every language including elven folk, driving cautiously he asks, "What? Where did you hear that from the elves?" Stevie sat there in the passenger seat and just nodded in silence looking forward ahead.

"High Hills elves are some what Gaelic and it means Shadow demon, and whatever you heard from the elves don't listen they're known to scurry up anything to start trouble." Nerd took a hard swallow and told Stevie to never mention this to anyone, not even your peers unless they ask you so.

"If I were you, whatever was said I wouldn't share it with anyone." Nerd gave a confident glance towards Stevie as they shared smiles, and nothing was said after listening to the radio continued driving late to Charlie's surprise birthday party.

"Yeah, then she came out of nowhere from darkness, very haste she was and a bit frightening I have to admit," Stevie chuckled nervously as he entertained the party. "Wow and the power of the light from the elves and dark of the grand hind witch you described witnessing from both powerful foes never before has been matched, truly an epic adventures of a cableguy," Valarie said, as it was the first time she ever showed compassion towards anyone placing her palm hand over Stevie's hand for a moment as she sat next to him.

Ashley was concern about the matter she brought up the elves, "I can't believe they kidnap you," then Charlie said, "The Librarian is such a towering woman."

It was Ashley that elbowed Charlie at his side rib as he jolts and was tisk at his exclaimed.

It was a quick discussion about Madam the Librarian after being shot down by Charlie and Ashley that told them the Librarian is on a constant alert now after she has taken the role of the grand hind witch she'll be absent a majority of the time. There have been threats towards her from scattered revengeful and rebel witches throughout the world that would challenge her power or any one of under her command so why we must be on our toes."

Ashley then speaks out again, "Ever since Madame has taken the role of the grand hind witch she has been gone most of the time and no one knows where she goes."

But it was Kris who ended the conversation being the only practice witch in the room, "she's now queen of witches, leader of she-demons of this world what do you expect from a grand hind witch."

When everyone thought the conversation was over for a brief moment, Charlie finished opening his other birthday presents and later on the night then Stevie spoke out of place having everyone's attention by surprise luckily he knew every Seer in the room closely and consider them his close friends along non-Seer his old roommate Shay.

"But the one thing that struck me the most?" Stevie paused with everyone listening, "After leaving my house, I mean my parent's house I thought about the pleasant conversation with a new Sup buddy I met the other day."

Stevie laughed into his story joking with comical gestures explaining how he meets his new friend and continued, "So then the gnome told me how magic is fading and a new world is standing on an edge of a knife and there will be a time when all is decided."

Everyone took shock about the story of Stevie meeting a mystical legendary creature but it's ironic how a Seer could be living with a history of the civilization of gnomes right underneath his nose set in his backyard where he grew up grew up and didn't even know it except for Charlie he had the biggest grin with his arms cross studying everyone listening from standing back behind everyone leaning in the wall sipping from his drink.

"The gnome would say, nothing is a coincidence and everything is meant to be by the stars you make that your destiny."

Valarie began to enlighten the conversation with her surprise vast knowledge of the supernatural and mentions about gnomes, or "the Forgotten Folks," as she would say. "They were sometimes known, tiny small humanoids are known for their eccentric sense of humor, inquisitiveness, and engineering prowess. Having had few overt influences on the world's history but many small and unseen ones there are and to only appear to saints, knights, and royalties such as only good kings and queens."

She also mentions gnomes were often overlooked by the powers that be, despite their craftiness and affinity for illusion magic. Valarie then read through her Seer guide booklet,

"Gnomes were said to wear conical hats and to be able to move through the earth itself as easily as we humans walk upon it."

Kris did share his part knowledge being a witch and raised by one, "My mother once told me a great war between the Faes of light and creatures of darkness, it's rumored the Gnomes are the reasons goblins aren't around anymore."

The party began to socialize with tunes to the radio and playing card games, cutting the birthday cake while Stevie, Kris, and Valarie stayed back sitting on the couch while Ashley was passing out the cake.

"It's good to see you guys," Stevie said. Kris digs into the cake while Stevie took bites but it was Valarie who never took a bite beaming at her cake like it was a staredown between her and the calories.

"How did you do it?" Valarie said asking Stevie as she gawks at playing with the icing on her fingertips. "Excuse me," Stevie replied taking a sip from his party cup. Everyone else was attending to the guests socializing while Stevie, Valarie, and Kris who then got seconds for cake then participated in their conversation.

"The scarlet red door challenge," Kris exclaimed stuffing his fifth bite of the birthday cake.

"The Librarian?" Stevie said as he asked for assurance while Valarie and Kris both nodded in reply gathering closer in on their little conference.

"It's known the red door challenge along with the Librarian not many have been able to pass her test." Valarie said with Kris then asking, "you beat the grand hind witch at her own game, you do realize what you did but the question is how did you do it?"

"Stand still and be known, for you are loved," that's what my mother always told me."

Valarie and Kris exchanged looks for assurances as if they understood.

"That's how I did it, hold strong!" Stevie showing his clinch fist. "It's a gut feeling to not be afraid and know your place. I think that's how I passed through the scarlet red door, I just thought of it."

It was Valarie's interest she murmured very quietly to Kris's ear, "he has fore-strong past all spells and charms thwarted at him and he doesn't even know he's shadowing."

"What!" Stevie exclaimed lost in the conversation.

Then Kris replies to Valerie loud enough just for Stevie to hear, "we should tell him."

"Tell me what?" Stevie asks desperately striving for their attention, with Valarie and Kris still starring at each other exchanging their deep thoughts.

"We think you're in danger?" Kris said to Stevie.

"It's the Librarian isn't it?" Stevie asked and again Valarie and Kris's exchange looks with each other like their mind was just read.

"Look," Valarie said and began with a sincere look upon her face and continued. "That night when you encountered the grand hind witch Baba Yaga, something happened to you that every witch has been seeking to get their hands onto." Then it was Kris being experienced in witchcraft his mother was a trained dark witch in the arts and said, "That was no ordinary grimorie book Stevie, it's rumored to be powerful among witches that the old Crane for centuries Baba Yaga possess its dark power first of its kind and before it was passed onto Merlin's medieval nemesis Morgana le fay was given as a tribute from Circe the legendary witch of Colchis received from the high goddess of witches Hecate give to by Death."

Valerie then explained the theory origin of the dark book, "Before creation and before the light was even around, Death himself alone conjured the Dark black grimoire that beholds dangerous forbidden secrets and unknown dark knowledge that could destroy our world and in the wrong hands that just might happen. "

Valarie then spoke, "It's famously known as the book of shadows."

Stevie was out of touch for a brief moment stoned cold remembering the touching effect of the black book back at the Baba Yaga's chicken feet hut and chills just ran down his neck to his spine leaving the hair on the back of his neck standing leaving an uncomfortable stain of a cold frozen palm hand, breaking his silence he keeps the conversation on the down-low looking around to make sure no one else was listening in and exclaimed among to his two close parties of friends, "I touch it!"

Kris claps in exaggeration and exchanged their open bet with Valarie, "I knew it!"

Then Valarie gave off a long sigh closing her eyes and Stevie wasn't sure if the sigh was for relief or stress but she opened her shut eyes and started asking important questions.

"Was the book open or closed?"

"I open it! Stevie also told them after he explained the black book to Madame she mentions to Stevie that no one wasn't able to open that book and began to awkwardly smile and sneered at Stevie making it a difficult rocky weird relationship that Stevie couldn't figure out if he was liked or hated by his Librarian.

"What we know is the Librarian has the book of shadows and when the chicken hut was confiscated we believed you activated something inside you, we mean you activated the book of shadows that contains dark incredible powers that now resides inside you and we think the Librarian is after you for it."

Stevie then asks again, "Wait, you mean our Madame the Librarian?"

Kris had to speak up to let Stevie understand, "You possess dark powers known as Shadowing, this could be coincidental to your repetitive dark vivid dreams about you being lost in the void with a sleeping mountain did you describe and not only that I think that's how you beat the Librarian at the red velvet door challenge."

Valerie studied Stevie's face letting Kris finish, "I believe to my knowledge this dark magic from the grimoire of the book of shadows has only been used by a few powerful dark foes, one was known to be in a witches fairytale my mother use to tell me and the other foe is our very own Librarian who can possess this dark shadow magic."

Valarie then continued, "You beat her at her own game, she's the grand hind witch and you're predicted as the witches Bane, you're a threat to the Librarian and all witches, you're a force to be reckoned with Stevie."

Stevie took upon admiring Valerie's complement or was it just a suggestion he keeps stewing over and overthinking about the praise gesture in his mind, "does that mean she likes me or she's just being nice?"

The big blow came from Kris that hit Stevie like a ton of bricks with a big drop in his stomach. "Every witch and their coven would want you dead, you literally killed their leader and replace one that is a rebel to the dark and you took their most possessive prize, you have what they want."

Stevie shivered, "I never did tell Madame or anyone about my encounter opening the grimoire, she was very resentful towards my accusations and now she possesses the book of shadows?"

It was Charlie who then called out Stevie to come over to meet and greet a new arrival guest getting up from the sofa excusing his friends walking away, "Guess that's my cue," Stevie sighed.

"Man, I feel for him." Kris said to Valarie lowering his voice as she replied watching Stevie smiling taking in the boosted morale from others but knew he carried a heavy burden, "We have to do something."

"Stevie, my unexpected surprise guest wants a word with you if you don't mind," Charlie asked Stevie picking up another party cup to sip a drink overhearing upon arriving at the social gathering there was a Beta require to a trouble-call charge for a leader Seer it was a conversation between Charlie and Ashley with their unexpected guest.

"Guess it not a rumor anymore," Ashley said then Charlie was baffled at the recent news and was elbowed by Ashley to end the conversation before he could finish his sentence. "Fairy tale investigations imagine that hearing Snow is still missing?" Charlie asks but Ashley was quick to respond with a short conversation, "We found clues with major leads of enchanted illegal magic mirrors that could be connected to the top residences of the Austonian."

What startled Stevie holding his drink in his mouth from almost spitting it out there he recognizes the guest was the unpretentious character, it was the flashback of seeing Mr. Ying back from the old creepy Chinese shop that spooks him.

"You do remember Mr. Old Ying when he subtle your Aeon weapons?" Charlie said introducing a submissive acknowledgement between the two late arrival guests. "How could I forget, I didn't know you guys were more than acquaintances?" Stevie replied was bothered to look for any fangs or serpent eyes behind the Chinese's golden round spectacles.

Charlie then replies, "Mr. Old Ying and I go back old school has been accommodating such craftsmanship in the mystic trading he sorta of did raise me watching over me ever since I was a troublesome kid in my teens plus if it weren't for Mr. Old Ying I wouldn't have become a Seer."

Afterward, Mr. Old Ying smelt and probe Nerd's broken gift to Charlie not being shy about unfamiliar technology acting like the gift was wasteful and toxic as if it was tainted with poison holding his breath using one hand and the other hand with the magic nullifier barley dangling off from his claw fingernails before it drops again on the table.

"Destiny precedes us, dear boy, I see you still have the fortune cookie?" With a deep respectful foreign accent, the amused old Chinese man said with his oddly pinky finger ring with a golden cap stroking his long white beard with his long sharp golden nail pinky talons.

Having it memorizes Stevie recited and read his fortune reaching into his pocket and awkwardly looking over the pulled out luck paper from the Chinese cookie he saved and said to himself, "You are kind-hearted by nature." upcoming battles."

"Have you thought of my offer dear boy?" Asked Mr. Old Ying with Stevie comically replying, "and you're still offering five hundred souls?"

By smiling ear to ear revealing sharp teeth once again the old man revered to his Aeon earphones wrap around Stevie's neck, "Ah, I see you've finally come out of your shell and started to play well with others."

Taken back awkwardly Stevie thought for a moment that Mr. Ying was speaking to his Aeon earphones wrap around his neck as usual.

The old man who's was still surprisingly spry chimed the whole party by bringing cultural merchant delights showing off strange magic and with a birthday surprise gift for Charlie.

With strong Chinese accents, the ancient man handed his gift-wrap present in a unique shape of a Chinese take-out, "This gift, a remembrance, and gratitude of our friendship." Fire char colors from the burnt flames out of the wrapping paper the moment Charlie opened his birthday gift. "Oh spiffy… Chinese fire magic, I love it and it's a magic eight-ball!" Mr. Ying took gratitude and the pleasure to start off with the karaoke machine having music in the background with a mic in his hand. "Good for only one wish I captured for you a shooting wishing star that I collected high among the Chinese Nepalese border."

Charlie was then in static as you could tell he was close to his dire friend with everyone else in awe at his gift. "Red, you shouldn't have, you caught this at the highest peak of the world?" Mr. Ying with a strong accent went straight back to sing the song, "Can we pretend that airplanes in the night sky are like shooting stars…."

"That old man caught a wishing star and was able to contain it and give it as a present?" Kris asking for everyone else in the room knowingly they all thought the same thing. "It does sparkle, but look." Ashley applied as she pointed out the black sphere changing colors from black to silver glaring from the inside it sparkled. Charlie shook his eight-ball gift back to its original color black as if he knew how to play the game placing his gift on the table next to his other gift that came from Nerd was the nullifier button unnoticed as the magic eight ball rolled over fortuitously pressing the button that began to tick without anyone noticing.

With Mr. Old Ying never giving up the mic, there was a trio performance with Charlie and Ashley singing to the Spice girls stealing the show midway during the party it was Kris who caught on to the two suspicious gifts left on the table.

"I swear I saw that gift box twitch, look! The eight ball sphere began to shift colors with vibrant electrifying colors making the table shake while Nerd's gift the nullifier began to hop around the table.

With his deep foreign accent again Mr. Ying sang along to space oddity on the karaoke mic, "Ground control to Major Tom." (SC Music/ 10)

An explosion of loud surprise fireworks that everyone thought at first with sparkles jetting out from the wishing eight-ball filling the room with flashing strobe lights being a nuisance with and everyone shouting at one another.

It happens so fast spontaneously it was a rush while the room was full of stars and sparkle magic discharging but ironically Stevie would notice he was flashing by while time and everything stood still. Magic has always proceeded to be visible around Stevie ever since he became a Seer but he knew this magic was way different and was off the chart taking a few more steps around the table with the room frozen in time to probe the odd situation at hand he wondered when the time would unfreeze itself.

Taking steps viewing the room frozen in time with everything floating in the air untouchable in place Stevie could witness his friends in slow motion with a state of shock and complexity on their faces with Charlie spraying a fire extinguisher into the midair collecting foam and stardust while standing still stuck in time.

In a split second with the corner of his eye, Stevie was certain he saw Mr. Ying take a quick sip from a teacup as he sat there on a recliner like a creepy mannequin that looks like it came straight from his antiques foreign shop with his eyes hidden behind those dark round golden spectacles he wore.

Gleaming at Stevie with a smiling stare baring his fang teeth's with his white long Chinese beard rugged leather pearl face.

The next moment everything was unfrozen and no one could tell the difference of what just happen except Stevie but it was Kris and Valarie that took notice of Stevie's sudden misplace, finding him at a different location across the room seeing he was stirred into curiosity and was a bit nervous.

The astound commotion died off with half of Charlie's living room soaked in foam and scorched ceilings. "What happens?" Asked Kris. "That was witnessing a wishing star dying in front of you," Ashley said as she held up the burnt magic nullifier.

Everyone's reaction was surprised at the sudden unusual event and they were charted on the Birthday boy waiting for Charlie's next riposte.

"THAT WAS AWESOME!" Charlie jumped and celebrated shaking anyone around him, "DID YOU JUST SEE THAT!"

Matching his excitement to those around him disoriented and taken back from the sudden attack surprise.

Right after Charlie's revered birthday surprise, it wasn't the accident that bothered Charlie it was his protocol alert keeping up the old fashion having his own beeper going off on his waist side that disturbs him.

"Duty calls got an alert." Charlie and Ashley followed by everyone in the room turned to Mr. Old Ying sipping on his teacup drinking tea drastically with his gold dagger pinky up. "Don't look at me?" Mr. Old Ying announced sarcastically.

Charlie began gathering his coat and keys "Beastmaster duty calls something triggered the North Austin barrier disturbing the Monster gate between Loop one and I-35 an invisible entry standing between the tall corridor of the underpass freeway the Monster bridges. Best for me to go check it out."

Stevie's curiosity has always got the best of him, "The Monster Gate, I did read up on that in the Seer's guide hand-booklet." Charlie took the chance and asked Stevie if he wanted to tag along knowingly this is a rank third-level class duty for the only experience in defensive magic.

The response from Stevie was no surprise to anyone, "Monsters under bridges, how can I miss that!"

On their way out when it was just Charlie and Stevie alone outside Charlie's home and warned Stevie, "Hey one more thing before I forget what happens here on out in your city's backyard stays in your back yard." And then winks at Stevie.

17

The Monster Bridge

IT WAS GETTING LATE AT night after Charlie explained the important location loop bridges that connect around the city of Austin, unrepentantly Stevie then asks Charlie how he felt about his gift the wishing star dying in front of him as they journeyed arriving in Charlie's black EV Hummer at a location of the Monster loop bridge parking beneath on a feeder road with heavy commercialization under a line of large corridor concrete bridges with support beams pillars built for a castle that constructs the freeway just as high as a six-story building as it elevated a viaduct narrow right away bridge.

"Sad it broke but it was a thoughtful gift, wishes are only meant to be no big deal?" Charlie said surprising Stevie who took Charlie's comment with great magnitude, as they lead each other onto the middle medium of the oncoming traffic road right under the U.S. Route 183 freeway bridge off of Research Blvd.

They continue to walk downward the middle medium with Stevie's curiosity getting the best of him asking Charlie, "What is Mr. Old Ying?"

Charlie wasn't prepared to answer the unexpected question but was admiring Stevie's sudden anticipation.

"I really don't know, but what I do know is he's a good man and we have a lot of things in common, we both like dragons and he's a Xian from China possible to be immortal maybe." Stevie murmured to himself and repeated, "Mr. Old Ying is a Xian?"

Charlie couldn't help grinning knowing he took the risk to reveal more than enough information of what he knows, Charlie immediately drops the conversation and jump course to the direction of the reasoning they were there in the first place pulling out his smartphone.

"Right here where we stand is the gate to the monsters." They both stood under between one of the many stacks large concrete corridors holding up the highway bridge starring at large open medium with Charlie beginning to take pictures with his smartphone of the vandalize graffiti that look like a suit of hearts and spades dagger into the spray painted heart tagged along the bridge concrete corridor pillars.

Stevie was confused but he wouldn't be surprised if Charlie has his own fan base being that guy having a personal network platform for social media, but then again Stevie's been surprised a couple of times.

"No trespassers tonight just urban art graffiti," Charlie said taking photos holding his smartphone, and taking his last snap photo he said, "I think it's a good hobby just not here."

While Charlie pulled out a silver Seer remote from his cable tool bag hung around his brown leather tool belt wearing his usual one piece jumpsuit he then randomly spoke out, "Don't let puzzles define you when you can make your own magic." Charlie smiled then winking at Stevie.

"What's with the silver remote?" Stevie asked. Charlie raising the silver remote in the air aiming it towards the middle of the terrain medium of the road, "this here remote is the only key to the monster's gate, watch and learn." A humming sound began to progress louder around them while Charlie pressed a few codes onto his silver Seer remote.

Waving his remote, "I wasn't kidding when I said you can make you're own magic and this bad puppy isn't just a weapon sting-ray or a phaser gun against the dark of the supernatural or using eraser charms casting fade away memories but it also holds the key to my dear heart."

Charlie vanished right after he spoke taking a few steps forward pressing a few buttons on his silver remote, "you want to know why they call me the beast tamer? See you inside," Charlie took a few steps forward and vanished into an invisible pathway door with Stevie immediately thinking about the elves realm having to explore their pathway world it was very similar he wasn't surprised.

Stevie step through right behind Charlie closing his eyes then reopening he saw he was no longer under the Highway commute freeway bridge but instead walked into a huge gigantic space of an underground cavern that could fit a street block of a twenty-floor building. "What is this place another underground temple," Stevie asks in amazement at the sudden space that is occupied in thin air.

"This place my friend is like a portal some would say to my underground dimension directly right under the nose of the monster bridge," Charlie suggested a gesture pointing upward as he opens his invitation letting him know they were directly under-neath the freeway.

"This is my favorite my place in this whole wide world, this magnificent spacious secret is a place of unending roaming space is magic leading you back to where you started one of the great mysteries under the Quachita Mountains here that are beneath the Balcones faults of Texas, plus it is my second home to my family a sanctum of beautiful misfit creatures."

Grabbing a fire torch out of nowhere Charlie mantled it onto a cavern wall still beyond dark and gloomy inside but what capitulated the scenery were scattered sparkling light floating enough to see through the cavern's darkness, many fiery globes carrying the light with thousands of firelights dancing in the air. "Watch this," Charlie exclaims.

Able to see the otherworldly quarters lit up by the mysterious floating fiery flames but Stevie could sense no threat but with a rush, through his body, he could tell they were not alone tucking his cold left hand into his pockets for warmth. "You alright there, buddy?" Charlie asked confusing Stevie while stripping his clothes off bare skin revealing another side of Charlie covered in a full set of artistic tattoos on a chiseled body his tattoos began to glow like he was part of a displayed exotic light art show.

Stevie knew he was about to witness something amazing skeptical of any sort of show production but closely related to a scene straight from a barbarian warrior movie standing up Charlie began to shift in body movements like a praying monk in yoga formation.

In that particular moment witnessing Charlie's powers, he magically pulled out a flaming sword straight out from his chest tattooed with a glowing flaming red heart. The dark void was then penetrated with the flames from the fiery sword in Charlie's command possessing light of fire through the fire he said calling out in an enchanted command.

Then the next scene was indescribable with flames floating from above appeared a massive fiery figure taking shape gathering and collecting all the scattered dancing tiny light particles taking shape into a gigantic bird a flaming phoenix on fire.

Shone below from the fiery spectacular from above that lit up the whole place, not even the dark could escape the corners of the uncanny cave.

There shone under the phoenix's fiery light was a few stone mount of pillars accom-panied in between resting was a great green scale serpent dragon screeching with wings spanned the length of a bus as it flew onto a top tallest pillar and below was its companion a great beast twice the size of an elephant that yowl with deep low bellow it looks to be a large hybrid of both mammoth and a unicorn rhinoceros.

"They are incredible, mystic monsters aren't they?" Stevie asked taking his breath away. "This here is Rep," pointing his blazing sword towards the tall pillar standing guard was his green dragon. "She's known for her reputation among the lizard world if you know what I mean." Charlie nudged at Stevie with his elbow sticking his tongue out reflecting his sense of humor.

"And this handsome beast is Uni, not your average unicorn but he is the real deal very old." Charlie was close enough to pat and stroke its shaggy brown mane hair feeding it a wheel-barrel of cabbage while tossing one in the air showing off his companions with Rep flying in swooping for the tossed air cabbage.

"And that magnificent firebird is torch! He's such an adequate utility, he is what makes this place habitable" The giant flaming bird squawk loud enough to be compared to the dinosaurs in the movies.

"Such a fascinating specimen, its fire flames so bright it's light burns the freight in insight. Torch can also opt-out as you saw manipulate into multiple light particles, he mostly prefers to stay spread out and just be light."

Charlie chuckled giving Stevie some relief to breathe taking everything in all at once of what he just witness great monsters before his eyes, but Charlie did suggest it can be sometimes too much but it's a better world in here than out there.

"Harmless, these guys don't eat meat, my abandon eccentric friends are lost creatures no longer have a world among humans after magic left for they fear of neglect and extinction ever since."

Charlie briefly explains his role as a beastmaster and how these creatures have been under his kept ever since.

"Uni was a rescue from Siberia been here ever since two hundred years ago I want to say, and Rep is the last of her kind reserved from the Germans since the nineteen-thirties," Charlie then explains, "where and how about I found this green monster friend back at one of the abandon metric warehouses along with illegal international import papers."

Stevie couldn't count how many times he's been flabbergasted, "Legends of our old world are trap and coop up in here what it sounds like."

Charlie's gesture was forgivable as he patted Stevie's back and then his shoulders for his concern and thoughtfulness. Charlie began sharing how his creature buddies admire to be here than out there and don't want to go anywhere else knowingly what's out there in that where they know they don't belong.

Charlie then explains reality can hold many spaces, some like the gods have worlds of their own and hearsay Charlie gave in a little rumor that their Librarian even has her own little black forest dimension, immediately Stevie thought of elves again and their hidden sacred giant tree-world. But then Charlie warns, "I wouldn't wish my worst enemies to the black forest a very ill place and not many can possess this unique gift mostly the talented are the most dangerous ones, count me and Madame the Librarian are the only ones of central Seers base that is capable of conjuring spatial magic which is alternate dimension."

Stevie knew it was possible to witnessing whole different worlds from his experiences being at the tower of babel arena court of the gods he was a strong believer of spatial magic.

Stevie's mind thought process went over the roof with Charlie picking up Stevie's thought process replying, "it's somewhere in the dark forest that I know, just in case you wanted to know."

Cutting to the chase Charlie could tell on Stevie's facial expression he was desperate for more knowledge and was glad to share it with a friend, "this here little place is my own little dimension I found with just using my conscience mind.

"I manage to possess a little bit of willpower with proper frequencies and with the help of the Librarian it was basically practice of mediation, yoga, plenty of sunshine, and various esoteric methods, oh iodine is the secret and drinking lots of water."

Charlie laughs and reminisces about an embarrassing short story as he chuckled about how he got dehydrated once and continued to finish. "Now able to bend time for a short moment this is known as astral-travel and I manage to find a crack portal traveling through time dimensions just like this one here. Like the library having multiple secret passages sitting on top of a major supernatural pathway ley-lines but here my place it's safe and right behind the dark shadows." Charlie then points to the large boulder in the corner under the shadows build like a huge house giving Stevie a cold chill through his left hand then throughout down his spine. "Leads to places that we were able to catch a straight line to a Siberia region full of snow for them to escape too when they can get a chance for brief moments of fresh air and that's tonight."

Charlie put on a great show with himself being a walking light show with his unique ability to give life to his glowing artistic tattoos on his hard tone body.

"With my powers allowing me to draw sustenance from my body tattoo into reality, its tribal ink magic passed down generations in my family."

A set of tattoo chains artistically spiraled around his right arm sprung to life manifest into a chain whip as he yanks his chain tattoo straight out from his arm whipping his chains. "The beast tamer," Stevie jokingly said but bedazzled at Charlie's appeal powers but most of all he admired Charlie's compassion while he went on a short narration about his mystic friends.

Stevie brought a suggestion that bothered him, "Charlie you mention these guys don't eat meat, what were you referring to?

Out of nowhere, a goat was pulled on a rope tied around its neck. "Where did you get the goat, and I thought you said they were vegan?" Stevie asked Charlie watching him leading the goat into a narrow gorged pathway tunneled behind the large shadow boulder that led into another dark chamber quarter inside a large mountain inside an open wide range underground cavern with crystals above like waterfall chandeliers. Charlie with his muscles and charisma glistening covered with bright tattoos with mighty weapons in his hands it was ironic he cheerfully responded, "They are, but you think the Siberian unicorn and a Scandinavian dragon are monstrous? He perceives Stevie as a warning to not pass the tallest pillar not thinking twice and mentions taking arms setting the remote caliber to a high stung-mode cause he said you'd never know.

"Check this monster out." There was a rise within the entrance to the chamber quarters with a foul whiff of a wet animal permeated in the air occupying Stevie's nostril with a stench of death and sulfur. Stevie took heed standing guard behind Charlie and then asked, "What is that?"

There hidden within the shadows lays in waste in a eerie large puddle in the middle lays a thick stone broken pillar surrounded by black water dark as coal amidst from the light from being seen there Stevie can hear rattled chains rattled chains and a gigantic humanoid figure can be made out in the dark hiding behind a thick pillar peeking around as if shy to be around strangers.

Stevie's left hand went off on its senses as his hand began to freeze uncomfortably placing his cold hand into his pocket for warmth, and was profound what he began to hear.

"Stevie... Stevie... come here..." It said calmly in a familiar voice calling out from the shadows from behind the daunting thick pillar under the darkness a shadow a voice Stevie knew. "Mom," Stevie replied. Out of the shadow view from a smaller figure could be made out into a shape of his mother Stevie recognize immediately taking steps forward too quickly forgetting the rules to not pass the tallest pillar Stevie being just a few inches from breaking that rule. Meanwhile, there was Charlie to busy fastening the night-black goat in its place tying to a pillar After Charlie tied the goat the monster under the shadows was not interested in its meal and Charlie thought that was very odd, cause the monster was feasting on Stevie prowling his mind with an image of his mother and to close to losing his life walking straight into den of the monster.

Took seconds for Charlie to witness the threat upon Stevie succumb to the monster's dark spell as Charlie shouted to alarm Stevie but nothing could be heard being too late, tone deaf was part of the predator's ability as it hunts its prey.

It was Stevie's Aeon headphones he wore around his neck suddenly charmed in and began turning on playing itself as usual normally when Stevie is alone but this time it was different like a warning with blasting music so loud even the near surroundings was enchanted with music like being in a place of an arena rock concert playing a song.

(SC Music/ 11) "I'm a Believer" by Smash Mouth.

Instantly everything happens all at once, but for Stevie, he snaps out of the trance with everything being played out like time slowed down itself, and from the side of the corner of his eye he saw pouncing outreaching from the shadows was a terrible dark green abdominal creature with a muscular spotted shape charging at Stevie with a wide open mouth ranging to be equipped with sharp foul rotted teeth that could probably grind metal with having a foul mouth that could gobble Stevie in one whole.

Luck was definitely on Stevie's side saved by the distracting loud music almost walking into the monster's den Stevie fell backward escaping onto the ground away from the monster on his back pasting and catching his breath being thankful for his clumsiness he thought looking above from inches of the surprise attack by a one-eyed green giant Ogre bound to three stone pillars with a set of triple chains gold, silver, and steel black lock around a large metal collar attached to its neck viciously reaching and ravishing at Stevie as it petrified him.

Stevie stuttered in quick freight asking while Charlie rushed over to help Stevie off the ground, "Wh… what.. what is that?"

"That is the last of its kind, they were dark, old, and dull, and it prefers to be alone." Stevie wasn't too sure if Charlie was being sarcastic while Charlie chuckled and continued. "That's Roger, he and the firebird were both found here alone like this and to believe it was no coincidence but anyways Roger can't get you past that tallest pillar over there." After looking around inside the black boulder rock with a quick glimpse of the huge burden of imprisonment Stevie then shared his epiphany, "So the fire of the phoenix has been guarding this wet green monster of black water for ages that nobody knows about? All Charlie could respond was with a nod and shrugged his shoulders with his killer grin and glistening white teeth. "Ogres can look stupidity innocent with no threat but its black magic possess strong will intentions to fool its prey in a range that can be stupidly terrifying with a threat on a whole different level, but I have to say it is odd that Roger went after you, he's normally to himself and would never give me a time of day?"

"So Ogres do exist?" Stevie replies as Charlie commented and continuing his duty chores as being the beast master, "fascinating creatures they use to be but they'll eat anything including humans sometimes if this one ever gets a chance, I've come to learn they can never be civilized."

Then Stevie asked, "I thought I saw my mother?" Charlie paused from washing the cabbage collection from a small corner cave waterfall and turned to Stevie and ask for reassurance, "What did you say?" Stevie replies, "yea I got distracted and I thought I saw my mom but it wasn't her." It was Charlie that broke the ice between the conversations, "Ogres can be vicious especially when it comes to what they want and it's rarely known they prowl even to its extreme of using dark magic." Stevie had his Seer guide booklet out reading upon Ogres. Charlie was finishing up with the daily labor of the Beastmaster shuffling a wheel-barrel full of cabbage watching Stevie took practice in concentrating each time failed at summoning the mysterious white sword he once possessed back at the arena of Gods. "I think Roger really likes you, he probably senses you like your addictive candy of some sort." Charlie briefly mentions a tale of ancient's times when the world was full of monsters one out of the many was rare that could eat anything especially darkness for whatever reason it loves to eat darkness, especially in the mornings. It was then Charlie that points out the black goat with its color pitch black was its meal still tied to a rope long enough to let the goat pass a foot or two into the danger zone from the tallest pillar. "That's the first time Roger skips his meal, it's usually his favorite." Watching it creeping back behind the shadows to only see its giant humanoid figure slouch over behind the thick pillar with both knowing what the giant green Ogre wanted, with Stevie sensing a feeling of dire cold stare directly from the shadows with chills running down his spine. "Can we get out of here?" Stevie briskly heads towards the entrance they came from following Charlie out with another load barrel of cabbage for his two vegan friends.

Stevie could see that Charlie spent a lot of time with his beast companions watching Charlie do a trick tossing a cabbage right after he used his flaming sword as sports talent slicing the cabbage in half one to the Siberian unicorn beast and the other swoop in the air by the Scandinavian green dragon.

"Why my mother?" Stevie had to ask Charlie for it would be on his mind till he asks the question. "You don't have a girlfriend Stevie?" Stevie was clueless, not sure how or where that specific question came from. "Uh… ," " is all Stevie could sum up with. Charlie chuckled again, "An Ogre can fool one with black magic like fairies they can manipulate into one's heart most desire, it's such a dirty trick." Charlie then exceeded his question to ask, "Never had a girlfriend before?"

Stevie wasn't just taken back but with the man-to-man question that was spot on, he could never hide his modest happen to be a slight bashful character. Blushing, Stevie looking downward at his boots with nothing to say.

"I respect that. Being a major player back in my bad boy days before I cleaned up my act." Charlie then mentions and gives Stevie a radical surprise tip, "some girls like it when a guy can take charge if she's one of those you got to snatch her and be under around her arms and lay one on her a big smack kiss she'll never forget."

Took a while for Stevie to think that one over and look over at Charlie with a gaping mouth acknowledging he understood his metaphor.

Charlie took the assumption to acknowledge Stevie and decided to share a few pointers of his own over a bomb fire. "Like ogres, girls can be monsters as well." Stevie's response was comical as he giggled.

"It's not nice but it makes sense?" Charlie replied as he giggled along, "I know right, but go with it." While Charlie continued to feed the last batch air gaming with cabbage while his friend Rep the green scaled dragon swooping for a cabbage while Stevie took pleasure to feed Uni the beast unicorn while stroking its mane.

"Have you figured out how your Aeon works, I think it's pretty rad you can listen to music and wear it as an accessory, it fits you?" Charlie pointed out to Stevie's headphones around his neck, Stevie then answered Charlie, "besides my headphones playing random music when it wants to, I was only able to manifest that awesome white sword only once." Stevie quickly explained how much he's been practicing to summon the amazing white sword to reform again, Stevie also mentions he even had Kris to help practice with other ideas some he wasn't too please with knowing Kris uses dark arts and it didn't work out.

Stevie just remembered where he got his Aeon headphones that were tribulation gifts even though they were asked not to share their adventures guessing what weapons were destined from realizing his trails were also from spatial magic.

Stevie randomly began describing his encounter tribulation to Charlie mentioning how spiritual and pure of whiteness the place was as he journeyed through explaining he felt such purity it felt like his aura was cleansed describing a sweet warm rush came over his body.

Stevie knew he went silent purposely skipping the part with the scary weeping creature at the beginning of his tribulation then remembering almost like teleporting into another realm encountering the scary loud red heavy lights.

"If I could just figure out where and what kind of Aeon weapon gift I'm dealing with then maybe I might get a chance."

Charlie then said, "I'm pretty sure you'll figure it out, you said you were able to use it when a friend of yours was in peril was it not?" Charlie was always good to bring up the significant importance of a task that can play a good part in it, asking while boosting up morale in their conversation. "At the Tower of Babel arena of gods I did, and I was able to save my new friend at that very moment, his name is Trixs by the way, and he's fairy literally."

Stevie smirk at the thought of Trix's naïve innocence's being a complex of a moronically adult-child but with having fairy wings that can be summoned by magic.

"Maybe it activates with your emotions, at least it works." A great thought came from Charlie as he was pointing out his heart to his head. "You think so?" Stevie asked.

"I know so, I'm kinda familiar with that field," Charlie replied showing off whipping out his fancy light weapons equip with his flaming sword and a rile neon chain whips that glow. "A little push is sometimes required to achieve our manifestation." With his shirt off a display of diversity array light of tattoos coming to life, a hammer hacksaw reappeared out from his left back shoulder hurling it into a boulder as it crushes into rocks with suddenly a bow and arrows were equip within his arms showing off his skills with an arrow slashing a thrown in the air cabbage in half.

"My weaponry skills and magic are connected to here," again Charlie was pointing to his heart. "Allowing me to summon my tattoo mimicry, it wouldn't be possible if I didn't put my mind to it." Charlie fancies his charm weapons and began his passionate skill combat showing off a phenomenal fight performance with multiple ranges of weapons.

Stevie realizes he was having a moment-to-moment guy talk with Charlie mentioning how well Stevie has been fitting into the group.

Charlie explains to be aware of your surroundings especially when you're always the prey to someone or something, opening a dialogue to girls hinting Stevie, "you do know that Valarie has a thing for you," Charlie said. "Really, you think so?" Stevie asks, with Charlie responding, "Dude, did you not see the way she looks at you during your Intel story at the party." Stevie then turns pink easily bashful to the truth while Charlie nudged Stevie's shoulder with his fist, it was the first sign of generosity of their friendship towards each other.

Stevie rebutted and absurdly ask Charlie who began scratching his back anticipating knowing what the upcoming question is, "what about you and Ashley?"

He could only just laugh and Charlie kindly told Stevie it was nobody's business but if he must know there was nothing there between the two, and then Charlie mentions to Stevie he and Ashley are going on a very important reporting investigation around high places tonight a house call mission, not for a novice but only for qualified Beta house calls and I'll be checking in with you first thing tomorrow morning that requires us to go over procurement plans.

"Hey, I'm no expert or anything but want to know what I would do," Charlie said with Stevie nodded his head in complexion to find out the answer from a well-known good-looking bachelor who knows the game. Charlie mentions, having to sum up the courage in asking Valarie out on the next any coming event like a date to get to know one another, one on one to see if your compatible he said. "When the next opportunity opens even if there's the slightest chance of one percent." Charlie's humor was charming but being serious at the same time but trying not to be so serious in the subject both knowingly were holding back laughs with Charlie playing around acting like a strong macho guy nodding his finger flexing his muscles. "When the heart skips the beat and your adrenaline is high take the rush and run with it." It was the screech from the green dragon Rep that broke a few seconds silent and woke Stevie from deep thought. "That's it?" Stevie asks waiting for any other reasons or tips from Mr. charming. "Just waiting patiently and see what happens is the best part, like I said be aware of your surroundings especially when you're always the prey."

Charlie laughed at his rhetoric structure of life. "Hey, and with that comparison when you were the prey to the ogre just to mention," Charlie asked raising both his palms innocently." But wasn't it odd that your Aeon headphones went off playing to Smash Mouth by a song from some Ogre movie?

18

As Above so Below

IT WAS SATURDAY AND IT took a whole day for Stevie to even sum up the thought process of what happened the last night on Charlie's Bday having their "guy-talk" bonding moment afterwards Charlie invited Stevie over his secret base hide-out base hide-out sharing and learning the abilities of Seers things like monsters, parallel realities and portals back at Charlie's cavern domain which was hidden in spatial magic under the entire north loop of 183 and research Blvd. Stevie gave the freeway bridge a name called the monster loop reserved with pocket dimension to keep the beasts and monsters from coming out interfering into the human world.

It wasn't the fact that Stevie recognizes his reality is filled with monsters and gods being real and alive that have been here as their myths and tales are just story memories from their past but the possibilities of having your own spatial time magic that persist a dominion space of your own in dimension planes also learning that only known few are capable of achieving other small world pockets and portals between time and space let alone like Charlie his dimensions are homes of monsters in large caverns, and then there's the Tower of Babel that host gods and the dimensions of the elves sacred home Stevie recently explored.

"The Chairman that's what we call the leader of Seers. Madam the Librarian is the chairman and the grand hind witch. Turns out many witches deny this and so many witches will go after the Librarian when they can." Charlie opens up a little snippet about their arcane superior.

Thinking back at the conversation last night it was Charlie that decided to share a little secret and mentions the Librarian is so secretive having her own spatial dominion many have gone missing in search for her library and it goes with saying, "The Librarian has her own adjacent dimension go exploring through the library passage below the bowels of the bellows of the earth, there among a massive hollow underground is her world lost to those who find it."

"How can you get lost in a library?" Stevie asks inquisitively.

"Sshh…" Charlie then whispers trying to keep it a secret even though it was just Stevie and his tamed beast. "Her library is known to be located in the middle of some sort of dark forest on the other side in a great spatial rift that no one has ever come back from her library is well hidden." Then Charlie said at the end very cheery like it was something to brag about, "except for me!"

Stevie asks, "You've been there what's is the great rift?"

Charlie response back, "It's a crack between time and space hidden in the middle of the earth of the Ley way lines. I call it the TIME OUT place before you hit the beacon of the library there's an outside layer that is called time out literally means time out. Best to explain is time happens to freeze there like a portal in a box middle of purgatory being the central prime ley lines of dimensions, it's basically like being stuck in the middle of the universe."

It wasn't the details of the Librarian or learning there are possessions of dimensions that struck Stevie to the core that made him feel a bit nervous but it was the genuine guy to guy talk that got Stevie ruminating his mind play by play, game to game on how to ask Valarie on a simple first date suggesting he should take the advice from Charlie.

It was quite a simple plan he spared up at the heat of the moment suggesting he would just sum up the courage at the right time to ask Valarie on a blind date when the next chance arrives he was so motivated to ask her right now and willing to take his opportunity.

It was already at the end of Stevie's shift midway through the day on a Saturday and they still haven't heard from their Beta leaders since last night from their last night reporting house call mission. Without the supervision of their leaders being a cable guy repairman to check one's cable services while the other house call was offering a customer being a happy elderly couple that would argue with each other with the prudence of harsh love the couple giving each other a hard time as they were offered a free trial retail subscriptions as they investigated into the customer's complaints as they open up like a book to complain on their new mysterious neighbor that was a newly registered supernatural resident out in the public open that looks more so of a fairy grandmother wearing a large bow around her neck it being twice the size of her head like she borrowed mother goose's clothes the complaint old lady neighbor would say.

"You definitely not too far from the truth." Stevie would say after seeing who their neighbor was looking out from their window.

Trouble came along ever since the stranger moved into our retirement community neighborhood the old man said and complaint about her owning a noise giant geese one that Stevie has never seen that size before it was so large Stevie could imagine the crazy old neighbor lady hitching a ride on. He was told that supposedly makes the old couple's dishware's get up and dance while one claims to see a cow jump over the moon with their little dog laughing at them.

Stevie notices it's coming to the end of the day since he still hasn't heard from Charlie or Ashley that made the rest of the day drag on a little longer than usual training with his Aeon weapon still figuring out the kinks and getting to know his new companion Kris a little better being next to his side throughout their training days.

At the end of his shifts, they were Seers disguise undercover as the cable guy being beginners patrolling around the supernatural along with Austin's parks and creek sides was one of Stevie's favorite things to do. Charlie and Ashley have been missing all day since last night and haven't reported back must be on a secretive mission Nerd suggested to them it is not like them to not report back this late and Madam has her own secretive world as she comes and goes but hasn't been around the library lately either.

Kris- "Ever since finding out Charlie and Ashley has been missing I've tried casting a tracking spell but got no luck finding our Beta leaders and Nerd is up to weeks paperwork having no leadership and also no clue where the Librarian has skip too."

Kris preferred to be a witch rather than be called a warlock always correcting another when suggests he's a warlock when his power relies on the dark arts he picks up from the past years from his troublesome deceased mother.

"I still can't figure out how to freaking use this thing?" Stevie complied wearing his Aeon headphones while picking up gears and remotes from combat training with his Seers remotes and swords enchanting with their Aeon weapon gifts.

Stevie was getting ready to end the day at home with a plan to binge-watch reruns of Buffy seasons with an oven-pan pizza for the rest of the night.

Kris then began to bring up their past recent history throughout these couple months to Stevie's attention, "At least you got the seer remotes figured out, you were pretty awesome and brilliant settling the feud at the walnut creek trail between the wind nymphs and the creek Nereids over a yellow robin imagine that, what a house call and tricking them into a dispute dance off was brilliant."

Stevie replied, "Erasing memories of the general public it's protocol but it not my favorite but the abnormal is it seems to be every Seer's expertise."

"Yeah it's like your meant to be an expert of the supernatural with some hidden talents you have there impressing the nymphs gaining their trust now that was the cherry on top back over at the walnut creek-park Kris mentions to Stevie before retiring for the rest of the day, then grabbing a black bag of gears and ropes putting on a helmet arrange with a flashlight

"Their existence in and of itself is magical alone." Kris could tell Stevie said that with a direct sincere within his heart and admired his new best friend's qualities and truthfulness.

Stevie comically replies but notices Kris was focus on his recent activity packing up hardware equipment thinking was Kris planning on robbing a bank tonight?

"Are you going on a scavenger hunt on a Saturday night?"

Stevie asks and immediately there was a response directly behind Stevie who surprisingly was also in elbow knee gears, "You mean WE ARE! After the fairy tales of a Witches brew."

Stevie was confused and flustered with having a smile on his face staring back at behind Kris, seeing that Valarie arrived teaming up with Kris to reveal as if they have a hidden plan all along behind Stevie's back.

"Isn't it so suspicious how our leaders have gone missing?" Kris asks then explains the possibilities as to why their Madam the Librarian is so rigorous and so mysterious having to fight off witch assassinations to bump her off the throne but still Madame is nowhere to be found or heard from and our runner up leaderships are no better missing all day with everything that seems to be in chaos with the outside world.

Stevie recently brings up his recent past and talks about the eleven clans how he was captured by the elves and then rescued by Madame saved him that's when Valarie and Kris were talking about madam could be the one after Stevie and why Valarie convince the boys to go after their objectives against mysterious dark witches.

Kris being a witch knows in and outs about being a witch and that the grand hind witch owns secretive power and handed down knowledge.

"We took consideration into your threat seriously." Valarie said with Kris explaining to Stevie, "We believe the grand hind witch is a very dangerous person especially around you Stevie and that is someone to not take so lightly."

"Isn't it obvious the librarian loathes me?" Stevie signed and said taking the consideration of letting out his distress.

Kris also mentions, "We believe you of what you said about her harsh intentions directly towards you earlier."

Valarie points out how suspicious Madame the Librarian is around Stevie seeing him as a threat to the grand hind witch, reminding Stevie as Valerie recites the old mother English witch Shipton's fortune from the millennia party portraying Stevie as titled the Witches Bane is a major threat towards the mistress of witches Madame being the grand hind witch, Valarie convince Stevie how peril to the situation he really is in it for himself, "We believe she's after you."

"Well, I don't think there is such a thing that can protect me from the great and powerful grand hind witch?" Stevie politely asks.

The expression from Kris and Valerie's faces again as they look at each other gave Stevie near hope barely holding back a solid smile showing competition among two of his friends to see who will spill the beans first. Valarie then gave the respect as she smiled nudging Kris on the shoulder, as he was excited to go forward to explain their surprise knowing the arts of witchcraft was Kris's background.

"There might be such a power it's known in our fairy tales of a witches brew we believe there's a magic place of her domain that could behold such power."

Stevie announced, "spatial magic." Kris was shocked at Stevie's keen response wondering how he knew that and continue to finish, "a magic Hex place of her own sovereignty that exists somewhere here of her own secret library that we believe will help us find something of a protection spell against her, its a place of the Librarian's personal domain that holds grand power, some say it's the Librarian's source of power a library to be exact if the legends are correct its full of vast sacred knowledge of old power and wisdom that would be fit for any Librarian."

"Ok, and what's with this fairy tale of the witches' brew?"

Stevie replies wondering where this is leading too then it was Valerie that sold it.

"We came up with a plan for you Stevie in order to protect yourself especially witches including against the most powerful one out there would require some major type of power or protection."

Valerie then raised an eight-teen century-old book she came across and detailed after she explained she snoop into old books through the open library, "It's said here in the numerology book of witches, the tales of the witches brew shows it was conjured curses from united witches spread throughout the world.

"What does it say about the Librarian?" Stevie curiously asks.

It read the Librarian is mainly known as the arcane witch just years before in the dark ages when she was a terrible dark witch.

Today she is to be known as the fiercest witches of them all in this lifetime that beholds arcane magic, its combine sources of magic from many other enemies, victims, and foreign attributes but mostly gains knowledge through bookerty spells.

"So what did you have in mind?" Stevie ask.

Kris and Valarie were shocked looking at each other expecting a different result from Stevie but he had no remorse or empathy just a still face without a poker table. "Yeah, I figured ever since I was blamed for killing the first grand hind witch let alone having the title the witches' bane doesn't help either and for that, I don't blame the Librarian." Stevie appeared to be lost in a brief concentration of thought in taking a seat and started to huddle down to himself rubbing his own arms for comfort.

"Then it's settled," proclaimed Valerie taking charge of the situation. It took a couple of minutes gathering her gear dress in pink that always drew in Stevie's attention towards her, he always thought the pink silk ribbon scrunchie was a settled color in her brown blonde hair tied strung pulled back into a strong ponytail.

"Are you sure about this?" Kris reassuring their thoughtful plans while Stevie was asking Valarie for validation.

Kris explains after Valarie gave a strong nod to comply she was still going along with the plan knowing there's no turning back.

"You can never be sure with witches especially the grand hind witch but ironically you'll have to trust us on this one, I'm even a witch and I don't trust any of them that should tell you a lot."

It was like an encyclopedia at that moment giving a lot of comfort to Stevie winning him over with valued friends Kris and Valarie combining their thoughts for what's best playing out their execution plan to save Stevie from future harm.

It was Valerie that came close to Stevie padded his shoulders again with a semi-hug.

Stevie's heart was thrusting he felt his heart was going to jump out of his chest with his nerves getting the best of him he felt awkwardly embarrassed wondering if he turned pink while Charlie's memory was encrypted in the back of his head reminiscing the memory of Charlie mentioning in Stevie's daydream, "When the heart skips the beat ride the adrenaline and take your chances."

"We can find something about anything in the Librarian's library that would benefit us helping you for protection against any witch including the grand hind witch," Valerie mentions getting back into putting her gear bag in place from over her side shoulder continuing to go through her gear showing who's taking charge.

"You guys actually believe this whole spatial magic?" Stevie questioned without hesitation.

Kris replies, "It's a witches myth, and that is why I'm willing to take the chance to see for myself if the legends are true." Kris has shown his passion before but they could tell this meant a lot to Kris. "If the legends are true the Librarian posses some of the darkest arts of witchcraft among in her library well hidden like every grand hind witch before her. Can you imagine Stevie this will be our second grand hind witch hunt adventure and this magic library of hers is lost to be never found but we know it's in?" Stevie cued in and interrupted to complete Kris's sentences for him, "the dark forest?"

Stevie repeated to make sure he was heard right, "the dark forest?"

Valarie spoke out, "The dark forest is called Wormwood but how did you know?"

Stevie shrugged his shoulders and replied, "Charlie did, but that's all he told me and mentions it's dangerous describing her Library is in its own bubble dimension in something called a great spatial rift lost to those who find it."

The great rift lit up Valerie's face as a clue that gave her a lead head start that she might know where the location to the Librarian's dark forest that beholds the Librarian's captivated mysterious library.

Valarie took comfort sitting next to Stevie and began to share her research.

"So we did some looking ourselves into the grand hind witch and came across a few books and collective stories detailed about the bookworm-witch rather known as the librarian.

Here we found a few marks of history about the Librarian tales of her snatching a few children taking them into her dark forest and there it's known to be her sanctum grave-yard place now reserved for the revengeful dead of walking witches that escapes death's grips that fall prey to her concealment that want her dead for revenge. It's a witches binding realm of some sort like you said its very own bubble dimension that could be acres of horrors."

Valerie gradually then exchange smiles as they meet eye contact then Stevie's nerves caught up to him and he repeated what Charlie mentions about the Librarian, "as above so below." Valarie in utter shock and amused at Stevie's epiphany sudden knowledge, "Why yes, how did you know that?" She asks Stevie with his reply, "It's always been the Librarian's go thing to say around me for whatever reason, plus Charlie told me about projectile astral-travel explaining it to me to picture it to be a bubble of wide range open area between time and space."

They had already gathered their things with Valerie gathering her little handbag of collections strap over her shoulder with the boys following Valarie's lead into the sanctum library surprisingly she had the best intuitive memory while the boys were lost about their sense of direction confused about their whereabouts into the Seers library maze walking through labyrinth chambers discussing their plan quietly among themselves reaching their final destination at the hallow point bridge.

"Why here?" Stevie ask.

"This is the great rift?"

Stevie remembered Charlie's response back at Charlie's secretive spatial dimension pocket he could hear Charlie's voice in his head. "It's a crack between time and space hidden in the middle of the earth of the Ley way lines. I call it the TIME OUT place before you hit the beacon of the library there's an outside layer that is called time out literally means time out. Best to explain is time happens to freeze there like a portal in a box middle of purgatory being the central prime ley lines of dimensions, it's basically like being stuck in the middle of the universe."

Valerie began to point out their hidden mission, "The hallow point bridge has the only markings to be above the great rift that is known to below the Seer sanctum library among the labyrinth directly on top of the main ley lines. Here are the encrypted as above so below symbols," pointing out the symbolic triangle on both sides of the bridge one side triangle downward and the other side is a triangle side upward.

"So this is it, this is the grand hind witch's hideout?" Stevie said reaching over the bridge looking downward into the everlasting dark pit below with a sense of cold and loneliness after Kris and Valarie took their turn looking downward.

Valerie explains Madame's headquarters is the entry of the course magnitude for this mission, in order to get in you have to shift your perspective.

Kris then mentions he didn't mind checking out what the grand hind witch has got in stored in her own library exposing his boosting old habits of being a five-finger thief for a living. "There's no way I'm not going to sore out this time on another grand hind witch plus I've been wanting to test this black flame fire of new magic that I can conjure."

Kris pulling out his black Aeon lighter, "testing out this bad boy to its extreme has got the best of me it'll be just like the first time back at Baba Yaga's hut and to come to think of it you weren't the first to liquefy a grand hind witch knowingly we won't run into grand hind witch this time." Stevie replies back, "Let's hope not!"

Then Valarie responded, "Whatever happens don't forget to shift your perspective and no one freaks out, we don't have time for that, and see with Kris's powers, my skills, and your charm Stevie, we will make it!"

Kris ironically out of nowhere hiding his exposure of excitement the best he can being usually dull couldn't help his personality exclaimed with raising a rare silver acorn at them before they began their hunt. "Hey and try to stay alive! We got places to be, cause we got tickets to an actual fairy ball at the stroke of midnight the Fairies Eve and we all know those parties are legends, it's happens every season solstice year and that's tomorrow night." Kris quickly explains this is something they can't turn down as he left out one minor detail perceiving to be bashful as he was turning pink, "oh, yea it's a couple's thing only and Trixs was interested to invite me to court him to the fairy ball and thought maybe…" Kris starring desperately at his new unique friends as he kept holding up the silver acorn invitation forcefully in front of his friend's face's in an awkward display like a mannequin noticing neither the two Valerie nor Stevie weren't as excited as he was placing the silver acorn back into his pockets. "Just let me know when one of you ever decides if you can make it, I really don't want to go alone."

Then it was serious from thereafter, "Are you positive the Librarian will be absent?" Valarie asks Kris before she began her plan ruffling her small pack bag surprisingly pulling out strap ropes and rock climbing gear clamp onto the arch bridge and strapping on a small headgear over her head with a flashlight.

"It's the third full moon of the month, the Librarian has her hands tied being the grand hind witch she has matters on her own to deal with tonight, I'm positive the book-witch will be out all day and maybe tomorrow." Kris wearing his dark jacket over his company attire was familiar with the witch world and its recent black arts community being raised by a thief mother who was a witch.

Stevie was in a steady mood not moving one inch lost in his thoughts of the open invitation fairy-ball couple invitation even though he's supposed to be thinking about his future safety for the purpose of this suicide mission and his friends he thought but what stuck out the most behind his thoughts was the tip Charlie gave to Stevie taking the guts to jump onto the next open opportunity to ask Valarie out.

Is this it, is this the open opportunity Charlie was trying to spell out to Stevie he thought. Taking Charlie's advice was a lot harder than Stevie anticipated dumbfound loss of words struck by his emotions with high adrenaline starring lost into Valarie's eyes as they meet eye contact. At that moment he realizes his heart skip a beat and remembered Charlie's tip, "When the heart skips the beat ride the adrenaline and take your chances." But little did Stevie know that his love, at first sight, was about to be Russian roulette.

"Do you trust me?" Valarie asks Stevie snapping out of his deep thoughts realizing he was already strapped and buckled onto a rope with a belt harness seeing that Kris was also strapped on with his harness having a grin on his face as they each three stood there standing beside the ledge of the hallow point bridge.

It was a shock thereafter of what just happen when it was all in slow action as if time was about to hold still Valarie rushed in showing off her athletic skills starting off doing a Spartan style with her foot pushing Stevie suddenly off the bridge keeping eye contact with his eyes as she jumps off after him with Kris jumping behind her as they jump off the arch bridge together.

Stevie saw it coming before it happens, he was terrified for the moment till it was the look in her gray soft eyes that spoke to him before he was pushed off keeping eyesight with each other throughout the push fall off and he knew he had to hold on to the adrenaline and run with it.

With all the hype and the excitement from the unexpected free-fall Stevie let out a cry, "I didn't even say yes!" Stevie ended up dangled like a ripe cherry flushed red in the face ready to be pluck along with Valarie and Kris hanging onto their strapped ropes attach swing under the hallow point bridge dangling about twenty feet under the arch bridge seeing the darkness of the bottomless pit beneath them.

"Is this what you guys had in mind, bungee jumping off of a bridge hanging about in the darkness?" While swinging Stevie asks with concern about their recent scenario of them stuck just hanging with an unshared plan, jerking around dangling their feet desperately onto his body strap harness as they hang with their ropes lock onto the point hollow bridge.

"The symbol triangles on each side of the arch hollow bridge is a clue to our key," Valarie mentions as she regroups from swinging grabbing her gear. Then she motions the boys to look up above hanging under from the arch bridge was an upside-down arch bridge with Valarie caught a Greek word mantled below the arch bridge barely missed, read the word Skotos on one side and the other says Pneuma. "It's Greek for soul of darkness—jumping off the bridge falling into the darkness of everlasting, it's falling down repeatedly it's a dimension magic puzzle trick."

Kris shared his thoughts judging on the dark arts of the puzzle magic trick, "we'll fall forever literally."

"They say the Librarian holds great power in the sub-conscience like an omen place with no ending."

Valerie continued her plan, "Direct your attention at your thoughts changing your body to reality. It's the oldest witch trick in the book for mazes and traps for those who know little to nothing of magic. Create this illusion of know thy self." Valarie could tell she was losing confidence in her companions.

"You mean it's all in my head?" Stevie ask. It didn't help much knowing you're swinging off below from a cliffhanger bridge but thankfully for Kris who could relate with Stevie metaphorically shared his two cents he knew Stevie was a fan of movies, "it's like the part in Star Wars from the Empire Strikes back when Luke was trying to get his X-wing out of the swamp water and he said he couldn't do it it's too big and Yoda said, there is no difference, it's only different in your mind."

"Who's Yoda?" Valerie ask.

"Star Wars the movie?" Now it was Stevie and Kris that exchange looks with each other as they hung around like rag dolls with Kris baffled exclaiming at Valarie's paucity of pop culture. Valerie then replies as she gathers her collection bag hanging about in her harness stuck under the point hallow bridge reaching for a hair clip and began swinging while executing her plan she said with a faint accent, "Yoda is such a great wise actor one of my favorites I must say, but hanging around much isn't going to get us far." The boys still look confused at her unwitting last comment hoping she meant her favorite movie.

"So what did you guys have in plan?" Stevie ironically mentions as he and Kris just sat there with Stevie dangling his legs still wondering what's the next trick watching Valerie swinging back and forth. Valerie then gave Stevie a smirk adjusting her harness jacket.

"How does this as above so below work again?" Stevie asks taking notice Kris and Valerie was about to release themselves from their harness.

It started to get skeptical for Stevie looking downward into the deep bottomless void of nothing feeling doubts of his redemption outcome. A thought came across Stevie's mind, he must be hung strung towards this mystery girl realizing he knows nothing about her and yet was willing to risk their lives for his future life was so absurd but that's what attracted him the most.

"Now the trick is up and down," shouted Valerie with a stride momentum swinging from her rope harness back and forth preparing to detach herself. She continued to look upward over the bridge and shouted, "Picture the up there is the ground!"

Stevie was petrified for Valerie as she unclips her harness but instead of falling down into the dark pit, she shot upward opposite of gravity landing beneath the upside-down arch hallow bridge standing upside down on both feet.

"How did she do that?" Stevie confusingly asks Kris as they were left dangling like little children on a swing set. Kris took his turn and started swinging in his harness, "Hypnokinesis, you trick your mind what is and then," Kris let go looking upward after he said that with a big swing he too landed with both feet onto the bridge upside down.

"You got to be kidding me!" Stevie shook and dangled his feet like a tantrum child for a quick second feeling defeated and realize it was something he had to get over and challenge himself. He remembered looking upward at Valerie standing upside down seeing her charisma always posing to be delicately posting her gears into her bag straightening her hair into a ponytail tied with her usual silk pink scrunchie it's what gave her the touch of being a lady. "When the heart skips the beat and your adrenaline is high take the rush and jump with it!" Stevie said under his breath then shouted as he then jumps from his swinging harness never took his eyes off Valerie's eyes as he continued to fall past upward missing his landing fall catch onto the bridge while Valerie reaches out to the edge of the bridge missing his grip as he continues to fall.

Stevie continued to free-fall spiraling upward originally downward not to be confused to be falling upward as it felt like plummeting to his death into the black pit that lays ahead of him as he skydives into the dark.

Almost thirty seconds into the scary fall with the motion of his body reduced gravity to a space-time curvature to a degree of feeling weightless that felt like forever falling but there was a speck of light that gradually expanded the closer Stevie plummeted deep into his fall further away from the arch hallow bridge.

Stevie's face rigid with pain supplement to the body being stiff and having chilled aches from his back muscles from weightless air cold cushions beginning to wonder if there was no ending to his free-fall as he continues to fall closer into the light falling into a large familiar open area. Having an ironic sense of humor Stevie began to laugh when he figured out he wasn't falling to his death but a repetitive continuing pattern with no end after he had fallen past the point hallow bridge with Kris waving back at Stevie now aware of the strange puzzle magic trick beholding him and remembered, "as above so below."

It was a repetitive fall that began to be of annoyance, a third time around when Stevie hopelessly kept falling again passing the arch hallow bridge it was then Stevie's right hand and arm was caught onto a swift pink silk fabric wrapping around his arm being pull onto the arch bridge landing on his feet falling on his back.

It was almost like a whip except it was pink Stevie thought saved by a tenacious simplistic foreign girl full of surprises that used her pink silk scrunchie from her ponytail maneuvering into a weapon whip collecting Stevie by his arm.

"Well aren't you full of tricks and surprises?" Stevie asks and thankfully pasting to catch his breath while being fish out onto the bridge together by Valerie and Kris.

"After tiring the arts of the Russian ballet I quickly joined the gypsy acrobats touring with the Russian circus where I learn my secret trade," explaining her distinguished abilities Valerie said while she gathers her long pink silk streamer back into a scrunchie tying with her hair back into a ponytail.

Stevie wasn't even fazed from the fall being upside down on the other side of arch hallow bridge but was still in his little trance with his heart thumbing confused and admiring the attribute stats of a hero from Valerie's quick response rescue. Stevie couldn't tell which adrenaline he felt for was it the life after near-death falling experience or was it, Valerie.

Stevie brought up attention after his sudden rescue, "what the heck guys, what was that?"

"There are stories about witches and there's a biography of the Librarian's domain matches in details that leads to relating the symbolic upside and down triangles on the side of the bridge, as above so below," Kris said revealing to Stevie their plan as he recovers a few books from his bag figuring out a map of the magic puzzle's domain that they got themselves into while a souvenir of black rusty compass fell out from his bag he quickly places it into his pocket.

"It's a reverse parallel spell upside down beneath the bridge is the only way in, but by the looks of it were not dealing with little league stuff, these magic traps to Madame's sacred library are for pros that knows their magic."

Stevie then shared a thought being in the middle as they walk while following Kris with Valerie behind Stevie, "For a quick second before I jump missing the bridge I didn't believe." Kris was focusing on his witch maps figuring out the Librarian's manual spells to her domains being an expert in witchcraft and a burglary since childhood being taught by his witch mother who is now deceased. "That will do it to you," Kris slightly mentions and replies again pointing out their destiny while leading them into a dead end to a small-enclosed black stone brick wall, "a witches room?"

They were very fortunate realize the talent Kris possesses familiar with the dark arts being raised in a community of witches that they wouldn't have known where to began without him.

Kris examined the brick wall and said profoundly, "another magic puzzle, its Tetris magic, a witches game." Stevie then asks Kris confusedly, "like the game puzzle?" Kris smirks back at Stevie, "how do you think the game got its name?"

Stevie took notice and have witnessed this before where seeing Kris sitting on the floor Indian style with his legs crossed like he was meditating.

"Are you sure you can do this?" Valerie politely asks hiding her impatience while Stevie was anxious as they were all on their toes. Kris was collective and calm for a while till he began to twitch a little. "I've seen this before, back at the greenbelt this was how we got into Baba Yaga's chicken hut in the beginning," Stevie mentions to Valerie as they are witnessing Kris's talent.

Whispers turn into unknown voices surrounding them as the shadows gathered closing around them it was Valerie that broke into her worries she then reached into her bag right before Stevie padded her on the shoulders alerting her for comfort.

There was loud screeching at the end in total darkness for a second everything went silent it was then Kris snapping out of his trance gulping for air.

"Are you ok?" Valerie quickly gathered Kris helping him getting off the floor.

Valerie gave a gravely concerned look at Kris, "That magic of yours is dangerous and dark I believe you know this?" Stevie picks up being aware of Valerie's keen objection towards Kris's use of magic, thinking what doses Valerie know about Kris that he doesn't know.

Kris then pointed out to Valerie at the dead-end wall taking in deep breaths while the black bricks began to shift and twist turning into an open gap enough for one individual to walk through the other side one at a time.

"We are entering in the domains of the legendary Librarian known to be the darkest witch alive this is pretty spectacular!" Kris was consecrated as well basking in his goosebumps with anxiety taking notice of his short breaths he then glorified taking in a deep breathe of the cold aroma of bark from the dark woods that filled the air surrounded by a forest of thick black trees being so dark light barley peered through above the thick black forest with the ground covered brown musk ankles high with dead leaves you couldn't see the ground dirt.

Valerie sheared her courage, "I don't see what the fuss is all about, just random old woods dark trees, and leaves in the middle of nowhere."

Kris interrupted Valerie to mention, "some say the Librarian's black forest is in the middle of Germany that consists relating of many fables and fairy tales supposedly located just southwest of Germany to be exact, but this particular region of the forest is well hidden magically barred from society and is well famously associated with the brother Grimm fairy tales."

Kris held an iron rusted witch compass that he would secretly check from time to time from his pocket. "This path leads north, this is the way through the dark forest but it's crucial we must stay quiet even better to be silent for we are in the library of the dark Librarian.

Their set headlights gear guided them through the forest, Valerie wearing a flashlight headgear with Kris head of the group held his Aeon black firelighter and Stevie used his smartphone flashlight wearing his Aeon headphones over his head.

"Do you think the Librarian can hear us?" Valerie said as she whispered following a trail as they peered through the forest brushing through the dead leaves and small bushes quietly as they can while they each explored their dark surroundings in the musky smog of the forest trying to peer at what's in front of them.

Kris response by looking at his black compass again, checking which direction to take his team upon ahead before them was a pass three-way trail taking heed in a rush to the middle little path. "It's not the Librarian I wouldn't worry about right now, it's the Boggart's she leaves behind to guard her library."

Stevie knew that sounded concerning basically being left out of the plan was the spare moment he took upon himself to look up Boggart in his creature section of his Seer guide booklet following Kris behind with Valerie behind him as he quoted. "A Boggart is a household spirit or a malevolent shape-shifting creature that will assume the form of whatever most desires to encounter its prey.

Nobody knows what an actual Boggart looks like, although it continues to exist, usually giving evidence of its presence by rattling, shaking or scratching the object in which it is hiding."

The booklet also mentions Boggarts cause household mischief but the dangerous ones are boggarts inhabiting marshes or holes in the ground are often attributed to more serious evil-doing, such as the abduction of children and leading its victim to astray. Then Kris brings up a fact history about boggarts, "it was believed by the witches that helpful household sprites, or brownies, could turn into malevolent boggarts if offended or ill-treated. In ancient times powerful foes and dark lords could summon boggarts to heed their deeds."

Oddly enough it was silent and too quiet Stevie then took a pause and look up from his booklet and found himself to be lost alone on a dark trail in the middle of the black forest. "Kris! Valerie!" Stevie shouted out of instant panic and began shuffling his feet in the dead leaves heading towards the trail using his smartphone to direct his path in the light. It wasn't that Stevie suddenly found himself lost that disturb him it was the stir and eerie growl over behind some wild bushes to his far-left behind his shoulder about six yards away. Stevie remembered the Bogart abilities are to make one lose it way assuming he would be that one to be in some cast of a spell. Five minutes being lost alone it felt like forever going in circles Stevie's left hand gave warnings began to tingle being cold but then there was noticeable shuffling and heard twigs snapping ahead in front of him in a shrubbery bush Stevie took arms with his Seer remote set ready to sting gun still wearing his Aeon headphone over his head.

A sudden wild deer peered from the shrubbery bush revealing itself that startled Stevie for a shocking moment.

In Texas, it's common to see a wild deer roaming in the open country field or on the side of the road when traveling but it was unusual when a deer walks towards you. "Whoa, hey there buddy you wouldn't happen to see any of my friends around or better yet a boggart to be around here somewhere?"

Stevie lowered his weapon remote reaching to pet the wild innocent deer when Stevie was startled again hearing nearby shuffling in the bushes unsure of the direction it came from sounded it was surrounding Stevie and the calm deer. Looking left to right turning around to look behind there was nothing but a twig snap in the trees was heard above Stevie as he slowly looks up.

When Stevie look up already emotionally drained but this was different with his heart that felt like it drops to the bottom of his stomach with goosebumps and chills came after running down his spine while his left hand went icy cold-hot as he was about to pet the deer.

It was the sight that Stevie saw above him in the tree that struck him with fear was his two companions in strife standing still motionless watching with Valerie having wide-open eyes hunch on a tree limb with her knees up tuck covering covering her mouth with disbelief and standing behind her was Kris with a silent petrified alarmed look signaling Stevie NO! Stevie knew then he just messed up looking back missing all the clues barely touching the wild deer with his hand about to pet its head revealing sharp fangs from the deer's mouth.

Stevie freak on the spot immediately raised his hand up right before the deer carnivore Boggart could take a bite out of his left hand.

It was then Stevie's arms were raised above wrap again fasten with a pink silk streamer exhilarating to miss near death again pulling Stevie's body upward while Valerie and Kris ride it out jumping off the tree limb holding on together to the other end of the pink streamer raising Stevie off the ground saving him from the carnivorous deer.

With Stevie and Valerie landing on the other side of the scary boggart deer with Kris blasting it with his stun-ray gun seer remote and as they took ground the boggart deer screech stun frozen on the spot.

It was enough to flutter Stevie's heart as he landed on his two feet retrieving ground nervously hyped-up from his near-death experience again he felt he could just go up and ask Valerie with his heart skipping a beat and he wondered is this it, is this the sign when your adrenaline is high to take the rush and run with it?"

Stevie knew his heart was uneasy but it was the wrong time to ask Valerie out

It gave them enough time to regroup escaping together with Stevie following Kris and Valerie through the black forest heading north away from the surprise attack of the boggart.

It wasn't exactly what Stevie had in mind taking Charlie's tip to the heart, literally it felt like a rush to Stevie and now he's running with it.

"That deer has teeth it was going to bite me?" Stevie asks profoundly looking for reassurance from his friends.

Kris replies while checking his iron compass again, "the carnivore deer are the witches boggart." There were suddenly few howls from where about surrounding them as they ran north. Stevie comically responded to the eerie howl, "I didn't know deer can howl?"

Kris shouted leading the group, "We must hurry and reach the library before we get split up again." Stevie then asks, "Is it following us?" Valerie replied being the last one behind the pack taking a few glances behind her keeping her pace with the boys as they continued to run.

"No, but they will be on us soon if we don't reach the library in time."

They were soon coming across a giant wall of trees with a tower lock gate surrounded by fallen dead trees with giant trunks exposed from the ground and withered tree vines scattered across and over the limbs that lay ahead of them blocking their path with a small tight opening gap for one to slip through in between the dead tree limbs hidden just over the lock gate.

Before they could turn around they were already surrounded by the Librarian's minions with Bogart deer's prancing in their view with multiple carnivore deer's arriving and appeared to be baring their fangs like a scenario straight out from a horror movie trap behind a dead-end unless they climb over or under the dead tree limbs to their escape as they get shredded from behind.

"I don't have my clicker."

Stevie panic never taking his eyes off the closest Boggart deer being few feet away eyeing each other slowly Stevie reached for his Seer remote stun gun in his cable guy handy bag that hung on his belt around his waist.

"I don't have my clicker either?"

Kris was quick to respond implying their luck.

Valerie stuck out again tagging the Boggart deer's defending them off with her electrifying pink scrunchie streamer weaponize as a whip that she was able to tame three boggarts at the same time that jump out at them.

"I'm not sure how long I can keep this up," Valerie said as she hesitated to whip the seventh carnivore deer that jump from the side surprising them. Without thinking Kris began to ignite his Aeon weapon black lighter given to him from the titan Prometheus, conjuring the dark to inflame his lit flame.

They were already familiar with Kris's creepy dark conjuring coming with the echoes and screeching of its little dark hell but this was different. The air got colder within a second stealing the warm air out of their breaths making them gasp as they turn to Kris who held his lighter with a little flame that lit a sparkling flame turning its flames black and his eyes were also charcoal black.

Stevie and Valerie didn't realize that Kris meant what he said, "wanting to test the flame of his new magic."

19

The Witches
pendulum prism

KRIS'S BLACK FIRE MAGIC NEEDED to pull this one through, for they were surrounded by maleficent spirits the boggarts were scattered all around the place of the black forest the group was back up to a dead-end wall made up of dead roots of a fallen twisted giant tree laid within the dark unless they climb over the limbs of the dead tree but by then it would be too late infested with commanded crawling dark boggarts that shapeshift into carnivore deer's roaming to defend its black forest.

"Anytime would be good now!" Valerie exclaimed holding off as many deer's that attack them with her pink streamer whip that can manifest into a weapon from a play less pink scrunchie that's used to tie her hair back into a ponytail.

This was nothing that they've seen before from Kris trying to draw in his unique dark power but this time they knew this spell was different.

Sucking all the warm air suddenly and every moist airborne droplet went dry they were parched and cold after sapping all the air from their surroundings it was Kris who was dark with his eyes enchanted in black, spoke in tongues and released a major amount of heat energy that ignited his little bright flame into a black flame wrap in its dark fire scorching its heat radiant like hot lava consuming all the light in the room into the void of the gloomy fiery flame but the contrast of the fire was just as black as Kris's eyes his magic encircling them inside a protection black fire ring backing them up behind the dead tree wall protecting their behind backs from any attacks from the leaping carnivore deer boggarts.

Valerie stood back taking alert of the dark flame, "the incredible Black fire, it's the highest sacred level of holy fire and known to represent material world and light."

They could hear some of the boggarts lit on fire screeching and hollering in agony as they back off dashing into the black forest.

"The black deadly fire is said to be the fires of hell and to burn as hot as the sun itself burning any material including spirits and consuming other flames until nothing reminds that its black flames can continue burning for several days in some case can burn forever."

Momentarily it was Kris that almost passed out after waking up from summoning his new spell with Stevie and Valerie catching him before he fell with Valerie aiding to explain the conjuring magic from such technique it puts a great deal of strain on the user, usually causing their eyes to bleed.

"Your eye is bleeding?" Stevie told Kris helping him gather himself as he wipes the small teardrop of blood from his right side check. "I won't be doing that again any time soon, fusing my magic to create the holy fire takes a big toll," Kris said as he was pasting to catch his breath.

"I don't think the boggarts will be coming back anytime soon?" Valerie mentions their accomplishment with Kris replying. "Hellfire burns fairly slowly, once caught ablaze you're already too late." Kris catching a gulp of air to continue, "better off removing the burning body parts before it spreads throughout."

"Hot tamale!" Were the only words that Stevie could fluster out of his mouth keen on his hopes to survive through this survival mission but the courage to asking out Valerie on a date was harder than risking your own lives he thought.

They knew it wasn't the time to discuss the values of their predicaments about what they just witness in their current events with Valerie still in charge taking lead and began climbing over into the wall tree limbs entering the librarian's sacred chambers.

"There it is."

Approaching at the top entrance of the giant dead tree wall made up of house size tree roots with Valerie already at the top helping Kris over the last wall it was Stevie who approaches first at the top seeing the sight of an eerie terrain of a theatrical library set with its personal spotlight in a middle of the dark forest on a terrene flat ground surface with high shelves of books just as tall as the trees the shelves were filled with thousands of books with measurable sizes and objects displayed.

"shsss… Tread lightly… and don't let the Librarian hear you." Valerie whispered signaling the boys to be quite taking caution as if spirits were listening in as she handed them each their own library card.

"They look like tarot cards?" Stevie ask.

"You guys have no idea what I went through to retrieve these library cards, it took a great ordeal." Valerie explained, "It summons to allow us to get access passage through the library without any harm from ghastly spirits and maleficent ghosts."

"One for the dark soul," she gave a black library card to Kris with a graphic picture of a dark heart cover in black tar.

Then she said, "one for me the enchantress," she raised her library card to show a decorative red figure of a young girl.

"And the last one is for the innocent." She said to Stevie, as his card was a Shepherd boy leading his flock.

Stevie was confused at the anoint words but didn't question Valerie but it reminded him when his heart skipped wondering if this the chance to ask Valerie out and then Stevie ask, "I thought you said the Librarian wouldn't be here?" It was Kris that replied and noticed Stevie turning pink-red with his skin tone coming back to his original color. "The grand hind witch has many spies especially in her keep always be watchful for anything suspicious."

They ran past multiple passageways full of tall shelves occupied with books one caught Stevie's eye shelves line around like dominos circling around a lock small door surrounded by four corner tower stone pillars with hieroglyphics and key symbols with a hierarchy of power Egyptian symbols. Running through as if they had no time Stevie pondered how many other enchanting surprises does Madame's library possesses as they continue to rush through the black forest of the library halls the giant bookshelves kept growing larger the deeper they traveled following Kris's lead using his surreptitious black compass.

Slowly they came about upon the library studying the books within the shelves occupied with mystic dark arts and ancient magic having some of the unknown markings and no title labels while some others books look hundreds maybe thousands of years old and ruins.

Treading with light feet through the library passageway Kris explains a little more about the Librarian after Stevie asked, "what makes you think the Librarian is occupied and you doubt she would show up?" Kris explains about the roles of grand hind witch the librarian being called out by other witches who oppose her only then on the third full moon on the day before the Sabbath. The Librarian will be tending matters of her own as we speak, rumors have it she has a class of assassin witches after her desperate longing to dismantle her grand power for being the supreme witch. As you can see her sanctum is very well guarded, not only by her powers alone but also guarded behind Seers as well. Very clever she is…the librarian very well indeed, they all agreed. "Are you saying she's using us?" Stevie asks for clarification then Valerie replied, "The Arcane Witch is a legend that is known to have a malevolent past gone rogue betraying her purpose and the dark lord himself taking revenge on those who defy him good or bad. They say she was destroyed by the devil, but underground witches know better" Kris finishes off by saying, "Hiding in disguise as a bookworm Librarian the Arcane witch is very well alive and among us and is now revealed as our headmaster who is now the grand hind witch."

"Wait, and you're just now telling me this?" Stevie acted shock but wasn't surprise giving them a wink back applying he was at least glad his friends were looking out for him.

Coming to the middle of the black forest library a passageway that Kris lead into an empty room shape in an octagon with slender trees as thin tall bookshelves full of books taller than the average forest trees but before stepping pass onto the hollow eerie library grounds there placed a large stone with a hole to see through from the other side standing tall alone before the entrance.

Slowly coming upon the eerie library entrance passing the tall hag stone with the hole they began studying the books within the thing tall tree shelves with mystic books of dark arts and ancient magic with some of the unknown markings while some other books look thousands of years old and ruins

Valerie points out a clue, "A hag stone, back in my country one of the claimed supernatural attributes of holed stones is that of a person looks through them at certain times they will glimpse the Otherworld."

Kris being a witch was able to read the encryption in druid language inscribe on the hag stone he mentions he believes he can make out what it says, "on the thirteen stroke."

Right on cue, thirteen bell rings could be heard as it rang all awhile Valerie look at her watch, "Well what do you know perfect timing it's strike one in the morning." She then took charge and began to give away hints by starring into the stone hole facing the other side from their entrance. "I knew it, look there what do you see?"

Allowing the boys to take a turn looking into the stone hole they could make out displayed in the middle ground of the library was an odd old large grandfather tree clock taller than the average person ticking away invisible to the naked eye. It was Kris's witch iron black compass that leads them to their destination viewing the witch's ancient clock.

The library grounds came with fog of the black forest being so dark there was hardly any light from the outside being shielded from the inside trees being so dense and dark even the dirt grounds were covered with dead dark leaves among the black autumn forest with Valerie studying the great grandfather clock through the stone hole then circling around the clock that is now visible to those who once seen through the hag stone hole.

Valerie then notices a few books that stood out by their labels drawing her interest in the thin tall shelves of the trees of the black forest library she picks out a red leathered bared ancient book with encryptions of a metallic picture of arrow birds but Valerie knew how to read Greek. "Birds of Ares."

Stevie digresses from exploring into the books on the thin tree shelves and awfully recognizes something that haunted his attention seeing the same familiar wooden creepy ragdoll from the past that could possibly be following him he thought finding it as the doll sat there placed sitting down on one of the large thin bookshelves set across from him as the ragdoll was daunting on him he then became speechless of the doll appearing suddenly as Stevie thought he was going crazy then Kris saw it as well.

At that same time, Valerie dropped the red book, and immediately within moment opening it shot out and flew into the dark above were a flock of red black feather-darts known as dropping birds that began circling back around to guard the black forest library flying back in patterns to attack its intruders aiming straight towards Valerie as she dodges using the ancient Greek red book to protect herself from being stab alive deflecting darted birds that some stabbed through the red book still in her hands taking cover coming around to hide behind the grandfather clock.

"Ornithes Areioi!" Valerie exclaims shouting to warn the boys. Mythical rapacious birds straight out from the tales of Herakles as the sixth of his twelve labor identified like arrows that are deadly shooting birds." It was Kris that figured out the magic behind the library, "Mysticism spell creation, it transforms any book in this library into real life!"

It was Stevie that took the next dodge rolling across the floor from being attack by the red-black voracious birds of prey known to history to attack men.

Kris trying his best rapidly would pyro the air with his Aeon black lighter avoiding the trees creating a fire shield only lasting few moments from the swarm attacks but it was the birds that began to multiple before them armed with brazen wings from which they could shoot out of their feathers like arrows.

Feather arrows whistled by their ears barely missing them as they continued dodging throughout the forest library finding any way to stop the dangerous flying attacks of the charade.

"Water! Water is their weakness!" Valerie shouted running across the library taking cover again standing behind one of the library trees.

Right there and then Stevie climbing one of the trees shelves for shelter from the darting red birds just passed an interesting blue book exposed just high above him on a lone shelf in one of the trees across from him that caught his attention climbing towards the book that read, "Aegaeon the God of Dangerous Oceans and Sea monsters."

Unexpected surprise lighting struck from out of the blue book immediately opening it Stevie could feel the rage of the sea god's power dropping the book while it zapped lighting to the last flock of the darted red birds in results that fulfilled the library within seconds of ocean deep waves splashing in from every four corner direction of the library with a sea pool of swimming sea monsters that came out of nowhere slithering in and out of the deep waters. It was Valerie that tied herself to a tree stub library shelf being underwater so quickly she realizes the coming dangers that hid beneath the waters of the forest library.

Kris and Stevie scrambled to climb to the top of the tallest library tree shelves collecting sea algae on themselves from getting drowned by the magical small ocean tides that came out of nowhere with slithering sea creatures swimming in and out from the water surface of the forest library sea pool.

"Where's Valerie?" Shouted Stevie as loudly as he could over the mischief rainstorm sea clouds above the library holding on desperately still climbing to the top tree shelves while the small storm brews with coming waves splashing higher and reaching higher with each wave.

"I'm going after her!" Stevie yelled in a frantic shear moment about to dive in the ocean bowl of monsters just when thrown out of the water flying through the air was Valerie who then manages to cling onto the side of the tallest tree on its shelves following behind her right out of the water were a spare of red giant tentacles from a sea monster hidden beneath the dark waters with body size suction cups sprouting out to attack.

Everything went slow again and the admiration fire inside Stevie made his heart skip again inhaling the icy storm ocean weather was it a fever taking sport in watching Valerie conduct her extreme courage slicing each tentacle that came close within range with the magical pink scrunchie that undergoes changing into a sharp pink silk streamer as a gauging weapon leaving with a luminous streak dancing above her as she slice.

"We have to do something?" Valerie shouted loudly in the storm with such demanding leadership her performance showed that her physical exhaustion was not in her gene.

It was Kris who took on the next deadly magical dupe trap of the library with his unexpectedly wide eyes sizing a primeval book concealed with old black brown dead leather ruins opening the book with needs of desperate measures of life and death something had to be done.

Within an instance the entire habitation library with the ocean rage storms manifests its entire environment flipping the surroundings of the forest library into a hidden remote desert wasteland shifting ocean waves into violent gale winds and flying sands barley they can see making out a view of stones and strange shadows. Through the sandstorm, they couldn't make out the deserted forsaken landscape that was notable for being the Demon City that has become a dark world with flying sands and stones, and to behold strange shadows.

Only the strongest and toughest to survive the devilish winds howling through the vast dry land transformed from inside the ancient brown leathered book but what can be heard roughly were sounds of the sand slamming against the desert rocks and faint shouts from Valerie that sounded afar. "Close the book!"

Having to leap into the nearest fissure at the top of the giant tree of the library Stevie had shielded himself from the desert's unforgiving winds of wrath in the nick of time for as soon as he has done so, a wave of sand swooped across carrying anything in its path till the sandstorm disintegrated.

"Is everyone ok?" Kris announces clearing the way kicking dried-up squids and sea-weeds within the small sand hills making a path towards the invisible grandfather tree clock.

Stevie was surprised trying not to blush finding himself alone with Valerie both were in the same tree sharing the space gap from taking shelter holding his hand accompanying him.

Charles's charm could be whispered in the back of Stevie's mind, "When the heart skips the beat ride the adrenaline and take your chances."

It whispered again from the back of his mind.

"When the heart skips the beat ride the adrenaline and take your chances."

Was this the clear chance Stevie considering the signs in taking the chance of the coordinated destiny that laid before him.

Stevie stumbled to get any word out of his mouth taking a deep breath being in the virginity of dating this was Stevie's first to approach a girl. "Ahm?"

Trying to not beat himself up so much he was too dumbstruck to even take away his eyes off Valerie and tongue-tied having stunned wordless vocabulary he could jeopardize his life a couple of times, but he was obscured through his instant thoughts of reasoning to miss the chance opportunity of asking out his first date.

"Hey!" Kris said surprising his cohorts peeping into the encaged shelf gap split tree protected from the conjuring magic book sandstorm and began helping them climb out from the tall tree.

"That book?" Valerie slammed Kris with a hopeless question while he walks away making a trail over the freshly made sandhill towards the visible grandfather tree clock displayed in the middle within the strange library of the black forest now covered in sand and sea.

"You're asking about the desert sand book I lost the moment I close it," Kris replied as he revealed to open a one half-man size door from the grandfather clock as it ticked the time away and began slowly to draw all the sand and its mystic mischief wonder of the library books spells seeping into the clock disappearing into a path what lead a dark deep stairway into the ground floor.

"That was the book of the lost black city, the windy city is formally known as the Demon City as you can see summoning that book here sulfides all book charms," Kris answered and then completely shuts down the conversation pointing out they can now see the grandfather clock is visibly out in the open.

Leading them downward onto the ground inside through the small open door grandfather tree clock was a passage with a steep narrow stairway case it was childlike following one another traveling downward the staircase with their heads tilted down body tuck low luckily neither were claustrophobic finally reaching to open a similar small door walking out back into the same custodian forest library they walk away from but nothing has changed. Valerie mustered in annoyance and asks, "It's like a timeless loop we're back to the beginning?"

"This place is Hex not charmed." Kris retorted presenting his patience that was beginning to wear off sounded doubtful in his voice beginning to regret their surprise mission.

"Now wait, in the book about the Librarian, the legend says the arcane witch's power is timeless on her sacred grounds," Kris responded back with an epiphany clue that startled him. "It's the grandfather clock, that's the witch's power, as above so below, it's the oldest witch trick!"

"You must make the final blow Stevie."

It was Valerie that spoke with Kris as they suggested Stevie sticking his hand into the clock's opening door revealing the dark shadow inside of the grandfather clock supporting the idea of its bend with shadow magic.

"Just like the red door challenge you can imagine in your mind create this illusion of know thy self." Kris shared to mention but when it was Valerie who tried to joke but was being serious, "let us not forget the famous words from the great actor, "There is no difference, it's only different in your mind."

It was only Kris who wasn't sincere and questioned Valerie's joke, "you do know Yoda isn't real right?"

"I got something!" Stevie cried out with his hand's grasp reaching inside the shadows of the grandfather clock and he was feeling left out not obligated to the team but at least something he could do since it was the one thing he can manage to do. Stevie notices it's the same concept in his sleep dreaming off into shadow worlds. "Ever since I've been in and out of control of my dreams getting the hang of traveling through shadows but this even seems so surreal."

Carefully Stevie pulled out to their astonishment was another clock in mantle case with a glass dome covering the clock that has a rotating silver pendulums attach to the clock.

"it's no brew it's a witches' pendulum prism!"

Valerie and Kris awkwardly announced together relate to their sheer excitement coming from two odd worlds of characters not too fair together in same social skills.

It was Stevie that characterize their prize. "This is it? It looks like one of my grandmother's clocks back in the day. What's so powerful about this witches' pendulum prism?"

Careless to share their enthusiasm and curiosity they were delighted to explain.

Valerie held onto the glass dome clock that beholds the witches prism, "We found the legendary witches hexes that we needed to protect ourselves against the threat of the dark and against the grand hind witch Madam the Librarian."

Then Kris took off the glass dome and studied the little clock and pulled out a scroll, "and the witches' prism was purposely made to destroy any witch on this earth specifically to bring down the grand hind witch if ever to go rouge and chooses to reign in chaos." Kris then takes a baseball from Valerie's shuffle bag hung around behind her shoulders. "Magnifestio secqarum, double copy."

With the baseball in Kris's hands using a spell it transformed into an exact duplicate of the witch's clock pendulum prism. "It's a mirage a simple witch trick, disguise one as another."

Kris handed the disguise replica to Stevie knowingly what to do next using his shadow charm again placing back the fake copy into the grandfather clock.

"Man, you guys thought of everything in this plan." Stevie said amused with the recent strategy with Kris continuing after following up to repeat Stevie's recent question by asking, "so how does this thing called the witches prism work?"

Kris opens up his story as they reviewed the witches' prism in Valerie's grasp.

"A tale among witches since the dawn of Hecate the goddess of witches when she was supreme the most powerful of witches from the dark ages her powers drove her mad her threat was so powerful even the gods were threatened by her dark uprising apocalypse. So being the new threat to the world the dark and light were summoned to gather from across the corners of the earth successfully containing their new coming threat by combining and sharing their most deadly enchantments known to all witches and rumored to be a soul-spell."

"Soul-spell, and what is that?" Stevie asked right away being drawn to the witches' tale.

"The one thing we need for protection." Kris then replies, "A spell not only exterminates you on the spot but as well removing your very true essences your soul." Valarie then interrupted to add, "eliminates your entire existence from this timeline history."

Stevie smirking at the thought of the idea, "If this so-called Goddess of Hecate was erased from existence then why do we still remember her?"

Kris bestowed to answer since being the witch in the group, "No, I'm pretty sure I said it was Hecate's twin sister." It was then Valerie that was speechless of the news and cried out, "The witch goddess has a twin sister?"

"Hecate use too but not anymore?" Kris said very amusedly of his profound conversation.

Stevie then replies, "What did Hecate use to have but not anymore?"

Kris began to regret his decision to tell the truth behind the witch goddess curse explaining the story, as one who is not a witch will never know behind the spell but he retaliated and responded, "Her twin sister."

Valerie then asks and was suddenly confused, "whose twin sister?"

Kris replied with annoyance, "HECATE'S sister!"

But it was Stevie that always puts the cherry on top, "so when are you going to tell us this so-called Goddess of Hecate was erased from existence?"

Then Kris began with his grunts and picks up where he left off knowingly too well the effect power of the witches prism, "They say the dark enchantment is possessed on a scroll in the ark hands of the grand hind witch lock away in her chambers that we are in at this very moment with the scroll and the witches prism in our hands!"

A riled-up of confusion came across Kris's face contemplating to acknowledge the power he posses in his hand wondering if the legends are true.

"Do you know how much this would go for in the witches' black market?" Valerie's disappointment was nippy after responding to Kris's old habits as he uses to be a theft quickly shifting gears taking back the witches scroll and placing the clock that holds the pendulums into her handbag. "Let's keep this for safe keepings."

"It's just a spell?" Stevie responded.

Then Kris replies and coughs to laugh in sarcasm, "A spell that can cost you a lifetime of presidential paychecks!" Kris came forward to Stevie and padded his companion's back or his support and retorted to reply smiling back at Stevie, " but I guess its all well worth saving a friend."

"Are those Boggarts?" Stevie implied.

Wails could be heard in the background of the dark forest with Valerie's sensory of being a huntress taught in the past how to track and hunt among the wildlife when living with the Russian circus, "They brought friends," She said. "We must hurry, there's no time to dawdle we must leave this place now!"

Valerie leads the way out of the forest library strayed into the black forest feeling secure knowing they have what they were looking for, now, their top priority was to get out alive.

Valerie's vast skills were extraordinary leading the trail through the black forest for a good five minutes keeping the pace while the boys were slowing down behind her.

"Go!" Valerie exclaims taking her breath showing she was not all perfect thwarting the boys to take lead in front of her. "About mile end straight ahead is the witches brick wall gate entrance where we came in from. I'll run behind and distract the Librarian's boggarts they come in packs now and whatever you do, don't look back!" Off they ran like a cross-country race except they knew this was a race for their lives with their prize in their possession Valerie caress the clock and slowly handed it back to Kris placing it back in his bag.

At that moment a lot went through Stevie's mind as he ran through the dark woods behind Kris who was ahead holding dearly to their prize as they ran it seems to be running forever for them.

Was it a possibility that Valerie may not make it back Stevie pondered concentrating his breathing skills while running to maintain his stamina shock to see Kris was well athletically kept up in the running atmosphere?

Coming into a deep narrow valley of a field with acres of high grass and no trees reaching at the top of a basin on a flank of a hill breaking one of the rules Valerie had set for him riding on his adrenaline Stevie had to look back recognizing his heart skipped causes he knew his chances for once in a lifetime was behind him.

It validated everything he thought about Valerie possibility of being some Russian elite soldier may be reflecting her handy scouting as she was so captivating a performances of a huntress warrior an expert in whips as she dashes through the shrubs and trees bouncing off small exposed boulders and side hills holding back four Boggarts' deer slashing at them as she delicately flips and pounces back tumbling away then charged at another deer of one that almost made it coming at Stevie.

She then responses back gasping for air seeing she was tiring pretty gradually she then pulls out from her over shoulder gear bag was a strange wooden comb and a small rag doll fell out from her bag and Stevie thought how unusual to carry such personal items but it was the creepy doll that he then recognizes once again. "I told you to run Stevie I got this!"

It was almost a sudden nightmare something straight out of a twilight zone spin-off to pet cemetery but times three showing in strengths than last time packing in groups the black forest was filled with Bogart's surrounded by hundreds of luring ferocious red demon deer eyes baring with fangs peeking out from the black forest shadows revealing one another one by one and some in groups to be a hundred.

Stevie had to pause at the dreadful sight that laid behind him and couldn't even phantom what monstrous army of Boggarts carnivorous deer could just reappear within a few seconds unable to finish his sentence, "oh my…."

Stevie was alarmed watching Valerie as he faces her back and was shocked to see she was speaking to the familiar haunting creepy rag doll and then dropping an odd wooden comb from her bag kneeling to the ground before burying it.

She then quickly patted the buried comb into the burrow dirt and came within seconds sprouting forth ripping from the ground grew dozens and dozens of growing forest trees trapping all that came forth covering all around the valley basin were thick sprouting trees after trees dangerously growing over the top one another and from under other trees holding off a barrier stopping more than a few boggarts at its place.

Without wasting any time like a track star, Valerie manages to catch up to Stevie with her surprising swiftness momentum at hand but too bad it wasn't a real race it would be better than running for their lives.

Valarie yelled, "Pick it up slowpoke, the worst ones are right behind us!" Stevie contemplated to asking while sprinting for his life. "You mean it's not over?"

Valerie rushing to get ahead of Stevie did a side backward flip flop jumping over Stevie in time to greet a surprise attack that crash in out of nowhere from the ranging dark forest dashing in front of them was the biggest terrible Boggart buck carrying giant antlers being three times the size of an average deer barring its fangs and strength with glowing red eyes as it barge through the trees.

Just in time Stevie took cover while Valerie whip out her pink scrunchie into a long flexible vane into a whip that she would whisk lashing a blow managing to make the monstrous boggart deer jumping up above over them so high including jumping over some short trees landing at least forty yards behind them.

Valerie took in very slow motion in reaching for her over shoulder bag trying her best to not startle the great beast with its hooves pounding the ground and its huge antlers taking a bow to alert for another rampage attack. "Whatever you do." Valerie quickly told Stevie never to take her eyes off the beast as Stevie too copied cat Valerie daring to not make another move. Valerie swiftly pulled out a personal handheld mirror this time right out of her bag that flashed with a reflection light that startled the great Boggart beast from getting a jump quick start to attack as she yelled at Stevie, "RUN AND DON'T STOP RUNNING!"

Stevie kept running and running emerged into the darkness of the trees and finally quickly kept running coming across a clear opening upward hill path with each second pass his heart would beat louder with excitement and fear.

The witch's magical library held both the promise of their salvation and his compassion, with the threat to their destruction is at hand for he may have a chance.

The last thing Stevie could remember back there was smitten by Valerie's majestic acrobats when running so fast he had to turned to look back and could see Valerie's backside dropping her shiny hand mirror occupied with the same creepy old rag doll in her other hand. Then place before her a bright blue light came forth and shines so bright the ground felt like it was lifted being blind for a second by the ghastly blue light he kept running and realize the ground soil began to be heavy suddenly seeing that the ground was wet.

Finally reaching at the end of the top bowl valley basin hill behind him which was now magically transformed into a lake of trees with a display of multiple deer Boggarts stop at bay on the other side of the bowl valley with Stevie meeting Kris at the top turning back to see that his heart was fulfilled and began thumbing as it skips a beat when he saw Valerie running up the hill he took notice of his greatest extent chances is to ride his adrenaline taking Charlie's advise and just straight up ask her out.

"A lake? How the heck did you summon a lake?" Kris began to ask while Stevie began to fathom wondering who is this mystery girl he happens to fall for? "Yeah, and you manage to summon a forest with a wooden comb?" They didn't even mention the creepy odd doll let alone that it was in her possession.

Valerie's reasonable pragmatist objection was to be silent willing to show the boys her inclination by reminiscing her feat.

"It was something quick and useful I found from the grand hind witch's forest literature collection it was the best that I could do." She then pulled out two storybooks to prove her story; the first book was in green color, "A Trip into the Woodlands" and the second was a gray book, "Tranquil upon the Pond." A personal item was then exposed while pulling out the books the familiar mystery rag doll fell out of her sack onto the ground.

Stevie and Kris wary of the small creepy mystery doll stood there motionless baffled and eager to ask about the sudden awkward predicament but waited for an explanation from Valerie to appoint her odd behavior in possession of the creepy doll.

After Valerie reclaimed her explanatory she brushed it off marching towards the exit as the team followed and she promptly picks up the creepy doll to place it back into her bag sack, "not to be so sensitive but I found this antique Russian doll on the shelves back there and I find it to be such luck, plan on giving it to my grandmother in the motherland who collects such items, people can turn to childhood items for comfort support sometimes."

Then Kris replies, "We believe that doll is possessed?" It was the answer that worried the boys as Valerie scuffles to laugh and says, "so far that doll has been luck and I wouldn't want it any other way." As she stuffs the doll back in her bag with gratitude she hugs Kris and flashes the precious prize of hard work that was almost worth their lives as she takes out the witches clock protected in the glass dome pulling it from the bag and hands it over to Kris as they reach their exit at the witch's black brick wall.

"We make such a great team!"

It was Stevie's intimate heart that gave in again feeling his heart skip a beat for a mysterious foreign girl who then hugs Stevie rejoicing to share their accomplishment.

Staring into each other's eyes ironically Stevie's Aeon headphone is known to play his playlist music tapping in to match Stevie's emotions that began to play a song.

(SC Music/ 12)

They had a perfect moment to share together holding each other lock into each other's eyes as Stevie's palms began to sweat nervously at the rare opportunity to spare a genuine smile from Valerie and were lost in her mysterious gray-blue eyes.

This was the chance Stevie had anticipated riding on his anxiety all night to epitomize on his adrenaline surviving to stay alive throughout their mission and to finally have the courage to ask Valerie out.

Kris was able to summon the exit entrance of the witch's black brick wall as it began to open slowly and knowingly they were about to walk out with their grand prize bargaining more than what they ask for Kris knew he held one of the most powerful dark magical weapon known on earth.

"When the heart skips the beat ride the adrenaline and take your chances."

It was Charlie's quote that rang and haunted Stevie echoing in the back of his mind and it was the reminder hanging at the tip of his tongue exploring his courage and was about to get his words out then Kris interrupted and began walking out towards the exit, "now that we have what we need against the grand hind witch will you guys hurry up and figure on that double date tomorrow night I'm not going alone."

Stevie could tell his face was turning pink and his cheeks were cherry red disarrange to muster what words to say as his heart was racing he was lost in his dignity humiliation manhood defeated by his tied tongue and to top things worst his Aeon magical headphones started to cue Stevie hinting messages by playing love songs as if his Aeon has the mind of its own.

Love is like magic it can be surreal only then time itself bows down allowing you to cherish that moment that can take a split second but seems like a lifetime especially when it's love at first sight.

Stevie stood there lost in time enjoying every moment still holding Valerie's hands lost in her ash-colored light blue eyes as every piercing word from random love songs began shuffling its music track a compliment from his Aeon headphone and its silly actions were thoughtless of what to say.

After all, taking chances and risks when the heart skips for love it's paid off for Stevie it was Valerie who was riding on her adrenaline that beat Stevie to the punch line asking him out to the fairy festival.

"When the heart skips the beat ride the adrenaline and take your chances."

20

Love has a price

IT WAS A QUICK SHOCK one ear out of the other to Stevie snapping out into his ordinary reality easily accepting the lifestyle of many changes and challenges coming across among the supernatural but when it comes to girls he knew he had no game cause clearly he missed his cue from Valerie's punch pick up line.

"Stevie, I'm asking you if you would go out with me to the Fairies Eve?"

It was shellshock for Stevie beaten to the agonizing desire question lingering to ask her out but it was without difficulty for Valarie that baffled him grinning as he thought his heart was going to jump up in his throat.

"Well, I could always ask someone else or if you had someone else in mind." Valerie retaliated to Stevie's slow silent reaction, as all he could do was chuckle and quickly scurrying his mind to say something.

"No, wait that's not what I meant, I mean you beat me to it," Stevie said still scrambling for words.

"Beat you to the question huh, so is that a yes?" Valerie smiled and was amused by the implicating awkwardness from Stevie as she waited for his simple answer.

Stevie's discouragement of his sudden shyness reactions was bittersweet mortified at his let down manhood to pop the question first but grateful towards the rewards of his outcome favorable conditions.

"Of course! I mean YES, I would love to."

In response, Valerie then smirks and asks as they walk over the hallow point bridge, "for a moment there it looks like you almost saw death."

Stevie then asks, "I can't believe we just survived all that, now knowingly we have something that can protect us from witches especially the grand hind witch but isn't this stealing?"

"Not if it's for your own protection against the dark and did Kris not tell you?" Valerie mentions on a serious note, "Kris being a witch its best we decided he handles and figures out the prism hex for a cautious reason and we're going to return it back as soon as we figure out the clock's protection spell and by then we should know what the Librarian is up too?"

Stevie's conscience was more at ease but his manhood questions the traditional manliness, graced with her countenance smile as he was lost starring into Valerie's eyes admiring her strong feminine audacity with her blonde hair pulled back and her natural beauty that brings out her gray-blue eyes transfix into her gazes.

"So we're going to the Fairies Eve together?" Valerie asks with redemption while Stevie replied in a sudden realization. "That's tonight at midnight isn't it?" Leading over the hallow point bridge starring into the abyss together very early in the morning.

"The fairy's Eve from what I know is a Fae festival that is also called the changeling that begins at sunset with their ceremony of a Dj concert of some sort on the eve of the spring equinox that opens all fairy realms starting at sunset till sunrise that allows the fairies to run amuck with their mischiefs and games but every seventy-two years mortal men are invited with an opportunity to spring with fairies in the fairy realm sharing their magic deeds and little secrets that will be tonight."

Stevie retorted, "Sounds like a party!" Valerie replies with laughs to elaborate, "every seventy-two years humans are invited to spring with fairies that's literally sounds like an carrousel, where do you think the story of William Shakespeare's *A Midsummer's Night Dream* thrives on?" She continues to laugh it off, "They say the party lasts till the next sunrise. I don't think Kris knows the exploration of a fairy festival." Stevie was dumbfounded unable to figure out which part of the party with spring fairies would be settled for a decent date. Valerie winks at Stevie and begins to walks towards her exit. "We'll attend the beginning ceremony but not the whole event. I'm looking forward to hanging with you." Stevie was still and astounded about how bashful he came this far and still can't conjure a word to say anything to her, as it was Valerie who said the last word. "So we'll meet at the Fairies Eve at the greenbelt before midnight?" Stevie smiles and nods as he contains his excitement feeling childish and could feel his insides burning up with an embarrassment of red flush blood arise though his cheeks on his face. "Great I can't wait!" Valerie ended taking heed towards the exit.

Valerie then turns behind before exiting out ending with a gracious smile, "by the way I despise fairies and I hate parties."

There been rumors passing around among the Seers of Charlie and Ashley still been missing since Friday night and haven't reported back must be on hold-still delayed with their secretive trouble call mission Nerd being smart out of his wits for his own-good suggested it's not like them to not report back and Madam has her secretive world as she comes and goes but her presences haven't been around lately either, pointing out it feels like we're invisibly under the attack of what have they succumb too?"

Its been known for awhile stirred among seers with recent news before Stevie could leave the sanctum library restless from a long late-night mission it was Esma the Gypsy queen with concerning matters of her own she caught up with Stevie walking out acting weird around him as if she caught him in the act upon curiosity of his reaction asking to why he was still attending the library after hours early morning regretting to let Stevie reply with an answer she quickly showed she cared less and rapidity skip to the next question fishing for an answer asking an direct important question that had Stevie in a loop, "Have you not heard from your charges lately, its like everyone has gone mad and it isn't like your Beta peers to not report their tidings while the chairman Madam the Librarian is absences gone to important obligations of her witching hours demanding her requirements are important elsewhere being the new grand hind witch in all it does have its dark delicacy and ongoing thwart assassinations. The Gypsy queen let out a slow sighed after her sentences as if she regretted it.

Stevie replies, "Your saying Charlie and Ashley are still missing and the Librarian is too busy from constant under attacks?"

Esma suspiciously looks at Stevie while he hopes it wasn't true what they say about gypsy that could always tell if someone is lying.

"I'm saying time flies when our frontrunners and leaders have not yet return from their trouble call missions nor sent any message in their lack of appearances. It seems dire and mischief is happening suddenly everywhere, I'm to resume here at the library consulting with Nerd demanding orders in the absence of our head leaders until further notice.

Stevie then confirms to share his testimony to ease his guilt and calm his nerves before the queen of gypsies catches on to him, "weren't they last seen together and Charlie did mention slipping something at the party conversations before Ashley stop him about doing some investigation along the side to do with illegally imported magic mirrors and something to do with a princess I think her name was Snow?"

The gypsy queen studied Stevie's answer eyeing him for a brief moment with her open gap mouth exposing her keen eyes Stevie swore she was so still she staggered to respond as if something should not have been saying and quickly brash before retiring asking Stevie, "You should get some rest I think we both know you have a long day tomorrow let's not ever mention the millennial party for this topic was never discuss again and please do report back to the library if you hear anything from your Beta consort leaders."

That Sunday night the spring equinox, hours later after getting rest with haste and excitement while getting dress taking the advantageous chances of his luck since they requested the next day off, Stevie reminded himself this was a well deserved celebration that was much needed during their worry times among his new friends achieving their personal mission escaping with their lives already sipping on energy drinks for this peculiarly night is the day of his first date in a long time having his nerves in check.

Stevie stepped right out of the shower taking cautiously to his mirror but this time there was no shimmer. He would daydream all day of last night's fiasco recent craze about their secret mission going out of the whim nearly escaping their lives reaping their rewards were very well satisfied and happy with their accomplishments.

His becoming new close friend holds the most powerful defensive spell known on the planet against any opponent or adversary especially made for threatening powerful witches mainly for the grand hind witch and all that Stevie could think about was he won his girl.

Arriving just before midnight the timing felt uncanny to Stevie meeting up with Kris after dark at the Barton creek greenbelt one of Austin's hidden secrets with multiple entrances to the Greenbelt from Barton Hills resided in the middle of a middle of a residential neighborhood near a running creek.

"Hope you brought a flashlight for your date? Kris said with a smeared smile planted on his face looking at Stevie as he replied asking a question. "So why the double date?"

"It's the new de rigueur for couples they say, but all honestly thanks for being here," Kris said after Stevie ask why the dates.

"The entrance leads to multiple hiking trails as well as the one we're headed to is Campbell's Hole located about less a mile upstream from Barton Springs to the Barton Creek. It's a popular family-friendly swimming hole but to the fairies, this place is called the Werifesteria and that is where the party is at!" Following Kris leading downward hill slope to a creek taking a narrow trail path to the left along the creek into the woods about half a mile, it was a quite remote dried up spacious pebble beach waterhole.

Kris gave Stevie the witches prism in a cotton linen bag that holds the silver pendulum spheres from the witches' clock, he trusts Stevie should have the witches prism finding out it was only the silver pendulum of the clock that are magical trait properties leaving the clock behind.

"I trust it'll be safe in your hands. The small scroll is in the bag that possesses the words to activate its deadly magic, only use if necessary and I mean only use it against the grand hind witch if it ever comes to it."

With such gratitude all Stevie could do was thank Kris with a smile as he took and tighten the silver rope of the bag in possession of the witches' prism and securely place the bag into his pocket.

Stevie did feel a sense of protection come over him oddly a comfortable feeling but it was satisfying to have a powerful offensive weapon against any witch sublime in his pocket.

"There's nothing here but woods, rocks, and a large spacious dried up creek hole but when there's enough water in the creek bed I bet this place gets popular for outdoor enthusiasts and those who are looking for a quick and refreshing getaway to nature from the tiring city."

It was about the size of an acre field in the middle of the woods in the dark in the middle of the night.

Kris then gave off a sly reaction under the flashlight showing his teeth and smiling, "that's the best part."

Following Kris off the side along the creek trail path that leads to a circular area of grass that is darker in green color than the surrounding grass with growth mushrooms encircling into a huge ring.

"Look there, for thousands of years it's been the trademark, their sudden appearance of a ring of mushrooms was a sure sign of otherworldly presences."

Kris points out a fairy mound, or sometimes called a pixie ring he tells Stevie.

"These rings would seemingly appear overnight, or travel from one location to another, sometimes with no clear rhyme or reason, but tonight is different if you were to step into the fairy ring…" After Kris demonstrates stepping into the fairy ring he suddenly vanished in thin air.

Taking cautious Stevie followed and slowly took his turn stepping into the fairy ring and immediately his surroundings of the quiet dark nature of Greenbelt disintegrated in the same concealed outdoor space with bright lights of fairy walls around the magical festival rave with blasting music and magical pixie dust bright as day throughout the light realm with everything opposite to glowing with sparkles in the trees, to the grass even the black skies sparkled that everywhere looked like diamonds with batches of flowers everywhere shining bright as day opening up to play sweet music to you and even the fairies clothes were made out of sparkle leaves and flower petals.

Stevie was lost in the amidst in wonder of fairies so many to a crowd attributing to the dance floor raving that leads Stevie to sway with the fairies chiming to the music of pop-house that would be easily recognized in a club or concert with an upbeat tune that would pump Stevie's adrenaline, thinking this could be the happiest place on earth?

It was definitely a happy place with smiles and cheerful gestures or was it the charms that made everyone high on their ecstasy with fairies being the flirtiest in their nature were always half naked in their supermodel bodies touching each other for it was their culture to be bare in floral or greenery attire that look like gems and green aluminum steel giving their attire a shiny look.

Upon them was one of the beautiful triplet seirene fairies admiring their recent new coming human guest greeting Stevie with a flirtatious hostile-merry salutation as they began to feel and massage his upper body torso, "children of adamanite inhabitants of Eridu that finds their way are very welcome, come celebrate!"

There was a male fairy of the triplets with the two twin fairy girls began to proceed to lead Stevie into a slow motion mosh pit of appealing fairies with the two fairy sisters clinging onto Stevie on both sides of him swaying to their racy charms dancing away upon each other to a soft high frequency to the vibration rave. It was almost like a energize trance but only Stevie was in total control but felt compel to comply with the sensual dance hook onto an unsullied conclave.

Was this all fairy magic and games Stevie thought starting to feel a sensation of euphoria settled in a happy realm of bliss basking in a pleasure atmosphere being forgetful of all his worries as if time did not matter?

There was a sudden strong pull from behind Stevie yanking him out from the mass ecstasy of the fairies' charm's influence under their ecstatic rave.

"Stevie, have you seen Kris?" Valerie surprisingly came out of nowhere asking and sapping out all the desire ominous glowing light out of Stevie's eyes.

"I, I remember walking through the fairy ring, and then here I was."

He then looks strangely confused taken back at the ecstasy party that portrayed him earlier.

"I was in that ball of fireflies?" Valerie then responded to Stevie, "fairy pixies are like bug lights to mosquitoes, you're drawn to them, only your mind is the bug spray." Valerie then pointed at her head to draw her mind and then continued to flirt with Stevie admiring his shirt, "I really do like that shirt by the way."

Was she possessed? Stevie thought as she broke into a role-play, "Back from my hometown we take dating seriously with a first kiss is mark beginning with a new relationship."

She said it with unfamiliar foreign accent deep roots to a sounding of European culture and part from Siberia, a very awkward moment for Stevie that didn't think twice of it.

"Dis shirt looks good, you do work out?"

While it was obvious to tell that Valerie must have taken step lessons as she began dancing flirting around Stevie like an exotic performer out of a ballerina symphony feeling up his flex arm muscles she was playing tapping with her fingers on his special Aeon white color splash headphones that hung around his neck while she sways along to the enchanted fairy rave music.

Stevie couldn't resist telling the truth, "I was hoping you would notice, but I gotta be honest, I've always had a thing for you since I first saw you and I've never had an actual girlfriend before." Stevie nervously turns around to look at Valerie and starts to pick up on the music beat and began to dance with Valerie face to face with hers he began to feel the blood rush through his face flushing red.

"What I meant is that I've always been attracted to you."

She then took her turn to blush and she spins dancing in gentle haste rushing up to Stevie she then asks him, "You want to kiss me?"

Stevie closes his eyes as Valerie reaches in for the spare moment once of a lifetime for a guy who never laid his lips on another was just kissed by a girl barely puckering his lips it gave away a gentle soft touch perch his heart full of intent racing adrenaline with the exhilaration of a profound new feeling of a short circuit that struck him to his core having his stomach full of butterflies making his knees weak.

"Warning to my handsome suitor when it comes to my kisses."

Stevie was at least a bit shock but his eyes were wide open enough as her words spilled from her mouth holding each other to dance and he then mocks with sarcastic concerns, "now a warning?"

Valerie continues with a smirk and a sly remark, "For my virtues are high earning kisses are effervescent rewards but heed my warning attempt a second kiss just might be deadly if you wish for it."

Very clear of the strife warning knowingly what risk Stevie is gambling for taking his chances in the heat of the moment with urbane courage of an unknown knowledge to be a polish gentleman straight up sealed a second kiss onto her lips not wanting to keep her waiting as they both close their eyes it seemed forever but only lasted enough for mere seconds that felt for a lifetime.

"Kisses are deadly," Stevie said when they found themselves opening their eyes looking at each other finding themselves surrounded by a circle of acquaintance audience of fairies in awe sighing fans with their eyes drooping of their love admiring the new recollection human couple that spurred a love play before them. Stevie was melted between the valor romantic and puppy love feeling he was on top of the world.

Valarie broke and excuse their fan circle of fairy audiences displayed before them by taking Stevie's hand leading him away from the fairy crowd as he asked, "Does this mean you're my girlfriend?"

Valarie with her strong attributes of independence particularly her vain in a mystery she only then replies by leading the way with just a smile pulling his arm as they scuffled into the dancing crowd of half naked fairies to pass through.

Stevie wasn't sure if Valarie had heard him through the loud fairy music and wouldn't dare say it again as those were his last words clinging onto the edge of his heart.

"We need to find Kris before the fairy realm closes if not we will be stuck here for the next seventy-two years or maybe longer." "We just got here?" Stevie replied.

"It would be three o'clock Tuesday in the morning already," Valerie said turning to her watch to confirm.

Valerie claps at Stevie's face to make him snap out of his puppy love, "They're nasty fire devils they are, they're fairy magic and realm reveals the innocents of their hearts showing upon their sleeves that affects on those to succumb to an alluring behavior." Valerie then gave off a discord look on her face remembering why she loathes the fairy realm she then was concern asking Stevie for Kris, "We have to find Kris he holds the bag with the witches prism," but it was Stevie who was grateful for the successful date pulling out to reveal he has the linen cloth bag with he witches prism.

"I would do just about anything for you, knowing that I can trust you." Stevie had started to spill his heart giving freely the most powerful Hex enchantments known on the planet but it was Valerie who forces Stevie's hand to put back the silver tied up purple linen sack back into his pockets putting a close cap to his puppy love compassion.

They were both exposing their pleasure holding each other in the middle of the fairy festival of a spectral colorful bomb fire turning out to be a mosh pit of fairies as they lit up in their own flames of magic. Stevie was promised there would be a keg and a bomb fire but he wasn't expecting this, "that rainbow bomb fire is called Werifesteria."

Putting her finger up to his lips Valerie got discouraged upset with Stevie for trusting her so much and loving her he would give anything to her he felt he could trust her. But she was cold-hearted with an old soul and reasonable to Stevie and explain to him never to trust or just do things for people or to anyone no matter how good their intentions are, asking him to always trust your instincts.

Stevie was baffled and lost at the direction of the conversation at hand wondering where all this came from as Valerie tells Stevie, "something about you is special, you are made for something much bigger than I realized I see stars in your eyes." She explains holding onto Stevie masquerading gradually around his face with her fingers then palms to his cheeks gazing into his eyes, "you hold the keys to your own destiny" and she took very concerned ill of that and mentions, "it's truly a blessing but can be very dangerous."

Then Stevie took advantage so dangerously interrupting Valerie, "kissing you can lead to…" AND STEVIE KISSES HER.

Stevie then remember time was different like in the elves realm an hour there could be days back on earth.

Stevie began to wonder looking around for an escape exit, "Yea, what a party but I think your right, I can see why you call them to fire devils and we definitely need to find Kris."

Peering from afar over through the large pixie crowd of fairies with their wings in sparkle dust and magic everywhere it was Kris that caught Stevie's eye waving them down to get their attention.

Surfing through the crowd into a wave of fairies prancing to the loud fairy music trying to approach to meet Stevie and Valerie reaching to get through the crowded festival with masses on the dance floor Kris has a follower behind him was their companion Trixs the fairy prince who was hosting his friends as welcoming guests.

Short momentarily from behind the scenery of the rave festivity in the background was a slit bright realm to their fairy kingdom world was opening with lots of awe and oohs from the fairy crowd, blindsided to those who were not Fae by the light shone so bright from the enchanted view from the slit crack in the middle of thin air that only lasted a few seconds upon Kris arriving with the fairy prince Trixs behind him to greet Stevie and Valerie, but it was tragic that shone on Trix's face upon arriving to greet but was found to be with dismay.

The intense dislike from Trixs the fairy prince's face stole Stevie's attention and suddenly everything happened so fast with a rush wave of fear among the fairies within the crowds with a blink of an eye as Trixs their fairy prince swiftly kidnapping Kris away back into the fairy realm portraying as if his guest friends were monsters shattering and confusing Stevie's consciences it was surreal seeing glistening fairies like a dream all pure light and the life of the fairies suddenly disappeared being suck dried at once back into the light crack of the fairy realm all was over that happen within seconds as it was so fast and so quickly everything went dark.

Next was something Stevie could not explain waking up falling into familiar darkness of shadows full knowingly he was back into his repetitive dreams he would go into a state sometimes in his deep sleep but this time it was out of the ordinary and he knew this dream would be different.

Why now, why would Stevie be sleeping he thought while he depicts looking around in his state usual dark dream checking his surroundings in the familiar darkness of the vast space feeling for the smooth rock pavement floor to the wall that can stretch for miles knowingly the outcome of his dream as he continues to walk down the accustomed dark path only lit up by his smartphone all awhile he was wearing his Aeon headphone and began running through the dark usual cold fog.

This time it was a lot colder than usual in his repetitive monotonous dream strolling through the dark haze maze on a recognizable trail path in the void mass echoed cave is what it felt like with no light but from his phone peering in peering in the darkness of the shadows Stevie always felt the cave would move sometimes come to life.

Coming to the end of his dream running and running into the endless fog of dark void it was the ground that shook with the stonewall pavement trembling, that's when Stevie for the first time witness he's been traveling on a gray-black mountain of some sort like being a flea as the dark geographical shadow area began to shift and change its range structure with waves of hills as the rough ground fluctuated from what Stevie could make out holding on to a rock structure in the dark with his flashlight smartphone in his hand wearing his headphones.

Experiencing something anew Stevie couldn't tell if this was a nightmare while being in his dream a chill shot came from his left palm hand a sense of warning intuitions signaling of dire boss coming of the supernatural into his situation brought goosebumps making his neck hair stand straight and with that a sharp gust of cold wind came out of nowhere still grasping on to the stone rock.

Stevie took shelter being a shield from the icy wind taking heed behind a half person-size gravel rock stone.

Stevie's surroundings began to change again with its geographic landmasses moving so swiftly around him structures with ruffled hills were paved through the shadows as the solid ground again shifted the dark environment moving rapidly feeling the cold ground like quicksand. In the dark in between the ice rushed winds was a voice commanding so loud it could be compared like thunder that it rang the whole dark void in Stevie's dream with a ringing stuck in his head as it roared into the dark from somewhere and blasted in a vibrant low bellow tone followed with a stray echo and it said to Stevie, "WAKE UP!"

Stevie stumbles upon waking up never before finding himself trembling thinking was his dream real covered with frost icicles where he awoke passed out again on the earth dirt ground laying in the middle of greenbelt looking upward at the brushing trees with silent winds in the middle of the sunset daylight ending but saw a coming storm brewing above him through the rushing trees.

Coming to his senses with a huge headache he studied his new setting surroundings and saw he must've been knocked out right before the freak out outburst disturbance of the festival that he could remember. He then remembers seeing the fairies sudden faces with fear among the crowds and the bewilderment anger on Kris's face after their new companion Trixs the fairy prince whispered something in his ear displaying defeat on their faces before they were magically forced to vanish into the fairy realm in thin air with Kris dragged into the fairies changeling light as well.

It must be hours he was out asleep as it dawns on Stevie he remembers time changes quicker in the fairy realm and wondered how many hours have passed.

Valerie was missing too, remembering she was last seen standing behind him was the last thing he could remember recognizing his linen bag was stolen with the witches' pendulum prism but what was odd also finding a rusted horseshoe stab into the ground with an iron pick in the middle of the fairy ring that once mushrooms now change into rotted fungus and sickly grass.

Trying to stay clueless Stevie couldn't comprehend the worst outcome as he was coming together to collect himself getting up from the ground realizing his headache was from being knocked out from the behind feeling a little knot on the back of his head but it was the knot in his stomach that hurt the most.

He was well aware it was a little past the afternoon finding himself alone silent among the greenbelt woods something did not sit right knowing his leaders have gone missing and now his friends.

A bright sparkle light started to appear before Stevie stepping out from a zapping sparkle crack that from out of thin air it was Kris that startled him.

"Kris, I saw you get suck in that fairy portal, I thought you were gone forever in the fairy realm, well for at least seventy-two years?"

"More like two days has already passed by out here and it's Tuesday night barely past seven o'clock just feels like only a few minutes in the fairy realm."

Kris replies and motions Stevie to follow gearing up their things and his belongings that were found on the ground, "Luckily it takes a royal fairy to open back a portal that connects to our world."

Kris then gazed at the subtle mutilation upon the fairy mound in complete utter silence. Stevie took the chance to swallow what feels like a golf ball was stuck in his throat. Before Stevie could speak it was Kris that broke the silence, "An iron pick through the horseshoe is like a deadly curse upon fairies, iron bounds fairies powers weaken them that can eradicate pixie's magic and of its surroundings, clever witch, she took the bag didn't she?"

"Valerie's a witch isn't she?" Stevie had to ask and then Kris replies, " That doll you keep running into, the summoning forest back there even a lake, I don't know what she is, but she lied, she lied to all of us!"

Stevie was silent just nods in disbelief and dismay he didn't want to believe it or was he just heartbroken and didn't want to show it.

Kris's senses kick in quickly acknowledging his friend's sorrow with the empathy of a burly temperament placing his palm over his friend's shoulder, "She not who she says she is and she played us, and now she has the witches prism."

"How do you know it was her?" Stevie asks hiding his scowled feelings keeping his composure calm and playing it cool awaiting Kris to reveal the truth.

"It was Valerie that kidnap Trixs days before we all met and she had some ties with Baba Yaga, something about raising a witch back from the dead that is what Trix's said."

It was the name Baba Yaga of the witch that taunts Stevie's memory to remember the trauma pain agony being frightened by the old crone witch that cast scars below the center of chest under the lower part of his sternum leaving two small side scars by his ribcage and stomach when last confronted by her it lead to the witch's death settled in her chicken house hut. Stevie's response was clueless, "And now our leaders are missing? Something's definitely not right?"

Kris motion Stevie to follow gearing up their stuff hiking back exiting green-belt explaining how Trixs told him immediately recognizes his capture as they were approaching Stevie and Valerie through the fairy crowd it was Trixs that alerted Kris right there and then. "And that's when we saw her with the horseshoe standing behind you and she…" Interrupted by Stevie that ended Kris's sentence who then asks, "I don't want to talk about it!"

"How's your head?" Kris asked politely with concern and Stevie replied with a shrugged shoulder and putting on his Aeon headphone over his ear. Kris respected his friend's wishes picking up the hint Stevie didn't want to discuss his newfound love with a betrayal broken heart but they both knew they must pick up their troubles and fix it.

Jumping into the borrowed Hummer EV from Charlie since he's been missing lending it Kris for their dates before getting wet from the coming storm it was then the boys decided their fate taking charge of the matter in their own hands.

Kris knowing how to get around the city of Austin began to drive and ask, "Hate to say it but we're going to need limited reinforcement to get the witches prism back regardless of the consequences, we're going to need Ashley and Charlie?" Kris then speeds up and drove like a getaway driver that just robbed a bank.

Stevie brings up a dire valid point giving each other clues, "our leaders are missing but here's what we know, Charlie had mentioned they were going to check out high places and Ashley goes absent looking for a missing princess who inherent the descendant of Snow White and that would be Snow to be exact she's the one that helps us the dancer from the Speakeasy burlesque club works for the dark Hindu goddess Kali who runs the show club."

Stevie then snaps into a sudden intuitive leap of understanding.

"I remember back at Charlie's surprise birthday party Ashley mentions there were clues with major leads connecting to the top building residences of the Austonian, but we know that it's occupied and then Charlie mentions high places.

Right there and then a light bulb went off within their heads with Stevie and Kris both announce echoing each other ending their sentence together,

"The evil queen."

21

Mirror Mirror On the Wall

ON A TUESDAY NIGHT WHO would have thought?" Kris says as he pulls up with Stevie with a Deja vu both starring up at one of the tallest residential buildings in the lone star state the Austonian in the rain underneath a storm with thunder brewing afar with a view of blue bedazzle lightning.

"Valerie told us to never come back here?" Stevie declared foretelling his emotions and thoughts.

Kris response to his friend as they smiled with a bro shake and a half of a hug before heading into the building, "You think the party will have food?"

The boys knew the elevators to the residential building's top floor require a card key to use the elevator so they took to height to the stairs.

Catching their breath finally arriving at the very top of the Austonian the 56th floor Stevie had enough time to think over his possibilities and his recent upsetting breakup he was now focused on working overtime.

"Wow, this evil queen has high maintenance for a fairy tale." Stevie quickly mentions.

Walking through the top opening exit stairway door was a dark hallway having a marble mirror glass floor with no natural lights from outside transformed into a mental mirror room like a crowded chandelier with more depth of an embellish twisted dark fairy tale adorned than the last time they visited the amateur queen's throne chambers. Kris briefly mentions being aware of assumptions, "This is mirror magic, watch your step."

Decorated with brown glass crystal green trees sprouting chandelier branches reaching from the wall frames of the hallway on both sides overhead a red carpet pathway with red shiny diamond apples hanging from the branches.

"Can't believe all this is on the very top on the 56th floor like a whole another castle on top of this building?" Stevie asked again as they continued walking towards a coming entrance of what looks to be inside of an old enchanted castle with the red carpet leading to a queen's throne. "Spatial magic is something else isn't it?" Stevie had to ask Kris reassuring a rational possible cause for the unexplainable extraordinary extra space known to only be at the top of the building.

At the end of the hall, the familiar golden throne peacock stood alone that was once occupied with a long diner party table full of psychic clairvoyance guests from the boy's last visit that made a name for the celebration called the millennial party.

Even the pillars of the dark throne room were so grand the columns are shape twisted into tall dark apple trees crystalize its fairytale in an enchanted forest inside a castle with glistening shine glass giving off light with body mirrors set on side of the glass apple tree pillars.

"It looks like we have more party crashers that have arrived?"

"You've been spying on me?" Stevie announced as if traumatized.

The amateur queen appeared out of nowhere sliding out of a mirror from a dark corner strutting to her peacock throne lounging over it clapping sarcastically and began jeering Stevie's name as she reveals her magic mirror peeping through Stevie's bathroom, "Starman… "

Stevie was alarmed and speechless while Kris was creeped out as they geared their remotes set to the stung mode in their hand ready for anything.

"Now boys, this is one party you are not invited to!"

Like a cat yarning a ball of string the amateur queen was fascinated with her presumption arrived guests and began to circle around her arms sitting inappropriate manner on the throne wearing stilt high heels with her legs cross in the air wearing black hosiery netting and gestures with a quarrel of extreme vanity annoyance entertained by her pleasure of flamboyant acts working with a giant metallic fan in one hand making it clap with an unnerving laugher that signature her as the crude villain.

"There's something you don't see every day, how does that nursery alibi for witches go, oh what's the saying?" Simply the queen was now making a mockery out of the boys for amusement, "When a Christian and witch walks together…" the amateur evil queen chuckled, but it was Kris who completed the queen's quote, "they say time itself will then bow down."

But it was the queen that ended the witches' alibi, "May the green eye monster consume their will."

Then the evil amateur queen said, "You know it was forbidden for any witch to walk among alongside a Christian."

Glistening with lavish red fingernail polish drench in black eyeliner with purple eye shadow makeup giving off the pale skin reflection that brought out the pink blush on her cheeks.

It wasn't just the penciled-on eyebrow that sported features of a dark sadistic sociopath of a wanna-be evil queen before them but it was the outfit that screamed major cosplay.

"I thought the big one would come out to play but instead I get two little runts." Stevie murmured under his breath enough so Kris could hear it, "Valerie is not here?" Kris responded not being shy to be heard, "Charlie and Ashley are not here?"

The amateur queen then began to mock with a local Texan accent, "where is your big mama dog now?"

Stevie was mistaken for Valarie but Kris knew better the amateur queen's threat was meant for the Librarian.

Wearing a purple long-sleeved ankle-length gown and a red rope belt tied around her waist. She wears a black balaclava that covers her ears, her neck, and her hair, leaving her pale face exposed. The amateur Queen also wore a long black cloak that appears to be part of the cowl. The cloak is lined with red inside and the bottom of the cloak is lined with white fur. She has a high white collar attached to her cloak. She also wears a golden pendant that seems to connect with the collar and in one hand she's a tune to work with the same metallic purple-blue fan dramatically known for her outburst feminine gesticulations.

The convicted ladyboy was very titled to look and play as if she was the very evil queen similar to a popular villain in a famous cartoon fairytale. It was the crown that gave the amateur drag Queen its royalty touch wearing a golden crown atop her head with five spikes on the front and a jewel on the tip of the middle and tallest spike. The color scheme of her attire represents her pride and vanity.

"No matter time is of the essence, and I don't mind a few party favors." With a swish hand, the amateur queen magically commanded all doors shut, color glass windows close tight, and dark red draped curtains flew up revealing the queen's dark throne as a hall chamber of mirrors with dark high chamber walls having sparkling diamonds lighting in the background.

"Great now were lock in, she magically binds sealed a spell that no one can come in or out," Kris murmured very quietly to Stevie.

"Picking up dear o auntie's bad habits and her bad antique wardrobe collection is way outdated by the way, and if you're thinking about raising a witch back from the dead you have another thing coming." Kris snapped back who wasn't shy towards any comrade or rival witch of the dark or light.

"All bark but no bite witch boy!" The amateur queen historically laughs then after taking her time looking upon the many mirrors throughout the throne room tramping over her dark vogue looks placing dark red lipstick with puckering lips she then replies, "and you know nothing of me!"

The amateur queen looks rather amused working with a feminine reaction corresponding with a metallic fan in her hand overdoing the flamboyant hostile drama of opening and closing her fan with her reaction was beginning to be of annoyance.

Kris being a witch himself quickly explains to Stevie standing beside Kris confronting the amateur drag queen seeing multiple resemblances of witchcraft in conjuring the dead pointing out a little display witch alter in the near corner with a summoning pentagram and magical dark ingredients like a tiny glass vial with red blood that requires a small cauldron in being used with foaming white fog hovering and pouring out of the bubbling burning pot scattering onto the surrounding ground floor.

"Let's not forget the most important ingredient, blood from a heart of a royal princess, WHERE'S SNOW WHITE?" Kris let out before he could make a move with their remotes in command to stabilize their oppressor vixen opponent it was the amateur drag queen that had the quickest draw.

"Mirror, mirror on the wall." The amateur queen exclaimed.

Another swish with the right hand the amateur queen manages to disarm their weapon remotes from their hands flying across the room into the dark corners.

"Please, it only requires a few drops of blood from the whiny princesses that's all."

Reveling a dreadful setting across the throne hall appeared soulless bodies trap in the pillars of the twisted glass apple tree mirrors something the two boys weren't ready for.

Knowingly the four bodies reserved in a state of a deep sleep, the first wasn't a surprise finding Snow the go-go princess dancer the actual descendant of Snow White motionless in a separate magic body mirror, and the other three captors was a shock to the boys finding their peer leaders Charlie and Ashley stuck inside their set mirrors as well in a deep sleep but it was Valerie that was the fourth body that sent Stevie on an emotional roller coaster.

"Making victim's eyes close forever, it'll make her breath still… and her blood congeal… and I'll be the fairest in the land…" The amateur queen then looks upon the boys with a sense of overdose dramatic facade and a stare from a hopeless psycho stuck in a fantasy fairy tale world of portraying to be the classic villain.

"Do you understand the gratification of conjuring and to use the exact poison named "The Sleeping Death" once cast by a despairing ambitious queen witch achieving her end as a sign of her determination of desperation and don't get me started GURLFRIEND?"

The drag queen snaps her fingers twice with attitude then placing her hand on her hips dramatically folds and flaps her long steel fan with the other hand in mockery peeking and hiding her sinister expression holding back her laughs behind her big drag fan pandering from the pure shock of her rivalries.

The attack was on and Kris was already focused on his offense paying no attention to the drag queen who hated to be ignored conjuring silently sitting with his leg cross Indian style while Stevie paid no attention and was also fix onto Valerie's mirror trap within the mirror the amateur drag queen was trying to finish her sentence but notice Kris was up to something and began to call him out.

"My family legacy of eight great generations will finally, hey you there witch boy I'm talking to you!"

Thankfully for Stevie's supernatural senses, it will strike his left-hand numb cold as he stumbles out of his heartbreak trance taking a step back with attention off Valerie then towards the amateur drag queen with a deep burn rooted in his heart.

The amateur queen snapped her giant fan shut and marched back fancy to her summoning alters like a stunt on a runway and pulled the red curtain behind the altar to reveal the legendary enchanted Magic Mirror that once belongs to Snow white's true arch nemesis, the evil queen Grimhilde.

The Evil Queen is historically known among witches to be a greedy and murderous despot queen from the exotic faraway land called Shaitan of the lost black sand the last to use the ancient culture of the dark ages of Babylon.

The ancient magic mirrors were grand in their particular way very old and shape in a large oval having its ring made out of pure silver around the mirror with coil designs around the body mirror were of snakes at the top design of an agony head of a woman with a snake coil coming out of her mouth.

Stevie standing near the trap glass mirror that withheld Valerie he was puzzled putting the clues together the missing warning shots from Valerie advising him to stay away from the mirrors was intentional as it was revealed the evil amateur queen was spying on him this whole time. After he saw the magic mirror just displayed for Stevie while the evil amateur queen laughed showing a feature of Stevie's bathroom through the magic mirror.

"Step away from the mirror Stevie," Kris said while sitting down with Stevie taking steps back till he was standing behind Kris that sat down on the floor with his legs cross between their foes and was now concentrating on their enemy the amateur drag queen.

"Valerie is not who she is," Kris announced to Stevie.

With pure shudder as Stevie did his best to hide his quake but it was Valerie who stole Stevie's attention taking control of the fuss chaos by surprisingly awoke from a fake deep slumber and slowly stepping out of the trap magic mirror.

Kris began to mention Valerie's fraudulent friendship and her deception of lies as he figured her out.

"You were in on it this whole time wanting us here didn't you that planted the trap in the beginning and it was you that slip the special guest invitation cards into Esma's bag so we may attend the special millennial party, wasn't it?"

All that Valerie chooses to do was just smile with a sly gesture suggesting with her raised shoulders acting mischievously with her reaction caught in the act while Kris called her out.

"One that carries a magic creepy straw doll that continues to show up out of nowhere undercover in time of need that's always been spying on Stevie."

The flames withdrew from Kris's Aeon black lighter surrounding the boys with a small circle flame to protect them from harm as he continues.

"She avoided the fairies cause Valerie was there before the congregation of tri-paradox that kidnapped Trixs and you've been working with the evil queen and Baba Yaga."

Stevie was speechless and confused by Kris's blunted accusations as he reaches to feel the bump on his head and asks Kris, "What are you saying?"

"She's the one that tricks us into stealing the witches pendulum, one that can conjure a lake and a forest, you're the protector of children and innocents from the one known as Baba Yaga as the legend is told but the tale is far fetched as you were only an apprentice, the only one who was able to surpass the crone witch Baba Yaga, weren't you?"

"You got me, guilty as charged, and do you know how hard it was to manipulate the library stone table into casting me to be one of you to become as a Seer."

Applauding with a sarcastic clap with Valerie using her dally charms being as pleasant as ever wasting no time as she said narrowing in-between the circle flames as it started to rise lower losing its fire strength starring straight at Stevie with stone misfit gray eyes.

Then she said as looking at Stevie then turning to Kris, "Baba Yaga's magic is what got me through and she was like a grandmother to me. This place's high rise palace is magically seal shut even a goddess would have trouble getting in here."

"Countless of your eccentric disguise being Valerie your real name is not Lisa Vasil, but playing with your words before us is the infamous Vasilisa the beautiful confidant of Baba Yaga a familiar sorceress known to be a legend among the witch community."

Kris announced the imposter Vasilisa who was once Valerie claps again in mockery strolling around Kris's summoning protection flame circle was weakening low enough for her to walk over and squat eye to eye with Kris as he sits still meditating pasting with heavy breathing.

"Not only are you a sensible bandit but a very evasive witch you are, what's wrong can't catch a break on your holy black fire." Vasilisa walks away from Kris with a smirk walking around behind the boys in circles to the other side from the front throne room with her condescending profound knowledge as if she was blackmailing Kris.

Kris had more to say after the amateur evil queen cut in with her sociopath feminine gestures to the extreme dramatic irritation on a hinge of gasping toying to using her fan in pleasure lounging on the golden throne peacock getting up walking over to her corner there was the dark summoning alter.

The amateur queen was heavily fractious with Vasilisa the relationship was pretentious she began putting on dark red lipstick sneering at her ally entrant through the reflection before summoning again with puckering lips in front of her grand magic mirror, "a lost devastating witchboy bound to darkness forevermore but maybe he could be plus to the team?"

Kris snaps back at the amateur evil queen, "I'm not lost and you conjuring a medieval dark witch queen of family issues with stepdaughter rages coming back from the dead… is not my cup of tea, especially if it's your protégé!"

"Don't you see Stevie Vasilisa has been working side by side with the amateur queen and witches ever since, I can't seem to summon my holy fire since I've last used it back at the library," Kris turns to Stevie with a dire look of an apologetic gesture for his unknown mistake that could have been mention earlier before jumping into situations. "It feels as if my black flame has been tap out."

Kris with mixed emotions of anger and confidence still sitting in pose position he continues to spill their plans all out to Stevie making him realize the puzzles that were missing revealing the surprise of what truly Vasilisa is, and what the amateur queen is up to is raising a fifteen century year old dead witch queen.

Stevie noted an important suggestion, "how was it she was able to convey with the Tri-paradox?"

"Vasilisa is a surpass pupil of Baba Yaga a well-known enchantress to the witch world of sorcery who possess the charms of twilight once danced before the gods that some say her twilights can even endure the might of gods even cut one till the stars burn out."

The boys grasp to understand the moment Vasilisa pulled out a familiar object that was stolen and was last seen at old Yang's Chinese antiques and magical items shop revealing the pink ballerina slippers stolen from lock in a mystic glass dome case.

"It wasn't an easy task convoying my magic from the Durga protection spell of the Seer's library to the tri-paradox so I came as a guest, and thirty seconds to be exact is all I need for my twilight."

Vasilisa elicits Kris's statement as she began to tie onto the pink ballerina slippers removing her cable boots and shedding her cable guy clothes and gears revealing her true form slip into a moderate tight suit for dancers pulling pink streamers from hair bow letting her hair fall loose that was pulled back into a ponytail.

"You stole?" Stevie ask baiting the question with Vasilisa replying, "I took back what's rightfully mine, I would not have gotten my hands on it if it weren't for witchboy's theft- boosting five-finger discount." Vasilisa then winks to Kris standing her ground blocking the exit way with her pink streamers at hand like she's ready for full combat at a dance recital.

Kris spoke to Stevie still sitting down legs are cross concentrating on his protection facing the amateur evil queen with Stevie behind him guarded with nowhere to go facing his deceitful opponent in a confusing mixed outfit between a ballerina and an assassin was hard for Stevie to take seriously with pink streamers adjust in her hands.

"Running into Baba Yaga wasn't intentional but was meant to be by destiny, at the millennial party it was revealed to be suspicious ever since Valerie who is Vasilisa, and her little quarrel between the amateur queen, the two teaming up with Baba Yaga, but not knowing we intervene destroying their main leader and their traditional plans, disrupted the grimoire book and stop their dark curses." As Kris mentions the last part of his sentence he slightly turns to Stevie with a warning look knowing the information they share disclosed about Stevie's dark curse slain upon him."

The amateur queen began to dabble in dark magic reciting to her magic mirror persisting to finish her necromancy ritual. "A nemesis skin white as snow." The amateur evil queen then opens an ice chest full of snow dropping a handful of chucks into her witch boiling pot.

"The color of your adversary is lips red rose as cherry wine," she pours drops of blood from the tiny glass vial she consumes in a syringe from snow white into her brewing witch pot. She then pulls a lock of black hair from Snow White tied with straw yarn from a small velvet purple pouch dropping it into the pot. "And the enemies' hair black as ebony." She then smeared her brew potion onto the magic mirror and summoned, "change mischief peddlers cloak to the queenly rightful heir, transformed her ugliness to beauteous that once behold so dear, mirror mirror on the wall bring forth death as her everlasting breath, ashes to ashes dust to dust thou wert art that once commanded this rite may thy soul come back to life!"

While the amateur queen began to continue her ritual at her grand magic mirror with the dark summoning alter lit by candles Kris briefly explains the collaboration requirements of the mystery occult legend about witches raising a dead witch that requires the fairest for her enchantment to work staying beautiful forever and to never age needs a sacrifice a soul for the price to become the rightful ruler queen of the witches, a dead witch that would come back to life to rule and reign as the grand-hind witch with keys to chaos following the forthcoming to the end of the world by her wicked ways.

"Every dark witch's dream is to summon the apocalypse dead witch queen to be at her side till the end. I just can't believe these boneheads are trying to pull this off and I suspected ever since we ran into Baba Yaga with the book of shadows losing its dark curse is now pulsing through you, Stevie. For every witch knows its purpose of the dark curse was to raise the legendary vanity dead Queen witch of Shaitan of all witches but the Librarian Madam will never allow it!"

It was perfect timing that couldn't be played out any more perfect at hand as if her name alone summons her existence a surprise appearance with a gust of wind coming from across the throne hall coming out from the darkness walking forward into the light wearing her trademark black glove in her trademark dark black Victorian silhouette with ruffled shoulders and tight black opal brooch stranded as a turtleneck.

Within her right hand holding her black oak staff summoning with a grand entrance with gushing dark winds coming forth behind her with a force so might busting through the chamber entrance doors shattering the glass mirrors holding its victims as they were released with Charlie and Ashley fell onto the floor still unconscious breaking through the amateur queen's bind spell that it was the Seer's commander in a chef who has no name but she is known as Madam the Librarian.

Madam always came off to appear as a very eminence and grim-looking, always carrying the lady figure upright posture that gave off a calm collect defiance.

"Where's your posture, stand up straight hold you're ground, and relieve the wounded." The librarian scolds Stevie and Kris careless of recent appearance events when the boys were ironically happy and confused to see their scary enigma boss in the flesh such a vigorous character she is of late with old fashion manners of a strict dark Victorian Librarian they couldn't tell if they were in trouble or not but then in some ways, they knew they were if looks could kill they would be dead on the spot.

"Ah speaking of the devil, the mama bear has finally come out to play."

The conniving amateur witch queen having her double-cross fingers hidden behind her back she swiftly bowed to the Librarian introducing herself announcing her unpleasant guest, "Madam the Librarian solely right of the grand hind witch, I swear by the ordinance of the sisterhood I come in peace."

Madam hush the amateur drag queen being so loud the typical librarian with her finger to her lips to shush the dramatic amateur evil queen wearing her creepy tight black leather gloves.

Then the amateur queen got outraged by Madam's short small mockery after standing on her stage before her peacock throne declared a condescending comment towards the surprise arrival of the Librarian within seconds moment after moment after her bow everything happens so fast it was happening all at once.

Without wasting any time Vasilisa quickly overhead threw her prize the purple pouch across the room to the drag amateur evil queen as she quickly signals to cast shrouded broken glass mirrors to attack the Librarian while catching the bag as she fastens to summon the witches' silver pendulum charms whispering the old casting spell of the witches prism.

With coming shrouded glass of mirrors attacking the Librarian, Madam was too quick holding her staff and slammed it on the ground and froze the oncoming shredded blade mirrors from their attack in mid-air and shattered into shattered into sand falling on the ground everywhere.

Suddenly the evil queen was enchanting to cast a prism hex towards the Librarian from the witches' pendulum spell as her eyes glowed purple casting its spell that was transforming into natural elements in her grasp from fire to water, changing to rocks then into the air as it was thrown at the Librarian.

A fatality spell was summoned made for any witch especially designed to dispatch any grand hind witch and then drag queen spoke, "we've been expecting you, here try this for sore eyes."

All was soon to be lost as their devastating rescue was in peril before their eyes the enchanted legendary hex prism of the witches was cast for its purpose but wrongfully so.

The Librarian holds her ground in defense holding her staff with both hands with the hex thrown at her it was so sudden it formed into a trap sphere of ring fires surrounding her as she was so cold hearted and still she vanished into the gushing bright flames that began to turn its color burning away so bright the ember changed into blue bright flames. There was an eerie shrieking cry coming from the flames that began to turn blue to green that struck the boys deep knowingly helpless to their leader headmistress was tormenting to death as the bright green flames spewing green mist inside the trapping sphere that now change into electric charge blue rings still invisible to see inside the sphere rings filled with smoke and electric shocks as it went silent hearing just vibrant shocks and crisp sound in the smoke of electric shocks.

The amateur queen didn't waste any moment taking the advantage to finish her summoning ritual, as everyone else was distracted it was Stevie in dismay of betrayal confronting Valerie with a broken heart while Kris took upon a mirror looking confused at the unfamiliar reflection of himself in pale dark eyes.

"Mummy dust to make me old;" The amateur queen took a glass bowl of cobwebs dropping a snip of old rags of dust into her boiling pot, then picking up a small tin box that flashed as opening bring darkness close to her spell and said, "To shroud my clothes, the black of night."

The sphere witches hex continued with its rings around its victim of elements changing its rings of destructions from water to lava, then to dark steel rings holding dark entities changing to nuclear bright light with luminous rings but it was the agony screaming that came from the hex sphere that shrouded Stevie's courage.

Vasilisa confronted Stevie with her pink whip caught in her web of streamers holding him tight letting it all out in guessing to comfort Stevie with her knowledge of knowingly to herself of the rising dead ritual secrets that the amateur queen is casting, a secret that is known to be very deadly asking Stevie, "Does it bother you I'm ancient?" Stevie replies, "You're just a character from a witches tale, what else is there?" Vasilisa asks, "My immortally doesn't scare you?" Stevie then replies, "besides that, you lie, steal, and you cheat." Vasilisa came close to Stevie's face, "Everything I said about you back at the Fae festival is true, don't ever forget that!"

"To age, my voice, an old hag's cackle; The amateur queen said as she cracks opens a giant black rock over her chalice with a harshly shrill laughing that came from the broken rock.

"To whiten my hair, a scream of fright," she screams with a screech as she pours a white liquid into her potion glass chalice.

"I'll tell you this, be careful with power for it will corrupt you from the inside out."

Vasilisa exchanges a serious look with Stevie and quietly said with a vindictive observation, "Just watch."

She took fancy to make Stevie watch the amateur queen finish her summoning ritual as she whispers in his ear. "Carefully watch as the hopeless despair reaches its eleventh-hour blinded by death that is to come to those who pay vanity." Vasilisa then makes a sour face and quietly condemns the amateur queen, "One that deserves a sacrifice deed is better off as death becomes her."

Stevie being trapped and withheld in Vasilisa's entanglement pink streamers he was forced to watch and ask Vasilisa while she stood behind him in guard, "She's going to die?"

Vasilisa snared Stevie's mouth shut with a whip of her pink streamer before he could alert the amateur queen and spoiled the fun for Vasilisa as she replies, "She's up on the last part of the ritual which requires a soul for a soul and this witless imbecile doesn't even know it.

Stevie was blown away by how much of a dog eat dog world it was for a witch even as family companions in their witch community he learns they can not be trusted as he looks over at Kris still bewildering and lost at the reflection of himself.

" A blast of wind to fan my hate;" A dark cold wind brush through in and out of the chamber throne hall with the amateur queen's purple cape flying rising her chalice high in the air.

"A thunderbolt to mix it well!" There sudden a frightening strike of lightning zapped her potion chalice raised in the air from the storm brewing outside that whiz through the hall coming from a high above color glass window.

"Now begin thy magic spell!" She takes a drink from her chalice with wide-open eyes starring at her magic mirror it was filled with terror of a shrouded old hag witch cackling the moment she took a sip dropping her cup clasping her neck signaling she was choking from poison.

"NO! YOU BETRAYED ME YOU DOUBLE CROSSER, YOU CANT DO THIS!" The amateur evil queen yearns at her magic mirror pleading the mistake for his life as the voice changes he begs losing his soul in a shriek of transforming into someone else that once was dead, "No, not me, you promise... you lied to me..."

Touching the magic mirror sapping of what's left of the amateur queen's life for mishandling dark magic costing his life was the price he paid transforming in a grotesque degree of death to an old brittle peddler witch hunch over cackling insanely as they watch with her back facing towards them from behind as they see the reflection of frontal dark transformation on the magic mirror.

The peddler hunchback was now transformed into a slender figure of pale skin, green eyes, with red lips, brownish-gray eye shadow, and pink blush on her cheeks, with red fingernails and seemingly penciled-on eyebrows.

Vasilisa released Stevie from the grasp of her pink tape weaponry whip fooled to be a simplistic hair tied pink ribbon as he fell to the floor stunned.

"Look there, Stevie, the spell ritual is complete, long live the wicked queen." Stevie was stunned to see the resemblance of how close the evil queen looks like as the one from the famous kid's fairy tale movie.

Vasilisa mentions as she collects herself to greet an unfeeling face of an icily beautiful woman with a serene of an evil queen that once was and famously known for her harden cold heart, violent, egotistical, and possessive tyrant behavior, and so she has an extreme vanity that made her utterly intolerant and conservative of rivals.

Keeping contact eye-to-eye Vasilisa slowly bowed towards her special lifeless guest before she approached the throne steps as the evil queen bares the void in her eyes that stare back cold heartily studying and scanning the vicinity getting one's bearings. Giving off a gratified smirk from the evil queen noticing the familiar lethal sphere rings of the hexes running its course from the witches prism now being cast as dark noxious spines spewing toxic lost inside its trap victim was the recent grand hind witch the seer's Librarian letting out cries of shrill shriek.

The evil queen began to speak foreign with Stevie putting on his Aeon wireless headphone from hanging around from his neck placing on his head to listen he understood the foreign language from where he picks up.

"Where is here am I to be from the dead?" Said the evil queen with Stevie's outspoken obdurate response applying with a Vulcan hand salute, "In Texas, Keep Austin Weird."

Vasilisa spoke in a foreign language and immediately Stevie rushes to aid his comrades still unconscious lying on the floor.

"Your majesty, phase one is completed we must hurry and contact the others immediately for the ritual, leave the boy to me with the dark curse the others are yours to keep."

It was hard and peculiar for Stevie to see Valerie as a different person, it was Vasilisa running in charge head-strong doing what she does best with a leader attitude always two feet ahead before a plan but this time it was for the wrong side.

"Your fair archrival Snow White carries misfortunes she has a manager superior a protector, the dark goddess that brings avenges to our doorstep as we speak, it is wise for you to hurry with your incarnation while I handle miss firecracker when she comes."

Vasilisa could be a fortuneteller a well-known secret of the many powerful abilities she may possess but sure enough, there was a loud bang brought at the front castle door as the floor quake and shook the hall with every loud bang.

It was too late for Kris display lost in the mirror in a deep sleep, walking into his own trap the vanity spell of the magic mirrors was too much for him but little did they know it was his dark reflection that came to life and snatches Kris from behind into the mirror.

Stevie felt vulnerable, alone, and useless but he knew being powerless he dared to retreat at what he does best taught with his mother's love, and a rock, like his father he fights with kindness.

"It's the one and only Queen Grimhilde its legend proceeds your name to be very..." Stevie paused to delay any negative labeling to evoke the evil queen.

"Famous among children literature." He smiles grabbing the evil queen's attention swallowing his last hope in achieving to impede the witches diabolic plan to at least linger till help arrives he hopes.

Don't listen to him!" Vasilisa retorted across the hall as she prepares the lifeless Snow White back into a mirror tree pillar.

Stevie retaliated with his sense of humor and a gesture of curiosity, "Hi I'm Stevie Ruiz and your powers must be enchanted to be enhanced since you came back from the dead and all, not that you look dead but drop-dead gorgeous!" Stevie's reaction was too sudden to his comment in hoping she wasn't offended it was his action that could give it away. "No, no, no... but not in a bad way but just saying without the dead stuff." Stevie was trying not to lose his chill as he was stalling but buffering to stay in the game. "One so great and beautiful to cast a powerful curse, one known as the sleeping death upon an apple to its victims, and in one bite break the tender peel to taste the breathe will still, and the blood will congeal till their death."

The Evil Queen paused from conjuring her magic mirror, and was very amused, and intrigue giving off a petition invitation for him to continue his flattering acclamation.

"Powers so might as yours and your outdo is no more, don't you want to know who now is the fairest of them all?"

The evil Queen stroke back in a pose of a summoning position with her arms wide and eyes open in a command to face her magic mirror.

"Come from the farthest space, through wind and darkness I summon thee… speak. Let me behold thou face," the Evil queen announces to her magic mirror with a short side-eye checking at Stevie.

The Magic Mirror spoke in a robotic tone with a deep low volume that stirred an echo - "What would thou know my queen?"

It was bronzed in silver lining with alive snakes slithering and hissing barring it fangs around the mirror the prize was entrapped inside a mysterious person was coming forth sticking out of the mirror halfway was a shape-shifting faceless robed man whose entire being is seemingly composed of the mirror that was liquefied to take shape.

"Magic mirror, mirror, on the wall, who is the fairest one of all." The Evil queen announced in a flattering desire with vituperative tendencies brewing within her voice disguising her sadistic motives.

The shape-shifting hooded glass robed Mirror proceeded, "I feel the splendor of your wrath, and despair, were I to name one as so fair."

The Evil Queen retorted. "There is someone else? Reveal her name?"

"There is none to name as fair as thee, my queen." The mirror responded.

Cold heartily the Queen responded back, "Mirror, Mirror, do not lie to me! I detest, do you behold another face?"

The Mirror corresponded, "None to match your queenly grace."

"You LIE! Why Do You LIE! Your Queen forsaken!" The Evil queen patronizes her magic mirror the thought that made Stevie think what sociopath could conjure threats to a magic mirror.

"Your majesty I was mistaken." The mirror responded.

The Evil Queen possessively asks then with a bi-polar utterly intolerant forward command, "You are magic, you can not lie!" She then points with a finger towards her mirror and shouted in command as it echoed throughout the throne hall, "IS THERE A FAIRER ONE THAN I!"

Slowly the magic mirror revealed the answer, "Hair so raven, skin so fine, eyes as green as jade stone fine."

"SNOW WHITE!" The Evil queen snaps clasping her chest after short hyperventilating breathes she then repetitively asks, "Say her name! Is it Snow White isn't it?"

The Magic Mirror complies to take a final bow to say, "Greed and envy comes in hand and hand brings up misery to a land."

But it was the Evil Queen that coincided with the truth of the magic mirror- " Do not summarize your Queen! Mirror, Mirror, Now Answer Me!"

It was this that magic mirror gave the last regard to its command in a deep low tone, "as time has past, ever fairer once a princess behold in tales, forever not the fairest in the land but the one before you age days of virtues that are scarcely expended, it is not she but HE that have surpasses before your eyes, Stevie Ruiz is the fairest one in the land."

Stevie was just as traumatized as the evil Queen staring at each other clueless with both their mouths open to the final answer from the magic mirror but Stevie felt the pain of remorse, and embarrassment as he turns red smiling in a gully with his hands to his hips as his plan backfired on him. "Ahh... Yeah... about the fairest... are you sure about that?" Stevie didn't hesitate to keep questioning the narrative answer hoping to draw out to conclude another answer, "Are you sure, I think I heard Mikey Ruiz..."

"Enough!" The Queen yelled pulling out from a mirror a silver sacrificial blade one so sharp a dagger made out of a mirror enough to threaten the situation for Stevie at hand as she began to flaunt the dagger to use it as she displays a growing cynicism performance of her theatric mirror magic.

While she spoke magically appeared through almost all the mirrors with multiple reflections of the evil queen that echoed her confession.

"Spells charms that can be cast out by fairest vitality one can manifest great powers that can multiply and summon all creatures of living and dead of dark and light." You possess something we need and so rightfully mine!"

Stevie couldn't make out what she meant by that, but he knew his life was in danger being surrounded by reflections mirrors of the evil queen.

Once again within seconds of peril for his life Stevie was spared a few more moments before any life-threatening action was made towards him they were interrupted by a new highly threat that came from a voluptuous angry dark goddess Kali with her long dark hair a flow moving on its own dressed in a striking red orange-red two-piece cocktail sequins matching her flames revealing a smooth stomach riled in abs adorn with sparkled golden cuffs and glistering jewels abode over her body. Braking through the force field an invisible binding seal spell with her hands lit on fire as she began to walk slowly like a predator ready to pounce towards her enemies leaving a trail of her footprints melting onto the marble mirror floor with orange-yellow flames igniting through her eyes disclosing a shiny color charcoal skin ready to crack to explode within lava running through her veins such power of weight of force can be seen that was emitting from the dark goddess.

"Release the princess and friends then shall I give you a swift death."

Too much was going on at the same time, Kali notices the conjuring witches hex's rings were activated that were transformed into large purple rings rotating each other inside captive was clutching a huge ball of green acid slime being a goddess knowingly well Kali knew who's caught in that deadly awful trap of the hex death sphere prism worst to go for anyone known on this planet along with the disturbing foul eerie shriek cry that came within the hex's spell.

Vasilisa stood between the goddess and Stevie standing before the evil queen but it was Vasilisa in her defense stance letting the dark deity know she was not to pass became prepared and began to put on her famously known legend of pink ballerina twilight slippers as it magically twined its pink laces around her legs transforming her outfit into a spandex sparkling suit giving off a menacing superhero alter ego of the pink dark ballerina assassin with her deadly pink whip. Her whip is a hidden weapon so sharp are the streamers it can slice a diamond in half equip in her hand as she split a decorated large golden ruby mantle in half. Vasilisa took armed and said to the goddess, "I upgraded my twilight even I can cut diamonds and gods now can't you tell?"

Kali then took the threat as a silly gesture and responded with a pleasure sneer a fixed deadly smile, "I remember you showing off your twilight before the glorification of the gods, not bad for a rookie." Kali flashed and flaunt her goddess aura and began to ignite turning into a walking fireball transformed into her recognizable size power of the dark goddess remembering the last time Stevie got the taste of her power when first met back at her club.

"There is nothing that escapes the all-consuming march of time even for you immortal."

Vasilisa began to goad taunting at the dark goddess sealing her ultimatum, "Kali-Ma, the nurturer, to shy to bring around Smashana… the destroyer…"

The goddess's relieved a glaring stare as her attire manifest in a terrible sight her necklace of severed shrunk heads and her girdle of severed shrunk arms signifies her killing rage but are also tantric metaphors for creative power and severance from the bonds of karma and accumulated deeds. Even her stance is imbued with dual meaning with Kali's goddess's eyes going mad with bloodshot red, growing two more arms after she took a step with her left foot ringing her ankle bracelet and even Stevie was anticipating fully aware of what is to happen next will be an offensive move.

Kali the Hindu goddess then sneered with pleasure with a semi-bow thankful to release death revealing her sharp fangs counteract against the shiny Russian enchantress, "You tempt me so what are you going to do now, throw lakes and tress at me?"

The dark goddess was quick to be sarcastic but Kali was stuck sinking where she stands her feet were melting into the glass marble floor was the evil queen summoning her magic mirrors to bend the goddess's will while Vasilisa twinkled around the goddess spinning with a replication power by multiplying herself shining bright managing to block and trapping the dark goddess by surrounding her by waltzing around spinning to get at least one cut in on the dark deity's arm before she escapes.

The dark goddess did have super agile powers as she broke from the floor vanishing and reappeared sideways of her dancing sparkling prey with a sneak attack looking at her freshly cut wound laughing insanely making the victim regretful.

In one of her left hands appeared a severed demon head of Raktabija the sign alter ego of the human spirit that must be severed in order to exit from the cycle of life and rebirth was used as a flagrant weapon opening its demon mouth spewing red fire lava at the pink silver twilight enchantress.

"Sixth form whirlpool!" Spinning into a sparkling cyclone Vasilisa being light on her toes she manages to keep up and match the speed of the goddess as she spins with her pink streamers building up a force field protected by the spewing fire lava surrounding around her as she twirls a sparkling bedazzled cocoon making a shiny shield out of her sharp pink slay ribbons.

The epic battle lingered around the giant hex rings of the witches' prism now casting inside trapping a huge thriving deadly toxic thorn-needles shrubberies with poisonous blooming flowers ejecting into monstrous flytraps snapping at its victims nearby with the distraught void screaming still coming from inside.

Stevie ran to the nearest corner to grab his lost seer remote to at least protect himself, but it was the evil queen's persistence that didn't lose sight of Stevie appearing magically in every mirror of the throne room jeering at him as she gladly took scorn.

"Kris, Kris wake up!" Stevie shouted banging with a close fist to the magic mirror tree pillar that was holding his friend captive.

Kris woke up from inside the magic mirror with black shade eyes recognized by an unfamiliar face that Stevie definitely knew it was not Kris taking a couple of steps back away from the mirror as the imposter cloned Kris walked out from the mirror agile with threats towards Stevie.

The evil queen took to her magic mirror throwing her arms casting long foul spells ignoring the hostile threats behind her as the match between the enchantress Vasilisa versus the dark Hindu goddess Kali below before the throne stage orbiting around the two millennia-old hexes prism rings continuing its powerful witches' curses holding its victim's poor soul tormented by thousands of evil charms displaying a dark figure inside that were changing into hallow pure light rings filled with boiled water sphere with blue-green liquid turning into pink-red acid water.

Kali took at ease from attacking with an unfamiliar sense feeling of her god aura is being absorbed as her powers are draining into the leeching surrounded magic mirrors of the throne room strengthening the evils queen's spell charms.

With a reminder, Vasilisa warned the vigilant dark goddess realizing this was the plan all along pitching a picture of walking into a giant glass box to trap a god to harvest its power, "You feel that Babylonian magic from the evil queen taking your divinity like energy batteries and don't think about blowing out all these mirrors around us won't do any good but harm to your friends, goddess of destruction."

Dealing with the dark cloned Kris approaching near Stevie that stepped out of the magic mirror was bad enough for he was now dealing with a more complicated issue that arises before Stevie right after the evil queen finished an enchantment spell five more unpleasant surprises step out of their own set of magic mirrors pillars.

Stevie tried his best to attack and defend himself but it wasn't enough against the magical doppelgangers of his dark six fellow close friends was being surreal when stepping out of the mirror were Charlie, Ashley, Madam the Librarian, and Snow White along with the dark Vasilisa mistaken for Valerie.

Stevie managed in his difficult situation with pure luck he found the tossed Seer's remote in a close dark corner rashly being surrounded by his black-eyed duplicate fake friends as the evil queen moves farther away still casting her malicious long spell from her magic mirror.

To Stevie's surprise, the phaser-shot from the remote didn't even work on the evil mirror look-like friends as he zaps the evil dark Kris coming closer but it reflected back with a light mirror spot on its shoulder where it got shot with electric shock static and act like it didn't phase them.

Stevie began to shoot from his remote and shuffled backward's up cornered to a dark wall to get away from getting caught he was trapped. The clone Kris out of nowhere maintained Stevie from behind in a lock with its arms holding Stevie's arms behind his back as they stood against the shadowed wall.

The other five mirrors cloned evil friend's hands began to glow in a familiar eerie green color and Stevie remembering seeing this back at the attack from Baba Yaga crawling into reaching Stevie's ribs before her death.

Kali being the dark goddess with four arms her straight focus was on her prey Vasilisa as goddess jumped onto the activated hex spell till it abolishes its prisoner that was cast inside were now giant sphere rings changed into a trigger earth curse changing into a pack up rock crater crust with mantle lava from the inside the giant magic hex rings cooling into a boulder with monster worms and critters coming in and out from its rock crater holes.

Ending the cat mouse chase standing on top of the hex sphere rings she then senses Stevie was in trouble but Kali wasn't going to losing any eye contact from the sparkling Vasilisa looking downward at her in her goddess flames.

Moment peeks at the last battle defying gravity Vasilisa matching her momentum with the dark goddess using her flying sharp cloth of deadly metallic pink streamers equivalents in agile strength dodging Kali's hands knifes with red sharp dagger nails aiming for Vasilisa's head as she flips and tumbles over the Hindu deity.

Having the dark mirrors everywhere from the marble glass floors to the walls were hindering the goddess Kali as she then instructed Stevie how to summon the dark, as she sensed his powers to summon his nightmares, "They want what you have that's inside you, you need to use it!"

"Feed the fears!" The dark Hindu goddess proclaimed and said again, "feed your fears to your power!" Stevie screamed back, "what power?"

Then the goddess command with a slight echo that punched the air, "Your shadow-binding are summoning forces from the shadows conjured by your fears either you control them or they control you!"

In learning so how to control and conquer his fears so quickly Stevie closed his eyes and thought of his fears bringing back one in particular memory from the interview while he felt a slight comfort burn deep in the bowel of his stomach.

As his usual left hand tingled as it was freezing cold using as a sensory guide him of any all supernatural around him and within that rush moment Stevie began to feel a sensation of haste finding himself itching to get nearer at the evil queens tail end from the back he began to walk towards her.

The evil queen was quick to sly in with her remark words catching barely catching on to the new world's culture, "what's that your closet monsters from under your bed?"

But it was Stevie that got to reply with a realistic comeback that forces the evil queen to recheck her attitude as she sneered, "the boogie man is real and you found him!" Stevie didn't realize he could summon again his American monsters out of the shadows.

(SC Music/13)

Stevie's music began to roll out through his Aeon headphones one of its unique power is rhythm.

Coming out of the dark shadow wall rolling in behind Stevie being cornered by the mirror replica clones that had the evil dark eye's the boys were no longer outnumbered were Stevie's retro eighties horror flick monsters in the flesh from the shadows taking their stepping ground backing off away the simulate clone replica of the false mirror evil friends as they too look fret and confused at their new wicked conflicting nightmare arrivals.

Barring before them the evil twin Kris with dark shade eyes took the chance to run off after sizing his over equal match coming out of the shadows it was the machete thrown by a wearer of a hockey mask thrust into its back as the evil replica mirror Kris shattered into many broken black mirror glass across the floor.

It was the alarming sudden sprout knee below that darted out of nowhere from the dark shadow wall behind Stevie armed with a dangerous kitchen knife it was screaming yelling living lunatic villain doll with red fire hair and blue baby overalls that ran up to the evil replica dark mirror Charlie that then roundup kicking the killer red hair doll across the throne room before getting a chance to go after the scary tough guy wearing a Halloween mask in an attire that consists of a dark blue mechanic jumpsuit meanwhile, another creepy burnt slasher was a monster from a nightmare wearing a stripe red-and-green sweater and a dark brown fedora with its Razor-sharp clawed Glove had its hands full literally dealing with the evil clone dark-eyed Valerie and the replica Librarian manhandling the burnt monster at the same time.

"And with that is shadow bending aiding darkness to your will."

The Hindu dark goddess took amused at the glorified battle between mirror demons and the darkness that spectacled arise from Stevie's newfound hidden tapped power he then understood he could shadow bend.

The last two horror monsters Stevie conjured to walk out among the wall shadow was one wearing a leather face carrying a chain saw and the other shadow villain was a bleach white sadistic character in a black latex punk trench coat with pins out of its head took care of the last party of what's left of the evil dark magic mirror double-alike clones.

After Stevie's implausible nightmares uncouthly annihilated off all six conjured equally match evil false imitation from the magic mirror's reflections of Stevie's memorable friends shattered into hundred glass pieces spread throughout the throne ground floor unpaused each piece of the mirror glass recourse it's Babylon black magic and all began to shift and twitch liquefying in changing its growing size formed into the same multiple clones of the six evil reflection friends but times hundred.

Vasilisa was dallying around with the Hindu goddess with such quick superhuman reflexes she was tumbling around the cures giant sphere prism hex rings in a bright sparkle light every time she's active earning the name dancer of twilight quick enough to evade the strike of like a cobra from the dark cheeky goddess Kali adoring Vasilisa starlight contest warriorship clinging to battle the goddess showed greeting gestures revealing her salutations confirms she was additive to combat.

Stevie was caught in a mob of multiple evil mirror clones and took note that even a mass of willing suicide crowd will eventually take down any original monster with Stevie's come to life nightmare monsters overrun and destroyed by the hundreds of dark replica clones manifesting in sequences from the broken clones mirror glasses.

Stevie was taken to the front of the throne with his shirt ripped off before the snick-ering evil queen lessens from lounging to get up off from her golden throne revealing an eerie glowing green hand. Immediately Stevie recognizes a sequel of the threatening green hand once familiar attack by Baba Yaga with his shirt removed revealing his rib scars on his stomach from his last witch attack.

Vasilisa dances away as a tumbling enchantment ballerina swaying in between the pact crowded magic mirror clones scattered across she made with haste like a leaping deer with the dark goddess behind her tail leaving the Hindu Kali entity slaying every dark mirror clones dispersing one by one ripping through like paper with god-like powers as she goes by occupied with swift blade fingernails lost in her battles as many clones then again multiplied.

Vasilisa depicts a danseuse ballet dancing her way up the steps towards glistening in an aura Stevie companied the evil queen upon the throne floor and began to explain. "I still don't know how your body can still maintain existences this long but that dark curse inside you from the book of shadows will destroy you let us take it out was never meant for you."

Stevie was released from being held captive after taking the trust in sharing the throne floor with Vasilisa and the evil queen but their motives have been scrutinized and impugned.

"You took something that belongs to us and we're taking it back."

After looking over after his friends passed out unconscious onto the stairway steps to the throne floor stage was the real Charlie and Ashley with Kris stuck asleep in a body looking glass mirror from one of the closets ornamental glass red apple tree pillar nearest to the throne floor.

"I trusted you and I believed you?" Stevie started questioning Vasilisa's faux character and she then replies looking over at her past once friends that accepted her as a Seer with open arms.

"With the Librarian's spies and her Seers eyes all over me being overly watch I knew my undercover was short with you, it wasn't long for these two to have figured me out but not as quick as your unfortunate witch friend."

Stevie had to respond, "You used me? Everything was all set up to get to me?"

Vasilisa-"But do know this that everything I've said about you is true and I meant every word!"

The impeccable goddess Kali pops right back up unscathed from the rough abnormally pile like a burning wick escaping from the little mountain hill of a hundred body glass dark clones that laid atop of her were now in flames desecrated into ashes.

Building momentum as she flips over off onto the high throne floor Vasilisa knew she had to keep the fiery ill-tempered goddess occupied crashing to meet her again in the cat mouse chase all awhile the evil queen carried on summoning her magic Babylon ruins of the surrounding mirrors draining Kali's powers even as where the dark goddess stands manifesting to absorb the deity powers to her own.

The dark goddess calls out to her game, "You dance twilight among the stars, let's see your best thirty seconds performance."

Before it was too late Stevie awoke to the great deception persuade by wiles and understood what was going on as a puzzle came together in a thought of how everything was set in plan from the beginning.

All big threats were eliminated with the help of achieving the witches' prism leading Vasilisa's victims to their own ploy bringing back their dead witch queen indulging from ending up in her grand palace design mirror box of a fused god-like trap battery feasting on Kali's goddess powers to achieve their plans without her even knowingly distracted by the formidable pursuit like a fireball chasing after a sparkling firelight.

Stevie was unable to move handled like if an invisible tight bubble was around his body magically forced to be dragging to the magic mirror on the wall where the evil queen stood upon next to her mirror mustering her arms chanting in sequences summoning a green glow from her right hand carrying a silver sacrificial blade in the other Stevie was then forcefully compelled to kneel on his knees.

"After midnight my power will reign over this land" The Evil queen cheered and continued her summoning as the bells struck the halls for it was midnight.

Caught in grim circumstances it was at this moment Stevie felt slight guilt of wishing he regretted his decision choosing to become a Seer but still believed in his faith in making his own destiny creating ties and connection to all the past friends and supernatural allies it was Trix that came across his mind the fairy prince a friend he unknowingly made a pact to be light brothers with that came to his rescue last time Stevie was in peril for his life back at the troll king's lair. Reminiscing Stevie endured to ponder if his light bulb fairy friend would flash appear once again randomly to evasive their dire life threatening situation but to his disbelief instead, an unexpected tune could be heard echoing a familiar whistle and there was sudden gratitude that flatter within deep Stevie's heart, calm was collected over him as he knew who it was smiling ear to ear on his knees at near-death again.

In their superior instant that's where the goddess Kali used her ghastly inexplicable tongue pink as red blood slithering its magnitude length used as a magnificent whip that counterfeited Vasilisa's deadly lash with her sharp pink streamers.

Then a cold blast flew open the sky rise castle throne room doors of artic north winds blew in throughout the hall there at the front entrance appeared a bright blue light enveloping a wide aura around a familiar short crouched elderly man with a thick white mustache and a braided beard wearing an eye patch in a janitor suspenders uniform underneath dressed only in a Hawaiian shirt. Standing in guard the old man yawned looking very spry holding a pushing broom in his right hand forming into a staff barely able to hold himself up.

"What bag of bones is this?" The queen sneered at her new uninvited guest.

The old man gradually began gaining strength stretching upward gaining heights he magically grew nine feet standing tall instantly and growing with growth stout muscles bulge in size, with prominent veins becoming visible he instead gained a slender gigantic figure, and his mustache becomes wilder with his face fully grown rough and robust, pointing upwards. He's also shown to emit blue light from his one eye with the left eye-patched, a result of his light ultra magic graced of being a god. The long breaded North king god has physical prowess which is enhanced exponentially while in this state, allowing him to partially destroy an attack of large shards of the black mirror glasses casting towards him with a single punch obliterating a dark mauve magic force that generated from the ancient magic mirror created by the evil queen that shrouded the entire throne hall.

Stevie was release from the magic tight grip of the evil queen all surprisingly the magic mirror clones broke into glasses all at once in pieces with the glasses pieces rejuvenating quicker again twice as much more into hundreds of clones by the seconds.

"Odin, the bearer Watcher of the North Star has blessed us with his presence the Norse king of the gods, tell me how is that sacrosanctity spell treating you now these days?" An immense vortex of infusion power was cast around the unpredictable evil queen snickering to an uncontainable cackling reacting apprehensively to her laughter as she then summons from the magic mirror to the glass tree pillar mirrors caged in a binding imprisonment projection spell inhibiting the great white one-eyed bearded god surrounded with light vibrant mirrors at his entrance was of a red-carpet runway to the queen's golden peacock throne.

Kali went berserk full illuminated power in her recognizable goddess state figure known as the deity with six arms and the terrible face she owns of a she-devil with her serpent tongue flying everywhere as a loosely grotesque sharp weapon growing additional four more feet taller in an out-of-control slaughter rampage against the thousands mirror clones that fell victim to her slaying serpent tongue unable to rejuvenate to their clones.

"The Omega is here in our presences, how did he leave the temple?" Vasilisa said with little angst, decorated in her splendor sparkles took her steps upon the throne floor stairway gradually towards Stevie escaping the chaos massacre from the wrecked grounds of the Hindu goddess with enticing haste as if time slowed down he was gazing into her appealing eyes as she approaches taking her last steps upward the throne stage and he knew he could not escape her.

"Stevie it doesn't have to end this way?"

But it was at this particular moment Stevie who didn't even know it had paralyzed Vasilisa on the spot, gifted in her full virtue power she foresaw a light in his eyes with a glimpse of his future as he stood innocently hopeless wearing his special Aeon weapon headphones over his head.

"You are the chosen one! I'm so sorry! It was a strange complex as Vasilisa took an immediate change and humbly bowed and stumbled upon Stevie's arms who was speechlessly grasping his shoulders to hold on to him staring eye to eye as she tears up.

"My thirty seconds performance show is up." Vasilisa's sparkling glimmer began to shimmer even more. "Let me know before I leave did you get what you came for, you must find what you need there's a world at your feet when you are standing next to me. Let me show you and if it's not enough you can take my love."

Stevie stood there confused and disheartened all he could muster up to say is, "but heed my warning attempt a second kiss just might be deadly if you wish for it."

In shock dismay, it was Vasilisa that threw herself at Stevie's face this time with a second kiss as they close their eyes lost into each other's comfort carelessly being connected as one through sensual lip contact in a splendor affection of one another in a shared moment.

The kiss was withdrawn shortly with a disorder shock upon Stevie's face finding Vasilisa's left-hand glowing green as he just smiles back at her darling with death on her face. There appeared what Stevie saw was a red sort dagger tip of a forked snake tongue in between her sternum that was pulled back out as she fell revealing the triumph dark goddess Kali that stood behind Vasilisa watching her falling prey savoring in licking the blood off her lips and fingernails that shrunk from daggers as she was still transformed in a degree of the goddess transfix in a misguided dark human form and proclaimed, "Endings and Beginnings, the old must be released so that the new can enter."

Stevie was on the ground on his knees as Vasilisa fell catching her fall, "Everything I said about you back at the Fae festival is true." Vasilisa dying in Stevie's arms with trickle blood appeared from her corner pink lips, "You are special and never forget you hold the keys to your own destiny and those who can see beyond the shadows and lies of their culture world will never be understood, let alone believed by the masses."

Revealing the last kiss was the ballerina enchantress prophesying as she tries to convince Stevie to snap out of it, choosing another path for the one he seeks will lead to death. Vasilisa was held in Stevie's arms without any explanation of the last kiss but quotes, "kisses are deadly," as Vasilisa died in his arms her body sublime into sparkles that disappeared in mid-air.

Stevie was confused to sadden then mortified at seeing Vasilisa dying as she was slew in his arms he stood up against the destruction goddess's then the reckless goddess rushed at Stevie going berserks barley miss him as Stevie took a fall from stepping backward was then caught cast downward falling off from the throne stage to the ground floor with the dark Kali goddess finding Stevie underneath her foot once again the embarrassment took over her taking back her mother self form with calm and ease from her goddess destruction force.

It was then the last battle that took place, Odin lord of the Norse gods commander of high chief of Seers protector of the library vs. the vanity legendary raised from the dead evil queen witch Grimhilde from the exotic faraway land of the black sand called Shaitan of the lost dark ages of black magic of Babylon, she continue on.

All awhile Kali awoke from her vile goddess form helping Stevie gathering his unconscious friends she picks up Snow her cohort legendary princess co-star entertainer in her two arms and Charlie and Ashley were carried on both each side of her broad shoulder with her two set arms while Stevie quickly recognizes the might of a goddess he grabs his friend Kris by his arms dragging him near to Kali beside a wall near to the closet wreck broken mirror glass pillar tree right side by the throne stage.

Kali took her respective bow after she saw Odin the great chieftain god grown in strength who was about to do his thing as she took charge to protect Stevie and Kris with the others as she shields them with her multiple arms while Odin revered to his eye patch ready for the evil queen to make her first move surrounded by her reflection from the majestic mirrors of shape tree pillars.

Standing before her magic mirror casting an ultimate spell in a frenzied state the evil queen rejoices and cackled. "Vanity affair let it be fair, magic mirror capture this mere so it shall always be here far and forever near!"

Waving her arms reaching the sky insulating drawn power her action was indescribable dark magic of old times using prominence astrology symbols off her magic mirror for her casting dark spell but it was then Odin who just simply lifted his eye patch.

Surrounding the great god a reflective energy attack with blast beams was summon from the tree pillar mirrors that hit the great Odin standing still casting a white light so bright it blinds everyone for a moment but there was a pure blue bright light that stood out and could be seen from the shone magic mirror spotlights coming from the direction to his great eye.

The evil queen skipping a beat unable to finish her summoning power ritual interrupted and caused by the exhilarant icy icicles around the hexes rings that were changing into elements structures of fire, wind, water, and rocks as rings spinning around rapidly faster than usual in place stage in the middle of the floor that held the librarian captive in an iceberg inside the giant spinning element hexes rings that exploded and busted with a surprise ice and particles everywhere with such a force there were too many explosions happening all at once.

The blast was so crucial hope couldn't be more keener that it was life-changing to the evil queen disturbing her incantation she cast her dark magic causing all the mirrors to shone so bright it brought blindness for a few seconds but with a counter-attack reverse spell from Odin lost in the bright mirror light opening his blue light one eye from his patch the evil queen's dark mirror spell backfired at her as the lights restored casting her into ambitious body size mirror statue of herself melted to the glass marble floor with her mirror glass arms and eyes wide open looking up but her eyes were staring down in a summoning position frozen upon this spot forever to be just an art backdrop, now that's an exhibition of her deadly sin stamp forever in time and space.

There in the middle ground floor crouch and kneeling revealed the Librarian all in one piece amazingly survived through the worst deadly hexes ever known to be created still clinging onto her black oak staff slowly arising to get up with ice and stone particles falling off from her shoulders as she smudges off the patches of black icicles from her dreadful black Victorian gothic silhouette that has always signified her power dark features and grot attitude as she leisurely studies her surroundings with her eyes.

Before Kali took off swiftly with Snow unconscious in her arms graced in her motherly form changing back describe now in days with an urban slang more as a cougar changing back into her red-orange two-piece cocktail sequins with a rock cut body she bowed as if she thanks telepathic and showing respect to the North god Odin relief from the Babylonian casting draining spell, literally the goddess was a trap in a giant magic glass box sapping her powers.

Madam with her cold stare at anyone she could freeze ice with a look who venture her undertaking she came across first with the great god Odin and spoke, "It must be Wednesday." They were having an awkward match of a stare down, each holding their staffs with the Librarian lifting hers and stomps the ground with Odin vanishing into light in thin air.

The Seers team right after that showed up and confiscated the place within seconds that would have been a lot helpful if they were here just five minutes earlier things would have played out differently with Madam the librarian being stiff and cold as ever strict with discipline lacking empathy she wasn't playing around giving sudden direct orders and refusing help from other Seers to lead her out towards the exit while Valerie had the book of shadows in her bag laying on the floor exposed as Madam swoop and took the black leather book it was another surprise from Stevie validating his disappointed with Vasilisa.

The Librarian passing by dropping Kris's familiar switch bait baseball and ignoring Stevie's loudest cry in the room as Stevie sat there starring at the floor watching the baseball rolled to his foot lost was written all over his face even though he was quiet and stranded in the middle of blaring investigation, being silent deep within his emotions as he kneeled resting on his knees was the loudest noise Stevie made in the room.

Then that's when Esma the gypsy queen with her crystal ball and Nerd rushed in with his gadgets and tinker bots began examining the place then uncomfortably to their shock the gypsy queen yelled, "Using foxglove, also known as digitalis should wake up…? WHAT the red devil's eye are you doing! This is a new century we have antidotes for that!"

Catching Stevie hopelessly with Charlie and Ashley handling their lifeless bodies laying them down side-by-side facing each other carefully tilting their heads helping to harbor a kiss from each other placing their lips together so they can wake up.

"What are you doing, first true love's kiss… really!" As the gypsy queen revives Kris from being unconscious from the deep sleep explaining, "This is not in six-teen hundreds we have antidotes for death sleeps!

But then Charlie and Ashley unwieldy woke up together at the same time made it uneasy for everyone else in the room except for them two unknowing the complex situation hugging each other to be busy being happy knowing they survived the outcome of waking up from their deep slumber.

22

The last dance

COMING BACK FROM A COUPLE of days of rest at being home with his parents and the little mini magical domestic family he discovered in his backyard by the windmill cellar recently becoming a close member to the Gnomes circle was a short vacation that was a must well be needed for Stevie as he recovery physically and mentally taking a break from a Seer's work with the over dramatic showdown past weekend with the unpredictable bad boss who's residency was at the top of the Austonian skyscraper.

Getting back into the city from his home town San Angelo, Stevie met plans to meet up with Kris to hang with his seer click friends becoming quickly his second family for a drink or two even though Stevie doesn't drink they all meet at Austin's Speakeasy cabaret the Lone Star bar/club run and managed by the one only motherly goddess of doomsday Kali rapidly becoming Stevie's friend with the firecracker entity walking in with Kris approaching and nod with respect at the goddess standing by the stage who just finish her show with a new performance every weekend with her co-stars famously charm princesses including legendary Snow who was on the stage winking at the boys as they pass the stage when they meet up with their leader charges at a cocktail round table were Charlie and Ashley standing cheering each other in high spirits.

Kali then cites bravery sensing justices needs to be validated being proud of the boys of their heroic accomplishments, "well look what just walk into a bar together, a Christian hero and a devil-witch boy, we are definitely living in different times.

Kali desperately mentions, "If it weren't for you and your friends who would have known what the evil queen could have made out of poor Snow putting her and everyone else in danger."

Charlie managed to buy everyone at the table free drinks and sodas being the sentimental guy that Charlie is he had everyone toasting one another, "Man, I'm still embarrassed how we got suckered into those magic mirrors." Ashley responded to Charlie with a sly look on her face in suggestion, "Not pointing the blame but I followed you and your shirt was off and you had to go off to start staring at yourself." Charlie began to be peachy settled off with an innocent smile and two thumbs up back at Ashley his skin blooming with embarrassment with his face turning pink as a peach.

Stevie brought up his companion friend with admiration by offering him and everyone else a shot around the house. "I wouldn't have been able to do it if it weren't for Kris at the end who saw through the shrouded charade of the deception which leads us to you guys trap in those mirrors with the evil queen's elusive traps we just barely made it in time.

That's when Stevie realizes he must have been the topic when he was out on his personal holiday noticing everyone being awkward and his close friends took cautious about mentioning Valerie who betrayed Stevie's heart and he wasn't naïve as they thought he be but it was the thought that counted reminding himself to put a smile on his face.

"What exactly happens to the evil queen after transformed into her own self statue mirror?" Stevie asks knowingly the Hindu goddess of destruction would know the answer since the surprise attack came from the Norse God Odin guardian of the library and minder of the Seers.

"She stands where she will always be still." Kali mentions with Charlie then asking with a chuckle, "The evil queen's vanity turned her into a full-blown mirror statue!" "The Gungnir." Kali refers to the magic spell that Odin cast upon the evil queen explaining the lord of the Norse's power.

"It was his Gungnir, its very rare to witness such power and to be standing alive, be lucky the protector of Seers keeper of the north frost blue star deflected the witch's catastrophic spell with just his eye returning heavy damage on whoever he perceives that has ill intent from their heart using the enemies own attacks bouncing back, that is his specialty leaving friends and bystanders completely unharmed."

Ashley is known for her hardcore soft Christian appetite opening to accept of all things for what they are and adequate of impious ideologies she mentions the bible with a verse as it is in her character to recite she began paring to the evil queen. "Romans 1:21, because that, when they knew God, they glorified him not as God, neither were thankful; but became vain in their imaginations, and their foolish heart was darkened."

Then it was Kris that explains the intent of the evil queen's last spell, "The evil queen's last spell was manifest to capture the entity essence from the Scandinavian King of the gods trapping it in a mirror for personal gain power that she thought she can just take but she was no match for his great power.

Snow came around and brought the crew a tray of shots on Stevie's request slipping a hug happily to see her heroes with her princess charms and delicate gesture flashing her eyelashes with her pinky to her rosy cheeks then folding her hands under her neck she quickly said, "I sure do love happy endings."

Chris and Ashley briefly explain their role revealing to the boys why they were the team to be together in the beginning. "It was easier to watch and manage you guys when you're together however you two managed to have the trouble finding you when inseparable," Ashley said with a smirk on her face.

Charlie budded in as a reminder to say, "With Odin being revealed of our sacred guardian already has been weak is now weaker from the effect of his defense spell that took a big toll on him being the guardian of the sacred library and we had been instructed to watch you guys very closely by the charges of the headmistress Madame to watch Valerie very closely but it was the Librarian Madame that knew all along that she suspected Valerie to be a double agent using you guys to out the advantage allowing Valerie to get close to you as our enemies plan was unfolding before us.

The boys then went into a questioning mode with Kris asking and Charlie answered, "You used us as bait?" "No, you guys were perfect pupils, we knew you guys were special it was just a matter of time to draw her out only you guys were capable of carrying out that job, I found Kris to be extraordinary with his powers and Ashley found you Stevie to be gifted." Charlie smiled back at Ashley, as it was confirmed by Ashley to finish his sentence. "She found light in Stevie's faith that's why she believed in him."

It was Kris that spoke out bluntly next about Valerie's mystery contour, "Valerie was known to be Vasilisa the beautiful predecessor of the deceased Crone formally was the Gran Hind Witch known as Baba Yaga, blindly we manage to fold their plan avoiding the witches prophecy."

Stevie then had to ask, "the witches' prophecy of the black queen of a dead witch was to rise to power one day to bring forth chaos?" Kris scoffs with giggles and replies realizing Stevie was cool about everything. "That's the one." Stevie claps back trying to be funny, "well… I'm glad we stop the prophecy, I prefer to get mad dogged by our own Grand Hind Witch that we have now."

Interrupting their little party as they included and cheered their surprise drop in guest from the dancing crowd doing the robot coming out of the dance floor was Nerd wearing his science spectacles proudly in his common wardrobe and his famously known suspenders like a spin off version from the classic character from a nineties family matters sitcom and just as clumsy but is known to be the smartest man alive is what makes up for it.

"Don't sweat it, look at me, she loves me?" Nerd said sarcastically taking a friendly swig drink from Charlie's beer mug.

Everyone broke in fun gestures and laughs after Charlie and Ashley broke ties with Stevie and Kris having every excuse for their supreme leader Madame the Librarian.

"Stop she does like you." Ashley retorted to Stevie's comment about the Librarian and continued. "She can be very promiscuous with silent cold gestures of hers but it's her gratitude that is shown to be uncanny." Stevie slyly remarks to his peer leaders, "at least she can crack a smile once in and while."

Nerd had to include, "She won't be smiling sooner or later now that she's a target of witch assassins after her she even told me she would be dangerous to be around." Kris replied, "It's already happening with the attacks and it was the first full moon the other day?" Nerd response left everyone hanging, "Yep she wasn't too happy after I surprisingly found her in my medic lab as she normally isn't ever around me but after last night we got attack just right outside the parking lot working late after midnight I had never seen her outside of work but this was the first and she manages to defeat the assassin witch, she does have a lot on her plate."

Charlie- "The Librarian has been out for a while and hasn't been seen since I'm guessing the witches' prism took a big toll on her."

Kali- "Many will come for your witch leader challenge by many forces to come for the Librarian has shown the world supreme power like no other I've ever seen before from any mortal alike, even the dark forces of all the witches power combine couldn't stop your Librarian, rather than be called the grand hind witch I say she's fit to be the black queen."

Kris responded, "but the Librarian is not dead?"

Nerd then ask with a drop-dead response interrupting and went sideways with his personal question he just had to ask the dark goddess, "Hey the Great Kali form better known as the Mahakali form dose that related to your power possessing the ten dimensions that supports your title as Kalima?"

Kali chauffeur off ignoring the scientist direct interviews keeping her business to herself as if the cat was out of the bag running the goddess off to act as a waitress scheme collecting empty bottles as she hinted enough clues and change the subject as she said, "Ask your leaders who it was that tap your black firepower witch boy."

Charlie immediately had to react taking another shot fast down his throat breaking the ice interacting into the recent conversation responding, "Well I'm glad she's on our side that Librarian can be one tough cookie." Ashley knew better than to not delay or hide any more secrets from the boys. "Your power is the black fire it is the ultimate weapon we have thus far taking huge sustained damage on the Librarian she manages to restraint the tainted flames that can burn anything including the pure light of essences." Stevie gave Kris a considered look knowingly they both didn't know any better.

Charlie then gave the better inside scoop of Kris's newfound power being his guide leader, "Given as a gift by the Titan Prometheus the black flame is indulged with an unsullied legendary flame of absolute purity. The same primordial flame of spark from which the beginning of time soiled humanity and fashioned the world we now live in."

It was Stevie that would ask the random question that no one would know, "Why is the fire black?"

With a rhetorical answer, Kris replied and Stevie couldn't tell if he was joking having Ashley and Charlie exchanging thoughts as they look at each other, "Must it's something to, maybe something sinister is inside me more like."

Charlie intervenes to finish the conversation and said, "It was the Librarian who manage to tap out your firepower the black flames after your embezzlement plans with the enemy trespassing blindly and looting the Librarian's sacred grounds and worst catching the black forest on fire internally, I think that gives her every right to strip your use of power." Kris immediately had questions flowing through his mind being known to be familiar with the dark arts and his only response was, "She can do that?"

Charlie then had only one piece advice for Kris, "In time your powers will be restored back in judgment when the Librarian sees you are fit to claim your firepower back." Charlie then whispers to Kris and then winks, "Just be on your best behavior."

Before Stevie was rushed onto the dance floor with Kris tagging along favorable for Stevie's dance moves he was escorted by Kali's employers the cabaret princesses Kris had to ask Stevie what was stuck on his mind for a while. "What push you through to survive all those epic adventures… you manage to escape danger with the two most notorious dangerous witches known in history?" And this is what Stevie said surprising everyone with his answer, "HEART, MIND, and SPIRIT."

Stevie said explaining what he does when he runs into problematic or dire situations as taught by family traditions he uses his faith and belief to solely rest on the almighty God he believes wholeheartedly of his savior.

It was Ashley's last remark that stuck to Stevie like glue, "That's strength and faith, I knew you would push forward and reveal yourself for who you truly are when you doubt yourself."

Stevie knew he had learned to be agile by Valerie, and to keep tamed was learned from Kris while being cordial was taught by Charlie and was reminded to keep his faith was from Ashley, and still, Stevie couldn't manage to summon his own Aeon weapon quite yet.

"I haven't seen that kind of human spirit in a mortal since for almost two thousand years if he knew any better and I believe he could hold power just as like a god all in one pinky if he knew any better and if Stevie keeps it up that kid will be going to extraordinary places."

It was Kali who was willing to open her third eye taking her distance away from her party guest sharing a snippet of her grace premonition seeing a glimpse of the future that made her smile being a dark goddess among Stevie's colleague Seers as they watch Stevie dance away on the dance floor but it was Nerd's presence among them that disturb Kali's chi concentrating back to her club managing giving orders from behind the bar as the goddess kept taking incongruous stares back at the poor genius science guy who can't get a break with his newfound high-tech gadgets he brought to the club blind to see other girl's interest in him across the room with flirtatious looks at his way but it was in his nature being clumsy with lack of dating social skills stuck in his work with a notebook taking notes while scanning the surroundings with his electric EMP magnitude calculator.

Nerd began to break the stats of Stevie's epic adventure all while multi-tasking one of the many gifts of being one of the smartest people alive he would check-in and out of his notes solving equations to a scientific mathematical hypothesis, "Well let's see, Stevie has recounted to be known as the curse of the witches bane, a first time Adamite record as a diplomat among the gods and to be alive to tell the story, slayer of the Troll King, ambassador among the tree elves and Fae brother of the fairy kingdom and continues to be favored by many, but let's not forget the only one out of all of us who surpass Madame the Librarian at the red door challenge.

"You do know something big is coming being the goddess of destruction and all." The goddess said as she returns to serve them their second round of drinks. "We gods can sense these things such as negative energies that come and goes but Austin Texas carries it all and this time around it's going to be huge. I can see dark energy attracts to him and underneath all that black energy is a simple light like a flame on a lick in a dark room make sure you tend the flame vigilantly."

Skipping through her goddess acts and accolade rituals, as she was used to being worship by millions long time ago for her consecration blessings she then picks up the empty beer bottles and shot glasses on her tray with no reluctant remorse she was rather happy to be the star waitress at her own managing club heir to her labor as a cabaret dancer as she sways away to her own collective new coming fans growing by the day from the dance floor.

Ashley then had to ask the question that stood before them like the elephant in the room as they watch Stevie and Kris dance away on the dance floor to the iconic song (SC Music/14) "Born to be alive," which was highlighted by the goddess recent consent without Stevie even knowing who or what he is.

"We are sworn to never tell and this will be the last time we'll ever bring this up," Ashley mentions before anyone else non-Seer could hear.

Nerd was speechless taking a break from his notes taking a sip out of a mug studying the new acquaintance part taken by Kris and Stevie quickly becoming comrades with each other watching his peers dance the night away.

Then Charlie replied with little concern of possibility questioning his doubts as you can hear it in his voice but with confidence and strength as so as his character that he was recognized with or was it sorrow as he watches his pupil companion dancing away with no idea what's coming. "That's what we're here for, to protect Stevie from the darkness."

Then Ashley had to say her peace, "Even if it cost us our lives."

Music Track Story
Epic Adventures of a Cableguy: playlist Soundcloud

1. Ellie Goulding/ Anything can happen
2. Kid CuDi feat. Cee-Lo Green/ Scott Mescudi Vs. The World
3. Morteu(feat. Frida Sundemo)/ Beautiful heartbeat (Derro Remix)
4. Blastoyz/ Parvati Valley
5. Kazaky/Pulse
6. Devo/Whip it
7. Chaseholfelder/ The Anthem Minor key version
8. Selena/ Bidi Bidi Bom Bom
9. Louis Armstrong/ What a Wonderful World
10. David Bowie/ Space Oddity
11. Smash Mouth/ I'm a believer
12. Borns/Electric Love
13. DJ Herax/ Brooms- the Sorcerer's Apprentice
14. Patrick Hernandez-Bradboi/Born to be Alive
15. Doris Day/ Que Sera Sera

At the end of this book, it leads to Stevie Aeon's magical headphones ringing into a tuning music theme song leading Aphrodite singing outside taking fancy, and strolling downtown Austin city Streets. (SC Music/15)

"Que sera sera, whatever will be will be, the future is not ours to see, Que sera sera what will be will be."

The End Of Book 1 To The Opening Of Book 2
Epic Adventures Of A Cable Guy
Gods And Monsters

Epilogue

FOR WHAT HAPPENED NEXT COULD not be explained there were no mortals insight and from the west coming around from the corner of the Texas governor's mansion like time itself slowed down once again as the familiar scene of the voluptuous celebrity vixen singing, "Que sera sera, what will be will be."

Dress in a fancy ruby red diamond silhouette, dresses her chest of a heart shape with of an hourglass body walking down on the eleventh street wearing red glistening stilettos right before the Texas capitol removing her dark red shades flashing her luxurious shine blonde locks of hair all in slow motion while being in a spotlight of unseen cameras of flashes.

The goddess began to grow rapidly revealing their grace of magnificent power shot out of loving force as she applies charmed glistening red lipstick like cherry pink diamonds while puckering her lips posing for shots.

It was a whole another level of a trance watching a goddess grow into a giant of about thirty-six feet tall the world's most magnificent beautiful creature but in a strange way the goddess of love glowed in such radiant aura it gave off a warm feeling of loving anything glowing of sunset rays with a glistering after effect of the night stars that she touched reaching the skies, she could be the most beautiful woman on the earth.

Sudden dawn of glitter ray light of silver gleam from among the east clash in a subtle evenly match light sky over the Texas Capital against the west red burning sunset glistening into the starlight sky.

Walking proudly from East in a charismatic business lawyer attire straight out from Wall Street fashion statement in a gray skirt suit in black glistering pumps strutting the street from the east letting her dark hair lose from a fashion tight knot held by a pencil morphing into a glistening golden spear as she too began to grow gigantic sprouting by taking a few gigantic steps being a giant towards the Texas capitol with a large bird of an owl flying to her shoulder carrying a lawyer briefcase in the other hand before changing into her glistening golden shield.

Aphrodite was openly opinionated to ask, "I can't believe we're doing this, again!"

Then Athena goddess of wisdom appears equally gigantic to the goddess of love standing height and to share her honesty, "I can't disagree with you any more sister, it's the planets that have to align and the stars that once adorn again."

Momentarily colors burning ember green and blue of comets with a meteor shower rain across the enthralling sky there arriving from the south from the congress bridge in a classic motorcycle fit for god with fire trailing behind as metal chains were strapped onto the god's bike dangling dangerously lose with ember fire at the ends like a welding rod crackled onto the street.

Then Hephaestus god of blacksmith jump off his blazing meteor black bike and also began to grow just a few feet more taller than his two giant goddesses sisters and bow to allow himself to speak in their presences but was fashioned to ignore the goddess of love Aphrodite his ex-wife to say, "we all know anything that what sister owl has to say is true, what did father say?"

Athena in her delightful grace in silver aura then tells the craftsman god still on his one knee bowing, "You can ask him yourself!"

Then rushing the skies from the north taking over were blue clouds with blue lighting of deep ozone oxygen filling the air rolling in black thunderstorm clouds zapping lighting out from the middle skies into the capitol forcing the gates and front doors of the capitol swung open struck out like lighting was the grandfather of the skies the king of Mount Olympus Zeus growing forty-five feet tall just five feet taller than his son Hephaestus, and the sky king with a grey clean sharp warrior beard flashing with lighting in an appearance to be wearing a dark blue fitted muscular business tux's with buttons lose opening to revealing his muscle torso with a toothpick in its mouth like he just finished an elite steak diner meeting, wearing black shades with radiant electrifying blue eyes flashing behind it as he shakes his suit arm with glistening golden collar cuffs and silver rings creasing his neck to pop smiling with glistening teeth to announce as he ignores his children's anecdote.

"We're moving in."